MW01154015

Witch Queen's War

Also by Eric R. Asher

Keep track of Eric's new releases by receiving an email on release day. It's fast and easy to sign up for Eric's mailing list, and you'll also get an ebook copy of the subscriber exclusive anthology, *Whispers of War.*

Go here to get started: www.ericrasher.com

The Steamborn Trilogy:

Steamborn
Steamforged
Steamsworn

The Vesik Series:
(Recommended for Ages 17+)

Days Gone Bad
Wolves and the River of Stone
Winter's Demon
This Broken World
Destroyer Rising
Rattle the Bones
Witch Queen's War
Vesik Book 8 – coming spring 2018*

*Want to receive an email on the day this book releases? Sign up for Eric's mailing list.
www.ericrasher.com

Mason Dixon – Monster Hunter:

Episode One
Episode Two
Episode Three – coming fall 2017*

*Want to receive an email on the day this book releases? Sign up for Eric's mailing list.

Witch Queen's War

Eric R. Asher

Copyright © 2017 by Eric R. Asher
Print Edition

All rights reserved. This book or any portion thereof may not be reproduced or used in any manner whatsoever without the express written permission of the publisher except for the use of brief quotations in a book review.

This is a work of fiction. Names, characters, businesses, places, events and incidents are either the products of the author's imagination or used in a fictitious manner. Any resemblance to actual persons, living or dead, or actual events is purely coincidental.

Edited by Laura Matheson
Cover typography by Indie Solutions by Murphy Rae
Cover design ©Phatpuppyart.com – Claudia McKinney

Is it too early for a theme song?

CHAPTER ONE

S TREETS FILLED WITH fear and terror and blood. This wasn't what our home was supposed to be. No matter how close war had come before, no matter what we'd fought on the streets of Saint Charles, we'd always managed to keep the commoners safe.

The tourists weren't the only beings in danger here. The military had seen too many Fae, too many things they didn't understand. Now they were targeting our allies, and in that action, they were targeting their own allies. They'd set their sights on the Fae who stood with the commoners.

I raised my hand in a useless protest, too far away to reach anyone in time.

The tank fired.

Flames and death and smoke screamed from the barrel of that awful weapon. Aeros raised his fists, and a u-shaped wall of stone sprang up between him and the shell. The wall cracked in the following explosion, sending waves of shrapnel and debris into the air. Angus had barely escaped, grabbing two of the kids who had been too close to the line of fire, and launching into the air with them.

One of the kids he'd had to leave behind screamed and went down, clutching his leg. Aeros glanced at the child, then turned back to face the tank. The Old God dropped into the earth, vanishing into a circle of green light. The tank adjusted its aim, centering on the wall.

The next shot might take the wall of stone, but it was going to kill the half dozen people sheltering behind it too. If they thought firing on the wall would hurt Aeros, they were wrong.

"No!" I shouted, sprinting forward. If I could get close enough, raise a shield, do something. I wasn't that fast. No one was that fast. "Run!"

Angus dove back into the panicked crowd.

A loud thunk sounded from the tank, the same sound I'd heard before the first shot. I wasn't going to make it to them in time. Where the fuck was Aeros?

He answered with a fury, rising beneath the tank. One stony fist grabbed the barrel and bent it toward the ground before Aeros flipped the tank over and slammed it into the earth. Stone flowed over the armored metal shell, and the tank screeched as Aeros tore it apart.

"They are *children!*" the Old God roared. "My stone will bear your names for all time, and the world shall call you monsters."

"Aeros, no!" I shouted.

He paused with his fist raised above the exposed soldiers, his eyes flashing between me and the terrified men below him.

"Don't kill them," I said.

"He's dead!" A voice screamed, cracking and rising into hysteria. I turned to see a child tugging at the arm of an older man. The child's wails were the endless, undefined cries of a survivor. There are the cries of grief, and then there are the primal chords of loss no person can put into words. These were the hiccupping, terrible sobs of lives broken, and a world that would never be the same.

"Murderers." Aeros turned away from the soldiers and looked down at me. "They should be held accountable. Would you not slay them if they were Fae or vampire?" He walked back toward the screaming boy.

I stepped up onto the flattened edge of the tank. "Okay, look, that's a big talking rock who wants to kill you now. Congratulations on pulling that off. You also just murdered someone's grandfather, so fuck you very much. Now..." I called on the dead things around me, let the decayed ruin of the gravemakers flow up from the earth to coat my arms and chest. "I suggest you get your tanks the fuck out of here before I decide to let my friend flatten you like tin cans."

The nearest soldier's hand reached for his sidearm. All he found was a mangled strip of metal.

I let the gravemaker chaff close over my head. "Draw that gun, and I'll eat your soul."

The man next to him had a smarter approach. He placed his hand on his companion's arm, preventing any further attempts to draw his weapon. When the first man tried to protest again, the smart one grew more forceful.

"Stop it. Don't you see the thing standing in front of us? Do you want to hug your family again, or you want to die here?"

The man with the gun stopped fidgeting. I backed away, letting them climb out of the ruined tank. The wails of the child behind me cut through the silence of the men before me.

"Never forget that sound." I turned away at that point, not wanting to see what the men would do. Or maybe I just didn't care anymore. How had it come to this in just five days?

CHAPTER TWO

F IVE DAYS EARLIER, the bell had jingled when Sergeant Park pushed his way into Death's Door. I'd seen him enough lately to know the quick steps that led him to the counter weren't indicative of a casual pace. I sat up a little straighter.

"Everything okay?" I asked.

Park glanced around the room before setting his palms flat against the countertop. I winced at the creaking squeal of the glass. "Is Frank here?"

I debated for a moment whether to tell him Frank was actually there, wondering if Frank had gotten himself into some kind of trouble. After considering Park's stride and the anxious flashing of his eyes toward the back room, I decided I'd better get Frank.

"Yeah, sure. Wait here for just a second and I'll grab him for you."

Park nodded a little too quickly. I hopped off the stool behind the counter and headed through the saloon-style doors. I passed the grandfather clock and the Formica table before I came to the entrance to the cu siths' lair.

I paused with my hand on the ornately carved doorway. Foster and Aideen had whittled the once ragged hole into a beautiful array of Celtic knots. I ducked through the entryway, following the sounds of a snoring cu sith.

"Frank," I whispered, not wanting to wake Bubbles. I made my way farther down the sloping ramp that led into the basement.

Frank had his reading glasses on and was squinting at the runes on the wall. He held a book in one hand and was comparing the drawings inside to the sketches on the wall.

"Frank."

He jumped, surprised when I said his name so close behind him. Frank spun around, raising the book in his right hand as if he expected to swat an overly large, overly annoying bug. "Damian!"

Frank hadn't whispered. The cu sith startled awake, sucking her tongue in and flinging her massive furry form against the nearest wall. Unfortunately, I was between her and that wall. I grunted as the bristly fur smashed me into the stone. She bounced away, looked up, and then started snuffling at my shoes.

I gasped, trying to regain the breath Bubbles had smashed out of me.

"You okay?" Frank asked.

I nodded through a grimace and pointed up the ramp.

Bubbles understood just fine and ran right up the ramp to see what was waiting in the shop.

Frank, on the other hand, looked a bit more perplexed. "You need me to cover the shop?"

I took a deep breath and shook my head, my lungs finally recovering. "Park wants to see you. He's waiting upstairs." I took another glorious breath and gestured at Frank. "Still researching the runes?"

He glanced down at the book in his hand. "Yeah, with everything Calbach told us about the runes, I thought it might be interesting to see what else I could dig up." He snapped the book closed. "Haven't found much."

"Were you expecting Park?" I asked, leading the way back up the stone ramp.

"No. I mean, he drops by fairly regularly, but I wasn't expecting him today."

Bubbles started barking, and Foster cursed above us. The fairy shouted, and I could hear the rattle of his armor. I suspected he was trying to wrestle Bubbles away from Park. I picked up the pace and pushed through the saloon-style doors a moment later.

Bubbles had her paws up on Park's shoulders, licking and snorting, easily pulling away from Foster each time the fairy managed to free Park.

"Bubbles," I said in a low voice.

She froze, slowly licked Park one more time, and then padded back to flop on the floor next to me.

"Sorry about that," I said.

"Oh," Foster said, turning to Bubbles. "So now you listen to the necromancer and not me? Your ancestors would be ashamed."

Aideen glided over the swinging doors from the back of the shop and settled onto the cu sith's ruff.

"Park?" Frank asked. "Are you okay?"

"Yes," Park said, looking down at the cu sith before returning his gaze to Frank. "I think so."

Frank eyed him, and the suspicion on Frank's face was obvious. "Well, what do you need me for?"

"We lost a squad," Park said. He crossed his arms and blew

out a breath.

Frank grimaced. He glanced at me and then back to Park. "Who?"

"You don't know them."

Frank frowned slightly. "Okay. Then why are you here?"

"What is it?" Foster asked, clearly not missing Park's distant stare.

Park hesitated, and then said, "It was a fairy by the old railroad bridge. Foster, when we played back footage from the scene, he looked like you."

Foster frowned. "What do you mean, exactly? Like he had my face?"

Park shook his head. "No, I mean he had your wings. Huge wings like a moth."

Foster squeezed the dagger sheathed on his belt.

I was about to interrupt when Aideen did it for me. "One of the queen's spies?" She sidled up beside Foster, eyeing Park. "What else have you heard?"

Park shrugged. "Not much. Look, you already know some of the commanders in the area are concerned about the intelligence we have. I've heard rumors that some of them think it was you."

"Think I impersonated myself?" Foster frowned at his own words. "Never mind, that was a stupid question. But come on, Damian. This is clearly a setup."

"I'm not arguing that," I said. "But what are we going to do about it?"

"Oh, that's simple," Foster said. "I'm going to cut pieces off him and feed him the chunks before he dies."

I couldn't suppress a small smile. "Sure, but we don't even

know who he is. Which means we don't know how to find him."

"You kill enough enemies, you get the right one eventually." Foster massaged the hilt of his sword, and it was particularly menacing.

Aideen laid a hand on his shoulder. The murderous gleam in his eyes receded, but it didn't leave entirely.

"This isn't a time to be brash," Aideen said.

Foster nodded once. "The patrol was attacked at the bridge below the highway. That's where we buried Lewis. You think they dug him up?"

I blinked at the fairy, not quite sure where that question had come from. "No, but I wouldn't be surprised if it was a message. Someone telling us they know where we've been. They know where our skeletons are buried."

"Literally." Frank put his hand on the countertop and leaned toward Park. "Come on, man. You had to have noticed something. Something different? Something unusual about the scene?"

Park frowned slightly at Frank. "I understand what you're saying."

"What about the light?" Foster asked.

"Everything looked green," Park said. "Like they were bleeding green."

Foster's expression turned stony. "Green poison."

"Poison?" Park asked.

"The queen is back," Aideen said.

My fingers tightened around the blue obsidian coin on the counter.

Frank rapidly waved his hands, cutting off the conversation. "We need a witness."

"Were there any survivors?" I asked.

Frank looked to Park, who frowned for a moment and then nodded slowly.

"Casper," Park said.

I raised an eyebrow. "Is that a ghost joke?"

Park glanced at me, his brow furrowing. It gave me the distinct impression it hadn't been a ghost joke.

"Casper is a sniper," Park said, the mild look of confusion still not leaving his face. "She's in the infirmary, and I'm not sure if she's conscious."

"You call her Casper because she's pale?" Frank asked.

"What?" Park asked. "Why does everyone think that? No, we call her that because she's a goddamn ghost."

I raised my other eyebrow.

"No." Park shook his head rapidly. "Not that kind of ghost. I mean she's a ghost on the battlefield. No one sees her coming." Park paused as if contemplating telling us something more. The look passed, but Foster didn't let it go.

"What is it?" the fairy asked.

"She's an assassin," Park said. "Casper is one of our best snipers. She's a master of camouflage. But the Fae saw her coming."

"Is she in a military infirmary?" Aideen asked. "Or is she in the hospital a few blocks over?"

Park opened his phone and texted someone. "I'll find out." He'd just finished typing when his phone buzzed. "She's at the hospital."

"That's where we need to be," Frank said.

"She'll be guarded," Park said.

I shrugged. "Makes sense." I exchanged a look with Foster. "I'll go with Park," I said. "The last thing we need is for them to see Foster and mistake him for an enemy."

"I'm coming with you," Foster said.

"No," Aideen said, resting her hand on Foster's wrist. "Damian's right. It's too risky. I'll go. They're looking for a male fairy, are they not?" She looked to Park.

Park nodded.

"Then you have no argument," Aideen said.

Foster clearly didn't like the idea, but he said no more. His hand fell to his side, and he nodded once to Park. He turned to me and said, "Don't let her kill everyone. Leave some for me."

"I'm really hoping we don't have to kill anyone," I said.

Frank looked at the wide-eyed Park before glancing between me and Foster. Frank barked out a short laugh. "It's like you don't even know yourself."

"Give me a little credit. We usually don't kill people in a public place."

"Okay," Park said. "Okay okay okay. Now I know you're just screwing with me."

I smiled at Park. "Well, it's either that or bury you in the backyard. We prefer not to do that."

"When did we start burying them in the backyard?" Foster asked.

"Right," I said. "We just turn them into deadbolts now."

Park blinked.

"Long story," I said.

Park narrowed his eyes. "You only intend to talk to Casper, right?"

Aideen sighed. "Of course. We need information, and it

appears she's the only source at our disposal."

"Right," Park said. "Let's un-ass."

That was apparently all the motivation any of us needed. Aideen glided to my shoulder as I made for the door. Frank followed us out, and Park's posture relaxed a fraction when he saw Frank coming with us. I suspected the two of them had become closer, or at least more trusting of each other, but this was the first time I'd seen it so clearly on display.

"It'll be fine," Frank said.

Park nodded.

"I wouldn't say it if it weren't true," Frank said. "Eventually you'll learn to trust this bunch as much as I do."

"They've saved your life before," Park said.

"They've saved yours, too," Frank said.

Park gave one sharp nod, and we started up the block, closing on the hospital in relative silence.

CHAPTER THREE

"**A**IDEEN," FRANK SAID. "Why don't you stay with me? They're going to be watching Damian more than anyone. You'll be less likely to be noticed with me."

"You are right, Frank," Aideen said. I felt her pat my neck as if she was consoling a loved pet before leaving him at the kennel. She pushed off and landed on Frank's shoulder. Not only had Frank been right, but Aideen's black and white wings almost vanished against the busy pattern of his Hawaiian shirt.

"Oh, Frank," Aideen said, disgust clear in her voice. "You're sweating like a Burning Lands troll in a furnace."

"What does that mean?" Park asked.

"Some things you're better off not knowing," I said.

"How did you survive being a criminal if stress makes you sweat?" Aideen asked.

"By getting other people killed," Frank said, his voice solemn.

"I am sorry," Aideen said. "I did not mean to bring up bad memories."

Frank dismissed the thought with a small wave as we followed Park up to the receptionist's desk.

Park leaned forward, crossing his arms and taking a casual pose. "We're here to see Lincoln."

"Sure thing," the receptionist said. "We had to move Ms.

Lincoln. I'm afraid she took a turn for the worse. You'll find her in the ICU. Keep it brief."

Park tensed, and only responded with a nod. He led us through the halls of the hospital as though he'd been to the ICU more than once. I suspected, with what he'd told us about the casualties in the past, that was exactly the case.

"If she's on a ventilator," Frank said, "she's not going to be able to talk to us."

"I know," Park said. "If she was in *that* bad of shape, they wouldn't let us in. We can use a whiteboard if we need to. She still has one good arm. And if we lose her, we don't have anything to go on."

If it weren't for the tremor in Park's voice, I would've thought he was being cold. But he was worried. This was his friend. This wasn't a nameless soldier, a statistic to be run across the six o'clock news.

I didn't have to ask whether or not we were getting close to the ICU. I wouldn't have been able to block out the ghosts if I wanted. At least not without closing down all my other senses. And that seemed like a really stupid thing to do right then. Even without trying to focus, gray and black wisps crept into the edges of my vision. The weight of the dead grew into a crushing presence.

I hated hospitals.

Park turned the corner and nodded to an MP before slipping into the room the soldier guarded. The ICU wasn't all that different from any other ward in the hospital, other than perhaps having additional space for more machines, and much more strict criteria for visitors. I doubted we'd be waltzing in if Park wasn't with us. Park lifted the paper chart hanging off the end of the bed, an anachronistic sight in what was otherwise a cutting-edge facility. He cursed and turned his attention to the broken woman on the bed.

"She's dying," Aideen said, ignoring the chart. "Close the blinds."

"I didn't bring you here for that," Park said.

"I cannot heal her completely," Aideen said. "It would kill me to do so. But I may be able to give her a chance."

Park ran his hand through his hair, cursing under his breath. "Casper hates magic. I can't do that to her without her permission."

"Then we'll do it without yours," Aideen said. "Damian, restrain him if it comes to that."

"Aideen," I said, some part of me thinking that I should be the voice of reason here, and the other part of me thinking that speaking out against Aideen at this point would be the exact opposite of reason.

Frank closed the blinds, sending the room into an eerily lit darkness. Aideen exploded into her full-size form, showering fairy dust across the room, and the suddenness of it sent Park stumbling back a step.

"Oh god," I said. "Warning next—" I didn't finish my sentence before a huge sneeze almost gave me whiplash. I blinked tears out of my eyes and fought off another sneeze.

Aideen gently laid her hands on Casper's upper arm. It was one of the few areas of pale flesh that wasn't covered in bandages. The fairy moved delicately, careful not to disturb the hoses and wires and God knew what else coming out of Casper's body.

"*Socius Sanation.*" Those were Aideen's only words. The

room felt as if it had been lit from inside by a brilliant white sun. Seconds passed. Twenty. Forty. We were closing on a minute when Aideen's wings started shaking.

"Stop," I said. "We're not losing you to save her. You need to stop."

Still, she continued. A few more seconds, and the sun abruptly went out.

"You don't understand," Aideen whispered, slouching against the bed, her head hung low. "She was in so much pain. I couldn't leave her like that."

A burned stretch of flesh on Casper's forehead crinkled and fell away.

"What in the hell?" Park said.

"She's better," Frank said. And before he finished talking, Casper clenched her fists.

"Casper?" Park said.

Pale white eyelids fluttered and then opened wide, bright green eyes flashing between me and Park and Frank before finally settling on Aideen. Casper flinched away from the exhausted fairy leaning on her bed.

Aideen struggled to her feet and leaned slightly against my arm.

"Welcome back," Park said.

"What have you done?" Casper whispered in a hoarse voice.

Park frowned at Casper and followed her gaze back to Aideen. "She means you no harm." Park gently laid a hand on Casper's wrapped shin. Casper looked down at her leg, eyeing Park's hand, and staring at it in something like confusion.

"She means you no harm," Park said again.

"No devil will take my soul." Casper stared at Aideen. "You

may have taken my brother, but you will not have me."

Casper's accent wasn't thick, but it was there, so Aideen's next words didn't strike me as any great surprise. "You are of the old blood."

"The what?" Casper asked.

"From our homeland," Aideen said, placing a hand over her heart.

"Casper," Park said. "Please. You would've died."

"Did she tell you that?" Casper asked. "You cannot trust a fairy. All they are is lies."

Aideen stiffened against my arm.

"You have it all wrong," Frank said. "Not all fairies are bad. Some of the ones you see on the news, like Nudd and Hern? Oh yeah, they're bad. But what about the fairies that are fighting them? There are fairies standing against them to protect the humans."

Frank's words grew more passionate, more fiery. I wasn't sure if that was a good thing, or if it was exactly what we didn't need at that time. "There are things in this world we don't understand, things people think are just stories. Some of them are more than that."

"He's right," Park said. "She didn't have to heal you. She could've let you die, and I would've been none the wiser. She could've killed you, for that matter, and I would've been none the wiser. These people saved me more than once, Casper. And now they've saved you, too."

"And so they own you now?" Casper said.

"No," I said. "He's our friend."

Casper eyed me for a moment. "I doubt that very much."

"Your words pain me," Aideen said. "These things you say,

they are exactly why we fight the king and all he stands for. That, and he has killed many in my family."

"Then tell me," Casper said. "What do I owe you for this?"

"Information," Aideen said, with so little hesitation that I flinched. "Tell us what you know about those who attacked you, and I will consider your debt paid in full." Aideen shook slightly, and I wasn't sure if it was the healing that she'd performed, or exhaustion of another sort. She leaned on me a little heavier before changing back into her smaller form and fluttering to Frank's shoulder.

Casper didn't seem surprised by Aideen's transformation. I suspected that meant one of two things. She had known Fae earlier in her life and had seen one of them transform before. Or, perhaps more likely, those that attacked her unit had been very much like Aideen.

"You don't mean to drag me into Faerie?" Casper narrowed her eyes slightly at the fairy, causing more of the burnt skin to fall away and reveal the fresh flesh beneath.

"Should you ever find yourself in Faerie," Aideen said, "I'll do no more than give you a tour of my home."

"I wouldn't really recommend that," I said. "Every time I go there, someone tries to kill me."

"Damian," Park said, "That's not helping."

But a small laugh escaped Casper, and the tiniest hint of a smile played across her scarred lips. She took a deep breath. "I'll tell you what I know, but there's much more I don't."

"Anything could help," Aideen said.

Casper nodded. "We were on patrol at the far end of Main Street. It wasn't Main anymore, though. It was where it merges into that other road and goes down by the old railroad tracks."

"By the highway?" Frank asked.

Casper started to shake her head and then winced. "No, not that far, but in that area. It was just the five of us. We'd left the Humvee on the other side of the highway, closer to the base."

I frowned and glanced at Park, not sure what she meant by a base on the north side of the highway.

"It's not a full-blown base," Park said. "It's more of a staging area. Go on." He nodded to Casper.

"It wasn't just the one fairy," she said. "There was something else with them, but I couldn't get a good look at it. It was too damn fast." She tilted her head to the side and closed her eyes. When she opened them again, her brow furrowed, causing another scarred patch on her forehead to crack. The bright pink skin already looked healthier from Aideen's healing. Casper turned her gaze to Aideen. "I swear it had a helmet and huge claws. It was one of yours, wasn't it?"

"No," Aideen said, her voice tired. "That was one of the dark-touched vampires. They are agents of those we fight against. You would do well not to lump all supernatural creatures in with them, especially those who would be your allies."

"So you say," Casper said.

"Okay, okay, okay," Frank said. "Talk to me." He leaned on the foot of the bed. "Talk to me." He lowered his voice slightly, drawing Casper's attention away from the fairy on his shoulder. "We want to help you. We have to know what happened."

Casper glanced at Park, and then kept her focus on Frank, her gaze wandering to Aideen only once or twice. "After the … vampire picked off the back of the squad, there were only three of us left. The fairy made quick work of the lieutenant then. I didn't see where the vampire went. I was too busy screaming in the fire that suddenly appeared all around me."

"Fire that the fairy cast?" I asked.

"It looked like it," Casper said, "but you can't trust your eyes with fairies about." Her voice rose slightly, and then trailed off as her exhaustion rivaled Aideen's. Casper frowned. "There was one thing I noticed that was odd. When the fairy cut the lieutenant, he bled green. Green blood from a human. I figured it was some kind of magic, too."

"Yes," Aideen said. "Yes, it was."

I looked at Aideen, waiting for her to indicate whether we needed more information, or if that was enough for now. She nodded once as Casper closed her eyes.

"We're good?" Park asked.

"Yeah," Frank said. "Let's let her rest."

Casper was already snoring lightly by the time we all exited the room. Park nodded to the receptionist as we passed, and we started back to the cobblestones of Main Street, Saint Charles.

CHAPTER FOUR

"**Z**OLA'S HERE," I said, reading a text I must have missed while we were at the hospital. Foster gave me a nod.

"Did Casper help?" Park asked as we entered Death's Door.

"She did," Aideen said. "She confirmed what you'd already told us about the green blood. And she told us more; she told us the dark-touched are already here. As are Glenn's soldiers."

"Are you sure?" Foster asked as he glided into the room. He tilted slightly, and angled to land on Zola's shoulder.

"It's still speculation," Aideen said. "But the witness we spoke to says a fairy used fire."

"Many fairies can use fire," Foster said, crossing his arms.

"This spell was enough to engulf a human," Aideen said. "It was at a level of the Demon Sword."

Foster almost growled. "They're setting us up."

"That's no surprise," Zola said. "We'll see more consequences from Nudd's stunt."

"We're already seeing more boots on the ground," Frank said. "Tanks in Saint Charles, for fuck's sake."

"Yes," Zola said. "And now those soldiers have been attacked by a power thought to be wielded only by the Demon Sword."

"It's brilliant," I said. "In one ruse, he's driven a wedge in to prevent an alliance with the commoners, and now Foster looks like a traitor to his own cause."

"Gwynn Ap Nudd has seeded doubt," Zola said. "All he needs to do now is let it grow."

Park crossed his arms and took a deep breath. "A leader does not rise to power on compassion and understanding, at least not one who is a self-styled dictator." He looked from Foster to Zola in turn. "I've seen warlords use similar tactics. They only need to fill people with fear of the unknown, fear of anything different. And those who the man would hurt worst, rushed to help him first." Park looked like he wanted to spit.

Bubbles shuffled through the saloon-style doors, sniffing at the air before butting up against Park with her hip. When he didn't pet her immediately, she bumped him harder until he had to catch himself by throwing his arms out on the counter.

"Persistent," Park said.

"It is probably in your health's best interest to pet her," Aideen said. "She has been known to get ... bitey."

Park scratched the cu sith's ruff while the rest of us watched in silence. Bubbles arched her back, smooshing Park up against the counter until the sergeant finally had to push her away to keep from being suffocated. Bubbles chuffed at him, and then slowly stalked away into the back room. Park smiled at her grumpy exit.

His smile fell when Bubbles vanished from view. "Why here? Why now?"

"Because this is a war," Zola said. "Nudd does this to turn the commoners and the military into tools for his arsenal."

"You're saying that Nudd fellow ... you're saying he's or-chestrating this?"

"Yes," Zola said. "That is exactly what Ah'm saying. Son,

did you not just say your soldier saw a man bleeding green this morning?"

"Well, yes," Park said. "But that's different. I think. I'm not sure." He frowned and his forehead crinkled as he turned away from the old necromancer.

"You've seen enough of Nudd and his people to understand this," Zola said. "Damian, summon the water witches. You can use the disc to tell Nixie about this, but we need Alexandra or Euphemia here."

"What do you mean to do?" Park asked.

"I mean to hunt them down," Foster said slowly while sheathing his dagger, then slamming it back home, "and show them the true power of the Demon Sword."

It was a rare sight to see Foster use all his powers. My most vivid memory was when we found the child killer's van years before. Foster had turned it into so much slag inside a supernova of fire.

"So," I asked. "Did Nudd create a new Demon Sword?" I paused, wondering if that was even the right way to phrase the question. I didn't know much about how his mantle worked.

"No," Frank said. "Foster's still alive, so no one else can be the Demon Sword as long as he lives."

Aideen nodded. "Frank's correct. It's much like the mantle of the Sanatio. While Cara lived …"

"Aideen," Foster said. "If Nudd has declared a new Sanatio, could he bestow the mantle of the Demon Sword on another fairy?"

Aideen shook her head. "It's possible he has bestowed some power onto a knight, but no one may take the mantle of the Demon Sword so long as you live."

"How did you know that?" I said, eyeing Frank.

"It was a story," Frank said. "One Cara told us. I think we were at the cabin." He frowned slightly, and then nodded. "Yeah, I'm positive it was at the cabin. Sam was down there with us. You might've been elbow deep in a chimichanga."

"You never did listen to her very well," Aideen said, giving me a small smile.

"We know the fairy who attacked Park's men was not Foster," Zola said, "but Park's men, they may be harder to convince."

"Can you come with me, Frank?" Park asked. "You've met several of my soldiers. It may help to have you by my side while I'm briefing them."

Frank glanced between me and the fairies. "If I go now, I won't be able to help with the hunt."

"We can handle dark-touched vampires and an idiot fairy," Foster said.

"Why do you say he's an idiot?" Park asked. "He did manage to kill off one of my squads."

"He's an idiot," Foster said, "because now I have to kill him." The savage grin on Foster's face caused Park to take a step back.

"Oh yeah," I said, "that look will breed all kinds of trust with the military."

Foster's grin widened, sending a chill down my spine.

Aideen raised her hand to cover Foster's mouth, and it broke the somewhat creepy tension in the air. He tried to bat her hand away, but she held firm, the muscles in her forearm straining against his futile attempts to escape.

"Then it's settled," Aideen said. "Frank will go with Park,

and the rest of us will go hunting."

"Should we wait for nightfall?" I asked.

"No," Zola said. "Contact the water witches. Then we hunt."

"Zola's right," Aideen said. "They'll be expecting us in the evening or after nightfall." She let her hand fall away from Foster's mouth, and he gave her a bemused look. "We'll have the element of surprise by attacking in the daylight."

"You're more likely to be mistaken for the enemy in the daylight," Park said. "Some of the soldiers out there have only been in the reserves a few months, and a lot of them came in during the enlistment rush after Gettysburg. Many of them are out for vengeance." Park hesitated. "I don't want them getting in your way."

"Then we hunt," Foster said, "and I will remind this imposter of the true power of the Demon Sword."

✦   ✦   ✦

I TOOK THE Wasser-Münzen disc with me to contact Nixie, and headed toward the Missouri River. It wasn't dinner time yet, so the light crowds on Main Street weren't that unusual. The tourists had been replaced by media, drawn to the military presence as much as the tourists had been repulsed by it. Our city had become a crippled, zombie-like version of its former self. It limped along, the media acting like some kind of symbiotic parasite.

I crossed the cobblestones and asphalt, finally reaching the riverfront. I hopped down onto the bank so I could set my feet in the river. The water was cold, and the chill reached out for my bones.

I crouched down and set the obsidian disc on the river rocks beneath the water. Almost a minute passed, and I couldn't help the rising worry in my gut. Nixie was bouncing between Europe and the Obsidian Inn, violence with the queen had been escalating, and now we had evidence of the queen moving against humans. Nixie needed to know. We needed the water witches' help.

The knot in my stomach loosened just a hair when the disc pulsed with a soft light.

"Damian," a voice said, rising from the river. "What is it?"

"Alexandra or Euphemia with you?"

"No, they're on a mission with the Obsidian Inn. Why?"

"We might need reinforcements."

The water took on the rough shape of Nixie's face, just enough that I could see her frown. "What's wrong?" she asked.

"The queen has attacked some of the guardsmen stationed here. One of them was in the hospital, bleeding green poison. Sounds like the queen's troops were impersonating us, or at least Foster."

Nixie cursed. "I don't like this, Damian. The coincidence and the timing are too much."

"What coincidence?" I asked.

"I can't say over our connection. This isn't secure enough. I'll send someone to you when I can, but for now, use caution."

I nodded. "I will."

The light on the disc began to fade, but not before I heard her whisper, "I love you."

"I love you, too."

✦   ✦   ✦

FRANK AND PARK were gone when I got back to the shop. The bell on the door jingled as it closed behind me.

"Alexandra and Euphemia are both on a mission with the Obsidian Inn," I said, glancing between Zola and the fairies. "Nixie will send someone when she can, but I don't know when that will be."

"Good," Foster said. "That gives us time."

I started toward the back room to grab my backpack, filled with beef jerky, bullets, and other things that were essential to any mission. It was only then that I noticed Foster and Aideen were both in their armor, the intricate details of Celtic knot work flowing over their silver cuirasses and down their greaves. Foster held his helmet under his left arm while Aideen left hers resting between her feet on the glass countertop.

I scooped my backpack up off the shelf and patted Bubbles on the head when she stuck her snout out of her lair's entrance. I thought about bringing the cu sith with us, but the pony-sized dog might attract more attention than we needed. I looked to the corner where I had often kept the demon staff before it tried to kill me. I still couldn't break the habit of wanting to grab it when things were going sideways.

I pushed my way through the saloon-style doors and adjusted my backpack. "Ready."

"Stealth," Aideen said. "This is no time for theatrics." She stared at Foster as she spoke, but he didn't shy away from her words.

"Do you think that armor is low-profile enough?" I asked.

"No other fairy wears this armor," Foster said. "Even if there is an imposter Demon Sword, there are some things he cannot duplicate."

I wasn't exactly sure how much I believed that. I'd seen some pretty crazy glamor put on by fairies. They were the kind of illusions human perception couldn't pierce. But I didn't think this was the time to pry.

"Are we driving?" I asked. "Let's take the car."

"Yes," Zola said, "because your car is so low profile."

We followed Zola through the back and out into the parking lot where my '32 Ford Victoria waited. Zola and I climbed into the front seat while the fairies took up a post on the dashboard.

"From what Casper told us," I said, "it sounds like they were attacked right by the comic store."

"Start there," Zola said.

I turned the ignition and pulled out of the parking lot, swinging down onto the cobblestones for a moment before the road mercifully changed to asphalt. We followed Main Street until it merged into N. 2nd Street, and the roundabout sent us off to the north. We briefly drove through a residential area before the buildings became strip malls. I turned right into one of the first of them, which held the local comic shop.

Aideen shifted the helmet in her hands. "We should leave these here. If one of Nudd's court is the imposter, it may make it easier to find us. Or, at the least, see us."

Foster let his helmet fall to the dashboard, the coif rattling as the metal slithered to a stop.

I stepped out of the car, and the fairies zipped over my shoulder, hovering just above me for a second before settling onto the roof of the car.

"Work toward the bridge," Zola said. "You hear anything, scream."

Zola was one of the most reassuring people I had ever known in a fight.

"We'll be right above you," Foster said. "If anything kills you, we'll kill it."

"If you don't mind," I said, "kill it before it kills us."

Foster shot me a grin before launching himself into the air. Aideen followed.

CHAPTER FIVE

"I THOUGHT PARK said they were closer to the river," Zola said.

I glanced up and one of the pale silver dots drifted back down toward us, until I could make out Aideen's form.

"That's true," Aideen said. "But that bridge is steel and iron. Unless they're very powerful, or very stupid, I suspect they will be quite predictable."

"What do you mean?" I asked.

"I mean they'll still be in the area, if they haven't already retreated to Faerie. No mere soldier will risk contact with a bridge that deadly."

Aideen flexed her wings and rose into the air, rejoining Foster far above us.

"Smart," Zola said. "We head for the bridge, follow it to the river, and search the grid."

I sighed and kicked a stone across the parking lot. It wasn't a long walk to the bridge, but Zola's plan meant we were going to be out there for a while, unless something decided to ambush us. I frowned at the thought. "So, you think we'll get ambushed?"

Zola smiled knowingly. "Bored already, boy?"

I chuckled and adjusted the pepperbox holstered under my arm.

The asphalt of the parking lot gave way to an unruly section of long grass and scrub brush. We reached the bridge a short time later and turned right, heading east toward the river. I remembered running Lewis down not far from here when Philip had kidnapped Zola. It seemed like yesterday, but it had been years. Memory felt heavy, and it took me a moment to realize that the weight wasn't from the memory at all. The dead were close. Very close.

Gravel and dirt made it hard to walk silently, but the roar of the nearby freeway helped mask any sound we would make. What concerned me was that it would also mask the sound of any attack that might be heading our way.

I glanced up but saw no movement. "You see them?"

Zola nodded. "To the south a bit. Ah believe they're behind this junkyard, or whatever it is."

Old rusted-out cars flanked the railroad tracks. The lot looked like it might be a body shop, but some of those cars had been there for decades. We passed the junkyard and made our way down the gradual decline that ended at a line of trees just before the river bank. Zola sighed and glanced back the way we had come. She stared at the river for a short time, and then turned to the south.

"This will take all night," she said. "You take one side of the building, boy. Ah will take the other."

"I don't like splitting up," I said.

"Neither of us are alone, boy. Foster and Aideen are with us."

Zola vanished between two buildings on the junkyard property. I waited for a short time before moving, and then when no one screamed, I started forward.

I neared the riverbank first as the trees thinned, hoping to catch a glimpse of whatever water witch had almost killed Casper. The witch who had killed Casper's teammates. The more I thought about running into an undine on that bank, the more I thought it might be a terrible idea. I didn't have one of the stone daggers that could kill a water witch. I didn't even have an arrowhead. Foster and Aideen might, but I'd be helpless outside of my shield if that river surged forward and struck out at me. That was enough to send me wandering off away from the water, down a path on the opposite side of the junkyard.

A shadow moved in the distance, and my heart leaped, calming only when I realized it was Zola's hooded form. Our paths crossed time and again as we walked the grid across the junkyard, and eventually moved past it.

The attack site was plain to see once we found it. The earth was disturbed, but that was the least obvious sign. The nearby tree line was scorched—parts of it ash and others charred beyond recognition. The sight gave me pause because it certainly looked like the fire had been spherical, and I remembered that searing orb of death Foster had once conjured.

I raised my voice. "Zola. Here."

She rounded the nearby building, which I suspected was the office for the salvage yard. She paused for a moment, taking in the sight of the torched copse of trees standing between us.

"Ah did not expect it to be this obvious," Zola said. "This is not the subtle work of the Fae."

"You think?" I said, my voice flat.

Foster glided into my line of sight for a moment before settling on my shoulder. "Not subtle?" His eyes rolled from the trunk of the tree off into the scorched canopy. "Someone wanted whoever found this to know it was Fae." Foster cursed. "They want people to think this was me. And if people think I did this, they'll think it was one of Nixie's witches that stabbed the soldiers. That they used the poison blades."

"And imagine how convincing it will be with your armor strewn across the battlefield," a voice screamed from our right.

We all turned toward it, and that's when the attack came from the woods behind us.

For a split second, I thought Stump had come to help us. But the face of the Green Man was twisted in rage, and he was far taller than Stump. The fist I thought might be angling for our attacker was actually coming for me.

I raised my arms and shouted, "*Impadda!*" The shield burst into brilliant life a second before the Green Man's attack connected and a shower of sparks flew into the air. I stumbled backward, barely staying on my feet as the Green Man struck again.

I didn't think shooting him with the pepperbox would do any good. Maybe it might if I channeled fire through the gun, but I knew how that could end up. That had been what had sent Leviticus into the darkness during the Civil War. Instead, I reached out to the gravemakers, called the dead to me, and raised the Fist of Anubis. My shield flickered and died as my concentration waned before the protective light snapped out of existence. The nauseating rusted flesh surging out of the earth around me replaced the glow of the shield.

The Green Man was already committed to his attack. There was no way for him to slow. No way for him to avoid the attack. The Fist connected with a satisfying crunch, snapping one of the larger branches from his chest and sending a cascade of leaves and debris off into the woods behind him. He fell to one knee while I let the Fist expand, the Hand of Anubis wrapping around the Green Man's head and pulling him forward, smashing his face into the earth.

Foster's bellow drew my attention away from my foe. The Green Man rolled to the side, but he did not attack again.

A sword streaked in blood glistened from the back of Foster's armor, piercing him. To land the strike, Foster's opponent had had to open his guard. Foster didn't miss his chance. He lunged forward, impaling the Fae knight much as the fairy had impaled Foster in turn. Only, when Foster struck, his sword cleaved through his opponent's cuirass and sank into the tree behind him. The blade pinned the knight in place. The fairy struggled, but could not free himself.

I looked around for Zola but couldn't find her. "You good, Foster?"

"Yes," he snarled, his dagger sinking into the other fairy's shoulder.

I ran past Foster and rounded the corner of the short building. Aideen's sword clanged off the helmet of a dark-touched vampire. Zola was there too, crouched on the ground, a scorched ruin beneath her left hand. I don't know what, or who, it had been, but Zola had made sure they were no longer a threat.

Aideen closed on the dark-touched vampire and feinted left. It gave me enough time to line up a shot with the pepperbox. I took it, the boom thundering across the battlefield. It didn't do any real damage to the vampire, but it caused the creature to pause and look, and that was the last thing it ever did. Aideen slid her sword through the thing's eye socket. It stiffened, and then fell to the ground.

"Are you hurt?" Zola asked.

Aideen shook her head. "No, where's Foster?"

"He has the fairy knight pinned to a tree," I said.

"Alive?" Aideen asked.

I shrugged. "Probably not for long."

Aideen hurried past me. Zola and I followed.

"Who sent you?" Foster growled.

The fairy tried to speak, but Foster cracked the side of his face with an elbow. "If you try to use that incantation again," Foster said, "I'll tear you into 1,000 pieces before you burn to death."

"The Green Man is awake," Aideen said. "I thought you would have killed him."

"I may have gotten a little distracted," I said, glancing at the prone form that was struggling to rise.

"This is good," Aideen said. "We have no need of the knight."

"Then I shall remind him of the true power of the Demon Sword," Foster snarled.

Evening turned to a bloody sunset as Foster wrapped his hands around the knight's neck. A hellish incantation of fire whirled to life. The grass and the earth burned away as the roaring cyclone of flame and rage scoured the knight from the earth.

CHAPTER SIX

OSTER'S FIRESTORM FADED, and our group's attention slowly turned toward the downed Green Man. He still hadn't regained his feet, but his emerald eyes were wide, aware and staring, fixated on Foster.

"Noble one," Aideen said, "why did you attack us? Why did you attack the Demon Sword of the Royal Court, son of the Sanatio of the city?"

The bark-like flesh of the Green Man showed what I could only describe as a frown. Layers of flesh shifted as his mouth slowly opened. "The word of the Demon Sword himself told me there was an imposter here."

"Clearly I didn't." Foster pinched the flat of his blade and ran his fingers down it, clearing the edge of blood and ash. "And you were wrong."

"You must tell us who sent you," Aideen said. "Our lives, and those of all who stand against the king, are at risk."

Aideen certainly hadn't exaggerated about our lives being in danger. I did wonder if our lives being at risk, or our dying, would affect the lives of all who stood with us. Even if it didn't, it still put the lives of all humans in front of a homicidal king.

The Green Man considered Aideen's words. He slowly sat up, bark and broken branches cascading from the left side of his body where I had struck him with the Fist of Anubis. "I did not know. One of Stump's most trusted advisors, an old friend, an ancient Green Man, told us that the imposter would be here. I do not understand why he is not."

"The imposter is dead," Foster said, indicating the pile of ash with his sword.

"Please," Aideen said, drawing the Green Man's attention away from Foster. "We need to know who told you this."

The Green Man hesitated. "He does not have a human name, like Stump does. Many of our people have taken human names."

I didn't really consider Stump a human name, but perhaps to an ancient and immortal tree, that was as human as it got.

Zola circled behind the Green Man, her forehead wrinkling as she peered into the woods and back.

The Green Man continued. "He was crowned with flowers, a unique feature I have not often seen in my many years, though Green Men like him were once known to roam the lands around what is now named Kansas City. It is a smaller city, a sub-city." The Green Man frowned. "I do not believe that is the word used for your sub-cities, and it is not the heart of the city; it is the smaller city around the heart of the city."

"Your point?" Foster said, impatience showing plainly on his face.

"I do not know the Green Men around Kansas City anymore. Perhaps one of them can tell you more about the imposter Demon Sword."

Foster splayed his fingers out across his silver chest plate. "*I am the Demon Sword.*"

The Green Man stared at Foster's armor for a time before nodding.

"The imposter is dead," Foster said, pointing again at the charred corpse on the nearby earth.

The Green Man stared at that circle of death for a time before he said, "That is not the armor of the imposter. The imposter is said to wear the brilliant silver of—"

"I think that's enough of that," a voice said as a sword exploded through the Green Man's face. I caught a glimpse of silver armor before the Green Man burst into a hellish, swirling fireball. The Green Man's scream grated against my ears, drilling his horror into my mind before thunder sounded, the shattering of a tree trunk as if impacted by a cannonball. The Green Man's flesh charred and popped and exploded, sending tiny splinters to ricochet off Foster's armor as the fairy backpedaled.

I raised a shield and watched the edges of the fire, waiting for something to circle around. Waiting for something to attack us. I was half blind from the inferno, and it would be almost impossible to see anything until it faded. But the attack didn't come from around the flames. It came from within it.

Had Foster not been between me and that fireball, and the white-hot sword lancing out, I might have had issues.

Foster roared as he deflected the newcomer's blade. In one smooth motion, he sent the sword skittering along his own cuirass before ramming the hilt of his sword into the face of the other fairy. The attacker stumbled backward, surprise lit across his now-bloody face.

Zola fired off two bolts of flame as Aideen dove from above, her sword angled to remove the attacker's head.

The fairy threw himself to the ground, avoiding the bolts of fire and the sword meant for his neck. He sprang back to his feet an instant later.

I drew the pepperbox and leveled it at Foster's back. "Foster, left."

The fairy didn't hesitate. He threw himself to the side. As soon as my line of sight cleared, I fired. The round clipped the attacker's shoulder, but his armor was powerful enough to deflect the bullet. That showed us in an instant that it was no ordinary armor.

The fairy had barely recoiled, as if someone had merely punched him in the shoulder instead of shot him. He grinned at me. "I think that's enough of that."

He shot into the air, bringing his sword up in a backward arc. The motion opened a red wound in reality and the fairy vanished through it.

Foster and Aideen stared up into the sky.

"Did you see it?" Foster asked.

Aideen nodded. "He wears the armor of the Mad King."

"Who was that?" Zola asked.

Foster took a deep breath, and his nostrils flared. "Drake."

"Drake died in the Wandering War," Aideen said, her brow creasing.

Foster's eyes trailed down from the evening sky and focused on Aideen. "It wouldn't be the first thing Nudd lied to us about."

"You gave me a name," Zola said, "but that doesn't answer my question."

Foster wiped off his sword and nodded. The metal rang against the scabbard until the hilt slammed home. "Drake was an owl knight."

"How did he call that magic if he's not a Demon Sword?" I

asked. Foster had never been overly forthcoming about his abilities as a Demon Sword. I could understand why. The abilities of the Fae court were some of the most closely guarded secrets in their world.

"Drake is said to be descended from dragons," Aideen said. "It's an old story, from an older time."

"Descended from dragons?" Zola said, a hint of amusement in her voice. "I suspect Jasper would have an opinion on that."

"Drake was fireborn," Foster said. He glanced from Zola to me and squeezed the hilt of his sword. "You know most Fae cannot use line arts the way a mage can. Our powers are more organic, tied to our natures, and some would say our souls."

"You have the power to heal," I said. "I would think that says very good things for your soul."

"And yet we can die from it," Aideen said. "Destroyed by the very thing you think to be so pure."

A memory flashed through my mind. That terrible moment in the Burning Lands when I had failed, failed by accomplishing our goals, springing a trap that Nudd had set in motion. I remembered Cara's screams, and the last time I'd ever seen her.

"I know," I said. "And I wish she was here now."

"So, is Drake Nudd's assassin?" Zola asked. "It would seem unwise to attack us as a group. Ah would expect more from one of Nudd's elites."

"It could've been a show," Aideen said. "It's clear the Green Man knew something, and Drake needed to silence him."

"Drake opened a portal," I said. "Does that tell you anything?"

Aideen nodded. "He's descended from the court to some degree. No one can simply step into the Warded Ways without a fixed entrance, unless the court's blood runs in their veins."

"If I have learned one thing," Zola said, "it is this: when dealing with the Fae, we cannot assume the answer is one or the other. He may have come here for us. He may have come here for the Green Man. Or he may simply have come here for the soldiers they killed. I suspect the answer lies with all three."

Foster nodded and blew out a sharp breath. "You're right. Killing the soldiers and making it look like me breeds hostility, or at least distrust, between us and the military."

"And because we live inside Damian's shop," Aideen said, "the military is far more likely to distrust him. I don't like to ponder what the situation would be if it was not for Frank's relationship with Park. I only hope it's enough."

"We need to find them," I said. "Park needs to know what happened here."

Something slithered through the grass behind me. My heart hammered in my chest. I raised a shield as I turned to face the sound.

CHAPTER SEVEN

"**W**ELL NOW," A sultry voice said. "Why the long faces? And why are you drawing a soulsword on me?"

I let the blade fade, hardly remembering drawing it in the moments before. As my eyes adjusted to the evening light, I could make out Alexandra's features and her long black hair.

"Christ," I muttered. "You about gave us all a heart attack." I glanced behind me, and noticed that no one else seemed to be having a heart attack at all.

"He's jumpy," Zola said.

"And I think I have a right to be," I said. "Have we already forgotten the fairy knight that tried to kill us, and the dark-touched vampire, and the Green Man?"

"What?" Alexandra asked. "Nixie wasn't exaggerating. What's happening?"

"The usual," Foster said. "Someone that should be dead, isn't."

"No," Zola said, "I doubt very much that anything she said was an exaggeration."

"Come back to Death's Door with us," I said. "We need to find Frank and Park."

Alexandra opted to take the river back to the store. Foster and Aideen went with her, leaving Zola and me to take a short walk back to the car. We were silent most of the way, walking into the bloody sunset as it scorched the sky.

"How late is it?" Zola asked.

I checked my phone. "Eight o'clock."

"I'm too old to eat this late."

"Oh man, why do you have to say that?" I said. We climbed back into my car and headed back to the shop. And, I suspected, dinner.

Sam's black SUV was parked outside Death's Door, and I hoped that meant Frank was back too. Although we hadn't been gone that long, it might have been long enough for him and Park to do whatever they were planning to do.

✦　✦　✦

"NOT DEAD YET?" the snide little face said from the lower deadbolt at the back of the shop.

"Why haven't we just killed him yet?" Foster asked. "It's not like Mom's still around to torture him. We should just put him out of his misery. And ours."

Foster glided to the ground and stood before the twisted face. He drew his sword, and the deadbolt laughed.

"Foster," Aideen said, "stop."

Foster glanced back over his shoulder, eyeing Aideen. "What is it?"

"He has never taunted us like that. Not once."

"Actually, that seems to be all he's ever done," I said. "But I guess I'm special."

Foster's gaze snapped back to the deadbolt. "What have you done?" Foster pulled his sword back, ready to strike.

The deadbolt laughed again. "You think to threaten me with that thing? You think to threaten me with death? When I have been trapped here so many years?"

Foster smiled, and there was nothing friendly in the expression. He lunged forward, his sword piercing the outer edge of the deadbolt's face.

The eyes in the dark bronze widened, and Foster released his grip on his sword, leaving it embedded in the metal.

"I can't hear you," Foster said. "I can see you trying to scream. Can you feel my blade inside your head? Can you feel the power inside that thing? Does the legacy of the Sanatio not run through your veins?"

The deadbolt shook, and fluid leaked from the edges of its eyes.

"Foster," Aideen said, placing a hand on her husband's shoulder.

Foster pulled the sword from the deadbolt and slid it gently into its scabbard.

Sound exploded from the bronze face, a shrill cry that had me covering my ears to stop the piercing wail.

"Silence yourself," Foster said. "Or I will cut you from that door, and let the humans have you. Imagine what they could do with their iron and steel if a mere fairy blade can do *that.*"

I crouched down and crossed my arms, resting my elbows on my knees. "What do you know?"

"Do what you will. My fate is sealed regardless."

"Your fate may be sealed," Zola said, "but the amount of pain you endure meeting that fate is not."

We stayed there for a time, at a stalemate with the Fae trapped inside the deadbolt.

"He knows something," Aideen said. "That he's not willing to tell us likely means it involves someone who'd hurt him far worse than us."

"I thought you knew us better than that," Foster said, baring his teeth at the deadbolt.

The face winced.

"It could've spoken to the humans," Aideen said. "A hapless commoner, maybe?"

Still no response.

"Let's go in," I said. "See if Frank's back. It's not like we don't know where to find this guy."

Foster frowned for a time and then nodded. When he stepped to the side, I pulled back and kicked the face right in the nose with a steel-toed boot. The deadbolt popped open.

We filed through the door and slammed it closed. The deadbolt grumbled on the other side.

A stampede sounded above us, and two barks, as deep as hell itself, filled the air.

"Upstairs," Sam shouted. "Bubbles!"

Bubbles tried to stop on the stairs when Sam called her name, but inertia can be a real bitch. I frowned at the mountain of green bristly fur that had just lost its traction.

"Shit," I muttered. Foster flashed into his full-size form, grabbing Zola and leaping over the railing, sparing her from the imminent collision.

Bubbles made about one half a rotation before she collided with me. It wasn't unlike getting hit by a car. More fur, a little less blood. But it still hurt like hell when my tailbone bounced off the hardwood at the bottom of the stairs. Thankfully, my stomach had provided a soft landing spot for Bubbles, and she was just fine. She licked my face with great enthusiasm, and then rocketed back up the stairs to Sam, who was now choking back laughter.

"Ouch."

"Well," Sam said, "Alexandra is already upstairs. She said you were attacked."

"Yeah," I said, "but they did less damage than the cu sith."

"Thanks, Foster," Zola said. "I much preferred to observe that from a distance."

I grunted and climbed up to my knees, wincing at the pain in my shoulder. My back. My left knee. My right ankle. "Ouch."

"I can heal that, Damian," Aideen said.

"That would be great. Let me go flop into a nice soft chair." I glanced up at Sam. "Is Frank back?"

Sam shook her head.

"Have you heard from him?" I asked, starting up the stairs. Slowly.

"He's on his way. We're supposed to go out for a late dinner."

My stomach rumbled at the mere mention of dinner.

"I thought the corpses you placed in the river would have deterred attacks more thoroughly," Alexandra said as I crested the stairs.

"You'd think," I said.

I was still hobbling my way down the hall when Foster glided past me. He swooped down on the coffee table, raising a hand to Sam in greeting as she settled into one of the overstuffed chairs. I glanced over my shoulder to find Zola moving a lot more gracefully than I was. Aideen was hanging onto one of her braids, but I couldn't make out their conversation.

The bookshelves upstairs were full enough they didn't give me much room to hold on. I stumbled a bit as my ankle tried to give out, and I began to regret not taking Aideen up on her offer to heal me downstairs.

Zola raised an eyebrow in judgment as Aideen climbed one of the bookshelves beside me.

"Oh, Damian," Aideen said. She didn't give me any notice, simply said, "*Socius Sanation.*"

I winced as the tendons and muscles in my ankle knit back together. It wasn't until the healing hit my back that I really understood how much damage Bubbles had done. Something cracked and shifted, and my vision went white for a moment before the pain faded.

"Thanks." I took a few deep breaths and still clung to the bookshelves. The fairies had healed me enough over the years that I knew trying to walk immediately would just result in a quick face plant.

"Try not to be so stubborn," Aideen said.

Sam flashed me a grin.

"Shut up." I made my way to the nearest overstuffed chair and settled in with a sigh as Aideen landed beside Foster.

Something crinkled. Like stiff plastic or foil. I glanced around the group and my eyes settled on Alexandra. Her hand vanished into a Ziploc bag, pulling out a huge strip of beef jerky.

"Food," I said, drawing the word out.

Sam sighed and raised an eyebrow. "Are you not going to survive?"

Alexandra looked down at the bag of beef jerky in her lap. She smiled and leaned forward to hand it to me. "We don't have anything quite this spicy in Faerie."

"Not unless it's being used for torture," Foster said. "I wonder what would happen if we fed that to the deadbolt."

I took the bag from Alexandra and winced at the fiery aroma. "I didn't realize this was Frank's death jerky."

"Lord," Sam muttered. She scooped another bag up off the floor and tossed it to me. "Less spicy."

I handed the face-melting bag to Zola, who seemed very happy to accept it. She was reaching for her second piece when Bubbles's tongue shot out and stole it. The cu sith chewed, and then froze. Her head cocked to the side, and she tried her damnedest to spit out the fiery piece of jerky.

Bubbles vanished and thundered down the stairs. I suspected she was heading for her water bowl.

"That's something I've never seen before," Alexandra said.

I popped a piece of the bland jerky into my mouth. It was a great teriyaki recipe, a fantastic blend of salty and sweet.

"I could get you a piece of old cardboard instead," Zola said.

"Just because something won't burn your face off," I said, "doesn't mean it isn't fantastic."

Alexandra smiled and took a few pieces of inferno jerky from Zola when she offered.

"What's been happening?" I asked Alexandra. "Nixie said she couldn't come here herself, and that you and Euphemia were both tied up."

Alexandra nodded. "Things have gotten worse in the far east of Falias. It isn't only the queen's attacks in Europe we must be vigilant for. She's been striking the military patrols along the coastal waters."

"Not surprising," Aideen said. "You told us yourself some of the queen's soldiers don't wish to set foot in Saint Charles."

"Of course not," Alexandra said. "You've lined the rivers with the corpses of their sisters."

Sam's fingers froze over her phone. "Well, that sounded creepy." She resumed texting a moment later, her fingernails beating out a rapid staccato.

"Regardless," Foster said, "we're glad you're here."

Alexandra nodded. "And I'm happy to come and see you all, but why have you summoned me here? It seems you have everything well in hand, do you not?"

"One of the soldiers bled green poison," Foster said, dropping any pretext from the conversation.

Alexandra froze. "What?"

"Any idea who could've done it?" Sam managed to relay the question without making an accusation. I could say something as simple as "hi" and it sounded accusatory. Sam had much better people skills with some things, but at least I didn't eat them.

The water witch shook her head. "The flower only grows in Faerie, its roots bound in Magrasnetto ore. The last I heard spoken of it, there were none left alive."

"There are already weapons out there," Aideen said. "They don't lose their power so easily."

"It will be lost, eventually," Alexandra said, "but it takes millennia for it to be worked out of the blade. In a mortal's eyes, the poison would never leave."

"I don't believe there can be much doubt who brought those weapons here," Aideen said.

"No," Alexandra said. "Even so, the military here has no understanding of the subtleties of the queen of the water witches."

Aideen frowned.

"I think you understand," Alexandra said with a nod. "Why would the military believe that a water witch stationed in Europe would attack any of their forces in this country?"

"They're setting you up?" Sam asked.

Alexandra nodded. "That's all that makes sense to me. And now you tell me the military here has been attacked with one of our poison blades. There aren't many witches with access to such a powerful weapon."

"Are they as rare as the stone daggers?" I asked.

"Not so rare as that," Alexandra said. "Many believe the stone daggers can still be forged. They are correct. One of the ironborn, or even someone of Calbach's skills could create another. But the very flowers to make the poison daggers are no more, long since extinct."

"Only water witches with access to the Queen's Armory could get their hands on those blades," Aideen said.

Alexandra gave one shake of her head. "There are a few more, in Nudd's Armory. There aren't a great many, but those aren't the only places to get one of the poison blades. Nixie has at least two that I'm aware of."

I cursed.

"You understand," Alexandra said. "It would be an easy thing to frame Nixie for the attack. The military believes that the water witches of the rebellion are to blame. That logic will take a natural course."

"That would lead them back to us," Zola said. She squeezed her knobby old cane. "We cannot sit by and wait for this to play out. We must move."

CHAPTER EIGHT

IT WASN'T LONG before Frank returned to the shop. I hadn't heard the bell on the front door jingle, but Bubbles's barking shook the building. It wasn't the hostile barking that said "Yes, I'm going to eat your face now," but it was loud enough to wake the dead.

I smelled the pizza Sam had asked Frank to pick up. The smell wafted up the stairs before he crested the top, Bubbles trotting along behind him. "Two pies from Talayna's and a dinner salad to go." Frank placed the boxes on the coffee table before slipping into the oversized chair beside Sam. I really thought they would have grown out of the cute stage at some point, but it didn't seem it was ever going to end. We were all just learning to live with it.

"Park is still tied up," Frank said. "Casper was better for a while, but she's not doing so hot now."

"Who is Casper?" Alexandra asked.

We filled her in about Park's sniper. It didn't take long to recite what we knew because, in all honesty, we didn't know much.

"Drake," Alexandra said. "A fairy named Drake, wearing the armor of the Mad King?"

"We saw it ourselves," Zola said. "Ah understand that armor isn't a familiar sight, yes?"

"That would be an understatement," Alexandra said.

Aideen nodded. "Casper's an asset to Park. Would you help me rid her of the remaining poison?"

"That will drain us both," Alexandra said, rubbing the palm of one hand with her thumb. "I don't think it would be wise to be in a weakened state under the circumstances."

"Then we won't heal her completely," Aideen said. "We'll remove the poison from her body. We'll let her heal the rest on her own."

Alexandra contemplated that for a moment before nodding. "Understand that I'll do this to strengthen your alliance with the military."

"I know," Aideen said.

I pulled a slice of pizza out of the box and dropped it onto a paper plate. The rest of the group followed suit. We were silent for a time, and I wasn't sure if everyone else was pondering Alexandra's words as I was. Initially, they sounded cold, but I understood the logic behind them. We needed a stronger alliance with the military. Or one of Nudd's gambits, or the queen's, was going to succeed.

"Oh, wow," Alexandra said as she finished snarfing down her crust. "Where is that pizza from?"

"Across the street," Frank said. "It's not as good as an actual New York pie, but it's a damn fine substitute. Place called Talayna's."

"It's a wonder you haven't eaten there," Zola said. "You've known Damian more than five minutes."

I grinned at Zola.

"I have been to the fudge shop," Alexandra said.

"That's all that matters," Foster said.

"How are we going to get back in to see Casper without Park?" I asked.

The fairies all looked at each other, and a slow smile lifted the corners of Alexandra's lips. "You'll wait here."

"We know where she is, now," Aideen said. "There's no need for you to return with us."

"Foster should stay here, too," Zola said. "They're already suspicious of fairies that look like him."

"I won't be seen," Foster said.

"Zola's right," Aideen said. "You stay here and help Damian eat that pizza."

Foster frowned. "I *am* hungry." He lopped a piece of pepperoni off with his sword and started munching on it. I winced at the thought of where that sword had been in the last few hours. "I'll do it," Foster said. "Though it's a harsh sacrifice."

Aideen gave him a knowing smile. "We shouldn't be gone long. I know where Casper is. I'll guide Alexandra there."

I stuffed another bite of pizza into my mouth and nodded.

"Park isn't there," Frank said. "Don't get yourself caught."

"We'll be careful," Alexandra said. "Aideen and I are better about strategizing. We don't simply stab everyone when we first meet them."

Foster gave her a flat look.

Alexandra and Aideen made their way to the stairs and were gone a moment later. I turned to Frank, who had just taken such a giant bite of pizza I thought he might choke.

"Where's Park?" Zola asked.

Frank chewed his pizza for another thirty seconds or so before he swallowed and finally said, "Talking to one of Casper's squad's lieutenants." He frowned and shook his head.

"He may actually be talking to the major."

"Didn't he say it was the major's decision to have the tanks sent to the city?" Sam asked.

Frank nodded. "Yeah. He did."

"That could be very good," Zola said. "Park is a direct line to the major. He may have influence."

"Let's hope so," I said.

Foster nodded and chewed vigorously on another piece of pepperoni. "And the armor of the Mad King looked a lot like mine. It would be easy for someone to mistake if they weren't Fae. And it would be easy for a Fae to mislead someone if they wished."

Zola frowned. "That's not reassuring."

"Delicate situation," Frank said, "any way you cut it."

"And a good reason to keep Aeros close," Zola said.

"I would've thought the military would be much more trusting of Aeros now," Sam said. "After he helped stop the harbinger by the Arch."

"Police force is," Frank said. "Some of the patrolmen were on the bridge. They saw a lot of what happened."

"Hopefully it won't take something so drastic," Zola said, "to earn the respect of the men with the tanks."

✦   ✦   ✦

FRANK AND SAM left after we finished the pizza. Foster was wrangling Bubbles downstairs, leaving Zola and I around the heavy coffee table. Zola flipped through the pages of Phillip's old journal, smiling at something on one before wincing at some unholy nightmare on another.

"You still miss him?" I asked.

Zola nodded slowly. "Ah do, but it's complicated."

"He did some pretty bad shit," I said.

"I did some pretty bad shit, too, Damian," she said. "The difference is, he never stopped."

I turned the page of the Book that Bleeds, its blood pooling in the pizza box on the coffee table. As much as it had creeped me out the first time I'd seen the book bleed, now that I knew it wouldn't leave any stains, it didn't bother me so much.

"Have you found anything new?" Zola asked.

I shook my head. "There are some sections about the Wandering War." I rifled back a few pages and turned the book toward Zola. "It's not as thorough as I'd like, but there is a myth about the Mad King."

Zola skimmed the page and frowned. "What does it say?"

"You can't read it?"

"Some of it is clear," Zola said, squinting at the book, "but some of the lines shimmer. Like the text is hidden behind another spell."

"That's how the Black Book used to look. Why this page?"

"It's perhaps your bloodline. It can be hard to tell with all the magic."

I spun the book back toward me, flinging a bit of ghostly blood into the air, where it dissipated in an instant.

"We can ask Aideen when they get back," Zola said.

"Foster might know, too," I said.

A wry smile wrinkled Zola's lips. "We want information. We don't want them to stab the book."

"He does like to stab things," I said with a nod.

We studied in silence for a time, interrupted by the occasional bark of the cu sith downstairs, but otherwise left alone among the towering bookcases and musty scent of the old tomes. I hadn't found many writings on the Wandering War. The fairies didn't seem to be fond of putting their history down on paper. Perhaps it was harder to skirt the truth that way, which was a skill they prided themselves on.

Nixie had told me there were libraries, more in the past, but some still stood. One of them was in Nudd's court, a chamber guarded as closely as the king's life. Now that was a sight I would have liked to have seen. Vik and the vampires had some old books in their archives, but I imagined that the fairies likely had tomes that were much, much older.

A passage in the Book that Bleeds that was hidden from Zola's eyes and not from mine. It didn't seem to make sense. And when it came to the Fae, anything that didn't seem to make sense always earned my attention.

"This entire book reads like modern English," I said.

"We know enough to know that it shows a language most comfortable to the reader," Zola said.

"Right," I said, "I understand that, but then why are some of these passages either in old English or just disjointed gibberish?"

Zola frowned. "It may be as simple as the fact its spell has worn in places. If it's like Ward's ... well, wards," she said with a smirk. "The erasure of one small section can wreak havoc on the whole."

I ran my finger across the thin paper and nodded. That actually made quite a bit of sense. I didn't know how the magic worked in the book, but if each page had its own ward for its own binding, it made sense that some pages might be jumbled and others would be clear. But why was it the pages on the Fae?

Had someone revisited them more than any other pages? It was a mystery, and I'd had more mysteries try to kill me over the past few years than I cared to remember.

"I bet Cara would've known."

"Yes," Zola said with a sad smile.

Some days I missed my friend a great deal.

CHAPTER NINE

T HE DEADBOLT IN the back door squawked when someone slammed their foot into it and pushed their way into the shop. A female voice I didn't recognize was shouting, and a moment later I heard Foster shouting back. Zola and I exchanged a look. She scooped up her knobby old cane, and I regretted having left the pepperbox downstairs. I wasn't defenseless, but I also didn't want to accidentally tear the shop down with a badly placed art.

"Foster!" I shouted. "Everything okay?"

"Hospital was attacked," Alexandra said as she dashed up the stairs. It wasn't her voice I'd heard at first. Someone else pounded up the stairs behind her.

"Casper?" I asked.

"Pants," she said. "Foster said you have some pants."

I blinked and glanced at her charred hospital gown. "Why don't you have pants? What the hell happened?"

"I was in a bit of a hurry," Casper said. "Being everything was on fire."

"Some bloody fairy incinerated the ICU," Foster said.

"Killed two guards," Aideen said.

"The imposter was right next to me," Alexandra said. "I could have mistaken him for Foster."

"Same here," Casper said. She turned to face the stairs, in

the blind spot of anyone who might happen to come up. She glanced back at me and caught me frowning at the mesh underwear showing through her hospital gown.

"Enjoying the show?" Casper asked.

"No, I have, I mean ..."

"What he meant to say," Zola said, "is that he will get you some pants."

I nodded quickly, offered Casper an awkward smile, and ran down the stairs.

✦   ✦   ✦

WE KEPT AN array of extra clothes in the closet on the first floor. At one time, we had several shelves that were always full of miscellaneous junk, which made finding anything half impossible. Thankfully, most of that was behind the door now, and we didn't have to remember that everything was half impossible to find until we actually opened the door.

"Was that Casper?" Foster asked as he landed on one of the shelves above where I was rooting. "I didn't recognize her all unwrapped."

I nodded. "Aideen and Alexandra are with her. Apparently you attacked the hospital."

Foster cursed. "Drake?"

"It sounds like the entire ICU was burned up."

Foster cursed at length and then launched himself into the air, gliding to the staircase and rocketing upstairs. I caught sight of Frank and Sam as they returned from whatever post-dinner adventure they'd been on. I turned to the slightly dusty pile of clothes on the bottom two shelves. Casper was a bit shorter than Nixie, but she was solid muscle. Sam's extra sweatpants might be a little short on her, but I figured that would be better than having something too long getting tangled up in her legs. I snatched the black sweatpants off the shelf, grabbed a black T-shirt, and headed back up the stairs.

"It was a powerful glamor," Aideen said. "It looked like you, Foster. I mean every detail."

"Everything except the armor," Alexandra said. "For some reason, he cannot mask the armor of the Mad King, or chose not to."

"A tactical decision?" Casper asked, taking the sweatpants from me. "It's possible he didn't mask his armor so that his own people wouldn't kill him."

"As good a theory as any," Zola said. "How much damage was done to the hospital?"

"If there was anyone else in the ICU," Casper said, "they're dead."

"Drake burned out most of what we could see," Aideen said.

"I extinguished what I could," Alexandra said. "Once the sprinklers went off, it was easy enough to guide that tainted water."

"I'm so glad you were there," Aideen said with a shudder. "Who knows how much iron had leeched into that water."

Alexandra shook her head. "It couldn't have been much. If it was truly Drake, he isn't ironborn. That would've hurt him just as much as it would hurt you."

Frank coughed and turned away when Casper nonchalantly dropped her hospital gown and slipped into the T-shirt. "What ..." Frank started. "So they're really trying to kill Casper?"

"I'd say so," Casper said. "You can turn around now," she said with a smile.

Sam didn't say anything, but she gave Frank a small smirk.

"I'm glad everyone has pants now," Foster said. "Did anyone see you come into the shop? Did anyone follow you?"

"Foster," Sam said. "Who else could it have been? You think Drake won't know it was one of us?"

"I guess it's a good thing we have some defenses here," I said. "Although we need to put a muzzle on that deadbolt if it's really been talking to the commoners."

"You are strange people," Casper said. "I need to get ahold of Park. He needs to know what happened."

"You need to stay here," Zola said. "You're the only one Park will fully trust. Without you, he may believe Foster capable of attacking the hospital."

Casper shook her head. "You don't give him enough credit. He's talked about Foster and Aideen at length. Even the big rock that camps out by the river sometimes."

"Mr. Chatty," I said. "That's actually his name. If you see him, you should call him Mr. Chatty."

Zola sighed, clearly exasperated. "Just ignore him."

"Here," Frank said, "call Park on this."

"Thank you," Casper said, taking the phone from Frank. "Can I get a little privacy? Some of what I have to tell Park is not for everyone's ears."

"Yeah, sure," Frank said. "Just go downstairs anywhere you like. With all the books and carpet up here, we can hardly hear anything that goes on down there."

Casper nodded. I noticed her bare feet as she started descending the stairs.

"I think there might be some flip-flops in the closet by the table," I said.

"Thanks." She vanished around the turn of the stairs.

"We should try to keep her here," Aideen said. "If it's only the fairies hunting her, the blood shield is her best chance at staying hidden."

"She's the only survivor," Foster said. "They come for her, it's going to be fast. It's what I'd do."

"What happened?" Sam asked. "They literally attacked the ICU at the hospital? While impersonating Foster?"

Aideen nodded. "And the impersonator ..." She shuddered. "Their glamor was inscrutable."

I started back toward the chairs, settling into the one nearest the shelf on the back wall while the others filtered in.

Sam looked down at the Book that Bleeds and grimaced. "Gross. Did you seriously let that thing fill up the pizza box?"

"But why now?"

"Because he's gross?" Sam responded.

Alexandra smiled. "That is not what I meant. Why would Drake surface now? A man known as the right hand of the Mad King. He was believed to be dead. No one has seen him in hundreds of years."

Zola frowned and rested her hand on top of her knobby old cane. "What do you know of the bindings on the Book that Bleeds?" She glanced at me and then turned her gaze back to Alexandra and Aideen.

"With all due respect, my friend," Alexandra said, "I don't believe this to be the time to discuss that relic."

"Perhaps," Zola said. "But earlier today Damian was reading a passage that remained in the old tongues. A passage about the Mad King."

"The book is ancient," Aideen said. "It's not unusual for those translation spells to wear down. And I believe they were laid on that book long before any preservation runes were added."

"A coincidence then?" Zola asked. "A coincidence those pages were blurred to my eyes, but clear to Damian?"

"I can't read it all," I said. "Some of it's in a language I don't understand."

"But you can read some of what Zola can't?" Alexandra said, frowning. "If you can read the words on the page, but Zola can't, then whatever spell is hiding it is still intact. Why wouldn't it work on you?"

"Could it be his bloodline?" Sam asked.

"I wondered the same thing," Zola said.

"Perhaps not the bloodline," Alexandra said, "as much as the legacy of magic that resides in his soul."

"Well, there's an easy way to test that," Frank said.

We all looked at Frank. Alexandra raised what I suspected to be a skeptical eyebrow.

"See if Sam can read the pages. Damian's soul is in her aura, right?"

"Truly?" Alexandra asked.

"Was that still a secret?" Frank asked. "I thought everyone knew that by now." He pursed his lips and glanced between Sam and Alexandra.

"Nudd and the courts already want to kill Damian," Alexandra said. "I don't think anyone finding out at this point is going to do much damage."

"That's reassuring," I muttered.

"You think it'll work?" Frank asked.

Alexandra shrugged. "There's only one way to know."

"Show us the page," Aideen said.

I ran my finger along the thick pages where the last ribbon bookmark I'd inserted waited. The paper was almost glassy, and the feel was entirely wrong. It always bothered me about the book, how it felt like modern paper when it should have felt like mold or old parchment. I turned the tome toward Sam, Aideen, and Alexandra.

"Can you read it?" I asked.

"I can see it has words," Sam said, "but I don't understand them. It's not in a language I recognize."

"Interesting," Zola said. "But can we be sure Samantha's aura is the reason she can read it?"

Aideen took up a perch on Alexandra's shoulder, and they both gazed down at the old text. Foster glided off the bookshelf and perched on Alexandra's other shoulder.

They studied it for a time before Alexandra finally said, "There is no great secret on this page. I don't understand why this spell is different."

"It's about the Wandering War," I said, "right?"

Alexandra nodded. "There is mention of the war, and the Mad King, but I don't see what this … what this …"

Aideen hopped down onto the table, staring wide-eyed at the Book that Bleeds. The blood pooled around her ankles, just skirting the bottom of her wings. "That can't be. That's not what happened in the war."

"Whose account is this?" Foster asked.

Zola flexed her fingers on her cane. "What's wrong?"

"It has to be a mistake," Alexandra said.

"There's one line here," Aideen said, leaning forward and running her finger along the text. "It states essentially that the Mad King was locked away for all eternity in a prison of his own making. But that's not what happened."

"He was slain," Foster said. "The story of the battle between the Mad King and Gwynn Ap Nudd is one of our oldest tales from the current king's age."

"Perhaps Drake's appearance is not a coincidence," Alexandra said, her expression sober.

"Nixie said something about the poison blades of the water witches not being a coincidence," I said. "I meant to ask you about that."

Alexandra frowned, then glanced between me and the fairies. "Some of the poison daggers were stolen."

"Who knows about it?" Aideen asked.

"Those of us loyal to Nixie have started another armory. There is more than one location, which we thought would help deter the theft of any of the more dangerous weapons."

"I take it you were wrong?" Zola asked.

"No," Alexandra said. "The poison blades are not as closely guarded as the stone daggers. They were in a secondary location, but still heavily guarded, under constant surveillance. The only way the armory could've been discovered is if we have spies in our ranks."

"Is the armory here?" Sam asked. "Someplace close by that they could've taken the blades and used them to kill Casper's squad?"

"No," Alexandra said. "We have assets at the ready, but none of the poison blades were being stored in this country."

"I guess that doesn't really matter, though," Sam said. "If a

Fae took the Warded Ways, they could travel here in an instant."

"And I'm afraid the attack here," Alexandra said, "isn't the first that has happened in this country."

"Falias?" Frank asked.

"Yes. But why do you ask?" Alexandra frowned slightly at Frank. "Have you heard from someone there?"

"That's where all the friendly Fae are supposed to live," Frank said. "If the commoners are getting murdered there, and maybe even the military, it's going to shake up people's trust."

"Yes," Alexandra said, surprise plain in her voice. "I'm afraid that is exactly what has happened."

I cursed. "And that's what has the Obsidian Inn all tied up."

Alexandra nodded.

"Damian?" Casper's voice said, echoing up the stairs. "Damian!" Her voice rose in pitch, cutting off the rest of our conversation.

I hopped out of the overstuffed chair and jogged toward the staircase. "Yeah? What is it?"

"Mr. Chatty is squaring off with some Fae out front."

"What?" Alexandra said, hurrying after me.

Something crashed. A thunderous report like two giant boulders colliding shook the building beneath our feet. I cursed again.

"Aeros," I said. "She means Aeros is out front." I started down the stairs, hurtling down to the middle landing before jumping to the bottom.

"Since when is Aeros called Mr. Chatty?" Sam shouted as she appeared beside me, her sudden vampiric appearance scaring about twelve years off my life.

"Bad joke," I said, following Casper through the saloon-style doors in the front of the shop.

"Christ," I said as I opened the door. It was plain to see what the thunderclap that had shaken the building was. A bloody smear and an explosion of gore had erupted from Aeros's rocky hands. He had literally smashed the life out of something. Or someone.

The disembodied scream that echoed around us a moment later told me it had been a fairy. Ley lines sparked to life, siphoning away the Fae's body. Aeros spread his hands, and the gore-soaked armor within clattered onto the cobblestones.

"That was a clever trick," the remaining fairy said, calling my attention to the shadows outside a nearby shop. He glanced down at his arm, either checking for damage or checking for the viscera of his ally.

"Drake," Alexandra said, coming to a stop a half step ahead of me.

The fairy only glanced at the water witch. He kept his focus on Aeros, the cautious gaze betraying his nonchalant stride.

"Alexandra," Drake said. "I would not have expected you to side with traitors to the throne."

"Our king is a traitor himself. He had to betray the throne to take it. Regardless of the fact our last king was mad."

"I found them attempting to pick the lock on the front door," Aeros said. "They intended to kill the one blessed with the old blood."

"They keep trying to," I said. "And they keep dying." I gave Drake a broad smile.

CHAPTER TEN

"**Y**OU DIED," ALEXANDRA said, narrowing her eyes as she focused on Drake. "Some of our people were there when you fell beside the Mad King."

The smile that crawled across Drake's face gave me chills. "Your kind live to be old enough and wise enough to know that what you see is not always what is happening."

Foster exploded into his full-size form beside me, and Aideen immediately followed. Foster walked off to my left while Aideen circled toward the right. The wider our horseshoe formation grew, the farther away Drake stepped.

"I will kill you where you stand," Aeros said. His eye lights flicked to me and then back to Drake. I wasn't sure if he was looking for some cue, or if I had no influence over the situation.

"I've seen you strike," Drake said. "You won't catch me so easily."

"Enough talk," Aideen growled. She lunged with her sword, the attack so unexpected that I thought my eyes might be wider than Drake's. He barely raised the sheath of his sword high enough to deflect the blade, sending it skittering along his armor to take a small piece out of his forearm. If he'd failed, that blade would have been sinking into his heart. Drake's eyes flashed toward Foster and he launched himself skyward a mere second before the cobblestones rose to swallow him.

"I already told you, I'm too fast," Drake said, slashing the air with his sword and slipping into the Warded Ways.

"What were you doing?" Foster asked.

"That strike was meant to kill him," Aideen said.

"It's unlikely that you would catch a knight that off guard," Alexandra said.

Aideen nodded. "Yes, but that attack wasn't without fruit. Drake, or this fairy who claims to be Drake, was wrapped in a particularly strong glamor. His armor deflected my sword a fraction of an inch sooner than I expected it to. He shouldn't have been able to deflect that strike."

"Meaning what?" I asked.

"Meaning the fairy we just saw," Alexandra said, "was glamored to appear smaller than his true form."

"Why bother to hide that?"

"Damian," Frank said. He tapped my arm.

I turned to look at him and cursed. A squad of soldiers was swarming toward us down Main Street, and it wasn't a casual patrol. The men moved with their rifles raised and trained on us.

"Get behind me," Casper said.

"Bullets will kill you just as well as they will kill us," Zola said. "Be wary."

The squad moved like one long snake, slithering along the shop fronts, one soldier taking up a post inside the entryway of a shop while the rest filed around him. That rolling movement continued until the nearest stood only a dozen feet away.

The soldier in the front used the barrel of his gun to indicate the ground, while the others kept their rifles trained on us.

"Weapons on the ground."

"I don't feel comfortable doing that at the moment," I said.

"Weapons on the ground or you're going on the ground. I don't care which."

I exchanged a glance with Sam. She gave a tiny shake of her head, as if she knew what I'd been asking her with my unspoken eyebrow raise. She wouldn't be fast enough to take them all down before they got a few shots off. And I sure as hell wasn't going to just flay these men alive.

I lifted the holster over my shoulder slowly, setting the pepperbox on the ground as lightly as I could.

"Then the swords," the soldier said, training his gun on Foster.

"Right," Foster said. He and Aideen snapped into their smaller forms and were gone. I suspected they were perched on Frank or Zola's back, but I wasn't going to go looking for them now.

"They won't attack you," I said. "We're on your side." I hesitated at my own words, realizing that I suddenly sounded like a bad 1980s action movie.

"You kidnapped Casper," the soldier said. "Give her back, in the same condition you found her."

"The same condition we found her?" Zola asked. "That would require us to injure your friend quite severely."

Casper stepped out from behind me, and most of the guardsmen lowered their weapons.

"Casper?"

"You look like you've seen a ghost," Casper said. "Where's Park?"

"We heard you were dying," the guardsman said. His brow

furrowed. "You look … alive."

"Thanks to them," Casper said with a nod toward us. "I thought you were going to shoot them just now. And, yes, I'm feeling much better."

"Where are the fairies?" the nearest soldier asked. "We're supposed to bring the one that attacked you."

"You just missed them," Sam said.

"That's the vampire," the bigger, louder soldier said from the back. "Keep an eye on that one."

Frank slid in front of Sam, staring the guardsman down. Sam cocked an eyebrow at him, but didn't say anything.

Casper walked out in front of me, and I muttered a curse when I saw Foster clinging to her back. "Not the best idea," I whispered under my breath.

The fairy shot me a grin. Some of the shit that amused him seemed very strange to me.

"We just saw him," the soldier said.

"No," Casper said. "You saw my friend, Foster. His wife saved me. If not for them, I would've died."

The soldier frowned.

"Foster," Casper said, holding up her hand. "Do not shoot. Keep your weapons down, fingers off the triggers."

Foster climbed up onto her shoulder and flexed his wings. He hopped over to Casper's palm and said, "Hi!"

The louder man toward the center of the group raised his rifle and shouted, "There it is! Take it out!"

"Stop!" Casper said.

Two more soldiers raised their rifles. I took half a step forward and managed to summon a shield before the first shot rang out. The cobblestone street erupted an inch in front of

Casper. She stumbled backward into me, dropping her hand as Foster launched himself into the air. Bullets whined as they ricocheted off the vertical cobblestones left standing from our encounter with Drake. A booming voice said, "Surrender your arms or die."

"Aeros, don't," I said.

"Kill them," Alexandra snarled.

"No!" I said. "Everybody put their goddamned guns down. And don't you get any ideas about drowning people," I said with an eyebrow raised at Alexandra.

I studied our group and didn't see any injuries. I also didn't see Aideen.

"Where's Aideen?" I asked.

A soldier shouted, and Foster vanished too.

"Drop the wall," Zola said to Aeros. A cacophony of shouts and screams rose from the other side of the cobblestone wall. Two more gunshots sounded. Metal echoed and rang out as it fell to the earth, and I didn't need to see it to know that someone had dropped their guns.

"Drop the wall now!" Zola shouted.

Aeros did, the cobblestones returning to their original position, leaving no trace of the wall that had been there a moment before. All the soldiers were still standing, and I was worried that meant Foster or Aideen might have been hurt.

Casper stormed forward. When she reached the larger loudmouthed man from the center of the group, whose uniform proclaimed him Stacy, her elbow flashed out, catching the man in the neck and sending him to the ground.

"What was that?" one of the soldiers shouted.

I jogged after Casper and slowed when I saw what was on

the ground. Foster and Aideen had cut the guardsmen's M16s to ribbons, strewing the barrels and sights across the cobblestones.

"Oh man," I said, "I hope I don't have to pay for that."

"I don't care if I'm not in uniform," Casper said. "If I give you an order, follow it."

"Where the hell is Foster?" The horrible scream of a fairy being sucked back into a ley line was nowhere to be heard, so I knew he was at least alive. And Aideen, too.

"Up here," a voice shouted.

I glanced up, and found Foster and Aideen perched on top of the Talayna's Pizza sign. Relief washed over me. I glanced at the angry guardsman squaring off against Casper. I nodded to the fairies and turned my attention back to the confrontation.

"Where's Park?" Casper asked.

"On his way, sir," the young private said, coming to attention.

Casper looked back toward Aeros. Her eyes strafed our group. "Frank, come here."

Frank looked at Sam and then hurried forward. "What is it?"

"This is Park's most trusted advisor when it comes to the Fae," Casper said. "You opened fire on a valuable liaison. A known ally. And that doesn't even begin to approach the topic of the fact that you nearly shot *me*."

"Sorry, Casper," a few of the privates muttered in a ragged chorus. By the downturned eyes of some of the soldiers, I didn't think this was the first time Casper had words for them.

In that moment, I was very happy not to be one of those guardsmen. I thought Casper's iron gaze might flay the skin from their faces.

"You're green," Casper said, "but if you don't learn to handle a weapon, you'll be relieved of it."

One of the soldiers looked down at the ribbon-like remains of his M16, but was wise enough not to comment.

"Park is here," a voice said as a shadow turned the corner of the street behind us. My hand went for the pepperbox, which I remembered was still laying on the street. I walked back and scooped up the holster, nodding to Park as he assessed the scene before him.

"Why aren't you in fatigues?" Park asked, eyeing Casper.

"I apologize, sir," Casper said, coming to attention. "I was in a bit of a hurry trying not to get dead."

"As you were," Park said. I wouldn't have thought it possible, but his demeanor was stiffer than usual. Though I was fairly certain that had been a very dry joke with Casper, none of the other soldiers reacted.

"And where is the fairy?" Park asked.

One of the guardsmen pointed to the sign, and Park turned to look up at Foster and Aideen.

"Glad to see no one murdered the wrong fairy. I do have a request, Foster. If you and Aideen could be so kind next time, would you please only relieve these weapons of their triggers? They would be much easier to repair."

"We'll try to be more precise next time your soldiers decide to shoot at us," Aideen said.

Park pinched the bridge of his nose.

"Up on the sign," Stacy croaked out, his throat clearly damaged by Casper's attack. "Take them out. They're all murdering pieces of shit."

Foster placed his hand on his hilt, and Sam creeped up in front of Frank. It was subtle, but it put her close enough to strike if needed.

"Private," Park snapped, drawing the attention of the newly conscious Stacy.

"They need to be put down," Stacy said. "They all do. We owe it to Philly."

Park eyed Stacy for a moment, and then nodded to himself. "Take Private First Class Stacy into custody. Put him in the brig to cool off. The rest of you, return to base. I'll be reporting this to your unit commander. Dismissed." Park's closing words acted like the crack of a whip, and the soldiers scattered, two of them lifting Stacy and helping the injured man walk away.

Park kept his eyes on the retreating soldiers until they reached the next block and vanished up the street. Only then did Foster and Aideen glide down from the sign. Aideen settled on one shoulder, while Foster took up a perch on Park's other shoulder, like the fairy version of an angel and a devil.

"I'm sorry for that," Park said, the commanding tones in his voice giving way to exhaustion.

Aeros took a few steps forward, each footfall grinding and scraping on the stone street. "You need not apologize for the actions of soldiers of whom you were not in command." The Old God crouched down slightly so he was nearly eye to eye with Park.

"They're my soldiers," Park said. "Everything they do is my responsibility."

"It was more mine," Casper said. "I'm sorry I wasn't able to do more."

Park nodded. "Stacy shouldn't be on patrol in this area

anyway."

"And why is he up for a promotion instead of a big chicken dinner?" Casper said under her breath.

Park frowned. "I'm afraid we both know the answer to that."

"Would you care to enlighten the rest of us?" Zola asked. "Seems like it may be important to the people he tried to kill."

I flinched at the venom in Zola's words. It wasn't undeserved, but I didn't want to anger Park when he was one of our only military contacts. But we'd saved Park's life, and Zola was an artist with guilt.

"He's from Philadelphia," Park said. "He lost everyone. Enlisted right after Gettysburg."

"You shouldn't have brought him here," Sam said.

"No," Park said, his voice solemn. "It wouldn't have made a difference. Half the battalion has a story just like his."

"How many other loose cannons do you have?" Frank asked.

"They don't concern me as much as the officers with the same sentiments."

"Officers?" Casper asked. "I think you mean the brass."

"Not all of them."

"Stacy's a mess, sir." Casper crossed her arms and slouched just a hair. I realized she must've been exhausted from the healing. And yet she was still on her feet, still had enough energy to put Stacy on the ground.

"I know." Park's gaze flicked between Frank and Casper. "Casper, I need you to worry about the boots on the ground. Let me worry about the brass. I'll do what I can, but five more commoners vanished outside Falias today. The brass is skittish, and looking to act, looking for answers."

"Casper needs rest," I said. "That level of healing takes it out of you. It's like you've had the flu for a solid month."

"Is that what's wrong with me?" Casper asked. "I was beginning to think some of the poison was still inside me."

Thunder boomed in the distance, and a strong breeze rustled some junk mail in the gutter, carrying the scent of rain.

"Before we go," Park said, "I need to tell you something."

Casper was once again standing at attention. The woman had more stamina than I ever did.

I nodded at Park.

"We've done a great deal of surveillance in the area. And I believe we may have found the Fae's base of operation." He eyed Casper for a moment, perhaps taking in the small tremor that ran down her left leg as she grew less stable. "It's not far from here. And I shouldn't say more about it in the open. You need to be aware there are forces amassing within striking distance. If anything, we think the attack on Casper's squad was a probe, a test to see how we react."

"To see if you'd come and kill Foster and Aideen," Alexandra said, her voice low.

I blinked at the water witch. "Are you okay?"

She frowned at me. "I'm quite okay. I'm also quite familiar with what happens when a military force comes to exterminate an entire people."

"That won't happen," Park said.

"You already said the top brass want us dead," Alexandra said, taking a step toward Park. "You might not be able to hurt me and the other water witches, but my friends are not so invulnerable. Any of them—"

Frank rushed forward and stepped in front of Alexandra, holding his hands up. "We need Park."

The serenity I was so used to seeing on Alexandra's face was gone, replaced by a cold rage that sent ice lancing down my spine. And for a brief moment, I remembered the history of the water witches, their merciless affinity for drowning people. Alexandra took a deep breath and nodded. "I will not stand idly by when the killing begins."

She fell back, leaving Park behind Frank, and taking up a post beside Aeros at the back of the group. The Old God exchanged a nod with her, which told me all I needed to know about his thoughts on the local military.

"Christ," Park muttered. "I need all of your help. Casper, I wanted to avoid it, but I need you to take a squad into the base."

"That's a suicide run," Foster said.

"I know," Park said.

"You sure as hell aren't doing it without us," Foster said.

"You'd support Casper and her squad when they infiltrate the Fae's base?"

"Yes," I said plainly.

Casper's tremble grew into a shake, and she stumbled to her left, where Sam caught her and helped her stay upright.

"We should probably take our leave," Zola said, "or Casper is going to collapse."

The first drops of rain started as the thunderheads moved across the sky. Park glanced up and sighed. "I'll contact you again soon. How long will Casper need to recover?"

"Twenty-four hours," Aideen said. "Perhaps a bit longer. In our experience, a long sleep can help a human's brain understand that its body has been healed."

"Thank you," Park said. "I'll get her back to our base."

"We can drive you," I said.

"I'll take them," Sam said, volunteering. I didn't like the idea of Sam being on the military's radar, considering how much they already knew about our little group, but I was pretty sure all the vampires were on the military's radar.

I nodded. "Thanks."

"Anytime, Demon," Sam said with a small smile. She scooped Casper up into her arms. At first Casper protested, but she gave up after about ten seconds. Park followed them to Sam's black SUV. Frank helped open the doors, and they all piled in. No one said anything until the red taillights vanished up the next block.

"Strange day," Aeros said, tilting his head up to catch the rain as it started to crash down onto us. "I will return to my post, guarding the streets."

The cobblestones beneath him roiled until they had swallowed him completely.

"Back inside," Zola said. "You too, Alexandra."

"Ooo," Foster said. "Somebody's in trouble."

"That's helpful," Aideen said, smacking Foster in the back of his head.

Alexandra eyed the old necromancer for a brief time, letting the rain start to soak into our clothes. "I hope you're prepared."

CHAPTER ELEVEN

W E PLOPPED DOWN into the chairs around the old Formica table, between Bubbles's lair and the fairies' grandfather clock. I cracked open a bag of Oreos.

"Are you okay?" Aideen asked, focusing on Alexandra.

The water witch nodded. "I'm sorry. Park reminds me of a soldier we knew a very long time ago. He had good intentions, but he got many of my sisters killed."

"Atlantis?" Zola asked.

Alexandra nodded. "Yes, only a century before it sank. Perhaps a little more."

"You're not invulnerable," Zola said. "Ah'm not sure you should've said that to Park."

"We're invulnerable enough," Alexandra said. "Though I have found it unwise to underestimate the commoners. They're inventive, and murderous."

"They consider you pretty murderous, too," Foster said. "I mean, before you were reformed and everything. You did have a pretty nasty habit of drowning people."

I shot Foster a grin and my phone buzzed. "It's Sam. They made it."

"Good," Zola said. "The last thing we need is a confrontation with the military."

"You mean to support Park's assault," Alexandra said.

I nodded.

"Then you must understand," she said, "you'll be doing it without the assistance of the Obsidian Inn. Ward, the Old Man, Mike—everyone is out of touch. Whatever is happening there has caused them to go underground. None of us can reach them."

Bubbles flopped her head onto my thigh. She raised her yellow eyes to me, her sad, sad eyes. I slowly chewed an Oreo and glanced down at her as the tip of her pink tongue fluttered in and out of her pouting mouth.

"No dog should be that expressive," I said. "You give guilt trips as bad as Zola." I flipped an Oreo up into the air, and Bubbles's tongue shot out like a chameleon's, snatching the cookie before it crashed onto the table.

"I swear you two could subsist entirely on junk," Aideen said.

"Who's a good dog?" I said in my best baby talk. "Who's a good dog!"

"Thankfully, she's not a dog," Zola said, "or she probably would've been dead from Oreos a long time ago."

Bubbles flopped her furry braided tail back and forth a few times until she finally gave up on me giving her another Oreo. The cu sith trundled off, vanishing down into the shadows of her lair.

"We should go to Falias," Foster said. "If Nudd is making his move …"

"Or the queen," Alexandra said.

"Can we reach the Obsidian Inn through the Ways?" Aideen asked.

"No."

"What do you think it means?" I asked.

"An escalation," Foster said. "But how much of an escalation is it?"

"We can't abandon Saint Charles," Zola said. "What's happening in Falias may be a design to draw us out. Something to get Aeros away from here. Something to get us to leave our home unguarded."

"Then why would Drake be here?" Foster asked. "It makes no sense."

"I agree," Alexandra said. "It's Nixie who should be here. I should be in Falias."

"You believe that?" Zola asked. She crooked a finger at Alexandra. "I don't believe we should allow our forces to be divided any further. It's a simple strategy in war—one that has been used for centuries, as you well know—and we should be wary."

"It's predictable," Foster said.

"Just because it's predictable doesn't mean it's not effective." I blinked and glanced at Zola. That was something she used to say to me during training.

A smile wrinkled her lips. "We stay with Park. I believe he's the real target here."

"Just point me at someone to kill," Alexandra said.

"Are you related to Foster?" I asked. "It really seems like you're related to Foster. He likes stabbing things."

"A lot," Foster said.

"We are related," Alexandra said.

I frowned slightly. "I thought that was just Nixie?"

Alexandra sighed and crossed her arms. "Nixie is what you would call my second cousin."

"That's perhaps a loose interpretation," Aideen said.

Alexandra shrugged. "It's good enough."

I handed Alexandra a cookie. She eyed it with something like disdain. Or maybe disgust. She didn't seem to have much love for processed food, unless it was deep-fried and Irish.

"So," I said. "Are you coming with us in the morning?" I frowned for a moment. "Morning is probably relative. I'm pretty sure we're all sleeping in."

Alexandra looked around the table. "All of you intend to stay here? To fight alongside this commoner and his soldiers?"

"Yes," we said as one.

"That was creepy," Alexandra said. "For now, I'll stay by your side. As my queen has ordered."

"Bubbles makes a nice pillow in an emergency," I said. "You know, if you want to stay here."

"You're welcome to come to the Pit with me," Zola said. "Ah'm sure Vik wouldn't mind, and he has some excellent guest rooms."

"I appreciate the offer," Alexandra said, nodding to Zola. "I believe I'll stay with my cousins in their home tonight."

"I might have an air mattress in the closet," I said.

"That won't be necessary," Alexandra said. "Come Aideen, show me around your home."

Aideen flew toward the grandfather clock, pausing on one of the lower shelves by the swinging pendulum. "It's a little cramped. And try not to get hit by the counterweight. It's not healthy for magical beings."

I stared at Alexandra as she grew translucent and her body pulled in on itself as she stepped toward the clock. By the time she reached the shelf Aideen was standing on, Alexandra was no taller than the fairy.

"What the crap?"

Alexandra frowned at me and put her hands on her hips. "You … didn't know we can what? Shrink?"

"I thought you could just change and vanish into water." I held my hands out, grasping for an answer. "No, I didn't know you could shrink as small as Foster and Aideen."

"Oh," Alexandra said with a smirk, "Nixie's going to have some fun with you."

And with that, she vanished into the recesses of the old grandfather clock.

"Did you know?" I asked Zola.

She shook her head. "I had no idea. Perhaps nothing is stealthier than water inside of a body of water, but imagine their ability to spy by combining those skills."

"But Nixie never showed you that?" Foster asked.

"No."

He grinned. And he kept grinning.

"Are you having a seizure?" I asked.

"Oh no, oh no. It's nothing."

"All right, I'm going to do some studying upstairs and sleep on a chair because who needs a bed, anyway?"

"You should probably just move out of your apartment," Zola said. "It's like you're never there anymore."

I shrugged. "Good night, Foster. Zola." I stood up and walked toward the stairs.

"Damian," Foster said. "Next time you see Nixie, ask her to show you. And make sure you're alone."

I glanced back at the fairy, and he winked at me.

"Oh," Zola said. "It's a sex thing."

Foster burst into laughter, and I shook my head as I headed upstairs.

✦　✦　✦

I CURSED AND flopped onto one of the overstuffed leather chairs. The empty pizza box caught my eye, still filled with translucent blood from the Book that Bleeds. I rubbed my forehead and sighed, turning to the panel in the wall behind me.

The chest was well concealed, both physically and, more importantly, magically. I left it on the floor where I'd slid it from the wall, as it had grown quite heavy with all the various things I'd hidden away inside it. The lid creaked slightly, the wards etched into the top catching the dim light in the little alcove.

Inside was the slot from which I'd pulled the Book that Bleeds, and where I now replaced it, sealing it in a waterproof bag. I used to just toss it in haphazardly, but I must admit that opening the box full of that ghost blood was occasionally unnerving. The hand of glory, Gaia's hand, sat on top of the box's contents, wrapped in a black silk cloth. I moved it to the side, remembering the sight of Gaia's still form resting in the cellars beneath Rivercene. I wondered how much more to the story there was that the innkeeper hadn't told me, and whether I'd ever really learn the full story.

Beneath that were the extra blue obsidian discs Nixie had gifted me. It would be good for our allies to have one, and I also felt a hell of a lot more secure about possibly losing one. It was the easiest way to communicate with her and outside of a video chat, the easiest way to see her, though I was still known to take an impromptu trip with Gaia's hand to visit her on the rare occasions we both had a few hours to spare.

The splendorum mortem rested on the next level of miscellany, its deadly blade inside a brown leather sheath. I ran my fingertips along the cold iron and remembered the sickening crack it had made entering Ezekiel's skull, and the unnerving lack of resistance it'd found.

I frowned at the charred fragments of the shattered demon staff as I shifted the contents around. It was one of the few things I probably didn't need to conceal inside the trunk; there was really nothing anyone could use it for to harm me or mine. It was a stark reminder of how dangerous these objects could be. Of how close I had come to losing everything.

And perhaps that was most important to remember, regarding what lay beneath.

I lifted the Key of the Dead in my left hand and held Tessrian's bloodstone in my right. I still intended to return her to the Burning Lands. I'd given her my word, and without her, we might not have been able to release Vicky from her legacy as the Destroyer. For that, I owed Tessrian. Demon or not.

I set the mottled red and green bloodstone on the coffee table, beside the now-empty pizza box. There was no trace of the blood that had been there before; it vanished as soon as I'd lifted the Book that Bleeds and slid it back into its slot inside the chest.

I turned the dagger across my arm. Its blade wasn't particularly sharp, but I knew what power lived within it. And I had little doubt there was far more for me to learn. What I'd read about the keys of the dead in the Book that Bleeds unnerved me. They could be used to break Seals, the great Seals that separated dimensions. They could be used to rebuild them, or to help forge an entirely new Seal. What the Book that Bleeds had not told me, however, was what powers or incantations one would need to accomplish these things. How dangerous was it in the hands of the seventh son of Anubis?

I ran my thumb in a clockwise circle across the faded runes on the circular ornaments at the base of the hilt. Gwynn Ap Nudd had left the Key of the Dead with me when he could've taken it. A trap? After more research in the Book that Bleeds, I didn't think so. Gwynn Ap Nudd was not ironborn, and the dagger was forged from iron and nickel, diluted with Magrasnetto.

With the Key of the Dead and Gaia's help, I could step into the bloodstone with Tessrian. And legend said I would be able to step into any bloodstone, holding any demon. I don't know that Tessrian and I had what most would call a relationship, but I had something she wanted, and that kept us on fairly good terms.

Stepping into a bloodstone with a random demon, on the other hand, would likely be a long walk off a very short plank.

I set the dagger on the table and picked up the bloodstone. I wondered if there was something else I could do with the demons. Some way to manipulate them into helping us in the war against Gwynn Ap Nudd. But they were unpredictable creatures at best. And some of them weren't demons at all. Regardless of his existence as a fire demon, I could never lump Mike in with those creatures. A memory surfaced, a quick glimpse of Mike's true form, the long limbs, the twisted horns … but I'd also seen his gentleness. I'd seen the oath that he'd sworn. I'd seen his broken spirit when Sarah died. If he had ever been a demon, he wasn't one anymore.

I put the dagger and the stone back into the trunk before sliding Gaia's hand into my backpack. I closed the trunk and placed it gently flush in its nook against the wall, where it vanished. No mortal, nor many Fae, for that matter, would be able to see it. Much less open it.

I'd spent too many hours buried in the Book that Bleeds. I needed something, not necessarily lighter, but something that I could relax while reading. I picked a thin blue tome from the bookshelf on the wall above the chest. And I flipped to the third chapter of Leviticus Aureus and the Fall of Atlantis.

CHAPTER TWELVE

M OST NIGHTS IN the shop, the dead were silent. If anything woke me up, it was usually Bubbles or Peanut streaking into the room like a furry missile before slamming into me on one of the chairs. Tonight was different.

Someone called my name. I was unsure if the voice was there, unsure I'd heard the sound when it first echoed through my consciousness. I grumbled something unintelligible and cracked my eyes open to find a gray form standing nearby. I didn't think anything of it. I just figured it was Koda, using Ward's circle to do some research. My eyes flicked to the clock on the wall. When I realized it was the witching hour, a frisson of dread shot through my spine.

I snapped my gaze back to the form inside the ghost circle. It didn't have Koda's cloak, or his oversized prayer beads resting around his neck. For that matter, the ghost before me wasn't fully formed. It shouldn't have been able to get inside, much less place itself inside the ghost circle, unless it was Koda. That meant it had help, which meant someone else had to be here.

The ghost made no move to approach me. It only held up its hand and stared at the translucent fog that had once been its fingers. When it raised its eyes to me, each was black, struck through with a tiny bit of yellow lightning. "They are coming.

They are near."

My heart rate spiked, amplifying the dread wrapping itself around my spine. "Why? And how did you get in here?"

The ghost was a few feet away from me, and then it wasn't. It moved toward me, one moment a safe distance, and the next I was staring into gold-tinted eyes mere inches in front of my own. "They are coming." The ghost vanished.

"What the fuck?" I muttered. I was pretty sure I wouldn't be getting a lot more sleep that night. I figured I should probably warn the fairies, in case the ghost hadn't been off his rocker. I tried to remember details about him, what he'd been wearing, where I'd seen the patterns on his uniform before. But he'd had a vague form, as if someone had started pulling him apart. Perhaps it had been the aftereffects of being torn away from whatever battlefield he'd died on. I suspected that's what had happened, considering the soul that still waited within his eyes.

For a moment, I wondered if the ghost had been from World War I, like the ghost who had helped us near Rivercene. I frowned. I didn't think so. I was pretty sure his shoulder had an honor braid, and an old one at that. One like they'd used during the Civil War, one that Zola would've called chicken guts.

I hopped out of the chair and rubbed the sleep from my eyes, heading toward the stairs. I tried to remember any nearby battles where an officer might have fallen in the Civil War, as I suspected some of the shadowy forms on the ghost had signified his rank. But I couldn't think of any specific ones.

I paused when I reached the bottom of the stairs. Bubbles stared at the back door.

"You saw it, too."

Bubbles chuffed.

"Keep watch for me."

Bubbles settled onto the floor, her head on her paws, staring at the door. I had to admit, cu siths made good guard dogs. Of course, I also suspected she'd be back in her lair about five seconds after I turned my back.

"Foster, Aideen, you awake?" When no one answered, I knocked on the edge of the grandfather clock. Foster had once told me that was about the same as being hit by an earthquake, so I figured they'd wake up sooner rather than later.

It didn't take long before Foster stumbled out from the back of the clock, stepping onto what had been an empty shelf a moment before, the deep interior of their home hidden by whatever wards had been placed on the old wood.

"What the hell?" Foster muttered.

"There was a ghost."

Foster raised an eyebrow and stared at me.

"An unusual ghost."

"And why does that require you to wake us up with a bloody earthquake?"

"It was weird. All the ghost would say was, 'They are coming. They are near.'"

"Son of a bitch," Foster said. "Why didn't you say so? That's an old fairy warning." He ran back inside the clock, and I suspected it was to fetch Aideen.

✦ ✦ ✦

IT WASN'T LONG before the fairies reappeared on the grandfather clock's middle shelf, Foster in mid-sentence. "...telling you, it was one of the old warnings. Whatever it was, it told

Damian, 'They are coming. They are near.'"

"No," Aideen said. "That phrase is long dead. It hasn't been used in earnest since the time of Atlantis and the fall of the Mad King."

Alexandra's minuscule form sprinted out of the grandfather clock, swelling into her full height, translucent one moment, flesh the next. "We must tell Nixie." She turned her emerald eyes to me. "What did it look like? The ghost, what did it look like?"

"Like a Civil War soldier. Much of his body was ill-defined. I could see honor braids on one shoulder, but it definitely wasn't the uniform of a modern soldier."

"I'll be at the river," Alexandra said. She hurried toward the saloon-style doors, hitting them at a full run. "Don't let anyone into the store that you don't know," she shouted over her shoulder. "If I haven't returned in fifteen minutes, assume the worst. And make ready." She unlocked the deadbolt on the front door and was gone.

"What the hell is going on?" I asked, turning to Foster and Aideen.

"It was the last thing the Mad King's advisor ever said to him," Foster said. "Before one of his own knights took his head. So it's a safe bet that a ghost from the Civil War doesn't know the phrase. Someone manipulated an older ghost."

"Get your gun, your focus, and anything else you can kill with. And then we wait to see if Alexandra comes back."

"Let's follow her and make sure she comes back," I said.

"No," Aideen said. "I understand why you want to, but if this is the beginning of an attack, she has a better chance alone."

"A better chance than what?" I asked.

"A better chance to escape an army stationed outside your door, than having to worry about the three of us."

Bubbles picked that moment to trundle out of her lair and chuff as she looked up at Aideen.

"The four of us," Aideen said, gliding down to settle on the cu sith's head.

The first few minutes flew by as Foster and Aideen slipped into their armor, and I pulled the holster for the pepperbox over my head before sliding the hilt of the focus into my belt. Once the frantic rush to gather our weapons was over, time barely seemed to be passing at all.

✦　✦　✦

"WHO SENT THE message in Atlantis?" I asked.

Aideen and Foster exchanged a glance before Aideen said, "It was Nixie and Alexandra's queen, the last time the throne of the water witches was emptied."

Even though it was one of the few answers I expected to hear, it wasn't reassuring. In fact, knowing so many of our allies were out of touch—either on a mission for the Obsidian Inn or fighting a battle of their own near Falias—was downright unsettling.

"We need to warn who we can," I said, pulling my phone out of my pocket. "You haven't heard from the Obsidian Inn yet, have you?"

"No," Foster said. "Whatever is happening, they either don't need our help, or everyone's already dead."

I thought that was probably a little more black-and-white than reality, but it didn't seem like the time to argue with

Foster. I started texting Sam.

Shop might be under attack. Be ready.

She responded a moment later. *I'll gather the others.*

Hold off until you hear from me. We don't know what's happening yet. It might be a warning. Just waiting for Alexandra's report.

Keep me posted.

"Sam will have some of the vampires ready, if we need them."

I thought about reaching out to Alan, as I knew he was back from Kansas City for at least a week to spend more time with his family. But I didn't want to drag the werewolves into this if I didn't have to. That should be Hugh's choice, as alpha of the river pack. They'd sacrificed enough over the years for us, and to Philip's ruses.

I stared at my phone, a creeping sense of dread crawling up my spine.

"What's wrong?" Aideen said.

"A ruse. This could be a ruse. Not a warning, not an attack. A ruse to keep us here, on our toes, and away from another target."

"Casper," Foster said.

I cursed.

"One of us could go scout the base," Foster said.

I shook my head. "We're thinned out enough as it is. We haven't reached half our allies, and we've heard nothing from Alexandra. They could be waiting for her to come back."

Foster pulled his sword a fraction of an inch from its sheath before slamming it home with a click. "I don't like this."

"Of course not," Aideen said. "You haven't stabbed a single

thing yet today."

Foster gave her a sideways smile.

Aideen glanced at the clock. "Anytime now. If Alexandra isn't back before the quarter hour has ended, we must either make a stand or run."

CHAPTER THIRTEEN

T HE RELIEF I felt when the bell on the front door jingled and Alexandra reappeared in the shop was no small thing. I blew out a breath before asking her if she'd learned anything.

Alexandra shook her head. "Nixie doesn't know any more than we do. The queen's forces haven't moved. The bulk of them are still stationed near the Royal Courts in Faerie, and many more around Falias."

"Then what the hell happened tonight?" I asked.

"I would still believe it to be a warning," Aideen said, "or a distraction."

"Tell Park," Foster said. "They don't need to be caught unaware."

I was pretty sure Frank was the only one of us with a direct line to Park. I figured Sam had probably woken him up, so I texted him, asking him to tell Park to make sure Casper was secure and guarded. And if they had anything with iron in it, to keep it handy.

Frank confirmed the requests. He asked for more details, but unfortunately, I didn't really have any.

"I told Frank to let Park know to call us if they saw anything unusual. They see so much as a hint of a fairy near the base, they'll call us."

"That's good," Aideen said. "Now we must decide. Do we

stay here? Or do we head for the base?"

"Honestly, I think anything short of an army of Fae attacking that base would be a suicide run."

"Not if they're water witches," Alexandra said. "The military won't have the weapons needed to defend against an attack from a water witch."

"Park should have a weapon," Aideen said. "A fragment of the stone dagger, or even an arrow."

"I don't know if that would be the wisest decision," Alexandra said. "I understand your need to protect the humans, but there's a need to protect our own kind as well."

"If Park falls at the hands of the Fae," Aideen said, "at the hands of a water witch… The tensions between all Fae and the military could escalate exponentially."

Alexandra sighed. "And we know how the humans are in war."

"Scorched earth," I said. "We don't need that."

She nodded. "So be it. We can give him a sliver of a blade," she said, still showing hesitation in her words. "The effect would not be as instantaneous, or perhaps even as deadly, as one of the stone daggers. Nonetheless, any water witch who sees the humans strike with a weapon that has the properties of a stone dagger will think twice before pursuing them."

"Do you have the shards?" I asked. "This is something we can get soon?"

"If we could take the Warded Ways," Alexandra said, "they would be close, indeed. But without knowing what's happening near the Obsidian Inn, we don't dare. And the armory that houses them isn't far from Falias."

"Is it not in Falias?" Aideen asked.

Alexandra shook her head. "Regardless, we dare not take the Ways."

"If you can't take the Ways, then I'll have Gaia take me there."

"One cannot just walk into the armory," Alexandra said, an edge of exasperation in her voice. "The Utukku guarding it would kill you in an instant, shielded or not."

"I think I can handle the Utukku," I said.

"Their leader guards our weapons," Alexandra said. "Many of her people are stationed at the Obsidian Inn, and she'll kill anyone to protect them."

"I hate to say this," Aideen said, "but Damian does have a reputation with the Utukku. And their leader, in particular."

Alexandra frowned for a moment, and her eyebrows rose. "I had forgotten that you banished the glamor from the leader of the Utukku."

I nodded, remembering how frightened I'd been when I first arrived at the Royal Courts, only to blast the glamor away from a Fae who was more intimidated by me than I of her. A situation that could have gone very badly.

"You just said we shouldn't separate," Foster said. "And now you're talking about using Gaia to walk through the Abyss to the other side of the freaking country."

"It'll be short," I said. "And if I need to, Gaia can bring me back at a moment's notice."

"We can't communicate through the Warded Ways," Aideen said. "You'll be relying on a cell phone signal to reach us. And you know that area has had communications issues since Falias was brought onto this plane."

I cursed. "What else can we do?"

"We can wait to hear from the Obsidian Inn," Aideen said. "Though I'm afraid whatever machinations are moving may come to fruition by that time."

Taking Gaia's hand and going to the armory meant leaving the others there. Or I could take some of them with me, but I'd leave even fewer people to defend our own. Going alone left fewer people to defend Sam and Vicky, though Vicky had Jasper, which I suspected made her safer than the rest of us. But Saint Charles itself needed us. I cursed again.

"I don't know what to do," I said. "We can't afford fewer allies anywhere. Let me talk to Zola."

I had little doubt Sam had woken my master about five seconds after I texted her. And considering how fast Zola answered her phone, I knew I was right.

"What is it, boy?"

I gave her the rundown, what I saw as the advantages, disadvantages, and uncertainties about both plans.

"It's a hard decision," Zola said. "It's quite likely you'll be ambushed if you stay in Saint Charles. It's also quite likely you will be killed by the lizard people if you walk with Gaia."

"What do you think?"

"Boy," Zola said, "I have seen war. Ah've seen men bleed each other dry, and as powerful as the Fae are, there is nothing more dangerous than man."

It didn't take much to see what she really meant. "We need Park."

"Yes."

"Bringing him a weapon he can use to fight the water witches … it would help solidify us as friends, and that would make him an even stronger ally."

"Ah agree, boy. Regardless, be quick. Tell as few people as you can. From what you tell me of that ghost, it may still be inside the shop. Ah've heard of similar things, though Ah've not seen them with my own eyes."

"What is it?"

"It's much what you thought it was," Zola said. "A soul that had been trapped on the battlefield, torn away, and brought to some place that isn't its own. It may have tried to take on the form of another ghost, or a form that was forced upon it by whatever dark mage enslaved it. It's hard to say."

"Thank you," I said. "I'll let you know what we decide."

Zola ended the call. I was fairly certain she already knew what my decision was.

"You're going to Falias?"

I smiled at Alexandra. "Yes."

✦   ✦   ✦

AFTER CHECKING MY weapons and securing my backpack, I laced my fingers into the dead flesh of Gaia's hand and stepped into the Abyss. The cold gray fingers warmed and curled around my own, small motes of golden light floating down and congealing into Gaia's form. I could better see the things in the darkness as Gaia's light grew, and I recoiled.

A cluster of peaks large enough to crush a house loomed overhead, flanked by tree-trunk-like tentacles as thick as a redwood.

Slimy gray flesh shifted at a near-frozen pace, and I watched in awful fascination as one giant black eye began its slow rotation toward us.

"Croatoan?"

"It is indeed the one known as Croatoan. I have seen many of his kind lately, and stranger things have made their way into the Abyss." Gaia offered me a small smile before turning her head up and gazing at the massive beast beside us.

"Where are they coming from?"

"I suspect there is a fracture in one of the Seals," Gaia said. Her ethereal voice whispered through the darkness. "It is not the time Seal, though I feared it might be after what occurred in the Burning Lands."

I didn't have to ask her if she meant what had happened when we destroyed Prosperine. In the events leading up to that, I had become a Timewalker, as had Vicky and my sister. "Where do we travel to today?" Gaia asked.

"I'm not exactly sure," I said. "Can you tell me where Alexandra has been outside of Falias? To the south? They have an armory there."

"I am afraid I cannot. I will need more detail than what you have offered."

I'd been curious if Gaia would be able to tell me more, without giving her the exact destination Alexandra had shown me. Gaia was a Titan of the earth, and she had displayed an uncanny intuition in the past. But I supposed it did have its limits. "It's near Antietam," I said. "Where the Irish Brigade gathers, the werewolves led by Caroline."

Gaia shifted her head as if she was looking into the distance, able to see something halfway across the world. Although distance as I understood it in the Abyss likely meant we had already walked nearly that far.

"Yes," Gaia said. "I believe I see our destination." She frowned slightly. "You are walking into a trap, Damian."

"The Utukku," I said. "They are the guardians of the armory. I know them well." *Or well enough,* I thought.

"You go to a place with ghosts," Gaia said. "It may be unwise to venture there alone."

"I don't have a choice," I said. "But thank you for the warning."

"The Abyss will open on a hard corner. It may not be a soft landing, but I believe you will be alone for a brief time." She turned her golden gaze to me. "Are you ready?"

I nodded, and Gaia released my hand.

CHAPTER FOURTEEN

EXITING THE ABYSS was far gentler than exiting the Warded Ways, but sometimes it was still a hard landing. I didn't have any of the awful vertigo I'd grown accustomed to when dropping out of the Warded Ways, but the sudden stop in forward momentum was enough to put my stomach in my throat. The immediate impact that followed didn't help matters. Gaia hadn't exaggerated about it being a hard corner.

Even though I'd been expecting something, the room was still black as night. The stony surface beneath my cheek was a wall, or possibly a floor. It took me a moment to realize I was still standing. So it was a wall. Gaia had left me flush against what felt like stone and water and dirt. I blinked my eyes, but still no light came.

Something whispered in the distance as if it had just grown aware of my presence. I tried to listen, and the sound grew louder. What I thought had been a whisper became a hiss. What I thought had been a hiss became the slow scratch of a claw on stone. I was still blind, and I hoped the sound was the Utukku and not something else.

I had a matter of seconds to decide whether I would raise a light, or shout a greeting, or simply wait for them to discover me.

I decided instead on a combination of all three. The incantation came first. *"Minas Illuminadda."* The greeting came second, though I didn't know how effective it would be. "It's Vesik! Uttuku's friend from the Royal Court of Faerie. I fought alongside Hess in the ruins of Falias." The incantation had finished forming a small ball of light by the time I finished speaking. It looked like swirling flame in the darkness, but the pale white of a sliver of moon. The rhythm of the slithers and scratches on the stone didn't change. Nor did it grow louder. I understood why as my eyes adjusted to the light of the incantation.

A battlefield ghost, with more sentience than it had any right to have, dragged a shattered rifle in his right hand, the bayonet scraping the stones. It shouldn't have made a sound. Something was wrong. For that matter, it shouldn't have been underground, and by that point, I was fairly confident we were underground. The ghost swayed back and forth, closing on me. Its eyes never left mine. The crown of its head passed through ghostly roots that had forced their way between the minuscule cracks of the stones overhead.

I could reach out with my necromancy, but if this ghost was a trap, that might well be the end of me. Someone with either more power or more knowledge than I had had sent a ghost not so unlike this one into the shop. My other option was to flee, wrap my fingers into Gaia's once more, and run screaming into the Abyss. But I knew that wasn't an option, no matter how much I was tempted to reach into my backpack once more and grab that cold dead flesh. I gritted my teeth and sent my aura rocketing toward the old ghost.

Before my aura touched it, I already knew it wasn't natural. Its bayonet shouldn't have been able to spark across the stones.

Something else was at play, and as soon as I made contact, it all became clear.

A knowing began, not the life and love and regrets of a soldier fighting for something he believed in, fighting for people he cared for, or even an unlucky bystander from that bloody age; instead, I found the tangled remnants of a werewolf, masked and bound against his will to be what amounted to little more than a diversion.

I didn't see much into his past, but I felt the sword blade, felt the attacker physically change the clothes he wore and place the old Springfield rifle in his hand. If I hadn't been nauseated, I would've laughed when I realized it had been a modern bayonet duct-taped to the barrel.

Once I knew it was there, the threads of his binding were easy to see; a malignant, red and black miasma, just a tiny darkness behind the golden glow of his soul. I reached out with my aura and burned it away. I didn't much care which side had bound this werewolf or for what reason. He was in pain, and he needed to move on.

I wasn't sure exactly how long the process took, as sometimes when my aura was intertwined with something else's, time vanished. A moment could become an hour or an hour a moment. I heard the ghost's whispered "Thank you" as the dark magic faded from his soul, and his entire being began to fade in turn. The vision of auras, and incantations, and utter darkness, gave way to the creatures now standing at the other end of the corridor.

✦ ✦ ✦

ONLY WHEN THE mutilated ghost had gone did I feel the horrifying weight of the dead above me. The halberds of the

Utukku gleamed in the light of the *illuminada* incantation. One of them raised a blade with her right arm, pointed at me, and spoke sharply. But I couldn't hear it.

All I could hear were the stuttering screams of the dying above us, the likes of which I hadn't felt since Gettysburg. I summoned a shield as the first Utukku charged at me, but the electric blue power short-circuited in an instant, failing me as if it had been struck by a great power.

I frowned as I fell to one knee, the impact jarring my bones as the nearest Utukku threw her halberd to the side. It clanged against the wall. That seemed like a remarkably sloppy attack. My vision dimmed, turning into a tunnel. I wasn't sure if it was the dying light of my incantation or the rapid onset of a loss of consciousness. Either way, the room went black. The rapid thunderclaps of cannons firing back to back shattered the stillness around me. My mind felt as if it were drifting from my body, lost in the Abyss, while my physical self was gently pulled through a stony corridor. A whisper wound its way through the screams, too real to be my imagination, but too distant to be real.

"What's wrong with him, Hess?" the voice whispered. "Something's wrong. That barrier wasn't supposed to attack our allies."

"I don't think it was attacking him," a familiar voice hissed. "That thing that was in here with him, I don't know what it was. Take him to Utukku. Get him to the Fae."

The thunder of gunfire and screams of the dying silenced the whispers once more.

It felt as if I'd been dragged across the rocks for a day. I wasn't sure if I still had my shoes or my backpack, and panic cut through the pain inside my head as I realized I wasn't even sure if I had the hand of Gaia.

"He's waking up," the first voice said.

I wanted to tell them that I had always been awake. But had I?

"Get him into the light," that familiar voice said. Hess's voice. But she was supposed to be in the Obsidian Inn. What would she be doing in Antietam? I tried to ask that very question, but my mouth wouldn't move.

"By the gods," a new voice said. "What's wrong with his hand?"

"It's the flesh of a gravemaker," Hess said. "We need to wake him, for this could be bad for everyone here."

The gentle dragging grew into something more frenetic. My heels bounced off the uneven stone, and it felt as though my shirt had been torn as it was pulled across jagged rocks. The solid darkness around me slowly, painfully, brightened.

"Over the threshold," Hess shouted. "Clear the way!"

I heard someone bark a protest, but the sharp crack of flesh on skull silenced whoever had spoken. Glorious light stabbed into my eyes. The thunder of cannons and screams and gunfire slowly faded. Not as overwhelming, but still a constant cacophony that felt not so far away.

"Hess?" I managed to cough out in a shaky voice.

"Damian," Hess said, and I felt a gentle pressure on my left shoulder. "Can you understand me?"

"Yeah," I said. "Can you tell me how to get to the armory?" I squinted into the light, just barely making out the outline of her reptilian face. "The tour guide said there was an armory around here."

Hess patted my shoulder. "Yes, yes. Rest now."

CHAPTER FIFTEEN

I HADN'T MEANT to fall asleep, and I wasn't sure how long I had been out, but I startled awake when the sound of claws on stone echoed right beside my head. The Utukku waited patiently for me to stop having a heart attack.

"Damian Vesik," Utukku said. "Why have you come to this armory?"

"Utukku?" I said. "I'm glad to see you."

She gave me what amounted to a smile on her lizardlike face: a small curl of a thinly lipped mouth, and the flash of dagger-like teeth inside.

"It is good to see you, too, but you must tell me, why have you come here?"

I sat up and rubbed my forehead. "Alexandra said you had the shards of the stone daggers here, or at least the shards of a weapon with powers like those of a stone dagger?"

"We do," Hess said, stepping up beside Utukku. "But without one of the fairy blacksmiths, they are quite useless."

Utukku nodded in agreement. "Hess is correct, but why has Alexandra revealed the location of this armory?"

"We lost contact with the Obsidian Inn," I said. "Foster and Aideen can't reach them through the Warded Ways. We weren't warned about any kind of radio silence, and were worried there was an imminent threat."

Utukku gave a slow nod. "They are maintaining silence. I am afraid some of the queen's water witches are laying siege to the Obsidian Inn. Or at least they believe they are," Utukku said, a knowing smile on her lips. "In truth, they are laying siege to an unguarded outpost."

"Any communication through the Warded Ways could be intercepted," Hess said. "And that could reveal our ruse."

"We were all a bit worried," I said.

"As were we," Hess said. "Especially when you began summoning the flesh of a gravemaker in the catacombs."

"They are not catacombs," Utukku said.

"The term is still apt," Hess said, annoyance plain in her voice.

"Where are we?" I asked.

"Beneath Antietam," Utukku said. "I'm afraid the ghosts that we thought would conceal our activities had ill effects on your well-being."

"Yeah," I said. "I guess you could say that."

"Come with me," Hess said, helping me to my feet. "I'm quite certain that some of your allies will be anxious to see you."

I followed Hess after Utukku dismissed herself for an audience with some of her people. We left the light of the larger chamber behind, diving into the darkness of the corridors once more. These were formed of carefully cut, inlaid stone like the catacombs beneath Falias. They reminded me more of the burrow of some great creature, the edges rounded except where they became doorways. Several times, Hess paused before a branch, listening intently at the darkness, before tugging on my sleeve to continue.

It felt like we continued in that pattern for a good fifteen minutes before I once more saw light ahead. Hess had guided me well enough that I'd only landed on my face once, and I was quite grateful for that. The closer we came to the light, the more I realized it was in the shape of a doorway. Just a thin line of luminescence pierced the darkness.

"The armory is hidden here," Hess said. "We'll be above the ground again, and I hope the ghosts will not be too much for you."

"It's better now." My subconscious had been hard at work, focusing on the structure of the catacombs, muffling the thunder of gunfire and screams and cannon shots. This place was still alive in a way, like so many of the old battlefields I'd set foot on.

Hess raised the amulet around her neck, placing it at the edge of the door. Something clicked and cycled, followed by another and then another, before our dimly lit corridor echoed with the smack of dozens of opening deadbolts.

The door opened slowly, revealing a broad swath of an old painting. An old battle. As the door opened wider, I realized I'd seen photos of the painting before. It was one of several enormous works done not long after the Civil War, depicting the battle of Antietam. I frowned, not understanding why it was inside the water witches' armory. It dawned on me a moment later. They'd hidden the armory in plain sight.

Hess stepped through the doorway, and I followed. We were in a relatively small square, surrounded by the very paintings that I knew were on display at Antietam's museum. Glass cases sat in front of each, holding old swords, guns, and memorabilia from the battle that had happened here so long ago.

At the edge of my hearing, someone whispered, "It's Hess."

I turned my head to the left to see who had spoken, and blinked in surprise when I saw a familiar face at the top of the stairs. "Caroline?"

"I told you we were being too loud," the alpha werewolf said, almost hissing at the man standing beside her.

I couldn't stop a broad smile when he stepped into the light. "Hey, Damian."

"Dell?" I laughed. "You're about the last person I expected to see here."

"Me?" Dell said. "So, you only expected Hess and Caroline to be sitting on a pile of fairy weapons in the middle of the Civil War battlefield?"

"Well, when you put it like that," I muttered.

"Why are you here?" Caroline asked. "I trust you, necromancer, as did the Ghost Pack before me. What has brought you here?"

"We couldn't reach anyone at the Obsidian Inn. Everyone's in a communications blackout."

"And with good reason," Caroline said. She was far more serious than Dell. She gave me a critical eye as if the person standing before her might be an illusion. And at that moment, I realized that probably wasn't a bad state of mind to be in.

Caroline gave me the rundown of what had been happening with the Obsidian Inn, and why the werewolves were helping to guard one of the armories. To her, it was all strategy, taking small advantages where she could to keep her pack safe. Safe was maybe not the right word, but to keep as many of them alive as possible. And they'd completely locked down communications, fearing what was being intercepted by unfriendly ears.

"Hess told me much the same about the Obsidian Inn," I said. "Nixie's queen has been striking out against the commoners' military in Saint Charles. They lost nine men, Caroline. A squad of soldiers, killed by undines."

She was taken aback.

"They would've gotten all ten, as the survivor was poisoned by one of the water witches' blades. Aideen and Alexandra were able to heal her. Shortly after, a fairy calling himself Drake destroyed the hospital ICU where the soldier was being cared for. They barely got her out."

"Drake?" Hess said. "No Fae has taken that name in millennia."

Hess's words made my suspicions about Drake's identity settle like a lead ball in my gut. "He's a fire user. Nearly as powerful as the Demon Sword, from what Foster says."

"So this is why you've come?" Caroline asked. "But what do you need from the armory?"

"The broken shards of the stone daggers," I said. "Alexandra seemed to think this is the only armory that has some."

"I have only one question, necromancer." Caroline eyed me. "What was the name of the werewolf in the ghost pack who despised you? Who attacked you in the Burning Lands?"

"Jimmy?" I asked, immediately answering her question before fully contemplating what the consequences of a wrong answer might have been.

Caroline nodded. "It's him."

"As we told you," Hess said.

"And what if I hadn't answered back quite right?" I asked,

wanting to know what awful things could've happened to me.

Caroline slowly pulled a gun from behind her back. "Fae bullets. Euphemia seemed quite confident they could pierce the shield of most magic users."

I was both impressed and happy to be alive.

Caroline nodded, and some of the tension in the room slowly subsided.

"I'll get the shards," Hess said. "Wait here. I'll return shortly." She didn't really go anywhere, simply walked across the room to another display case and began touching the base of the podium with her medallion in a series of complicated gestures.

I turned to Dell. "How are you holding up? This place is worse than Gettysburg. Well, not quite that bad."

"I know what you mean," Dell said. "I think I put on about five pounds in the last week just from eating chocolate."

I smiled. Coming in contact with too many ghosts could be incredibly draining for a necromancer. Dell helped compensate with chocolate and sugar, but mostly chocolate. We had trained together with the Old Man down at Zola's cabin. And I fondly remembered our snacks, which had usually consisted of s'mores.

"They really starting to move on Saint Charles?" Dell asked.

I nodded. "Yeah, and against the military. We have one sergeant and a few privates who are probably on our side. I don't think the rest of them want to understand. They want us dead."

"What's new?" Dell said with a humorless laugh.

"How's the Old Man?" I asked.

"Good," Dell said, "killing a lot of things. It's what he does best."

"He's still working with the Obsidian Inn?"

Dell nodded. "Yeah, he's been tooling around with Ward. Morrigan's been sending them on special missions." He made little quote signs with his fingers when he said "special missions." I wasn't sure if he was bitter about it or just amused with the idea of the Fae goddess sending his rather infamous master on missions.

"I heard you had a run-in with the Morrigan," Dell said. "Something about an old city the water witches destroyed? And a harbinger of the dark-touched?"

I let out a humorless laugh. "You heard right. I also found out that old demon staff Gwynn Ap Nudd had gifted me hadn't been much of a gift after all."

"Beware the gifts of the Fae and all that jazz," Dell said. "It makes so much more sense when they just come at you with a sword, instead of playing with you for a year before trying to kill you. That shit drives me nuts."

"So what are *you* doing here?" I asked.

"Originally they sent me out here to test the barrier in the corridors they built under the battlefield." Dell shivered. "I don't know how you made it through that. They got me about fifteen feet into that thing, and I was done." He shook his head. "The power of whatever they used inside the corridor knocked me out. Flat on my ass."

"And you just decided to hang around here after that?"

Dell smirked. "Not exactly."

Caroline sighed. "He's here because of me. I asked his master for a favor."

"You asked the Old Man for a punching bag," Dell muttered.

"And there is no better punching bag than a disrespectful necromancer," Caroline snapped. I would have thought she was truly furious with Dell, but for the sly wink she gave me.

I thought I'd try to poke the bear, well wolf, a little bit. "This doesn't have anything to do with Dell dating someone from your pack, does it?" I turned an innocent wide-eyed stare on Caroline.

"Of course not," Caroline said, Dell echoing her precisely. Caroline ignored him as if they were siblings.

"Dell's proven himself to have a reasonable mind for strategy," Caroline said. "He's a welcome addition. We have Utukku, werewolves, and Fae guarding this place, but it still leaves us open to some of Nudd's more sinister powers."

"Dell is your Defense Against the Dark Arts teacher?"

"Shut up, man," Dell said, "I don't want to die today."

Caroline made a disgusted noise and shook her head. I think deep down she enjoyed our banter.

Echoes of nail on stone sounded behind me, and I glanced back to find Hess with a small leather satchel in her left hand. She held it out to me. "There are many shards here. They should be adequate for forging many weapons for your military allies."

I took the sack and nodded to Hess. "Thank you." The satchel was heavier than I'd expected, and I wondered just how many fragments were inside.

It occurred to me then that I hadn't checked to see if I still had the hand of Gaia. I couldn't remember if I'd managed to shove it into my backpack or not. My panic must've shown.

"What's wrong?" Caroline asked.

"The hand of glory," I said as I unzipped the edge of my backpack. "I'm not sure if I dropped it inside the corridors." Almost before I finished speaking, I felt that slightly pliable, cold dead flesh brush against my fingers.

"You seem really happy about touching dead things," Dell said nonchalantly. "You touch dead things a lot? And what kind of dead things do you touch?"

"Shut up, Dell," I said.

"So, is there an easier way out of here?"

"You have a hand of glory," Dell said. "I'm pretty sure you could walk out of this place whenever you want."

"If you would like to be cut into a thousand ribbons of stringy flesh," Hess said "then yes, you can use the hand of glory whenever you would like."

I frowned at the Utukku. "You could have warned me about that before I actually picked up the hand of glory."

Hess shrugged and slightly bared her teeth.

Caroline shook her head and eyed Hess. "Sometimes I think they have no sense of humor at all. And other times I think their sense of humor is just as terrible as a necromancer's."

I astutely ignored Caroline. "Where should I go to be safe? And please don't say it's back to those catacombs."

"You need not go back that way," Hess said. "Up the stairs and through the glass doors. You'll see a small church across the street. I warn you, there are many ghosts here. You need only reach the church on the other side of the street, and you'll be safe to use the hand of glory."

"Thank you," I said. "Can you get word to Mike the Demon?"

"Word has already been sent," Caroline said.

"Really?"

She nodded.

"Of course," Hess said. "There aren't many demon blacksmiths who are allied with Damian Valdis Vesik."

I thanked the group again and started up the stairs. Caroline caught my sleeve as I passed her. I looked down, meeting her fierce brown eyes. "What is it?"

"Have you seen Alan? Or any of the pack?"

"Hugh is still in Kansas City, and I know Alan has been traveling back and forth since the attack on the coven, to spend time with his family and his pack. I think it's been hard on him."

Caroline nodded. "It's been hard on a lot of people. Carter was a loss to many."

"He was also a terrible influence," I said.

"Why?" Caroline asked.

"If it weren't for him, you probably wouldn't be stuck here with necromancers for friends." I flashed her a small smile.

She barked out a short laugh and nodded once. "Tell Alan I said hi. And tell Hugh, if he ever needs me, I'll be there."

"You should call him and tell him yourself."

"I'm telling one of his pack members," Caroline said, glancing down at the curved half-moon of scars on my forearm. "That's as good as telling him myself."

I took my leave of them then. I strode toward the front door, remembering Hess's warning. If someone warned the necromancer there were many ghosts, it was unlikely to be a pleasant experience. This was no different.

CHAPTER SIXTEEN

I STEPPED OUTSIDE, and the presence of the dead wasn't the only thing that was jarring. I'd left Saint Louis only a matter of minutes ago. It'd been a rainy, saturated mess. But here the sun was out, still morning, but warmer and brighter and on the surface, beautiful to look at.

I knew the smartest thing to do was hurry down the concrete path, to stay focused on the little church across the street that was almost as plain as that old church in Pilot Knob. But something called my attention, tugging on my aura. And even as my feet carried me toward that church, something drew my gaze to the south.

Ghostly cannons stood along the ridge, manned by the dead. The earth didn't heave and move like that horrible corridor under the ground, but this place was terrible. My steps slowed, and I stared slack-jawed at the sunken road in the distance where, piled one on top of the other, lay the soul-bearing ghosts of countless soldiers. I knew enough from the stories Koda used to tell me that it had to be Bloody Lane.

My presence here drew the attention of darker things, and I could feel the gravemakers surging beneath the battlefield. There were more here than anything I'd experienced since Gettysburg. I didn't know if it was the mantle of Anubis, or just my own inherent necromancy, or some combination of the two, but I wanted to call to them. I wanted to see how many would rise. And that thought alone was enough to send the terrible bark-like flesh bubbling to the surface of the earth near that cluster of ghosts.

I shook my head and hurried away; I had to get to back Saint Charles. The faster I got back, the faster we could help Park, and hopefully solidify our alliance with the National Guard there. I stepped into the grass between the sidewalk and the asphalt road that cut through the battlefield. It was a mistake. The pavement had provided more of a barrier than I'd realized. My shoulders sagged with the weight of that place. It was no longer the gravemakers my powers wanted to reach out to. It was the countless souls tied to the earth, and tied to death.

I gritted my teeth and focused on the church, on putting one foot in front of the other. I closed my mind off as best I could, so the cries and screams faded until I could focus once more on the feel of the earth beneath each footfall. I wasn't sure what they expected Dell to truly do in a place like this. Either one of us would be at risk of being overwhelmed by the dead.

I hurried across the asphalt, and a few more steps over the tortured earth took me to the front door of the old church. I didn't wait. I glanced back, taking in the modern vista of the welcome center, and the ocean of dead behind it. I wrapped my fingers between Gaia's and stepped into the only place I thought might be darker than Antietam.

I TOOK A shaky breath as the comforting darkness of the Abyss wrapped its arms around me, and I savored the silence before Gaia had fully formed at my side.

"Are you well?" she asked.

I nodded. "Yes, you were right about that being an uncomfortable trip." I gave her a half smile. Uncomfortable was a hell of an understatement.

"Do you wish to return to Death's Door?" Gaia asked.

I didn't think I'd ever heard her refer to the shop as Death's Door. I wasn't sure if I was amused or disturbed. "Yes. Please."

I watched distant lights in the Abyss shift and move and blink out. I wondered what titanic creatures might be lurking in that vast space, slowed by the strange time here, locked in perpetual frustration, much like Tessrian.

"Can you help me return Tessrian to the Burning Lands?" I asked, trying to take my attention away from the leviathans that seemed to be growing ever-closer.

"It is possible," she said. "But you would need to travel with the Key of the Dead once more, and that is a dangerous thing to bring into the Abyss. Though I suppose it may be less dangerous than freeing Tessrian on your plane and bringing her here as a free being."

"I'm pretty sure I may have issues either way," I said. "Even if I don't release her here, I'll have to release her in the Burning Lands. Once she's out, and in a realm where she has much power, well, things could get interesting."

"She has no sense of time inside her prison," Gaia said. "You could leave her there."

"No," I said, "that's the one thing I can't do. I gave her my word, Gaia. And that has to mean something."

"The word of men can be coerced. Though I suppose, if you cannot trust your own word, then whose can you trust?"

I wasn't 100% sure if Gaia was agreeing with me or trying to make a point about people in general, but I was going to go with the former for now. We slowed, and Gaia frowned. "We are here, but there are more bodies within your shop than when you left."

"Living bodies?" I asked.

"Of course."

"Well, that's good. I guess I'll see you soon."

"Travel well," Gaia said, and she released my hand.

She still hadn't mastered the art of returning me to Death's Door. I wasn't sure if it was the wards, or the blood shield, or just the general chaos of magic around the shop, but sometimes I had a smooth landing, and sometimes Gaia sent me flailing into a brick wall.

I cursed when the back door appeared in front of me, and grunted when I smacked into it a moment later. "Ow, that was my nose!"

"Is it broken?" asked the deadbolt from the other side of the door, an edge of unabashed glee in its voice.

"I don't know," I said, talking into my cupped hands.

"You okay?" Foster asked as he glided into my vision.

I scrunched up my nose and winced at the pain, but I didn't think it was enough that it was broken. And honestly, even if it were, I'd be tempted to let it heal on its own. Getting my nose healed by magic was one of the most painful things I'd ever experienced.

"Gaia said there's an extra body here. Who is it?"

Foster blinked at me. "That old Titan is right. Come see for yourself."

✦　✦　✦

TO SAY I was happy to see that the extra body in front of the shop was not only alive, but was Mike the Demon, was a gross understatement. The bulky blacksmith raised a hand in greeting, his thick leather apron stained with recent work.

"Hey, Mike," I said. "Good to see you again."

"And you, my friend," Mike said.

"Where's Sarah?" I asked, when I realized his figurative and literal shadow was not with him.

"I suppose she has found her independence in little bits," Mike said, "now that she seems to have been reborn. She's with our allies at the Obsidian Inn."

"So everyone's okay there?" I asked.

"In a matter of speaking," Mike said. "With a conflict imminent, I don't know that I would say anyone is okay."

I nodded.

Foster landed on the countertop beside Aideen, and that's when I noticed the array of weaponry that had been laid out across the glass. A few clips of modern ammunition next to a dozen or more survival knives, and perhaps most odd, two ancient swords.

"Are you going to fashion a weapon out of all these?" I asked.

"They're already weapons," Frank said. He popped his head up from the aisle off to my right, scaring me half to death.

"Christ, Frank," I said, rubbing my forehead. "I didn't see you there."

A large form moved outside the front window, and I blinked at the shadow before I realized it was Aeros strolling by on the cobblestone street.

Mike glanced at the window. "I may have coaxed him out

of hiding. I hadn't spoken to the old rock in quite some time."

"What about Alexandra?" I asked.

"I came with a message of my home," Mike said. "She was needed back at the Obsidian Inn. Nixie and Euphemia had asked her to return."

"Let's hope we don't need them here," I said, wincing as I rubbed my nose.

"Are you well?" Aideen asked.

"Let's just say I had a rough landing," I said. "Although I did get to see Caroline, Dell, Utukku, and some of her people. That was an unexpected surprise."

Aideen frowned. "If Caroline was there, then I know what armory you were at. That would be a trying trip for any necromancer."

I nodded. "I didn't think anyone was supposed to know where these things were at?"

"I don't," Foster said. "And I don't want to. The less reason people have to torture me, the better."

Frank barked out a laugh. "Ain't that the truth."

"Oh," I said, fishing around in my backpack for the leather satchel. I lifted it, and held the aged leather out to Mike. He took it carefully.

"It's perhaps good that Alexandra isn't here. These blades can be somewhat unstable when they are shattered. I wouldn't want to see her come to harm."

"How dangerous is it?" I asked. "Is this dangerous enough that it could kill her?"

Mike blew out a short laugh. He untied the top of the sack and pulled out a curved sliver, which reminded me more than anything of an underwire from one of Sam's bras that had once jammed up my parents' washing machine. "They don't truly turn to stone."

"Those water witches they sank into the rivers sure look like stone," I said.

"So, what is it?" Frank asked. "Like rigor mortis for the Fae?"

Mike frowned and nodded. "An apt description."

"Rigor mortis is temporary," I said. "Do they become something else?"

"I usually burn my enemies," Mike said, "for I rarely had the opportunity to study what happens to them."

I blinked.

Mike continued as if he hadn't said anything mildly horrifying. "I'll need some place to work. I can do it here, but will need to set up an area where we can be sure none of the shards escapes."

"And if we miss any?" I asked. "Would that be like stepping on a Lego in the middle of the night?"

"A bit worse than that," Foster said.

"If one of the water witches stepped on it," Aideen said, "it would turn the base of their foot into what you refer to as stone. It would slow them down, and prevent them from transforming completely into water. It makes them susceptible to attack.

"The blades are forged from Magrasnetto. You need a creature of raw magical power to be able to detect the tiniest shards. Jasper would be able to do it."

"I don't want to take him away from Vicky," I said. "Not unless we absolutely have to."

"Graybeard, then," Foster said. "He's all magic and soul and bone."

"Is he close?" Mike asked. "I'd prefer not to delay. I need to get back to the Obsidian Inn. Much as you don't wish to leave Vicky alone without Jasper, I don't wish to leave Sarah in a dangerous situation."

I nodded. "All you need to do is turn on the news. He hasn't exactly kept a low-profile. Although I guess that would be rather hard to do with the skeletal ghost ship flying over the ground where rivers used to be."

This time it was Mike's turn to blink. "He's not in hiding?"

I shook my head. "He's ... well ... been spending some time with the researchers at Washington University. He apparently took issue with someone's reports on his namesake."

"It gets better," Foster said. "The ghost panda is down there keeping him in line." Foster laughed. "So, you have a ghost panda and Graybeard speaking to academics at one of the most prestigious schools in the area?"

I pinched the bridge of my nose and winced. "Yes, well, the important thing is we can get Graybeard here rather quickly. Or we could go to him."

Mike looked around the front of the shop. "Keep the store closed. I'll start preparing things. Summon Graybeard."

I closed my eyes and sent my aura racing toward downtown Saint Louis. It could be difficult to contact Graybeard, but Happy was always easy to find. In the background, I heard Mike ask, "What's he doing?"

"Summoning Graybeard," Frank said. "That's what you wanted."

The rest of the conversation faded as I made the connection with Happy. The panda raised his head at my contact, cracking it on the desk of a startled-looking research assistant. She probably couldn't see the panda, but he still had enough energy to move physical objects.

"Graybeard. Bring him to the shop."

It will be done. Shiawase's voice boomed inside my head. The thunderous sound reminded me of Aeros, but more ethereal.

When I opened my eyes again, no one remained. It only took me a moment to find them, tipped off by the sharp bark of the cu sith rising above the ambient noise of the old settling building. I walked into the back through the saloon-style doors and crouched down to climb into Bubbles's lair.

"That's not going to cut it," Frank said, looking at the old sheet in Mike's hand. "It's all linen. It'll catch fire like dry hay on the Fourth of July."

"No," Mike growled. "I told you it will not. I know the temperatures of my own forge, journeyman. Don't think to tell me otherwise."

"I'll tell you otherwise if you're going to try to burn the damn shop down."

I smiled at Frank, the smaller man glaring up at the fire demon. Mike finally exhaled, turning away from Frank. "Fine, what do you suggest?"

"A circle shield," Frank said. "The sphere will catch it all. If I understand your magic a fraction as well as you think you do, it won't be cut off by being encased inside a circle shield."

Mike the Demon frowned.

"It'd be hard not to pick up a few things, being around Damian and Zola."

Mike glanced at Frank. "You've done your research."

"I think we've established that at this point," I said.

Mike gave me a half smile. "I suppose we have, indeed. And yes, Frank, you are correct." He looked to Aideen. "What do you think?"

"I believe it should be enough," Aideen said.

"For outside, as well." Mike crossed his arms and frowned at the hollowed-out stone that formed the cu siths' lair. "So be it. This should be deep enough in the earth to at least partially mask my work with the hammer."

Something sizzled in the air, not unlike bacon slapped down on a hot griddle. I suddenly found myself torn between being hungry and being concerned with what the sound might be.

Happy appeared a moment later, his fluffy butt backing through a portal, dragging a pirate skeleton with a very grumpy parrot on his shoulder. Parrot was perhaps a generous word, considering the bird was half decayed and bore brilliant golden eyes.

"Get off me coat, you daft bear!" Graybeard swatted Happy, but the panda casually moved his snout away, so Graybeard gave him more of a quick rub than a slap. Happy nudged my thigh with his broad nose. I scratched him behind the ears.

"You can go if you want," I said. "We should only need Graybeard for this."

The panda chuffed and took two trundling steps back into the portal.

Graybeard glanced up at me, and the parrot glowered. "I was having a perfectly fine conversation, with a perfectly fine lass, before your beast dragged me off."

"Glad to see you're adapting to our time of technological

wonders, and not being dead."

I held out my hand to help Graybeard to his feet.

"What is it you be needing?"

"Mike's forging weapons for our allies," I said. "To use against the water witches. We need you to tell us if any of the fragments get away."

"If you need help forging those blades," Graybeard said, "you likely would've been better off talking to the bear."

"He's a samurai," Mike said, "not a sword smith. Not even a blacksmith."

"Bloody hell," Graybeard muttered. "Let's get on with it then. I'd like to get back to helping Miss Marshall with her research."

"Damian," Mike said. "Set the circle, and I'll begin."

CHAPTER SEVENTEEN

I'D WONDERED WHAT Mike meant to do about a forge, or if he'd just conjure some magic flame to make the metal more malleable. Instead, he did both. The earth moved beneath our feet as Aeros lowered the floor slightly and forced a stone table up in the center of the room, ever careful not to erase the line I'd drawn on the stone, leaving us ready to begin.

"You need only speak my name when you wish to return this place to its original form," Aeros said.

"Most recent form?" I asked. "I don't want this to be some granite plain. And I sure as hell don't want to go through the cu siths digging out their own lair again."

Aeros's eye lights danced with amusement. "You should not worry so much," the rock said. "It does not suit you." And with that, the Old God took his leave.

"Worry too much," I grumbled.

"That cane is nearly as cool as your old staff," Foster said, eyeing the simple walking cane in my left hand.

"Yeah, but this one shouldn't kill me. Unless I take the sword out and fall on it like an idiot."

I set the edge of the cane on the circle and spoke the incantation, "*Orbis Tego.*" A translucent dome snapped to life over Mike's head, closing around the stone workbench and the forge Aeros had raised.

"You good?" I asked.

Mike closed his eyes for a moment, and blue fire erupted inside the forge. The demon nodded. "All is well."

"You could have waited to summon me," Graybeard said, "at least until the demon finished banging around with his hammer."

I smiled at the parrot as it danced on the skeleton's shoulder. "But we have so much to catch up on. You wouldn't want to miss out on that, now, would you?"

The parrot grumbled, and the skeleton moved its mouth wordlessly, causing its scraggly beard to shift up and down. He leaned against the wall and sank to the floor.

"Where's your sister, lad?" Graybeard asked. "That lass always had a much more level head on her shoulders than you."

"You just say that because Jasper didn't try to bite her hand off. Only her Barbies' heads."

The parrot chuckled.

Mike pulled the blade out of the fire. The metal glowed from being in the heat for several minutes. The fire demon didn't so much as flinch at the white-hot blade as he pinched it between his fingers, and began wrapping the thin spiral of the shattered stone dagger around it. He made it about three quarters of the way down the blade before he had to replace it in the forge. He repeated the process with another, and then another.

Mike worked the white-hot ribbons of metal back and forth between his fingers. I half expected his flesh to boil at the contact with the superheated metal, but Mike's skin seemed to rejuvenate. The deep scars on his hand faded, as if the forge gave his flesh new life. It was mesmerizing to watch as the blacksmith's tired, ancient hands grew nimble and filled with purpose.

Mike dropped the first blade into the fire once more. He raised his eyes to me. "I'm going to strike with the hammer," he said, being sure everyone in the room was listening to them. "It will be loud, and the walls may feel as if they will collapse around you, but believe in this process. Believe in me. And all will be well."

Mike slid the Smith's Hammer from his belt, the old wood blackened near the head. It had the appearance of a simple cutler's hammer, the kind you could find at any forge at any given time throughout history. Only Mike's hammer was far, far different.

Mike pulled a blade from the forge and laid it on the stone platform. He made small movements, light hammer strikes near the hilt, until he raised the hammer above his head, and a spiral of flame burst to life. The strike was like a thunderclap, amplified a dozen times.

"Again!" Mike said. He struck the blade over and over until I thought my teeth might rattle from my head. Still, I kept the cane on the chalk line. Kept the circle shield raised between the Fallen Smith and the rest of the world.

Someone grabbed my shoulder and shook it. I turned to find Frank with gun muffs over his ears. He leaned closer and shouted between hammer blows. "I'll be outside. To see how loud it is."

I nodded, and he left, speeding up the ramp Bubbles and Peanut had carved into the earth.

Mike's movements took on a rhythm, growing into an intricate dance of steel and power and magic. He made quick work of the second blade, dropping it into the forge beside the first. The third was even faster, and I realized then that his flesh didn't merely look younger. His veins filled with light, a deep burning inside his being, perhaps the very essence of what he was, and as I watched, it swelled to fill the thick tattoos across his forearms. He said, "Again."

He raised the hammer, its head expanding with the surrounding fires, and he struck again. The walls boomed as if the harbinger of the dark-touched had stepped into the basement beside us and crushed a barge beneath its mighty foot. Mike raised the dagger, red-hot as it still was, and inspected the edge of the blade. Apparently satisfied, he let the dagger fall into a pool at the far side of the circle, which I hadn't seen before. The metal hissed, and steam rose at a furious pace as he quenched the steel.

Daggers came next, and where he'd had the long and thin shards of the stone dagger to work with the swords, it wasn't so simple with daggers.

"The trick," Mike said, his voice deeper and louder than usual, "is to make the metal pliable, without destroying the magic within."

Heat from the forge had turned the air around us into a furnace. I wasn't sure how much longer I could take it, but the fairies seemed to be fine. In fact, the fairies seemed absolutely enthralled with Mike's work.

Mike pulled a small cup out of the satchel at his side. What I'd thought to be an old coffee cup at first glance turned out to be a bit more useful. Mike sorted out the shards of the stone dagger, dropping in any that looked to be around a half inch to an inch in length. He slid the crucible into the forge and waited.

"Should just be a few minutes," Mike said. "Did we scare Frank off?"

"I think Frank just went to make sure the building wasn't falling down," Foster said.

"Are you sure you wish to stay so close?" Mike said. "There is a great deal of iron in these blades. I doubt it would be healthy for you to come in contact with a shard, no matter how small."

Foster laughed. "No shard of iron is getting through the circle shield."

"I believe Foster's correct," Aideen said. "Damian's shield is more than adequate to stop an iron filing."

Mike offered me a small smile. "Your friends trust you with their lives. That is a refreshing thing to see, after spending time with the Fae at the Obsidian Inn."

"They have a right to be paranoid," Aideen said. "The water witches have decided to stand against the queen, and the rest are taking up arms against their king. If they fail, they'll die."

"And they're sneaky bastards," Foster said. "No better spy than a Fae. It can be hard to trust someone who never lies but doesn't always tell you the truth."

Footsteps sounded in my muffled hearing. I glanced over my right shoulder to see Frank jogging back down into the lair.

"Everything okay out there?" I asked.

Frank nodded. "It's fine, but the bricks over the door lit up like a Christmas tree. It looked like one of those runes on the wall behind Mike."

Mike studied the runes that made up the blood shield on the back wall. It was old Norse magic, runic magic that seemed to impress even Calbach. "I would believe this magic to be far too old to have been placed after the front of the building was constructed."

"How bad was the noise?" I asked. I looked at the gun muffs around Frank's neck.

"It sounded like there was a little carpentry going on. As soon as I stepped outside the door, I could barely hear it all."

Mike frowned. "I wouldn't have expected the sounds of a hammer to be silenced so thoroughly."

"Foster?" I asked. "You want to go outside with Frank? Make sure there isn't something you can see, or hear, that a commoner can't?"

"Not a bad idea," Aideen said. "Journeyman you may be, some magics may remain undetectable."

Mike pulled the crucible from the forge with his bare hand and looked inside. "It's ready. Replace your ear protection, or leave." Mike gave the others only a moment, and they hurried up the ramp, leaving me and Aideen to watch the Fallen Smith.

"I will move as fast as I can," Mike said. "But be warned, to do this, you will see my true form for a time."

"Nothing I haven't seen before," I said.

"And something I haven't seen in a very long time," Aideen said. The light that had grown so much brighter on Mike's forearms split open as he dumped the contents of the crucible into his palm. Light gave way to a tortured darkness, the human façade of his flesh curling away and shifting into the blackened ruin of a fire demon. It happened in moments, but time felt slow. A tiny bead of sweat rolled down the nape of my neck as the rising flames peeled back the flesh from Mike's upper arms. His fingers lengthened, and his fists closed around the super-heated metal in his palm. The hammer grew into the flaming war hammer I'd seen only a handful of times on the field of battle.

The tortured flesh reached his neck, and his forehead elongated, sprouting horns that were as black and scarred as the rest of his body. His eyes increased to twice their normal size, taking on a terrifying blood red hue. But they were still Mike's eyes. I could still see the strange black flake in his left eye. A flake that Sarah had once told me was a piece of her soul, which Mike would carry with him until the end of all things.

The sweat on the back of my neck vanished, cooling as my shirt absorbed it. Mike reached his left hand into the forge. He followed it with the first of the daggers, sliding it quickly through the molten pool of molten metal in his palm as if he planned to make a blood oath in some godforsaken 1980s action movie. When the dagger escaped his hand and he lifted it from the forge, a thin line of white-hot metal was stuck to the point, tracing down one of the cutting edges. Mike struck the blade across his left horn, sending a shower of sparks across the forge, and earning a satisfied grunt and a nod from the demon's enormous head. He repeated the process four more times, but before he finished, he dumped the scraps of the remaining stone daggers into the crucible and slid it into the center of the forge.

"He's … magnificent," Aideen whispered.

"He also has good hearing," Mike said, giving Aideen what might have been a smile, but looked more like a snarl.

The first time I'd ever seen Mike's true form, it had been a terrible instant, a moment I'd spent terrified for my life and for those of my friends. Now that I had time to study him, I was coming to understand that he was not so twisted and scarred as

I'd once believed. This was the true face of my friend, buried beneath the façade that he wore to blend in with the commoners.

Mike pulled a satchel out of the leather pouch at his side. I heard the familiar clack of ammunition banging around inside it. And he poured out what had to be over 100 rounds of military ammunition. I thought Frank said it had come from their M16s.

"You know those don't mix with fire?" I asked.

Mike set the bowl on the ground beside the forge. He raised his head slightly, perhaps acknowledging me, or perhaps thoroughly ignoring me. Mike splayed his fingers over the bowl and the rounds all snapped into a uniform line as a flicker of orange and black flashed out from the demon's fingernails. The projectiles separated in unison, floating half an inch above the brass casings, while Mike slid his enormous hand beneath them. The gunpowder ignited a moment later, sending a blast of flame and smoke into the air for a brief second. Mike dropped the rounds into the crucible and gave the dozens of projectiles a quick shake before splashing the contents out on top of the forge.

He eyed each in quick succession, tossing those he was satisfied with into the pool of water at the edge of the circle. Angry bursts of steam shot into the air when the projectiles hit. Others he dropped into the crucible once more, giving the contents a quick spin before repeating the process over and over.

The last of the bullets splashed into the water, and he looked up. The black horns on his forehead curled inward, and the nauseating ripple of movement that had borne them reversed. Blackened red flesh dulled, replaced by the hair and scarred skin of a middle-aged blacksmith.

Mike frowned at the work laid out before him. "Not the cleanest, but it is done."

CHAPTER EIGHTEEN

THE WAR HAMMER shrank and once more took on the humble form of a blacksmith's hammer. Mike slid the tool back into a leather belt loop at his waist, at which point I noticed a spark out the corner of my eye. I turned slightly to my right and realized there were dozens of sparks stretching across the glistening dome of the circle shield.

"Mike," I said, "I think we might have a bit of a mess."

"What do you mean?" Mike asked.

"Look at the shield." I gestured with my free hand. "There are tiny shards stuck all across it. I count maybe a dozen at a glance."

Aideen flashed into her larger size, the strange light that omitted no luminescence engulfing her for a split second. She stepped closer to me, and followed my line of sight. "I see them. There are more than a dozen. Slivers yes, but there are many."

I looked down at Graybeard, where he sat with his arms crossed and his head resting against the wall. The parrot danced back and forth across his shoulder, squawking.

"See," I said. "That's quite a mess we have for you there."

"And you'll be wanting me to clean it up?" The parrot cocked its head to the side.

"We don't need you to clean up," Aideen said. "We need you to walk the area. Your presence should cause the fragments of stone dagger to light up. It's attracted to you."

Graybeard grunted and glanced up at the green and black snout on the ramp above him. "You have some mighty fine pups, lass. Grant me a favor, and we have an accord."

"What?" I snapped. "How about I don't feed you to the next harbinger we meet?"

Graybeard harrumphed. "You've shown your hand one too many times," he said. "You have not a sadistic bone in that body."

"I will consider it a favor you have done for me," Aideen said. "I'll not grant you a favor of your choosing, but I will aid you if it is within my power and does not harm me or my allies."

"Come on," I said. "He was going to help us anyway." I frowned down at the bird.

Its golden eyes looked up and it clucked at me. "You can't blame a dead man for asking a favor. Have some respect for your elders."

"Oh, Christ," I muttered. "Now you sound like Zola."

Mike stalked the perimeter of the circle, stopping before each of the sparking shards embedded in the shield. "These are all iron." He stopped and frowned at a particularly large shard. "Some of these are iron with flecks of Magrasnetto."

Aideen looked around the floor and grimaced. "We must be thorough. Graybeard, walk toward the edge of the ramp. We will see if the metal reacts to your presence, or if it needs persuading."

The parrot grunted as the skeleton raised itself onto its feet. "Last time I needed to persuade someone, used a short plank in some bad water. You know the kind?"

"Sharks? I asked.

"Too fast," Graybeard said. "Feed them to a Leviathan if you want fast. Drop them into a school of jellyfish? Now that's a show." The beard shifted on the skeleton's face, and I had a little doubt if there had been flesh beneath it, it would have been smiling.

✦   ✦   ✦

THANKFULLY, OUR CLEANUP project didn't require any persuading. Graybeard's presence within about a foot and a half of the stone dagger shards caused them to glow with a brilliant blue light. Mike followed Graybeard around the room, holding a stone lump over each of the shining spots, while Aideen waited at the top of the ramp. While the shards of stone dagger might not have been an immediate threat, I didn't want her close to any of the iron.

"So that thing's like a magnet?" I asked.

Graybeard walked into a new section of the circle, and Mike bent down to pick up another shard.

"That's an apt description," Mike said. "The stone was imbued with the power of the ley lines long ago. It attracts many enchanted metals, be they natural, or forged."

"Oh, wow," Frank said, poking his head into the lair at the top of the ramp.

Foster stepped in beside him, staying close to Aideen. "The outside of the shop lit up like a fireworks display," he said. "It didn't seem to be causing any noticeable output of power, though. At least nothing I could feel."

"What's lighting up around the pirate?" Frank asked. "It's beautiful."

"My charming personality," Graybeard muttered.

I smiled at the pirate. I gave Frank and Foster a rundown of what we were doing and chuckled as Foster ushered Aideen a few steps farther back from the entrance to the lair.

That went on for another fifteen minutes or so, Mike following Graybeard around the room. They worked their way up the ramp, and Mike nodded. "I think that should do it for the stone dagger shards."

"And the iron?" I asked.

"That's not my specialty," Mike said, a small smile on his lips. He spoke one word. One name. "Aeros."

The earth beneath our feet shook and rose until the sunken area around the forge grew flat and level once more. Aeros's voice filled the room around us. "There is much iron left behind."

"Would you be so kind as to address that?" Mike asked.

"Remove your weapons from the floor and I will do what was asked."

Mike did, scooping up the last of the stone-dagger-coated bullets as the pool of water vanished into the stone. He wrapped the swords and daggers in oiled leather cloth, swaddling them carefully, as if they were children to be coddled.

A memory of Mike's oath bubbled into my conscience. If any of these weapons were used to harm an innocent, Mike would die. It was an oath taken after the horrors he witnessed at the Battle of the Crater in the Civil War. The sight of his only love dying.

"Mike," I said. "Are you sure about this?"

"A bit late to be asking that," Mike said. "And don't worry.

Sarah and I had a long discussion about the risks of making weapons."

"But we watched you summon the fire for the forge. How can you be sure?"

"There's little in this world that I am sure of, Damian Vesik. The one thing I am sure of is that this world won't survive if the queen of the water witches prevails."

"You sure?"

"We've made our peace."

"Let's be honest," Foster said. "You could probably kill one of our water witch allies with one of those things, and not be any worse off. What really qualifies as an innocent life in regard to your oath?"

"That is a question that I will not answer."

"Alright," I said. "You're welcome to come with us to deliver these to Park."

Mike shook his head. "I'm needed at the Obsidian Inn." He drew one sword and one dagger from the stash before handing me the bundle and the satchel for bullets. "I won't leave Sarah unarmed against the water witches. I hope that's acceptable, for I have no intention of debating it."

I was somewhat taken aback at the finality in Mike's words. They concerned me, not being able to deliver all the blades to Park, but if the Obsidian Inn was under siege from the water witches, it was conceivable they would need the blades even more.

I nodded to the fire demon.

Mike slid the blades beneath his thick leather belt. "I thank you." He hesitated for a moment. "Aeros, take care of the iron. I am done with the forge. Thank you, old friend." A red wound opened in the air before Mike, and he stepped into that hellish vortex of flame.

The floor moved, a stone hand rising from the rocky earth. Aeros's arm swept around the room, coming up through the ramp, and nearly knocking me off my feet as he returned to the area that had been the forge. The hand hesitated before rising up the wall and vanishing into the stone once more. The wall beside me rippled, and a small iron ball slowly phased out of the stone.

"That's it?" I said.

"Some people would be thankful for having their house cleared of such debris. And not only cleared but delivered in such a conveniently portable package."

I grinned at the wall. "Thanks, rock.

"Would you mind discarding that?" Aideen asked. "I am sure Aeros could hide it deep within the earth."

"I would be happy to assist," Aeros's voice boomed.

I held the iron ball against the stone, and it vanished into the solid rock.

"Until next time," Aeros said.

I hefted the bag of coated shells in my left hand and said, "We need to get these to Park. Now."

"Park gave permission to give them to Casper," Frank said. "You need her trust more than his."

"He outranks her," Foster said. "I'm pretty sure it's more important to have him on our side."

Frank shook his head. "You're wrong. She'll have more pull with the troops. They see one of their best marksmen making friends with the likes of us? With the likes of the Fae?" Frank nodded. "That's more important. She spilled blood with them, had her own blood spilt with them. They trust her like family."

"Right then," I said. "Probably shouldn't walk in with swords and ammunition wrapped in a rag."

"I've got some old gun cases we can use," Frank said. "They should hold everything but swords. And I don't really know how much good a sword is going to do anyway, not in the hands of a modern soldier."

"There's a great deal of tradition and honor in swords," Aideen said. "Swords have been used as rewards and symbols of rank for centuries. The tradition repeated in many cultures. Do not underestimate what a simple gesture can accomplish."

Bubbles surged down the ramp, sniffing the walls and the corner where she and Peanut usually slept. It likely smelled a little different, now that Mike had lit the forge and perhaps felt different since Aeros had turned stones. Of course, I'd seen the cu siths fall asleep in the most uncomfortable of places before, and was sure they would adapt quickly.

Frank unearthed the old gun case, a dented aluminum thing, from one of the overcrowded shelves in the junk cabinet. He was right. We were able to fit everything but the swords.

CHAPTER NINETEEN

"**P**ARK'S AT THE camp," Frank said. "It's not far from where we saw Drake."

I frowned. "I'm glad you were there to see Drake with us. Like a crazy Foster. Which is a lot more terrifying than I'd expected." I shook my head. "Where is the base exactly?"

Frank dusted off the old gun case while we waited in the back parking lot for Sam. "They set up in one of the fields just past Fast Lane."

"There aren't any buildings in those fields," I said, skirting a particularly sharp looking rock off to the edge of the parking lot.

"Sam's here," Foster shouted, gliding down from the top of the building to land on my shoulder. A moment later, the blinding headlights of one of the Pit's SUVs cut through the darkness.

"Now I'm a deadbolt *and* I'm blind," the being trapped in our door shouted.

We all studiously ignored the complaints pouring out of our friendly neighborhood deadbolt.

"Take the front," I said, nodding to Frank. "These guys know you best."

I opened the back door and hopped in, expecting to find Zola, but she wasn't there. Foster took up his standard perch on the dashboard, closer to Sam.

"Where's Zola?" I asked.

"She's in the archives with Vik," Sam said. "They're still looking for more details on the dark-touched. At least that's her excuse for asking for help."

"Man," Foster said, "If you can't trust the intentions of an old necromancer, who can you trust?"

Sam held out her hand and gave Foster a tiny high-five while they both laughed, and cast quick glances back at me.

"You mind holding this?" Frank asked as he passed the old scabbard, which didn't quite fit the sword, into the back seat.

"Not at all."

I slid the sword part way out of the scabbard as Sam made a sharp turn and bounced us out onto the cobblestone street. As fast as Mike had worked to make the swords, they'd turned out beautifully. The addition of the shards of the stone dagger made the metal look something like Damascus steel—beautiful shades of color and waves of metal grains followed the addition from the tip of the sword to almost the center of the blade. I sheathed the sword and laid it on top of its brother.

The drive took us to the old roundabout—well, actually, the new roundabout—and sent us off past the field where we had faced Drake and the Green Man. This time we crossed under the railroad and the highway until we reached the road with Fast Lane, an antique car dealership. I'd be lying if I said I'd never visited before.

The orange glow of the sunset lit the horizon as we closed on the railroad tracks, cruising beneath the trestle.

"Something's off," I said.

The tornado sirens roared to life a moment later.

"It's barely sprinkling."

"It's not for the tornado," Foster said. "Don't you remember? They're using the tornado sirens as warning sirens."

"Something's attacking the city," Sam said.

"Yeah," Frank said as we crossed under the highway. He pointed toward the glowing ball that had nothing to do with a sunset.

I stared in horrible fascination at what I could now clearly tell was an enormous fire.

"That's the camp," Sam said. "Fucking hell, that's the fucking camp."

Something flashed in the distance, just on the other side of Fast Lane, revealing an outline of what I suspected had been a tent shortly before. Now it was fire and ruin. Sam floored the accelerator, and we hurtled toward the raging battle.

Soldiers and Fae sliced up from the river, closing on the camp in a half circle. Drake hovered above them, raining fire down on the unsuspecting soldiers. I wondered how many had died before they'd even realized they were under attack.

Beneath Drake, waters raged and boiled. We were a good quarter-mile from the Missouri River. The water shouldn't have been there.

"The water witches are here," I said.

Sam jerked the wheel to the left, and the SUV's tires screamed as we veered toward Fast Lane, cruising past the worst of the carnage on the front line.

"They don't have a chance," Foster said. "Let me out. Let me out now."

"Take one of the swords," I said. "Just don't cut yourself with it."

Foster nodded.

Sam squealed the tires as we darted into the smoking ruin of the base. The burned-out guardhouse wasn't empty. The charred flesh of its poor occupant dangled out the window. I didn't need to raise my sight to see the freshly dead aura weaving around the soldier.

Sam slammed on the brakes, bringing us to a halt behind a row of soldiers who were managing to offer some resistance.

"Go," I said, tossing one of the stone-dagger-forged swords into the air. Foster zipped out the window, bursting into his full-sized form as he wrapped his gauntleted hand around the hilt.

Sam and I pushed out the driver's side while Frank popped out the passenger side, staying low to the ground as he joined us behind the SUV.

Frank slid one of the daggers out of the case and hooked it into his belt. I gave the other sword to Sam and turned to Frank. "Get the case to Park. Or whoever's left in charge." Something huge roared at the edge of the battle, and a glance showed me a Green Man lumbering toward a guardsman who was armed with a flamethrower. "What in the hell are they doing here?"

"It doesn't matter," Frank said. "Just help them." He turned to Sam. "I love you."

And he was gone. Sam bounced her right hand up and down, and I frowned at the bullets on her palm.

"What the hell are you going to do with those?" I asked. "We don't have a gun that can fire them, and they're not even loaded into brass yet."

"I can throw them."

I blinked at my sister. She probably could throw them at a fast-enough velocity to do some serious damage to a water witch. I nodded. "Get some of them to Casper!" I shouted as I rushed toward the nearest group of soldiers, incredibly thankful that I had brought both my backpack and the focus on my hip.

"Shit's about to get a lot worse," I said to the nearest soldier who wasn't unloading an insane number of rounds down the field.

"You're that fucker who knows what the fuck all these fucks are?" He released a string of about fifteen more fucks before I finally got him to shut up.

"Where's Park? Where's Casper? Are they still alive?"

"Beats the hell out of me," he shouted back. He pulled out a grenade, and screamed, "Fire in the hole!"

I expected the detonation to be louder, but the sounds of gunfire and explosive incantations muffled everything around us. The grenade detonated, tearing a nearby fairy's wings to pieces, and sending the owl knight to the ground.

I saw Frank at the other end of the soldiers, shouting at them about the daggers he was handing them. I caught the last thing he said before he ran off between two of the tents that weren't on fire. "Save it for the ones you can see through. Stab them with it. It's the only thing you can stop them with."

One of the privates Frank had armed stepped in front of another who was frozen at the sight of the battle raging around him. He tossed a survival knife to the ground and slid Frank's dagger awkwardly into the sheath at his hip before unleashing a hail of gunfire.

I had little doubt that soldier wasn't as green as the petrified man behind him. If they'd seen action before, it hadn't been anything like this. For God's sake, how many commoners *did* see action like this? I was afraid the answer to that question would be vastly different in the near future.

Two fairies sprinted between a cluster of burning tents, and I didn't think anyone had seen them coming. They were still small, closing fast when I jumped out in front of the soldiers and shouted, "*Impadda!*" One fairy dodged to his right, circumventing the shield as he exploded into his full-size form. The other crashed headfirst into the crackling dome of blue energy, crumbling to the ground with a satisfying crunch. He was still moving until the soldier beside me shot a round through his head, obliterating the upper half of the tiny body.

The second already had his sword embedded in a stunned-looking soldier. I shaped the shield on my left arm and backhanded the bastard in the head. His helmet sparked and bounced off the dying soldier as the fairy turned to look at me. The slight hesitation, the curiosity in his eyes at who or what could've struck him so forcefully without him noticing was all the delay I needed. My soulsword lit through the hilt as I slashed with my right hand at an upward angle, careful not to catch any of the soldiers around me in the arc of that deadly blade.

The Fae's left shoulder and neck separated with little effort. The body collapsed to the ground, and both of the fairies' disembodied screams drowned out the horrors raging across the rest of the battlefield.

I watched as the vibrant aura of the injured private faded from blues and reds before solidifying once more at the screams of one of his comrades. His eyes snapped open.

I stared into the shell-shocked face at his side and wanted to help. These were just kids. These were just kids losing their lives in someone else's war. "Get ready. It's not over. Stay behind me, and try your damnedest not to shoot me in the back."

"Who are you?" someone said behind me.

"I'm just a shopkeeper. A weird shopkeeper. Who's in charge?"

"He was," a young female private said, indicating an injured captain on the ground beside her.

The captain tried to speak, and I thought I caught the name Stacy on his tongue before he passed out again.

I cursed under my breath. Perfect. So I could run to Sam, who probably didn't need nearly as much help as these kids, or I could stay here and fight with them, and possibly get myself killed trying to help them. Super.

CHAPTER TWENTY

"**W**HAT'S THAT?" A private shouted, pointing up at a fireball that continued to increase in size. I stared at the conflagration and cursed.

"His name is Drake, and he wants to kill you. Blow him out of the air."

Terrified though they might have been, the drills and training and repetition had paid off in spades. They raised their rifles nearly in unison, and the woman I suspected was the youngest of them gave the order to fire. I gritted my teeth against the explosion of sound around me. Half a dozen M16s firing at once were anything but quiet.

Electric yellow sparks flared and dissipated all around the whirling ball of fire. A stray thought flickered through my mind—would the Fae's elemental fire spell be susceptible to a water incantation? Maybe some good did come out of Sam and I spending more than one summer with our asses stuck firmly in front of a million different role-playing games.

With every shot that deflected or vanished into that maelstrom, I figured more and more that I had nothing to lose. I held the soulsword out toward the swirling mass and shouted, "*Minas Glaciatto!*" A shower of dagger-like ice condensed in front of me, rocketing toward that hellish flame. It hissed and popped, steam exploding all around it. Still, the fires closed on us.

The shouts of the soldiers grew more hysterical. I raised the sword again and screamed, "*Magnus Glaciatto!*" The very air in my lungs turned frigid, and icy daggers the size of softballs rocketed toward the incoming mass. For a moment, as the steam grew thicker and the momentum of that nightmarish thing slowed, I thought I might have bought us some time.

The fire dissipated, and laughter rose in its place. Drake's wings looked to be on fire, twice as large as they would have been without the flame, and the sight of that fairy having survived a *magnus*-level incantation sent a chill into my bones. "Fool," was all he said before the fires swirled around him again. This time, however, he didn't see the tiny winged form closing on him from behind.

Foster exploded into his full-size form and released a scream that could have pulled blood from the earth. Drake tried to spin to face the incoming fairy, but Foster's iron sword found its mark, cutting into Drake's shoulder, and extinguishing the fires on his wings.

Foster didn't relent. Drake slammed a gauntleted fist down onto the sword, tearing it out of his own flesh. Foster spun, striking low with his dagger before bringing the sword to bear once more, aiming for Drake's neck.

"You dare!" Foster screamed raising a knee into Drake's groin. The dagger found its home in Drake's side and Foster stabbed once, twice, before Drake could raise his guard. Drake dove toward the earth by the time I remembered to tell the soldiers not to shoot Foster.

Foster chased after the imposter Demon Sword. His body brightened until a sphere of fire erupted like the storm clouds of Jupiter. It made the magic Drake had summoned look like a distant star placed beside a sun.

The fairies vanished into the fires of the flaming tents.

"There," I said, gesturing with a soulsword. A water witch had slithered into the clearing, and was only then beginning to solidify. "You see one of those, use either of those daggers. That's the only thing you have that can take them down."

"Won't the fires hurt them?" one of the privates asked.

I thought of the apprehension of the water witches around Mike the Demon. I knew they were susceptible to some fire magics. Natural fire was no threat. I didn't think I needed to explain that to the soldiers, though.

Instead, I just said, "No."

"How do they operate?" the woman asked.

I blinked.

"What's their SOP?"

"Ambush tactics mostly. But they won't hesitate to attack in a group either. Watch for water on the ground. It could be a witch."

"Wait for them to get close enough, and then stab them?"

"More or less," I said.

"Set a trap," the soldier said, looking around the area. She slid a dagger into her belt. "I'm the bait."

There was only one stone building, which looked like it might be cinder block, and I suspected it was either their command center, or a low-budget abandoned office building. "There," I said, indicating the building. "Fall back to that. I'll send my allies to meet you. If I can't make it myself."

"Don't worry about us," the soldier said. "We'll take down as many as we can before you do."

The fairies roared, and a water witch at the other end of the clearing dashed into the smoldering tent city. I followed.

✦   ✦   ✦

STEEL CRASHED ON steel as the fires around me threatened to set my clothes alight. I followed the water witch's path as she created a narrow trail of moisture. I suspected the narrow band of water kept her attached to the river in the distance. I winced and batted my head as a hot ember settled on my hair, the stench nauseating, but quickly overwhelmed by the burning reek of the tents.

I aimed my hand at the stretch of water on the ground and said, "*Minas Ignatto.*" The flame created a gap in the water, and that farthest from the river swelled up and stretched to find the end of the stream. So long as the water witch touched the river, she could send word to any other witch connected to the same body of water. There were distances they couldn't cover, but for that, they had other means of communication.

Cutting the witch off completely might bring more. I didn't want to do that while I was alone. An arm of fire reached out from a nearby tent, giving me a small heart attack before I realized it was just more shriveling, flaming vinyl.

Something ran past me, crashing through the flaming tents with no regard for its own well-being. At first, I thought it was my imagination, until it happened again. The glint of gray metal helmets and the flash of silver teeth revealed a sight I had not expected. At least two dark-touched vampires had streaked past me. The soldiers didn't have a chance if we didn't get back to them.

This was no longer a matter of not alerting the other water

witches, this was a matter of regrouping, or they were going to pick us off one by one. I lit a soulsword as I rounded the corner of the last tent and found the water witch with her back toward me. The field in front of her was lit by the fiery glow of Foster and Drake hammering away at each other. I kept one eye on the water witch, and another on Foster.

"It was never your mantle to bear," Drake snarled, pushing Foster's sword aside.

"It passed on when the Mad King died," Foster snarled. "A fate you will soon join."

Drake laughed and danced away from Foster.

The water witch raised her arm as if to summon an attack, and I had little doubt of who that attack would be focused on. I sliced through her back with the soulsword, sending a gout of steam out through her neck. She writhed on the blade before collapsing onto the ground in front of me. The soulsword wouldn't be enough to kill her, but it would incapacitate her.

"Foster!" I shouted. "Dark-touched, here!"

Foster almost growled, his eyes glancing to me for a split second before he placed a boot firmly in Drake's midsection.

"You're already too late," Drake said through a labored breath. He used the momentum of his fall to open a portal and escape with a grunt.

Foster's body still glowed with the power he had summoned as the Demon Sword. "Get Sam," I said. "You're hurt, and we're going to need her help with the dark-touched."

Foster didn't say anything. He looked down at his bloodied forearm and frowned. "Take this," he said, holding out his sword. "I got lucky, Damian. I thought he had me."

"I'm glad he didn't," I said. "Now go."

Foster snapped into his smaller form and launched himself into the air. He tilted to one side for a moment before a strong stroke of his wings leveled him out. He glided over the rising heat of the fires and vanished into the darkness.

I pulled the sword out of the earth. I was under no illusions about my skills with a blade. The Old Man had taught me a few things, a few essential things, and the rest of the time I relied on the soulsword.

I walked back to the crumbled water witch at the edge of the clearing and rammed the sword through her chest. I'd seen what the stone daggers could do, turning a water witch into stone in a matter of seconds. The blades Mike had forged weren't so merciful.

Fire blossomed inside her translucent form, lancing out like a poison, creating a webwork of veins, like stone. The witch tried to scream, but her throat was compromised by the pulsing magic. I ripped the sword out of her, and stared in horror as the magic ceased working, and instead left her in a paralyzed agony.

"Fucking hell, Mike."

I raised the soulsword and cut through her neck. The stone shattered, and her translucent head rolled free. Slowly, the parts of the witch that hadn't been turned to stone spread. The liquid hissed as it bled into the fires.

The awful weapon in my hand drew my gaze for a moment before I jogged back to the burning tents. Rain fell in earnest, the sky opening up as the tornado sirens echoed around us once more.

A swell of magic tugged at my aura, and I glanced over my shoulder to find a hellish sight. The tornado siren was no longer merely a warning of the attack on the city, but a warning of the enormous water spout that had formed over the Missouri River.

I didn't think I could focus well enough to summon Happy without coming to a complete stop to send my aura out to find the bear, but I knew someone nearby who might hear me. "Aeros!" I shouted. "God dammit rock, if ever you're going to listen to me, let it be now."

Every glance over my shoulder showed me an ever-widening funnel cloud, saturated with water and debris. I had no illusions about the power of the creatures controlling it.

The earth beside me rumbled, throwing my sprint off balance as Aeros's face rose from the grass and mud. "Oh, dear," the Titan said.

"Get Graybeard," I said. "If anyone can fight that thing, it's him."

Aeros hesitated, looking like he might say more, but instead he vanished into the earth.

Shadows moved in the field. I couldn't tell if they were friend or foe, and the incantation fell from my lips without a second thought. "*Modus Illuminadda.*" A ball of light surged forward, revealing three dark-touched stalking the perimeter of the cinder block building. In the distance, more Fae clashed with gunfire and our other allies that I couldn't clearly identify. More heads were hunkered down by the cinder block wall than when I'd left. I saw two faces appear in the doorway, and then vanish back inside. I hoped like all hell they'd come up with a plan.

Exhaustion crept into my bones. I'd used too many incantations too fast, and it was beginning to take a toll. I reached down for the arts that had become little more effort than a reflex, and called the dead to my side. I curled my hand into a fist, feeling my aura intertwined with an ocean of the dead. The Hand of Anubis rose before the farthest dark-touched, causing it to run into the wall of dead flesh. All three of the vampires froze and looked around, likely trying to identify the source of the distraction, as the Hand of Anubis snatched up the nearest of them, and dragged it screeching into the ground.

What appeared on the other side of the stone building worried me most—two water witches I didn't recognize, with no trail behind them feeding to the river. These weren't scouts. These were members of a raiding party.

The light of the *illuminadda* spell faded, and I sprinted forward, the roar of the water spout a harrowing thunder behind me.

CHAPTER TWENTY-ONE

A SWORD FLICKERED through the fiery light at the other side of the field, and a brief glimpse of Sam untied a knot of worry in my gut. She vanished into the smoke and flames a moment later.

A bandaged head peeked out from the cinder block wall before ducking inside once more. Someone bellowed an order to fire, and the clearing lit up with the rapid clatter of M16s.

One of the fairies went down in that hail of bullets, and I realized the soldiers must have had steel-jacketed rounds. A wailing cry echoed up from the earth as the Fae dissolved into the ley lines.

It became readily apparent that I was standing on the wrong side of the field when a round shattered a tree branch by my head and whined as it ricocheted off a stone by my foot. I cursed and summoned a shield, willing to risk tipping off the dark-touched to avoid those bullets.

I almost missed the clawed arm reaching out for me, the gray metal nails swiping through the air, embedding in my shield with an explosion of electric blue lightning.

They might have caught the fairy with their rounds, but the soldiers didn't understand the dark-touched's weakness. Round after round pinged off the vampire's helmet and slammed into its obsidian flesh. Ten, twenty, thirty rounds found their mark, until the creature finally stumbled backward, dark blood pouring from dozens of wounds. But still, the thing came.

I reached down for the Fist of Anubis, thrusting my arm upward and splitting the earth beneath the dark-touched. The impact of that solid mass of dead flesh sent the dark-touched vampire spiraling fifteen feet into the air while the soldiers peppered it with more rounds. We'd caught the attention of the other dark-touched then, and their shadowy forms zipped across the clearing with terrifying speed.

A string of curses fell from my lips as I clumsily deflected the claws of the nearest dark-touched. The creature slowed as another hail of gunfire tore into it a moment before it managed to get its claws into me. The vampire tried to lash out with a foot, tried to slip a hidden attack beneath my shield. But I saw it coming and crushed the shield downward, so the dark-touched tripped and smashed his face into it.

Electric blue lights sparked all around us, and that awful face, dripping black venom from its mouth, inched ever closer. A series of booms echoed behind me, and the roar of the water spout as it tore through the flaming tent city grew louder.

Through it all, I glimpsed the first water witch slipping into the cinder block building.

I ground my teeth, and the muscles in my forearm knotted, trying to aid the shield in fending off the dark-touched. Those horrible, pale white lines that showed the shield fracturing etched their way across the blue dome. I knew it wouldn't be long before the shield fell. I slid the enchanted blade into my belt and drew the focus. A soulsword snapped to life, lancing out at the first dark-touched, who was now back on his feet and stumbling toward me. The instant the blade made contact I said, "*Magnus Ignatto!*"

The spell was too strong, and drew power like a starving vampire. The hurricane-force winds of the fiery maelstrom did their job, hurling the dark-touched across the clearing to smack into the flaming ruin of a tent. But it drained too much power. I couldn't hold my concentration, couldn't keep my shield lit.

The half dome of power shattered. The screeching clatter behind me was a death knell of gods knew what. I gathered the dead around me once more to raise another Hand of Anubis, but it would be too late. My best bet was that the dark-touched vampire wouldn't cut through anything vital. But if it was on me for more than a second, I was already done.

At that moment, I remembered the Timewalker Seal. I remembered that my life was tied to Vicky's. If I died, she died. Sam died. Instead of inspiring me to action, that thought paralyzed me. Despair leeched into my bones. The vampires outmatched me.

Pain brought me back into the moment. "Sam!" I managed to bark out as a dark-touched's claws bit into my arm.

It was only then I realized what had happened to the third dark-touched. It was battling my sister at the far end of the field. "Goddammit."

The sword nearly cut my nose off. The skeletal arm that followed confused me. It had no flesh, no muscle to give it life. But its blade bit into the dark-touched's eye just the same. The vampire squealed and backpedaled, flinging his claws into the night air. That gave me a much-needed split second to raise the soulsword once more.

I found myself standing not beside Graybeard, but beside one of his crew. The old stained bones knocked his teeth together, glanced at me, and then surged toward the reeling dark-touched.

But if that skeleton had come from behind us, and it had come through the water spout … a glance behind me showed the water spout failing. The cyclone broke, and fire rose where there had been water moments before. The entire structure collapsed, sending debris soaring through the air. Water witches fell from that spiraling torrent, more than I would've thought possible. The water spout hadn't been the work of single water witch, but dozens working in tandem.

I cursed as I realized the spout might have been broken, but now we had more enemies on the ground. Two more of Graybeard's men charged past me. These didn't carry swords like the first—they carried long narrow spears. These skeletons had fought against the dark-touched in the Burning Lands. They'd honed their weapons and learned how to strike the dark-touched vampires when the odds against them were far worse than what we faced now. I didn't think the skeletons would be able to overpower the dark-touched vampires, but they didn't need to.

From six feet out, ten feet out, they struck at the vampires, their spears thrusting, returning, and thrusting again. The strikes glanced off the dark-touched's armor three times before one found its mark. The vampire collapsed as the spear pierced just the right part of its brain in its long sloping skull. Two of the skeletons were still beside me, but the third had charged-off to help Sam with the remaining dark-touched.

"I think you're better at this than I am," I said, earning what I imagined was a chattering laugh from the skeleton. "I'm going to help the others. We have water witches."

The skeleton nodded at me, a disturbingly human gesture. I didn't know why that had bothered me more than a reanimated skeleton, but something about it just seemed unnatural.

I glanced back one last time as I closed on the cinder block building. Far in the distance, I saw the ghostly masts of the Bone Sails, and the cannons on Graybeard's ship roared to life once more.

"Sam," I shouted. "Right!"

I didn't alter my stride. I stayed focused on reaching the cinder block building, but I caught a glimpse of Sam's sword slashing out to her right, catching a surprised water witch. The wounded cry was all I needed to hear to know Sam had found her mark. By the time I reached the edge of building, the skeletons had engaged the last of the dark-touched.

Or, at least, the dark-touched I could see.

I sprinted toward the cinder block wall, sliding on damp grass and slamming into the structure with my shoulder. The stone wall felt gritty beneath my skin. I edged to the corner and peeked around in time to hear a boom from inside the building. I took a half step back as a water witch's body flickered between translucent fluid and gray stone near the doorway.

She screamed, but the sound cut off intermittently as fragments of whatever had hit her moved through her body. Parts of the witch became stone, and then flesh, only to return to a clear fluid. Her face contorted, creased in agony until a soldier reached out with one of the daggers Mike had enchanted. The dagger embedded in her neck finished the job.

"Take her head off."

The soldier looked up at me in surprise, and I was glad to see that the youngest of them was still alive.

"Welcome to the party," she said.

"Get back inside. I'll finish this."

The soldier ripped the dagger through the water witch's neck before raising her M16 and firing point-blank into the wounded undine.

I heard the ricochet of a bullet before someone squawked in pain inside the building.

"You shot me!" a familiar voice shouted.

"Shit," I muttered. I followed the private into the building. Maps, posters, and documents I couldn't identify at a glance adorned the walls. Half a dozen workstations were set up with multiple monitors. Frank was in the corner.

"I'm so sorry," the private said. She reached out to Frank, and he yelled when her fingers reached the wounded arm.

"Isn't that exactly where the vampire bit you?" I asked, eyeing Frank's wound.

"Yes!" Frank snapped. "How kind of you to notice."

I frowned at the table behind Frank, where Casper was working furiously with what appeared to be a reloading die and three cans of gunpowder.

"Two hours?" Park shouted from the far corner opposite Frank. "We're under attack now! Get those reinforcements out here now, or it's your ass." Park angrily smashed his finger against the screen. It just didn't have the same effect as slamming a receiver down.

I snatched the first aid kit off the wall and tossed it to Frank. "Wrap it for now. The fairies can fix you up later. Just, you know, don't bleed out or anything."

"Your compassion knows no bounds," Frank muttered.

"Today's lesson," I said, turning from one private to the

next, "Don't shoot the water witches after they turn to stone. Bullets can ricochet off them as easily as a rock."

I tucked the focus securely into my belt and crouched down beside Casper. "Did you take that shot?"

"Of course," she said. "Damian, powder." I popped the top off the can and slid it to her. She didn't even look, just kept her eyes on the scale as she tipped a few grains into a small cup. She measured and poured the rest into some brass before sliding the entire assembly into a die, placing one of Mike's bullets at the tip. A quick throw of the lever and she had a fully functional round for the rifle on the table. "How many of those have you made?"

"Three left in the magazine," Casper said. "And don't ask if you can help."

Casper wasn't the first person I'd met who was very particular about reloading. She was, however, the first person I'd met who was very particular about reloading while in the middle of a firefight.

"There's at least one more water witch to the west. The others are closer to the river. Has anyone seen Foster? The fairy I came here with?"

"Not since he was fighting that fireball," a private said.

"I saw him at the other end of the tents," Park said. "Before I made it back here to command."

"Good," I said. "Oh, and if you see any skeletons running around, they're on our side."

Park blinked at me.

A private nestled in the front corner of the building, stuck so deeply in the shadows that I hadn't seen him, said, "Water witch incoming."

Casper laid two more rounds on the table. She left them standing on their primers and scooped up the M16. She leveled it at the doorway, and we waited.

CHAPTER TWENTY-TWO

S OMETIMES IT'S EASY to forget that an attack doesn't always come from where you expect it. The front door of the building had been pulled off at some point in the battle, leaving the only other covered entrance the reinforced steel door at the other end. The attack came from neither.

The private stationed just inside the doorway howled as a sword sliced through his guts, penetrating the cinder blocks behind him. Two more blades slid through the opposite wall, narrowly missing Frank's head. He stumbled toward the center of the room, and crouched down behind Casper.

"Get away from the walls!" Park said.

The wounded private at the front of the building collapsed. I dashed forward, scooping him up from beneath the shoulders and dragging him away from the entrance. It was exactly what the water witches wanted. One of them shot through the doorway, and I was blocking Casper's view. I tossed the injured private to the side, hoping that the landing on the table wouldn't do too much damage as he sprawled across it. I dropped to the floor as fast as I could, but the water witch followed me down. "*Impadda!*"

The shield sprang to life, and I caught the water witch before her dagger found my flesh. Blue sparks flashed and popped in the interior of the command building. I shoved the water witch up as high as I could and shouted, "Fire!"

Casper did.

The round tore through the undine's head, entering the eye socket and blasting a mixture of stringy viscera and watery stone out the back. It wasn't like the last witch. This one fell still. She was dead in an instant, and the parts of her that weren't stone returned to water.

I turned my attention back to the wounded private as swords continued to pierce the building. It didn't take long to realize they were following a pattern, compromising the supports and cutting their way in.

Frank wrapped the injured man's wound in a compression dressing as best he could, but the injury looked bad. I wasn't sure anyone could recover from that. But I knew Foster couldn't heal it in his wounded state. The man needed a hospital, and he needed one now.

I closed my eyes and pushed out my aura, seeking my sister. It wasn't hard to find her. The auras of the fast-moving dead surrounded her. I suspected that meant the skeletons were still taking up arms with her and were staying by her side. Graybeard had always liked her better.

"Sam, we're inside command. We need you. Water witches."

I got an impression of her turning toward the building, and then our connection cut off.

If Sam was closing on the water witches from the north, I'd surprise them from the doorway. "I'm going out. Anything comes back in that isn't one of us, shoot it in the head."

I darted out the doorway to the protests of those inside. I curled around the building to my right and spun on the bloody flattened grass beside a long-dead soldier.

The water witches were no longer attacking the building. They were focused on the vampire who was screaming like a banshee. Sam charged at them, her left hand spread wide as though her fingernails were claws and the sword bared in her right. Graybeard's crewmen followed behind her.

The first water witch struck, but Sam moved almost faster than my eyes could follow. Her sword cut through the water witch's arm before slicing up her torso, leaving a screaming, writhing half-stone thing on the ground for the skeletons to demolish. The next water witch hesitated, and by the time she realized that was a mistake, Sam's sword was already embedded in her head. Sam pushed the witch backward, her sword stuck through the screaming undine's jaw.

"You shouldn't have come here," Sam hissed. She slammed the water witch's head against the building until the cinder blocks cracked, bits of mortar falling away with the undine's life. Sam ripped her sword out of her enemy's head and turned to face me.

"Is Frank okay?" Sam asked, lips in a tight line. Her aura pulsed with a red rage I'd rarely seen.

"He's okay, but he got clipped. Have you seen Foster?"

Sam shook her head. It wasn't the answer I was hoping for.

"We need Aideen. The soldiers in there, some of them are injured."

A rhythmic clacking of bone on bone drew my attention back to the skeletons at Sam's side. One of them was almost hopping up and down, pointing behind us to a part of the tent city that was no longer a pillar of flame, but a smoldering cloud of toxic fumes.

Massive trees swayed in a wind I didn't feel. I frowned at the sight, the slow rise of that cloud, unaffected by the winds. "Son of a bitch. There's one more witch on the other side of the building."

Two claps of thunder sounded from the far corner of the command center, and my eyes snapped up to see a half-frozen witch collapsing on top of the roof.

Casper appeared at the corner of the building. "No more witches. Go."

"Come on, Sam," I said. Before I finished speaking, Sam snatched me up off the ground, and I was suddenly hurtling through space under the arm of a vampire.

She dashed through the burning remnants of the tents, where I would've had to go around. She held me high enough to keep the flames away, and moved fast enough I barely had time to register the super-heated air before we cleared the other side.

She sat me down, and I wobbled for a moment on my feet. I cursed and drew the focus from my belt. Clear of the fires, I could see two Green Men squaring off against Foster, while another clashed with Aeros. The creature facing the Old God was an abomination, a titan of bark and magic. I suspected it was at least twice as large as the other two. That put the Green Man close to thirty or forty feet tall. I couldn't be sure how tall the damn thing was, but the blows it rained down on Aeros were terrifying. The Green Man drove the rock god inches into the earth as if it had the strength of a harbinger and the speed of the Old God.

The sagging branches of the Green Man closest to Foster snapped out like a whip, and Foster's grunts of pain confirmed the hit.

"Get out of there!" I shouted.

I wasn't sure if he could hear me. I wasn't sure how much damage he'd taken, but I could see that the white of his wings was splashed with blood, and only one of his arms was striking back as fairy dust mixed into the red stream.

"Damian," Sam said. "What are you doing?"

I stared at my sister as the chaff of the gravemaker rose beneath my feet and crawled up my thigh. "You know what to do. If this goes wrong, you know how to stop me."

I didn't hear her response as the rusted black and bark closed over my head.

The forest of swords, as I'd come to think of it, wasn't much harder to conjure than the Hand of Anubis. But conjuring it made it a lot harder for me to remain inside my own head. The power required might not have been much more, but the potential loss of control terrified me. But if these guardsmen all died, and the only witnesses left were us, then Drake's frame would be a smashing success. And they'd all hunt us down, regardless.

To keep my city safe, my family safe, I had to take the risk.

The presence of that damned flesh around me felt welcoming, but that unnerving fact kept me grounded. It let me feel the shadows crawling across the hairs on my arms and the thousands of souls that had gone into its creation.

"Foster," I said, my voice twisted into the guttural howl of the gravemaker. I knew when the corroded flesh had pulled away from my eyes because the scene before me turned into a milky-white nightmare. I could see the ley lines running beneath the earth, making their way to the river. The tendrils of blue and green magic wound up into the Green Men, animating them, becoming their life force. But there was something else in that twisted mass of magic, something dark.

Foster stood out against the shadows like a beacon of light, a brilliant sun of bright reds and deep blues. I saw the form twist to look at me before it dove toward the earth, dodging another strike from the radiant Green Men.

"Vesik," Aeros's voice boomed through my mind. "Do not lose yourself here."

I opened my mouth to scream as my fists clenched and pillars of the dead streaked into the night sky. If I hadn't known what formed those awful things, I might have thought they were stone or metal trees that had rusted in some forgotten art installation. My palms opened with a snap, the elongated fingers of the gravemaker around my own, crackling and crunching as the power surged through them. Dozens of spear-like constructs erupted from the pillars around the Green Men, splitting bark and the softer flesh beneath. By the time the Green Men finished moving, all they had left to do was burn.

All it took was a thought, and fire burst from those pillars of death, racing across their branches until the Green Men ignited in earnest. I felt the flesh along my forearms again, felt the shadows seeking to dig their roots in deeper. I knew what the gravemakers wanted. They wanted me.

But if they had me, they had Vicky. They had Sam. And from there, our allies would unravel. If we lost here, we lost everything.

Something grabbed my shoulders, and my eyes rolled up to find Sam. Screaming. "Stop now!"

Slowly, painfully, I let Zola's training seep into my mind.

The same mantras she'd taught me to close out the voices of the dead when we visited places like Gettysburg. I remembered the peace of the cabin in the middle of the woods. The summer nights spent with no one but the frogs and the lizards and the wildlife to keep me company.

I felt the shadow dig deeper into my arms, but I knew it would find no purchase. Zola had trained me too well, and this was not my time. The flesh began sloughing away. The blackened ruin attached to my right arm gave way first, revealing the red and tortured skin underneath. It looked as though I had laid out in the sun for hours, days. My vision dimmed as the gravemaker flesh covering my head fell away, only to brighten as my eyes returned to normal and I under-stood fully what I had done.

The two towers of the dead had company. The Green Men, when they had no life running through their flesh, looked instead like displaced trees propped up by failing power lines. The power sparked and faded as the entire scene started collapsing. It gained momentum, until the dead flesh gave way in earnest into an avalanche of ash.

I surveyed the battle around us. Most of the field had fallen still, but bursts of gunfire and screams erupted over the crackling fires. A small circle of soldiers shuffled their wounded into their center, and chased a water witch off with a small dagger and a masterful distraction.

The rest of our enemies started retreating, what few had survived.

I took a deep ragged breath and looked up at Sam from my knees. "Thank you."

"You're an idiot," she snapped. "You got my boyfriend shot

and nearly set us on fire."

She trembled slightly, crossing her arms before turning her attention back to Aeros.

I blinked, trying to understand what I was seeing. It took a few seconds to register the fact it was Foster, with a flamethrower slung over one shoulder, screaming like some possessed warrior god. I didn't know if that flamethrower would be enough to take down a creature the size of the Green Men, but with Aeros following the fairy, the remaining Green Man had decided it'd had enough. I watched as it slipped through a copse of trees and vanished. The flamethrower cut off, and Foster released a guttural scream.

Sam had helped me back to my feet by the time Foster made it to us. He was walking beside one of the guardsmen, who now had the flamethrower Foster had been using strapped across his own back.

Considering the guardsman only glanced up at Aeros a few times, I thought he was handling the insanity of the battle quite well. The skeletons rattled off a brief staccato, pointed toward the river, and hurried back through the carnage of the burnt tent city.

"What the hell did they say?" I asked.

"They said Graybeard has summoned them," Aeros said. "It is time for the Bone Sails to dock."

"Here?" I asked.

Aeros offered me a broad smile. "Yes."

I shrugged. No energy left for arguing about why it might be uncomfortable for some people to have a ghost ship manned by a literal skeleton crew docked in their town.

"Did you do that?" the guardsman asked as he came to a

stop beside me and Sam.

"Yeah," I said. "Sorry if I scared you. Necromancy isn't always pretty to watch."

The man's uniform told me he wasn't a guardsman all. He was a Ranger, and I had literally no idea what the hell he was doing here.

"There are wounded in the command center," I said. "Foster, I don't think … I don't think Foster can heal them and survive."

"Come on," the Ranger said, "I'm well versed in trauma care."

Sam scooped the Ranger up and tore across the field.

"I don't know if that was a good idea," I said. "In fact, that may have been a very bad idea." I wobbled on my feet a little.

Foster put his good arm under mine, and we hobbled beside the Old God. A soldier nodded to us as we passed.

"What wasn't a good idea?" Foster asked. "Me going toe to toe with Drake? Who I'm fairly certain is *actually* Drake? Or you closing yourself up in that goddamned gravemaker again? Or maybe Aeros trying to take on a tree twice his size?"

Aeros looked down at Foster, and his eye lights narrowed. "Samantha Vesik is much more entertaining than you."

I flashed the rock a grin. We hobbled around the corner of the command building in time to see the Ranger staring slack-jawed at the brilliant white light that exploded from inside it.

The light faded, and as my vision cleared, I saw Aideen breathing deeply and staring down at the now-healed private. When she stepped to the side, I froze at the presence of Nixie, looking like a silver-clad warrior goddess. Her hair was tied back with a length of silver rope, and her piercing blue-green eyes locked onto mine.

"I'm sorry that I couldn't be here sooner," she said quietly. "But you have slain our enemy here, and sent a message stronger than any I hoped we could."

CHAPTER TWENTY-THREE

NIXIE LOOKED DOWN at the injured private and frowned. I realized who the private was in that moment: the same man who had threatened us outside the shop. The same man who had opened fire on us and vowed to kill us all. Stacy.

"Ha," I said.

"Did you let them touch me?" Private Stacy asked, tentatively pressing his stomach where his wounds had been.

"They saved your life," Casper said. "Now pull your head out of your ass."

"You let them touch me with their magic," he spat. "You damned me to hell."

"Did the military give you leave to die?" Park snapped. "These people are the only reason any of us are alive right now."

"You're wrong," the private said. "They're the only reason any of us are here."

The fact the man had a point irritated me. Part of me knew it was their commanders who had sent them here, so close to the river, but another part of me knew that it was true—they wouldn't have been there if it wasn't for us.

Perhaps they would have been there to watch over the ruins of Saint Charles if we hadn't been there to stop it.

"Park," I said, "This is Nixie. She's one of the leaders in the rebellion against the water witch queen and Gwynn Ap Nudd."

Nixie's eyes lifted slowly from the man she'd healed and settled on Park. An awkward smile crossed to the sergeant's face, as if he'd just realized how deadly the water witch standing before him was.

"It's a pleasure. And I hope I have not wasted my time healing your soldier."

Park composed himself quickly, and he turned to Aideen. "And thank you. None of my men would have survived if it wasn't for the intel and weapons you all provided. I'd like to have you brief the troops in a more formal setting. You know infinitely more about our enemies than we do."

Private Stacy glowered at Park.

Park held the man's gaze before saying, "Get him outside. The medic will be here soon. Take him to a hospital for evaluation."

"Gladly," Casper said. She and one of the other privates dragged the healed man out of the building. Before they were out of earshot, I heard Casper whisper, "Insubordination. He's a master sergeant, private."

"I can take him to the hospital," Aeros's voice boomed.

Casper shook her head just outside the door. "He's my responsibility."

"Very well, friend."

"I'd be tempted to let Aeros take him," Park said. "Maybe knock some sense into the idiot."

"What are you going to do now?" Frank asked, inspecting the bandage on his arm. "This place is wrecked."

"We have a secondary location," Park said, "but it's still too close to the river."

"You should station your people on Main Street."

I glanced to Frank and frowned slightly. He didn't miss the gesture.

"If they're on Main Street," Frank said, "and something happens, they can be there in an instant. There's plenty of space to set up by the art store and on some of the common lots. They'd be close enough together that each unit would act as a scout for another."

"You're talking about urban warfare in the middle of a historic city," Park said, before I could say much the same thing.

"No," Frank said. "It would keep the battalion far enough away from the river to protect against anything outside of a full-scale attack from the undines. Casper and the other snipers would have their pick of the high ground to fire on strays with the stone bullets. We've seen the Fae fight enough times to understand what they're used to. They tend toward big open fields, like an idiot army marching in a straight line."

"Hey, now," Foster said. "We're mighty fine at killing things, thank you very much." He winced as Aideen healed the cuts in his wings.

"Just ignore him," Aideen said. "He's probably delirious from the pain."

"You mean the excitement of battle," Foster said.

Aideen squeezed his arm, releasing a small stream of blood and a high-pitched yelp. "Oh yes," she said. "The glory of battle."

"It'll work," Frank said. "Put Graybeard out by the old shipwreck. The barge, I mean."

The mere thought of seeing the Bone Sails docked just off

Main Street made me consider Frank's words. Graybeard knew how to fight the dark-touched. His crew were startlingly efficient, bones though they were. And if the dark-touched ever descended on Saint Charles with a harbinger, Graybeard would know how to fight it. He'd helped us save the Arch not so long ago.

"The idea has some merit," I said.

"The idea," Nixie said, "is brilliant. Park, if you station your men here, we'll provide support on the river."

Park nodded.

"There are three points in this country we believe she will attack. One is near Falias, or inside its borders. One is here. And the other … is Rivercene."

I frowned at Nixie. "Rivercene?"

She nodded.

"Are you talking about the bed-and-breakfast out near Columbia?" Park asked.

"Well," I said. "You go there, get the soufflé."

Park blinked at me, a blank expression on his face.

"Damian likes to base strategies on food," Sam said. "You'll have to forgive him."

I fought back a smile before I caught sight of Casper's down-turned face. She was looking at one of her friends, still on the ground outside. I could tell one of the dark-touched had gotten them, based on the claws that had ripped her friend's back. My good humor died. It was easy to forget that not everyone had seen the horrors we had. It was easy to forget that they might not consider ill-timed humor the best way to relieve tension after a battle.

"Thank you," Park said. "I'll make that recommendation

when I brief the commanders."

"If you need us," I said, "you can find us at the shop."

✦ ✦ ✦

SAM'S MOOD EASED a bit after Aideen healed the bullet wound in Frank's arm. We asked Park repeatedly if we could help stay and clean up the site, but he declined the offer just as much. He didn't want us there when his superiors arrived, afraid we would be too unsettling.

I supposed I could understand that. Park and his soldiers had likely never seen battlefield magic before. It could be jarring, and some of the incantations we'd thrown around would be intimidating, even to a seasoned mage.

The water in the shower of my old apartment sputtered, and I yelped when it turned to a freezing temperature for a moment before returning to normal.

"It's not that cold," Nixie said with a small laugh. "Now, am I going to have to drag you out of the shower, or are you coming willingly? We only have thirty minutes."

I turned to face her, the shower hammering on my back. Her face gleamed with the water running off her hair. I ran my fingers through the long strands, taking in the scent of the ocean that followed her everywhere.

"We'll see our friends soon enough," she said. "This is our time." She pressed her lips against mine before pressing a great deal more against me.

✦ ✦ ✦

"WHY DO YOU still live in this … shit bucket?" she asked.

I grinned at her. "I think you mean shithole."

She frowned slightly. "Perhaps, but the question stands, regardless."

I glanced down at the singed berber carpet before raising my feet up onto the old oak coffee table. "I guess it's still home."

She sighed and wrapped her arm around my shoulders. "At least the couch is comfortable."

"And there are chimichangas in the freezer."

Nixie blew out a breath and shook her head, before releasing a sigh.

"We need to go."

"I know," Nixie said. "I was just thinking about what Park said. About his superiors. He's going to show them some of the footage of that battle, and I'm not sure how they'll respond."

"Yeah, but like you said, we have bigger things to worry about right now. Best case scenario, it'll get some of the soldiers on our side. They know we're the good guys, and if Graybeard is actually going to dock the ship right in front of Main Street, they need to see you."

"Things were simpler when we were hidden," Nixie said. She threw off her blanket and stood up to stretch. She glanced over her shoulder and caught me shamelessly staring at her ass.

"We need to go," I said.

"What's five more minutes?"

I hesitated. "I'm sure five more minutes won't hurt." I grabbed her around the waist and pulled her back down to the couch into an ungraceful tangle of limbs.

CHAPTER TWENTY-FOUR

I'D RELUCTANTLY MANAGED to get dressed and ready to go while Nixie slipped back into her armor. I offered to help tie off the metal straps in the back, but she only smiled as power rippled through the armor, tightening the metal ties and locking the silver clasps closed.

"So, you mean you could've just popped that off when we got home?" I asked.

"Of course," Nixie said, "but where's the fun in that?"

I laughed and shook my head. "Why are you here?" I asked. "Don't get me wrong, I'm happy you are, but I thought you were stuck in Europe."

"I had an unexpected ally offer her assistance when she learned of the plot here."

"Who?"

"Morrigan," Nixie said. Before I could ask anything more, she continued. "She has served on the courts nearly as long as Nudd himself. She knows what a tyrant he can be, and she understands the damage he has already done."

"Can you trust her?"

Nixie was silent for a time. "To an extent, I suppose. She has long had a history of doing what will benefit her, but she has also committed selfless acts to strengthen the courts."

"And you think she sees Nudd as a threat to the strength of

the courts?"

Nixie nodded.

I hefted my backpack over my shoulders and frowned. "I sure as hell hope you're right."

Nixie led the way out the door and down the old wooden stairs.

"If Morrigan's in Faerie," I said, "who's in Falias? Who else is supporting the Obsidian Inn?"

"Leviticus, for one," she said, raising her nose to the wind. "You should move somewhere with less industry, someplace more like the cabin. It suits you, and it does not ... smell."

"Hey, now," I said.

Nixie shot me a cutting grin.

We climbed into my car, and I remembered the first time I'd seen Nixie get into the old '32 Ford. Her hair had been much longer then, almost to her knees. I'd worried about how tangled up it was in the seatbelts and the doorjamb, but she'd only given it a gentle tug to pull the entire mass of hair safely into the car. Sometimes I missed those days. I'd been able to see her a little more often than I did now. The times had changed. We had changed.

"Have you spoken to the werewolves?" I asked. "They've been tied up with some nasty business with the dark-touched over in Kansas City."

"I'm aware. Camazotz joined them. I imagine the conflict there will end soon."

"Maybe they can lend their support to Rivercene," I said. "I worry about the innkeeper being so far from us."

"She is far from everyone," Nixie said. "Without the use of the Warded Ways, none of our enemies can reach her at speed."

"The queen's undines can," I said, turning the wheel and pulling back out onto the highway. The car bounced over a small pothole, which felt more like a crater because of my car's ancient suspension. "The Missouri River practically cuts to Rivercene's front door."

"When the queen receives word that I'm here with you," she said, "I have no doubt she'll split her forces. She'll believe the Obsidian Inn to be weakened, when they are anything but. And she'll aim to strike both of us down in one assault."

"It's kind of dangerous to be your boyfriend," I said with a half smile.

"I believe the word is thrilling," she said.

A humorless laugh fell from my lips as we rumbled back onto the cobblestones of old Saint Charles.

I turned off Main Street and headed up Adams. I could see Park through the glass in the front door, true to his word, and a bit more punctual than me and Nixie.

"That man has a great respect for Frank," Nixie said. "I don't believe he would've allowed us to heal that private otherwise."

"Stacy?" I asked as we bounced in the rear parking lot. "He believed it would kill Aideen. And that if Aideen died, Foster would come for his head."

I frowned slightly. "He probably has a good point. And Foster wouldn't just come for his head. He'd come for tiny little pieces."

"Are you bothered by that?" Nixie asked.

"It would probably be a bit hypocritical of me." I glanced at her, and she eyed me. "If something ever happened to you, whoever or whatever caused it would have a fairly terrible fate."

"Such poetry," Nixie said. "I asked because you tensed. Your knuckles are still white."

I looked down at the steering wheel and slowly released my death grip. "There's too much at stake. We can't afford to lose …" I shook my head.

"It's a price every civilization has paid. It's the way of the world."

She leaned over and kissed me on the cheek. I took a deep breath, and we climbed out of the car.

The deadbolt started up before we even crossed the parking lot. "Disgusting. Mating with a mortal. A necromancer. What would your ancestors think? What do your contemporaries think?"

Before I could even respond, Nixie gave the deadbolt a swift kick to the face, and it snapped open. "Thank you, doorman," she said in an exuberant voice.

I frowned at the cringing face and wondered if we should have used the front door.

"Peanut! No!"

Peanut? I wondered, knowing that Peanut was still guarding the coven with Ashley. A furry green shadow hit me like a battering ram a moment later, a smaller yet still very pink tongue licking every inch of my face like wet sandpaper. I gasped for breath after I bounced off the wall. Peanut jumped up on his hind legs, still licking me as I fell toward the ground. He was nice enough to hop up and down on top of me while I tried to roll and get away.

"Oh, Damian," Ashley said as she reached the back room. "Are you alive? Are you drowning in tongue?"

So many opportunities for a terrible joke, but all I could do was try to fend off the pink monstrosity. "Help!" I squawked.

"Peanut," Ashley said. "Oreos."

The 200-some-odd-pound cu sith happily jumped up and down in my chest before using me as a launching pad to rocket back over to Ashley.

"Thanks," I muttered. Bubbles and Peanut bumped their heads together, excitedly waiting for Ashley to gift more Oreos to them. I groaned as Nixie helped me to my feet.

"You need another shower."

I took a towel from her when she handed me one from the shelf and I wiped my face off. "You're telling me."

"What are you doing here?" I asked. "I thought you'd be with the coven, hunkered down with that monster."

"It's Beth," Ashley said with a sad smile.

"Did something happen?" I asked, my heart pounding in my chest.

Ashley took a deep breath, her shoulder-length red hair rising and falling. "No, she's fine. She left for Rivercene with Cornelius this morning."

I raised my eyebrows, unable to keep the surprise from my face. "I was under the impression the innkeeper wasn't a huge fan of blood mages."

"I know, but Rivercene is a stronghold on a nexus." Ashley's voice took on the cadence of someone carefully reciting words that she only recently had to memorize. "Cornelius says that Rivercene is not only a gateway through Gaia, but there's an intersection with the shadow realm there too."

I cursed. "The shadow realm? As in where he and Beth summoned those giant freaky beasts?"

Ashley nodded. "It's why they want to help defend it."

"Well, shit."

"Master Sergeant Park is in the front," Ashley said. "He asked if the coven needed help. I thought that was very nice of him. He didn't have to ask."

I gave Ashley a small smile. "Park is good people."

"The shadow realm?" Nixie muttered under her breath. She was surprised, too. I didn't know if that made me feel better, or a hell of a lot worse.

"Let's go see Park," I said, making for the saloon-style doors.

✦　✦　✦

WE WALKED INTO the middle of an arm-waving, foot-stomping discussion between Frank, Sam, and Park.

"That's fantastic," Frank said. "I'm telling you, it's a tactical advantage to place some of the troops along Main Street."

"Command is considering," Park said.

"Did they say anything about the giant skeletal warship on the river?" I asked.

Park shot me a smile. "I may have left a few of the details out. We're grateful to you and your friends. I only wish all of my soldiers were."

"Soldiers follow orders," Nixie said, the stone in her voice surprising me. "It's those in command who forge alliances."

As much as Nixie's words bothered me, Park didn't seem upset by them at all. He nodded, agreeing with her to a degree. "And that's part of the problem. Some of command thinks your assistance is a ploy to get inside our own defenses. Others want you on the front lines so you and the other supernaturals can take each other out with minimal casualties on our side."

"We were just talking about how I need a new apartment. Seems relocating would be a bit more humane than murdering everyone."

Park shook his head. "I don't think you're in immediate danger, but some of my superiors suspect you're in league with Nudd."

"Do you know how many times that guy has tried to kill me?" I asked jetting my finger at Park before realizing it was a rather rude gesture.

"A lot," Sam said. "Like, a whole lot. Why aren't you dead?"

"Thanks, sis."

"You have to understand," Park said, "millions were lost in the Gettysburg tragedy. Falias' arrival signaled the single greatest loss of human life in a single day, in all of history. People are scared."

"They should be scared," Frank said. "But they should remember who *is* responsible, and they should remember who opposed them."

"I know Frank," Park said. "I know."

"How many men did you lose?" Ashley asked.

"Fourteen. The squad stationed closest to the highway was dead before we knew we were under attack. We'd have more dead it wasn't for Foster and Aideen, and Nixie."

"Where the hell is Foster?" I asked.

"He's with Casper and her squad at the hospital," Park said. "I don't know who's more exhausted, him, Aideen, or the troops. But most of them are already sharing war stories."

"Oh, Lord," I said. "Foster has a great deal of those to share."

"I have to get back to command," Park said.

"You're welcome to join us," I said. "Whatever happens next is likely to affect you as much as it does us."

"I appreciate that, Damian. Please understand, our orders are to protect humans, and our ranks are flooded with recruits who have a vendetta. Be careful. What happened in front of the shop earlier with Private Stacy could've been a great deal worse."

We said our goodbyes and watched Park vanish down the street outside Death's Door.

CHAPTER TWENTY-FIVE

A SHORT TIME later, we found ourselves on the second floor of the store, huddled in the oversized stuffed leather chairs. Frank and Sam squeezed onto one chair together, while Nixie, still in her armor, sat on the chair closest to me. Ashley pulled out a sleeve of Oreos, and the cu siths watched with forlorn looks on their faces.

"Where's Zola?" Ashley asked, popping a cookie into her mouth.

"She still at the Pit with Vik," Sam said, "at least the last I heard."

"The vampires won't be able to sit this one out," Frank said.

"You don't think so?" Ashley asked.

Frank shook his head. "No way. Vik needs to save face after he only sent a couple enforcers to Greenville. Now the dark-touched are in his own town? Every Pit from the Gulf to Chicago is going to be watching them for weakness."

"No one came to attack it after Vassili was revealed," Sam said. "I think you're being paranoid, Frank."

"Sometimes being paranoid keeps you alive," Ashley said. "Sometimes not being paranoid enough gets you killed."

"I know what you're saying about the vampires," I said. "Maybe Vik will join us in force, and maybe he won't. We need to plan like he won't."

"What makes you say that?" Sam asked.

I grimaced and held up my phone. "A text from Zola. She must've sent it while my phone was silenced."

"What does it say?" Frank asked.

"Well, in so many words, it says Vik is undecided."

"Undecided about what?" Sam asked. "Even if he doesn't want to help the military, these bastards are in our home. They're attacking our people."

"Camazotz is still engaged," Ashley said. "If Vik won't help, or can't help, maybe the others can."

I took a deep breath. "Fine. We'll see if Zola, or maybe even Sam, can persuade Vik. But for now, let's focus on Saint Charles. I'm guessing the deployment here is about to get a lot bigger."

"You'll be lucky if they don't send drones in," Frank said. "Those things are a lot more terrifying when they aren't on television."

I shivered at the thought of deadly force being executed in a populated area with so many commoners. Then again, it wasn't so different than what I had done.

"You're not alone in this," Nixie said, resting her hand on my knee.

I flashed her a small smile. "I know. I'm just worried."

"You'd be a fool if you weren't."

I nodded.

"Ashley," Nixie said, "is the coven safe? Are they still here in town?"

Ashley crossed her arms.

"It's why I was bringing Peanut back. They're off in the woods. I don't see how anyone could find them without directions."

Nixie frowned slightly. "They may be safer than they are here, but the Fae do have their ways."

Not the most reassuring pep talk I'd ever heard, but I wasn't sure what else she could've said. Offered tactical advice on the deep woods of Missouri? Probably not her area of expertise.

"I'll tell you what I told Park," Frank said. "I don't think you should set up another tent city. Sure, there's a lot of space by that gallery, but think of the common ground by the rotunda. They have a clear view of the river, they're uphill, and it gives them the advantage of visibility."

"It puts them too close to the river," Nixie said. "Water witches can be stealthier than you know."

"I understand," Frank said. "We saw some of that this evening. They can place scouts on the roofs, and the second story of several of the buildings have apartments they can commandeer. Most of the commoners who live close to the river have evacuated."

"Not to mention the fall off in tourists," I said. "If you weren't selling so much online for us, it'd be just like the good old days. No money, and ramen noodles."

"You're forgetting something," Ashley said. "Graybeard is going to dock by the old barge. The Bone Sails will be your early warning system."

"Who has the weapons?" Nixie asked. "The weapons that Mike forged?"

"Park and Casper," Frank said.

"I still have a few of the rounds," Sam said, fishing around in her pocket and presenting a handful of the stone-dagger-coated bullets.

ERIC R. ASHER

"You should hold on to a couple. And I do hope Foster retained at least one of the swords. If this place is overrun with water witches, I don't want you to be defenseless."

"I think we have enough shields to take care of the shop," I said. "Hell, we even have a blood shield. What I'm more worried about is what happens to everyone around us. I don't know that one sword will make that much of a difference."

"We should talk to the soldiers," Nixie said.

"You want to talk to Casper?" Frank asked.

"Yes," Nixie said. "I assume she's the leader of those soldiers."

"Technically, that's Park," Frank said.

"So odd," Nixie said. "Why would any species allow their men to lead their military? So many egos, and unnecessary wars."

Ashley clapped her hands together. "I knew I liked her."

I flashed the priestess a grin and turned my attention back to Frank and Nixie's conversation.

"But what about the coven?" Nixie said, turning her focus to Ashley.

"What do you mean?" Ashley asked.

"Your witches have power," Nixie said. "It may not be as blatant, or flagrant, as mine or Damian's. But they have a great deal of power."

"They're green witches," Ashley said, a tiny narrowing of her eyes changing her expression into a scowl. "I will not ask them to fight."

"I hope that's a choice they can survive," Nixie said.

"I've made sacrifices so they don't have to," Ashley said. "They'll never need to break their vows. Not for me, not for you, not for anyone."

Nixie nodded and let the conversation drop. I was happy she did. The coven had been attacked before. We all knew that. Ashley had almost been killed, and when she took up arms and learned the long-forgotten arts, she'd lost something, some small part of herself. But she'd lost part of her coven, too—those who could no longer abide a priestess who would dabble in the dark arts.

"Some truths are best left unspoken," I said, giving Nixie's hand a brief squeeze where it rested on the arm chair.

She eyed me for a moment, and then relaxed into her seat. I must admit, I was pretty proud of her terrible posture. It made her look a lot more natural around the mortals.

"I thought about following Beth," Ashley said. "But I can't help her and Cornelius. The things they can do, the horrors they can summon." She closed her eyes for a moment. "I know some of the coven don't like having her around. But I love her."

Nixie raised an eyebrow and glanced at me.

"Hey," I said.

"Oh," Nixie said, "I can relate."

"Hey, now," I said.

"Oh, I think we all can," Sam said. "I was stuck with him as a brother."

"That … is horrible," Ashley said.

I let out an exasperated sigh and sank into my seat.

"He's not that bad," Frank said. "Most days, anyway. Then there are those other days."

Bubbles chuffed from her resting spot beside Ashley.

I scowled at the cu sith. "Don't you start, too."

"Are you staying here?" Ashley asked, focusing on Nixie.

Nixie shook her head.

"What?" I said. "I thought you were coming to save all of us foolish mortals from our terrible fate?"

"That magic is beyond me," Nixie said with a small smile. "Alexandra's coming. I'll wait for the queen's arrival in Falias. If she doesn't attack us there, it's likely she'll come here."

"So, basically, you'll come back if we're all dead?" I asked. "I'd kind of like to see you again before then."

"And what is death to a necromancer?" Nixie asked. "It's only the beginning of your path."

"Yeah, no one actually knows that. I know, I know, we read about immortals in the Book that Bleeds, and dying sends them off to some other realm or some such shit. But have you ever heard from them? No. I didn't think so. Dead is dead is dead. I don't want to be dead."

Nixie flashed me a grin. "It's certainly more fun to be alive. Stay here." She raised her eyes to Ashley. "Nudd and the queen have both shown their interest in the city. What I suspect is that it's to make a statement. If they can take the stronghold of their enemies—the very home of their enemies—it will prove their strength and steal back some of those who joined the rebellion."

"I'm close to the coven here," Ashley said. "Close enough." She rubbed her forehead. "And it's not so far from Rivercene that I can't reach them if they need me. That I can't reach Beth. I have to return to the coven for a time, to ensure they're prepared for the worst. I'll be back tomorrow."

Frank glanced down at his watch. "It's getting late. We should probably go see Casper and her crew now, if we want to catch them while they're still awake."

I nodded.

Nixie turned to me. "Come down to Graybeard's ship after you've visited the soldiers. I would like to say goodbye before we part ways."

"I will," I said.

Sam made a retching noise, drawing my attention. As soon as my gaze settled on her, she took one broad lick of Frank's cheek.

"Eww."

CHAPTER TWENTY-SIX

W E DECIDED TO take Sam's SUV to the hospital—it was a hell of a lot more comfortable if you were trying to shoehorn three people into it. Not to mention the cobblestones were a lot friendlier to the suspension of a modern SUV.

"I wish Ashley would come," Sam said.

"Me too," Frank said, "but I think it's good for her to put things in order with the coven. She's lost people before. And it's probably better than spending time with Graybeard."

Sam made a disgusted sound. "No one needs to spend more time with that old pervert."

I frowned, trying to remember if Sam was referencing something particular. "Graybeard say something to you?" I asked. "I don't remember him saying anything to you."

"You don't remember?" Sam asked. "Damian, he used to sit on my windowsill and spy on Miss Bromfield when she'd be changing in the morning. And I had to listen to him spewing lascivious crap for half the damn day."

"I seriously doubt someone was changing their clothes for half the day," Frank said.

Sam shot him a glare that could've skewered him in place as we pulled into a parking spot. "You'd be surprised."

I chuckled. "I'd forgotten about her. You could say she was a bit of an exhibitionist, Frank."

"Yeah, you could say that," Sam muttered.

"She put up one of those privacy fences," I said. "One of those fences that wasn't really private. You know the type?"

"Yeah, I know the type," Frank said. "I staked out more than one place over the years behind high-security fencing." He made air quotes around "high-security."

"Miss Bromfield," I said with a laugh. "We knew some strange people, Sam."

"I think we still do."

We made our way through the main entrance, and I paused by the hallway that led to the ICU. Construction workers were already there, cleaning things up and likely getting ready to rebuild. It was a ghastly sight. They hadn't gotten all the blood off the walls yet, and there was still a metric ton of ash and debris.

"Come on," Frank said. "The receptionist says they're in the next wing now."

We let Frank lead the way, passing rooms where terrible coughs echoed through the hallways accompanied by the rhythmic beat of EKGs. We passed out of the wing, and found two MPs at the front of the next hallway.

"We're here to see Lincoln," Frank said as we approached the first man. "Park said it was okay to come in."

The soldier nodded, and we passed by without incident. Frank was muttering the room number under his breath, but I peeked into the rooms along the hall. Some of them were clearly soldiers, their fatigues either neatly folded beside their beds, or sealed in plastic bags on the floor.

A few of the occupants were wrapped in gauze and whimpering from the pain of burns and heavily damaged limbs. The last, before Casper's room, was being covered by a sheet. I tried not to look. I didn't want to know, but it was hard to ignore a new ghost, especially one who didn't understand what happened, and was now looking down at the body he'd known his entire life.

I fought down a pang of sorrow when the ghost tried to grab the shoulders of the doctor, to speak to her, when he no longer had the ability to speak. As a spirit, he was mute, which gave me some small relief that he would pass on quickly. And not be trapped on the battlefield as some ancient memorial for all time.

"Casper," Frank said. We entered the room, which pulled me out of the haze of seeing the newly formed ghost.

"Frank," Casper said, patting the edge of the bed. "Come in, come in. You guys really saved our asses out there."

Casper squeezed Frank's arm when he took a seat on the edge of the bed. I nudged Sam with my elbow when Casper's eyes widened and locked onto my sister.

"Friendly," I said. "No eating them."

Sam turned jet black eyes on me, and I gave her a nervous smile. "You look great tonight."

"Sorry," she said. "I don't know what the hell that was."

"That was jealousy," a voice said from across the room.

I stepped farther in, and saw the Ranger from earlier sitting on a small desk in the corner. It wasn't a desk, exactly, but more like one of those rolling tray tables they bring you that wonderful hospital food on.

"That was not jealousy," Sam said.

"That's good," the Ranger said, "because I'm Casper's boyfriend. And I'd rather not have to shoot Frank."

"Pretty sure I can handle shooting people myself," Casper said. "Thank you very much."

Frank chuckled and patted the edge of the bed, coaxing Sam over to sit next to him. I stayed in the doorway, leaning against the bathroom door.

"How is everyone?" Frank asked.

"Most of the survivors are okay," Casper said. "A couple didn't make it."

"I'm sorry," I said. "You seen the fairies?" Now I wondered where they were, and how much they had done to help the wounded soldiers back at the hospital. It wasn't safe for them to expend too much energy healing.

"They did what they could," Casper said. "And more of us are alive than have any right to be because of them."

Something shifted on the pillow behind Casper, and I couldn't stop a grin when Foster popped his head up. "Nudd's balls, she makes us sound so noble."

Aideen sat up and yawned, stretching her back before casually slapping Foster across the cheek. "Just ignore him," she said in a tired voice. Aideen hopped off the pillow, her body weight scarcely denting the sheets as she walked over to Sam and flopped onto my sister's thigh.

"You are what you are," the Ranger said, crossing his arms. "There's no need to fight it."

"Since when is it the smart ones that carry the guns?" Foster asked. "I've gotten so used to it just being Damian."

Casper fluffed the pillow for him, and he laid back down.

"Don't get used to that," Aideen said. "Or they'll have a reason not to trust us."

Foster beamed at Aideen, and Casper chuckled.

I wasn't sure how much Aideen was joking, and where she would draw the line. Fairies could be ruthless, and I'd been lucky to escape with little more than a scratch on more than one occasion.

"Have you seen Park?" Frank asked. "We wanted to check on you guys, but we were hoping to catch Park, too. Nixie had some great ideas about where to station the water witches."

"He's ... dealing with something." Casper glanced away, meeting the Ranger's eyes for a moment.

"Just tell them," he said. "If they wanted us dead, we'd already be dead."

"Stacy," Casper said, "the man who opened fire on Main Street, is being debriefed."

The Ranger snorted. "Debriefed? Park tore them up one side and down the other. And he made it damn clear who our allies are."

"Yes," Casper said, "the man who fired on you has a following of radically minded soldiers, mostly raw recruits, but not all."

"We can handle ourselves," Foster said through a huge yawn.

"If I had a flyswatter right now," the ranger said, "you wouldn't stand a chance."

"That's like a weapon of mass destruction," Sam said. "Hardly fair."

"Vampires can be such bitches," Foster muttered.

The ranger leaned back a bit and cast Sam a small smile. "I thought I recognized you. You're with the local vampire clan. Damian's sister."

"Oh, don't call her that," Foster said.

"Why not?" Sam asked. "Some days it seems like I don't have a name outside of 'Damian's sister.'"

"Sorry," the Ranger said, immediately recognizing the danger. "No disrespect meant. Your hair was different in the photos they showed in our briefing. I wasn't sure it was you."

"Failure to recognize a mark," Casper said. "What would your old sergeant think?"

"It's a little different here," the ranger said. "There's a lot less sand."

Casper laughed. "That'll make a great excuse. There was less sand, so I couldn't recognize anyone."

The hammering started a moment later. "Wow," I said. "Somebody's using some heavy-duty equipment pretty late today. Are they trying to get the ICU fixed tonight or something?"

Sam sprang to her feet a moment before I realized Casper, Frank, and the Ranger had gone stock-still.

"Do you have your gun?" the Ranger asked.

"Do I have my gun?" Casper asked. "They didn't exactly give me an option to bring an M16 into the hospital."

Aideen leaped into the air and landed on Sam's shoulder as Sam bolted to the door.

"Wait here," Sam said, pausing at the doorway. "I'll see what's happening."

Another hammer blow sounded, and then more. The unmistakable burst of automatic weapons fire. I cursed and followed Sam to the door.

"Aideen, stay here," I whispered. "You and Foster have done enough. You're too tired for this."

The fairy looked conflicted. Her fingers wrapped around

the hilt of her sword, only to release it twice in succession. She cursed and glided back to the bed beside Foster. I heard them whisper, but I didn't wait to see what they decided. Sam zipped out the door and I followed.

A form clad in nothing but a hospital gown moved past one of the fallen MPs, and then ducked into one of the hospital rooms. Another burst of gunfire sounded before a second man stepped out of a room on the other side of the hall. Only it wasn't a man, it was a newly formed ghost, the color draining from his aura as it became the calm winding flow of the dead.

Sam blurred into motion. She rocketed down the hallway, knocking a whiteboard off the wall before she crashed through the drywall, snapping electrical lines and God knows what else. Gunshots tore through the wall, and the man in the hospital gown backpedaled, firing wildly into the room.

"You took my brothers," he screamed, all reason gone from his voice. "You'll never take me. You'll never take another one of us."

He chased something around the room with the gun, and I knew he was aiming for Sam. A black blur erupted out the doorway, wrenching the rifle out of the man's hand and taking him to the ground. Blood dripped from my sister's forehead, leaving a stain when she'd head-butted the deranged man.

I was so fixated on her that I didn't see the second gunman walking out of the room across the hall. I didn't see him until he had raised a handgun the size of Texas and pointed it at my sister's head.

"No!" I shouted, and my aura surged forward out of sheer reflex. It wrapped itself around that newborn ghost, an MP whose murder had just happened. And in a split second, I understood.

Father, a major. Mother, a sergeant. Brother, a Navy SEAL. A family born in war, who gave everything to their country, followed their commands without fail. Loyal, as loyal as a member to their alpha wolf.

His great-grandfather had given his life in the first of the world wars. And from there, a family tragedy unfolded, decade after decade. When there weren't wars, they died in black ops. But this soldier was unique, this soldier understood that there were things in the world outside humanity. He'd known about magic for decades. He'd met Green Men and journeyed to the newly risen Falias in hopes of finding an old family legend. A legend that had haunted them longer than they could trace their own history. A legend known as the Morrigan.

A strange creature that had once saved his sister, before visiting him at his father's grave in Arlington. And a year later at his sister's grave, when she came home in a box from a war that never should've been. A war of blood and sand and merciless gods.

I screamed through the tears, "Stop him!"

The words were garbled to my ears as that horrible domino of life after life lost in war after war burned into my soul. His now-corporeal hand flashed out, knocking the gun away as the murderer pulled the trigger. It blasted a hole in the tile beside Sam's head. The man reeled backward in shock, but the ghost followed him.

Sam cracked the man's head on the tile floor an instant later, leaving him unconscious while the ghost watched.

"Go," I said to the ghost. "Find what peace you can."

"Thank you," the ghost said. And then he was gone, the

shadow of a crow escorting him into the darkness.

Sam was on her feet again, staring at me. "Damian, look at the size of that hole. Could that have killed me?"

"Maybe," I said quietly. "I don't know."

She wiped the blood away from her chin with a shaky hand. She reached out to me, and I held her tight. I felt the sorrow of that ghost who had lost his sister not so long ago. And it was an easy thing to understand how losing Sam would destroy me in more ways than one.

Park stumbled around the corner, leaning down to check the pulse of the very dead MP.

"He's gone," I said.

Park hobbled forward and looked into the first hospital bed before releasing a string of curses that Zola would've been proud of. Park made his way toward us, and I saw the blood trickling down his left leg.

"You're shot," I said.

"In the job description."

Sam sniffed and pulled away from the unconscious soldiers. Park flinched at the sight of her blood-covered face.

"He'll do no harm now," she said, indicated the first shooter. She pointed at the second man. "I think this one just misunderstood the situation."

"Come on, let's get you down to Casper's room. The fairies might be able to help a bit."

"I need to assess the situation," Park said.

"We stopped them in the second room," Sam said. "They're both gone."

Park sagged against me, and Sam hurried into a room before backing out, pushing a wheelchair. We sat Park in it, and

Sam rushed him down the hall. I jogged after them.

"I got the call button," Casper said as Park and Sam made it into her room. "Who was it?"

"Combat stress reaction," Park muttered. "Sometimes combat breaks a soldier. Usually we catch it, but sometimes ..." he shook his head.

Aideen glided to Park's leg. He winced as she landed, but didn't protest as the fairy sliced through the thigh of his pants to get a better look at the wound underneath.

"You're lucky. It's not fatal. I can stop the bleeding for now, but I don't have the energy to heal you completely."

"I'll manage," Park said, his face paling.

"Aideen," I said, "are you—"

I didn't get to finish the question.

"*Socius Sanation*," Aideen whispered. The spell was brief. A flash of light, and then it was over. Aideen took a deep breath and looked at the thin patch of bright pink skin that had closed over Park's wound. "Come by tomorrow. I'll see if I can heal the rest."

"Well, that's something I'll never get used to," the Ranger said. "That was like magic."

Foster let out a slow laugh. "This one's dense."

If the Ranger was offended by Foster's joke, he sure as hell didn't show it. He walked over and inspected Park's leg before shaking his head. "That's amazing."

"The work of an amateur," Aideen said. "There's only so much we can do in one day."

"This is fine," Park mumbled. "I'm going to get some sleep. Leave before the MPs come." And with that, Park passed out.

Casper cursed. "You should all get out of here. There's

work to be done preparing the city. You don't need to be holed up in an interrogation room answering questions that shouldn't have been asked in the first place."

"What about the soldiers?" Frank asked.

Casper flinched like Frank had struck her. "Christ." She rubbed that her eyes. "We'll take care of it. Park will let their families know, and if he's not up for it, I'll do it. As for the ones that are still alive, they'll face the consequences of what they've done."

"We'll be seeing you," the Ranger said. I took that as our cue to leave.

"Come on," I said, holding my hand out to Aideen. She hopped up onto it, and I raised her up to my shoulder. Foster climbed up onto Sam, and we took our leave.

"Well, that was a cluster fuck," Frank said as we exited through the stairway at the end of the hall, where Casper had told us to go.

"Yeah," I said, "let's go see Graybeard."

CHAPTER TWENTY-SEVEN

W E MADE IT back to the front parking lot without being stopped. By the time we climbed back into Sam's SUV, military vehicles were squealing to a stop in front of the ER. Six soldiers poured out of the first as the second and third vehicle roared up behind them.

Sam frowned at her rearview mirror, and I glanced back over my shoulder as we pulled away from the hospital.

"That could've gone better," Foster muttered.

"It could have gone a lot worse," Aideen said. "What if we hadn't been there? What if Damian and Sam hadn't been there?"

"More soldiers would've died," Frank said. "It could've been worse, but it was still a cluster fuck."

The smooth asphalt turned into the rapid bumps of the cobblestones, only to return to asphalt as we crossed over Main Street.

"I could use a drink," Sam said, glancing at the Trailhead Brewery as we passed. "I could really use a drink."

"You and me both," Frank said.

Main Street wasn't as busy as it would've normally been on a regular weeknight, but frankly, I was surprised to see anyone out and about. I guess some folks wouldn't leave their town, no matter what was happening. And I could respect that. Crazy as it might be.

I glanced down the other side of Main Street, catching sight of the Conservatory and an antique shop before we rounded the bend and the Missouri River stretched out in front of us.

"That's hard to miss," Sam said.

I leaned over so I could see past her head out the front window, and I cursed. The bony masts of Graybeard's ship stretched into the evening sky like some horrible Halloween float given life. We slowed at a stop sign before Sam gunned it and steered us toward a small roundabout and the empty parking lot beside it.

Trees flanked us to the north as we stepped out of the black SUV. From there, I could see the skeletons scampering across the sails. The strange flesh in the upturned skull of the harbinger was a bizarre sight before the grounded barge on the riverfront. A floating u-shaped dock led the way out to the old shipwreck. Graybeard lowered a plank of what looked like femurs and shin bones interlaced with thick sinew. The skeletons that surged across the deck wore no flesh. Some wore old and tattered uniforms, while others wore nothing but ancient leather shorts.

The staccato rhythm that the skeletons used to communicate echoed through the night air like a discordant symphony.

"It does send a message," I said.

Sam didn't look up from her phone. Her fingers blazed across the keyboard on the screen, before she blew out a breath. "Vik already heard about Graybeard," she said. "He's on his way with Zola. Wants to meet with us."

"Wants to meet with us in a good way?" Frank asked. "Or in a 'we should probably head for Rivercene' way?"

"I guess we'll see," Sam said, flashing him a humorless smile.

I whispered a curse and pulled out my phone, expecting to see a message from Zola, and hoping she wouldn't be pissed. It was a message, and if anything, she sounded as if she was in good spirits.

I read the message back. "I heard Vik's ass pucker from across the room when he learned about Graybeard."

Some of the tension left Sam's posture. "At least it doesn't sound like he's pissed."

"Vik's always been a gentleman," Frank said. "How many times has he let you down? I mean really? Once? Maybe twice?"

"Still a better record than me," I said, leading the way onto the wooden dock. My hand slid along the black metal railing. I glanced down at the water and jumped. "Christ. That'll keep people away."

Foster glided to the railing and hurried along it beside me. "Oh, he's got sailors in the water. Smart. They're more attuned to vibrations than anything else would be."

"I imagine that's so they can sense the water witches coming," Aideen said.

"They certainly sensed you lot," a voice boomed from the Bone Sails' deck. "Reckon if they can hear the most dangerous necromancer in two states, they'll be able to see the water witches coming."

Nixie stepped up beside Graybeard and rested her arms on the railing. "And it doesn't hurt that I helped him test that theory," she said with a small smile. "The crew makes a hell of an early warning system. Although some of them aren't too happy about it."

"Aye, some of them find the water a bit too chilly."

I supposed it made sense, in a strange way. The crew of the Bone Sails were used sailing on an ocean of fire. If they could feel temperatures well enough, the Missouri River would be icy by comparison.

Graybeard started toward the plank, and Nixie followed. They both made it look easy, walking across those rounded bones, but I'd been on the spongy deck of that ship before. I remembered how it gave and flexed, making it even harder to stand on than a regular boat. Except maybe a bass boat on choppy water. I laughed as a random memory surfaced.

"What the hell are you laughing at?" Sam asked.

"I was just remembering the canoe trip Dad took us on."

Sam groaned.

"What happened?" Frank asked.

"Sam kept trying to stand up," I said. "Every time she did, she dumped Dad in the river. Funniest damn thing I'd ever seen."

"Dad didn't think so," Sam said. "If I remember, it wasn't long before he stuck me in your canoe."

"That was tragic," I said. "It was a shame how you fell out in those rapids."

"Fell out?" Sam said, narrowing her eyes. "You had Jasper push me out."

I grinned.

"Lass," Graybeard said, "just spend some time on me ship. You'll have sea legs as sturdy as one of the Green Men."

"And maybe as sexy as the Green Men," Foster said.

Sam's scowl could've stripped the bark from the tree. "Watch it, bug."

Graybeard laughed and crossed his bony arms, the parrot dancing back and forth on his shoulder. "So, you already discovered half the plan for yourself. I have my crew stationed in the waters, and some deep in the mud."

"Alexandra will be deploying some of the witches here," Nixie said. "Down close to the old railroad bridge, and more near your coliseum."

"Our what?" Frank asked.

"Riverport," I said. "The amphitheater? Whatever they're calling it these days. Seems like they change the name every week."

"The queen isn't a complete fool," Nixie said. "Don't let the soldiers drop their guard. Or we could lose far more."

I crossed my arms and leaned on the railing between Nixie and Graybeard. "There's something we need to tell you. Something that happened at the hospital." I relayed the story of the soldiers gone mad; those who didn't survive regardless of the healings, and those who didn't survive because their own men gunned them down. "I saw Morrigan carry them from that place. Just a shadow, but I'm sure it was her."

Nixie's frown grew deeper as I finished the story.

"There are some things that were far easier when I was just a dead pirate," Graybeard muttered. The parrot's eyes flashed yellow. "I believe the vampires have arrived."

I raised my eyes to the parking lot and watched as one of the Pit's black SUVs parked beside Sam's.

"This will probably either go really well," Sam said, "or really bad."

"Happy thoughts, sis," I said. "Happy thoughts."

CHAPTER TWENTY-EIGHT

V IK STEPPED OUT of the driver's side as Zola slid from the passenger seat and struck her knobby old cane on the asphalt beneath her feet. They exchanged a few words, and then headed straight for us.

My confidence in Zola's mood on her text message waned when I saw the hard lines on her face.

"We can't leave you alone for an hour," Zola said. She smacked her cane a couple times on the wooden dock. One of the skeletons clapped its forearms together in a rapid staccato. Zola gave him a satisfied smile. "So they do understand Morse code."

Graybeard's eye lights narrowed. "Welcome to my ship, Zola Adannaya."

Zola nodded. I could never tell what those two thought of each other. I remembered Zola taking Graybeard away when I was a teenager, after I'd bound the soul of the old pirate into a dead parrot. But Graybeard had flourished in the Burning Lands, and I wondered if he still resented her, or if he had long since moved past that banishment.

"Samantha," Vik said, "you must be more cautious when involving yourself in the affairs of Faerie. You are a representative of this Pit, and there are things I must do that I do not wish to in order to uphold appearances."

"The dark-touched are here," Sam said. "You mean to ignore them again? It's what Vassili would've done."

The venom in my sister's voice made me take a step backward and lean into the railing. I knew that tone. I knew how close she was to exploding. And for a brief moment, I wondered if Sam could take Vik. Or if the old vampire was so far beyond her that she'd never stand a chance. I shook my head, casting out that dark thought of friends battling friends, and stepped in between Sam and Vik.

"Vik, she didn't mean that." I held my hand up to the old vampire. "It's how she talks to family. You should be flattered."

"Stay out of this," Sam said. "Those harbingers could've destroyed the city last month." Sam stepped around me. "You can't stay out of this forever. You can't stay out of this when they come for our home, our families. When they come for you."

"Samantha!" Vik snapped, a fury in his voice that I'd rarely heard. "I am not ignoring what is happening in the world around us. I am ensuring that we survive it. Zola has been helping me move some of our most important works from the archive."

Sam blinked. "What?"

"I have no intention of staying out of this battle. The dark-touched have plagued vampire-kind and humankind for millennia. Their return is an event that must be undone."

"And they stand with Nudd," Aideen said. "Which leaves you in a convenient position."

"Convenient?" Graybeard asked. "It sounds like it leaves him stuck between people who want him dead."

Vik gave a slight shake of his head. "Aideen is right. The

dark-touched are allied with Nudd's purpose, which makes it an easy task to convince people that he controls them."

"Doesn't he?" I asked.

"No one does," Vik said. "They're much like a rabid dog. The disease will progress to a point where they will turn on their own master. For now, I can use Vassili's betrayal as an argument for anyone who would question my motives. Nudd must be overthrown, and his allies must fall with him."

"I don't know if I'm more pissed or less pissed at you now," Sam said. "Why didn't you just tell me?"

Vik offered her a sad smile. "Because when our enemies see us at odds, they may believe us to be weak. It may encourage them to strike at a moment they believe to be opportune, which is anything but."

"God damned vampires," I muttered. "Here I thought you were all just assholes."

"Now," Zola said, "tell us of your plan to disgrace a queen and overthrow a king."

So we did.

Zola and Vik listened attentively, pointing out potential flaws in the idea that Graybeard's men could detect the water witches. And other issues, like relying on the humans, who could be deceived by a fairy's glamor.

"Stay close to Park," Zola said. "He's your line to the commanders in the area."

"Casper has the most respect, from what we've seen," Frank said. "I think it's best if we stick close to her."

Zola nodded. "Ah agree. Do what you are required to, to maintain their allegiance."

"No matter how distasteful it may be," Vik said, giving Sam

a meaningful look. I wasn't sure if that was his way of apologiz-
ing for misleading her the past couple weeks, or if it was his
way of asking her to keep her temper in check. But I *was* sure it
was the vague musings of a vampire. Which could be really
annoying.

"I am confident in the skills of your lieutenants," Vik said,
nodding to Nixie. "Alexandra and Euphemia are both formidable. I am not so certain about Rivercene. Is that our Achilles'
heel?"

"Don't worry," Sam said. "They're quite good with shadow
puppets."

Vik hesitated, waiting for Sam to expand what she'd said.
Sam just flashed him a beaming smile.

"She means they're probably okay," I said. "Whatever
comes their way."

"I'm sure Angus will be there," Aideen said. "Boonville is
his home."

"So be it," Vik said. "And you are sure of the blood mages'
ability?"

"Oh yes," I said. "What they did to defend the Arch was one
of the most unnerving things I've ever seen." I glanced at
Graybeard, and the parrot cocked his head to the side.

"Quit while you're ahead, boy," Graybeard said.

I smiled at the parrot. He could be unsettling at times, especially with his warship carved from the skull of a harbinger, but
those things Beth and Cornelius had summoned... I shook my
head. "You saw those things."

The skeleton nodded, its beard shifting down and then back
up with the motion of the bird's head. Each of their movements
was perfectly synchronized. "I've seen many things, Damian.

I've seen things in the Burning Lands, things beneath the Sea of Souls that would pale a normal man. But the shadows ..." The parrot shook his head. "I've never seen their like."

"Graybeard has centuries of experience under his belt," Vik said. "And not only in our realm. I am not sure if I find this reassuring, or unsettling."

"If you're smart," Zola said, "it is a measure of both."

"Doesn't anyone know where the Queen's Army is?" Frank asked. "It seems like we should be hunting them down, instead of making a stand here. There's too many commoners. Too many innocent bystanders."

Nixie paced a few steps back and forth. "Nudd has given them full access to the Warded Ways, Frank. Undines are hard enough to track when they can't vanish into another plain. But with the ability to use the Ways as they please, the task becomes impossible. We've found scouts, traces. And at times, victims."

"Victims?" I asked.

Nixie took a deep breath. "Near Falias. Two Coast Guard cutters were pulled to the bottom of the lake."

"I have heard nothing of this," Vik said.

"Neither have we," I said. "When did that happen?"

Nixie opened a pouch on her armor, and slid a thin, blue obsidian disc out of it, spinning it briefly between her fingers. "Late yesterday, we think. The Fae around Falias haven't been on the best terms with the commoners. Or the military, for that matter. Two vessels vanished, but no one thought to look at the lakebed. Euphemia found them, and neither was sunk by anything natural."

Visions of leviathans rose into the back of my mind, those massive titans of gray flesh and beaks and tentacles. A cutter wouldn't stand a chance. One quick snap, one brush against something that large, that violent, and anything would sink.

"What did they find?" I asked.

"The holes were cut out from beneath," Nixie said. "It's an old approach, one that water witches have used for millennia. It was easier when ships were made of wood and tar, but it's not so difficult if you attack the seams between plates. Attack the natural weak points, or cut away the rivets holding those weak points in place. Once the water gets through, it's an easy thing to guide it to fill the cabins, to wrap around the crew, and drag them to their fate."

I shivered at the thought. What that must've been like for those crewmen. What kind of horrible final moments were those? The screams of rending metal echoing all around them, the snapping bolts, and shattered rivets, before the water took on a life of its own. And what? Drowned them quickly? I doubted it. The more sadistic water witches had pledged their loyalty to the queen, and a spike of anxiety squeezed my chest as my imagination showed me increasingly horrible fates beneath those lakes.

"Who reported the lost ships?" Zola asked.

I didn't understand why she was asking. What did that matter? You had ships and a dead crew trapped at the bottom of the calm lake. What else mattered?

"Euphemia did," Nixie said. "She led a search and rescue team to the ships, and some of our witches helped to raise the remains from the mud. The ships were a loss, but they were at least able to recover their soldiers."

I cursed and looked out at the river, that dark body of water that seemed so peaceful on the surface. But I'd seen what could happen to water in war. I had visions from the souls I'd touched, from the men I'd raised. I'd seen those tiny peaceful streams become clouded and bloodied with the lifeblood of thousands. Stones River, the wights at McFadden's Ford. It was little more than a peaceful stream now, but in the distant past, it had been a horror. That battlefield had seen the deaths of thousands. But it still wasn't the darkest place my boots had tread.

Nixie's recounting of the events pulled me out of that dark memory. "They raised the ships enough to beach them," Nixie said. "There wasn't enough left to do more than that. Some of the crew had been buried in the mud. Euphemia stayed behind to help, making sure they recovered all the bodies."

"So Euphemia has made contact with the Coast Guard, then?" Zola asked. "She's on friendly terms with them?"

"As friendly as they can be, I suppose," Nixie said. "So close to Falias, there's been a great deal of lives lost. I don't mean only Gettysburg. The disappearance of commoners has escalated, and I'm not sure if it's the queen meaning to draw us out, or if it's simply Nudd's Unseelie allies' bloodlust."

Zola rubbed her thumb on the top of her knobby old cane. "Then we stay the course. I believe our decision to split our forces was the best we could make with the information we have."

"Agreed," Vik said. He glanced at Sam. "Keeping the vampires centered here, at least those of our Pit, may benefit the city as much as it benefits our home."

"This city is our home," Sam said. "That old house may be where we live, but these people, our families, that's what makes it our home."

Vik gave Sam a small smile.

"I don't think the old fang is arguing with you, lass," Graybeard said. "The fact is, I think he's agreeing with you."

Graybeard's words tumbled a few of the vampire-related puzzle pieces in my brain. And the realization of Vik's misdirection made me smile. He hadn't simply abandoned us to the fight in Greenville, he'd set things in motion back in Saint Louis. To preserve the archive, no matter what occurred. To keep that knowledge on the side of our allies, and summon his Pit back to his side.

"This was your plan all along," I said, not raising it as a question at all.

"All along?" Vik asked. "I do not believe I would say all along. These are rather new occurrences, Damian. We prefer a long game, of well-planned strategy and assassination in the shadows. The vampires do not yearn for an open war with the humans, or the Fae."

"A little late for that," Graybeard said.

Zola snorted a laugh. "The captain is correct."

"Dominic and Jonathan are preparing the others," Vik said. "We will cover what we can from here to the Mississippi. If an attack happens east or west of either river, I will not stretch my forces to assist."

"Ah assume," Zola said, "that old town behind us is included in your protection. *Lord.*" She emphasized the title, drawing an uncomfortable twitch from Vik's eye.

"Of course," Vik said. "I have little doubt that Sam will be stationed here, regardless of my orders. Which is why Jonathan and a small detachment will be nearby, with Frank as the liaison for the military."

Sam and Frank exchanged a glance.

"Seems reasonable to me," Frank said. "Are we just using open phone lines?"

Vik shook his head. "The Fae may not seek to intercept our communications over electronic transmissions, but we cannot be so sure of the military. Or so Dominic tells me."

Vik held out what looked like a dull gray plastic rectangle. "Dominic calls it a burner phone, and assures me that the military cannot trace it."

"That's not entirely true," Frank said. "With the right—"

Sam jabbed him in the side with her elbow, and Frank's dissertation on the vulnerabilities of Vik's electronics came to a sudden end.

"Thank you," Frank said, taking the phone from Vik.

"What of the one called Drake?" Graybeard asked. "Who is he?"

"We believe he is an old Demon Sword," Aideen said. "Right hand to the Mad King. His allegiance now lies with Nudd."

"If he is as mad as Foster," the parrot squawked, "I would prefer not to cross him."

Foster barked out a sharp laugh. "His allegiance is to Nudd," Foster said. "That means as long as Nudd lives, Drake is a threat."

"It seems like Drake is a threat no matter who's alive," Sam muttered. "A bloodthirsty fairy with control over fire?"

"Hey," Foster said, "I'm a bloodthirsty fairy with control over fire."

Sam frowned at Foster and shook her head. "You're not crazy, and that kind of makes a difference."

Foster gave a dramatic sniff, and wiped the corner of his eye. "That's the nicest thing you've ever said to me."

Sam reached out to swat Foster. He leaped off the railing and fluttered over to Graybeard's left shoulder. From there, he flashed Sam a broad smile.

"What do you need us to do?" I asked, glancing between Vik, Zola, and Graybeard.

"Prepare your house," Graybeard said.

"I agree with the captain," Vik said. "Prepare as much as you can, even if that means trying to get a decent amount of sleep. We don't know when they are coming, but they are coming."

Vik's words reminded me of the spirit who had appeared in the ghost circle. The spirit who had brought an ancient warning. I wondered if its warning had been about more than Drake.

"I need to check some things in the Book that Bleeds, boy." Zola rubbed her wrist. "Do you still have an air mattress? I'd like to sleep on something other than one of those damned chairs."

"Damned?" I placed my hand over my heart. "I think you mean most comfortable chairs in the world."

"Not for sleeping. I don't think my old back can take that kind of abuse anymore."

"I must return to Falias," Nixie said. "It may take more than an hour, depending on what I must avoid." She turned and looked upstream and then down at the river. "Be safe, all of you." I slid my arm around her waist as she leaned back to give me a chaste kiss over her shoulder. And then she was gone, slipping into the water.

"A strange gift," Graybeard said, looking down at the blue obsidian disc between his bony fingers. "A gift from a sea devil. Has been an odd life. A very odd life."

I shrugged my shoulders. "You've been dead a long time, Graybeard."

The beard around the skeleton's teeth lifted, and the parrot cackled.

CHAPTER TWENTY-NINE

"YOU SURE ABOUT this?" I asked, unrolling the air bed at the end of the bookshelves on the second floor of Death's Door.

"Of course," Zola said. "I've spent enough nights at the Pit. They buy those expensive mattresses like they're some kind of status symbol. But they're uncomfortable as hell. Put a terrible kink in my back."

"If you told Vik that, he'd probably just buy you a new one," I said.

"Ah suspect you're right, but it would be rather rude to insult those who house me as a guest."

"You insult me all the time," I said, chuckling as I threw the switch to inflate the AeroBed.

"That's different."

"I'm pretty sure it's not."

Zola gave me a grin and a low laugh. "Ah'll always be a master to you, boy. Even when Ah'm not."

It was a phrase I hadn't heard her use in a very long time, and it reminded me of nights around the campfires at the old cabin in Coldwater. The only reprieve from the brutal training she'd put me through.

"Did you know this would happen?"

"Did Ah know if the queen of the water witches and Gwynn

Ap Nudd would forge an alliance and rain hell down on this city?"

"Yeah?"

"Absolutely not. Why do you ask?"

"I don't know. Some of the training we did, the relentless training. Sometimes it just feels like you knew this was going to happen. Like you knew I needed to be ready for it."

"Things always happen, Damian. And one should always be ready for them. But no, Ah didn't know where the threat would come from. If anything, Ah thought it would be mages, or witches. It didn't occur to me that your fate would become so entwined with the Fae." She patted the end of the AeroBed as the mattress grew taller. "I didn't think my days would be so tied up with the Fae either, mind you."

"Me either," I said, frowning. "Just flip that switch when you're happy with the firmness."

Zola nodded, and I headed back toward the overstuffed chairs and the leaning tower of old books stacked on top of the coffee table.

"I still can't believe Vik let you bring some of these here," I said. "I thought for sure they'd be locked away in some long-forgotten vaults." I pulled the first tome closer, a garish oversized thing that reminded me of an illuminated manuscript I'd once seen in New Orleans. "How old are these things?" I opened the decorative leather cover, and read the title. The Diaries of Vassili Kurlenko, 1350 to 1400. I whistled and gently closed the book.

"You need not worry," Zola said. "Vik only allowed me to bring that which was warded against damage. Ah can't imagine why."

"Ward protected these?"

"Some. Ward is not the only master of the old runes. There are others, and some of them are very old."

"What are we looking for? I don't see how Vassili's old journals from the freaking Dark Ages are going to help."

"They may not help us now," Zola said, "but you know where Vassili lived during that time?"

"No, why?"

"He journeyed through the Americas at the time of Vikings and werewolves."

"Did he cross paths with Hugh?"

"Hugh believes it may be possible. We may learn more, but that's not for today."

I slid the tome to the side and pulled down another, this one bound in a rich red leather, entirely devoid of text or notation. It was sealed with an ancient lock that had been cut away long ago—even the metal revealed by the cut showed decades of corrosion.

Zola turned off the air mattress before flopping down on top of it. "My back feels better already."

She joined me in the chairs, opting to study some of the unbound manuscripts Koda had given me long ago. Most of them pertained to line arts and a few to wards. Some were filled with dangerous magics we necromancers shouldn't have access to. A few of the arts remained out of Zola's reach, though they responded to my call. Not unlike the growth magics of the Fae, they didn't respond if called by a normal mage.

With other spells, the difference was minor. Zola could still use some line arts, though legend said no necromancer could. Koda's manuscripts had revealed that some of what Mike had taught me were bastardized line arts. Zola could summon fire through a line art, but not a gravemaker.

"There's nothing here." Zola leaned back in her seat after we had poured over the manuscripts and books for another hour. Bubbles and Peanut had taken up positions like bristly loyal ottomans. I still didn't like the fact that the coven didn't have Peanut.

Zola pinched the bridge of her nose. "There's nothing about other weapons we might use against undines."

I pulled a thin blue tome off the bookshelf behind us. "What about this?" I held out the story of Leviticus Aureus and the Fall of Atlantis.

"How many times have you read this?" Zola asked.

I frowned. "Two or three?"

"And?"

I grimaced. "I don't remember anything about other weapons besides the stone daggers, and their poisons."

Zola rapped her fingers on her arm chair. "Ah suppose poisons might be helpful if given time, or delivered in a powerful enough dose, but that is hardly useful in the midst of a pitched battle."

Even the poison daggers of the undines didn't do much more immediate damage than a steel blade. It was what followed, and even then, it took hours at a minimum. Zola was right; that wasn't helpful.

"It could be something worth asking Ashley about," Zola said. "She's skilled with herbs and the art of the apothecary."

"Next time we see her, then."

"We should sleep. Ah'm afraid we don't have a restful week ahead of us."

✦   ✦   ✦

WE HADN'T FOUND much we didn't already know. There was an interesting excerpt from Vassili's journals, which Zola suspected might refer to the Wandering War. The time that Vassili had spent since, mired in war, with a description of bloodlust so graphic, I was surprised he had the presence of mind to write down anything. But the details were vague, and the most I could make of it was that at one time he knew the Mad King.

The journal spoke as if the War had been a long time ago, even at the time it had been written. I suspected the Wandering War had been far longer in the past than anything I could comprehend in my mortal lifespan. But if it was 1,000 years ago, millennia ago, then how old was Vassili? And how old were some of the Fae we knew who had lived through it? They might not have viewed time in exactly the same fashion as the rest of us, but none of them spoke at length about the Wandering War. It seemed to be more of an age they all longed to forget.

It was not a restful night. I tossed and turned, curled up in one of the leather chairs. Zola snored peacefully on her air mattress, reminding me that sometimes she was far wiser than I. Sleep did eventually come, but it was filled with visions of my dead and dying friends. I startled awake as the whispered voices inside my head grew louder, until a vision of the nightmare that had been Gettysburg crashed into my mind once more.

I shot straight up in the chair, half expecting to see trolls from the Burning Lands storming down the halls of the library toward me. Half expecting Ezekiel to appear, the mantle of Anubis corrupted and fractured over his mad skull. But all that awaited me was the huge furry head of the cu sith, flopped onto the coffee table and panting at me.

I sagged back into the chair and winced at the kink I now had in my neck. "I'm getting too old for this," I muttered, rubbing the stiff muscles at the base of my skull.

I leaned forward and took two deep breaths.

The door to the rear parking lot slammed closed, the sound muted by the stairs and the books around me, but still unmistakable. I stretched and scratched Bubbles's ruff before padding down the hallway, and making my way down the stairs.

Foster yawned as he and Aideen slowly made their way toward the Formica table, just returning from some excursion.

"Where have you two been?" I asked. "And where's the coffee?" I grumbled incoherently.

"I could use that, too," Aideen said. "We went back to the hospital, to help where we could."

"To the first question," Zola's unholy perky voice said from the other end of the room, "here's the coffee." She shuffled around and poured two full-size mugs and put a coffee stirrer in one of them. "Frank spoke to Park, and apparently these two spent much of the night healing what soldiers they could."

"You weren't rested enough for that," I said. "It's dangerous."

"It was the least we could do," Aideen said. "They're our allies, an uneasy alliance though it may be. We need them healthy, and ready."

"You're the best healer around," I said, focusing on Aideen. "We may need you sooner than we'd like."

The fairy hesitated. She pondered my words for a moment before she said, "What's done is done. I cannot rebuild that stamina through magic. We'll need rest, and must hope healing magic is not needed so quickly."

"With the help of the water witches?"

Aideen shook her head. "A little, perhaps. We're still drained, and I won't leave Foster without a wife, as he has been left without a mother."

I frowned. "I'd never ask that of you."

"I know. But you're not the only one of our allies who may request our aid."

Bubbles, apparently sensing the tension in the room, trundled over to Foster and immediately slurped him up on her tongue. The fairy vanished into her mouth, and she gave us a wolf-like grin before dashing back to the front of the store.

"Bubbles, no!" Aideen said, taking off after the cu sith. "You spit him out right now!"

Muffled shouting sounded from inside Bubbles's mouth, and I tried my damnedest not to laugh.

Bubbles rocketed back through the saloon-style doors, and Zola managed to reach out and just catch the edge of her ruff. The cu sith came to a screeching halt, her claws digging in the floor, while she spat Foster out into the air. The fairy cartwheeled and screamed about fifty obscenities before smacking into my shoulder. He hung upside down for a moment, the cu sith's drool dripping over his face, while he tried to peel his wings off my T-shirt.

He met my eyes and said, "Not. One. Word."

"I hear they make great guard dogs."

Foster made an exasperated sound before hopping over to a shelf in the utility closet and drying himself off on a towel.

"So, did you see Frank and Sam over there?" I asked.

"Yeah," Foster said, running a hand through his hair. He took a deep breath. "It sounds like they're going to redeploy into the Main Street area this morning. That's probably what all that rumbling is outside."

"Did they say what their schedule was?" Zola asked.

"All we heard is that it was supposed to be done this morning," Aideen said. "Casper's planning to set up on the second floor of the museum, overlooking the river. Park's overseeing the construction of command near the arts building."

"It's good to know that man can listen to reason," Zola said. "Ah've known worse generals who were far more stubborn."

"Well, he's not a general," I said.

"That wasn't the point Ah was trying to make," Zola said. "Drink your coffee. There's work to be done."

CHAPTER THIRTY

I T TURNED OUT Foster and Aideen had at least gotten some decent sleep at the hospital. That made me feel a little better, but I didn't like the idea of our best healers being out of commission. One thing was for sure, neither one of them were sacrificing themselves to save anyone. After what Cara had done, I didn't care what the reasons were, I wasn't letting that happen ever again—a promise I knew I might not be able to keep.

"Ah'd take it all," Zola said, answering my unspoken question.

I looked down at my backpack, half full of speed loaders for the pepperbox, and the extra rounds in my other hand. I shrugged and dumped the entire mess in my backpack. It was heavy, ridiculously heavy. I now had the pepperbox, the bandolier full of speed loaders, and about a dozen more speed loaders to boot.

It would've made more sense to strap the bandolier over my chest, but I didn't think the police, or the commoners, would appreciate seeing a civilian walking around armed to the teeth. Another section of my backpack had the hand of Gaia and the blue obsidian disc from Nixie. There was a woefully small department dedicated to snacks, which I'd stuffed with Frank's slightly less insane beef jerky. Zola, on the other hand, had

Frank's *completely* insane burn your face off jerky stashed in a satchel on her hip. I was pretty sure she'd be able to weaponize it.

"We should probably let the fairies sleep a little longer," I said, glancing at the old grandfather clock.

"Agreed."

I led the way to the front door. This would be the second day in a row the shop wasn't open. I didn't like that. We needed money from our regular customers, and staying closed was a crappy way to accomplish that; especially with foot traffic so low to begin with.

I was surprised to open the front door and find Aeros at his post on the street beside the parking lot. One of the local kids gestured at the Old God, and I wondered where his parents were. Aeros lightly tapped on the kid's helmet and said, "Are you sure such a flimsy device can protect your head?"

The kid laughed.

Aeros raised his eyes to us as Zola and I started crossing the street. He turned his attention back to the kid. "I am afraid it is time for me to work."

"You don't work," the kid said. "You're always out here."

"I am always out here working."

The kid shook his head and hopped up onto his bike, wobbling a little bit before his balance was restored on the sidewalk.

Aeros watched him go before returning his gaze to us. "Good morning."

"What's he doing down here?" I asked.

"I do not believe some of the commoners understand the severity of the situation. The military has not evacuated them."

"It should've been mandatory," Zola said.

"To say the least," I said. "Even with what happened to their base last night?"

"It was not Park's decision," Aeros said. "Or so Frank tells me."

"How late did we sleep in?" I asked. "You've already talked to Frank? What about Sam?"

"Samantha was not with them. Frank seemed bothered by that."

"That's right," I said, "she's probably at the Pit still."

"Foster and Aideen are resting," Zola said. "If we do not return in the top of the hour, please awaken them."

"And try not to knock down the shop," I added with a smirk.

Aeros narrowed his eyes, his granite flesh crunching with the motion. "I will make every effort."

Zola patted the Old God's knee before we turned and headed south on Main Street.

It didn't take long to see the military wasn't sticking to Park's plan. At the first intersection, I turned my gaze down toward the river and cursed. A small cluster of tents had been set up, tents not unlike those that had been torn to pieces and burned to the ground less than a day before. Uniformed men milled about, approaching the river and pointing downstream. I had little doubt they were talking about the Bone Sails. Graybeard's ship was hard to miss.

"What the hell?" Zola's grip tightened on her cane, and she cracked it against the ground in one sharp blow. "What the hell are they thinking?"

"Who knows," I said. "Maybe it's a ruse? Something not as obvious as standing on the riverfront and getting killed by undines?"

Zola barked out a humorless laugh. "Keep your eyes peeled for anyone we know, boy. Ah'd like to find out more, before one of these fools tangles with a creature they do not understand."

We continued down Main, and I grew more uncomfortable with every step. The tourism had been light for a couple weeks, but now, outside of a few brave souls who remained behind in their homes on the old historic street, all that was left was military. Most of the restaurants were closed, and some of the gardens and dining areas outside were now swarming with soldiers. The presence of more soldiers than I'd expected made me uneasy.

"It's like they moved an entire battalion in," I said, rubbing the back of my neck. "I don't know if this will deter the queen, or entice her."

"The queen lost witches," Zola said. "That fact should at least give her pause. Unless she's gone as far off her rocker as Nudd."

We passed one of the bars and one of the few open restaurants. It looked like they were drumming up quite the business. I didn't think I'd ever seen them serving breakfast, but a clapboard outside had "Omelets & Bacon" written in bold letters.

My eyes trailed back toward the sign, and Zola chuckled.

"Ah'm sure we can find time to stop for food later."

"I feel like maybe I should've had more than a Pop-Tart." I took a deep breath and blew it out in exasperation. "But bacon, Zola."

"Oh my God, boy. I just flashed back fifteen years."

I paused at the next intersection and frowned at the personnel carriers parked along the cobblestone side streets.

"Well, that's an awful sight."

"Look to the river," Zola said.

I followed her gaze and cursed. Some of the wrought iron fence had been torn down or flattened. Two tanks were maneuvering on the neatly trimmed riverfront, one angling its main barrel upriver, and the other downriver.

"What in the hell do they expect to do with those?" I asked. "Don't they realize those guns, no matter how large, aren't going to do shit to a water witch?"

Zola slowly nodded her head. "Ah do wonder, though. If one of those tank shells exploded next to a water witch? Would it at least disorient them? Leave an opening, perhaps?"

"You let me know how that goes," I said. "I'll be the one in the back with the bacon."

Zola smiled, the skin around her eyes crinkling in the bright morning light. This was a place that had not seen much in the way of war. Many ghosts lingered, but they were not those unnervingly bound to their souls, rooted to a battlefield for God knows how long. But there were other things here like the werewolves, and other Fae that we saw on occasion. It made me wonder what else lurked behind the walls and stones of some of the older buildings.

We eventually reached a tent city where I suspected we'd find Park. Several tents lined the common area, with more under construction. It was obvious where the command center was, as that tent was at least twice as long and three times as wide as the others.

Zola paused while the sounds of men and women driving

stakes into the ground with hammers echoed around us. She put her hand over her heart and watched as one pair repositioned a stake after they hit a large stone in the ground, and then drove it in at another angle.

"You okay?" I asked.

"If these tents were linen, and heavier cloth, you could mistake this for an encampment from the Civil War. It's … Ah didn't expect to see that. It caught me off guard." She shook her head and nodded to herself. "Let's find Park."

We wound our way between the tents, and around the third or fourth corner, I realized that they had been placed in a very specific pattern. It would make it hard to for anyone to charge blindly through their base camp. It was defensive, and I suspected a sound strategy, but I didn't think it would slow the deadly arts of the water witches. It was a much greater distance from the river though, so I supposed they'd learned something.

We reached the command tent a minute later, and the MP stationed outside the door was the first to question our presence.

"What's your business here?"

Zola gave him her best old woman smile and leaned heavily on her cane. I'd seen her do it before, and it was damned effective at eliciting sympathy. "Ah was told my friend Master Sergeant Park was here. Do you know if that's true?"

"He's inside …" The soldier frowned, as if realizing he shouldn't have given that information away so freely. He studied Zola for a moment and seemed to relax.

I managed to keep my composure.

"Could you give him a message for me?" Zola asked. "Ah don't want to interrupt if he's busy. Although it is mighty hot out today. And Ah could use some shade."

"Let me see if he's done," the MP said. "Just wait a moment, and I'll get you a chair."

The MP vanished into the tent, and I wondered just how fresh out of boot camp he was. I was afraid Zola might've gotten him a good punishment.

"Ah do like him," Zola said.

"I bet." I gave her a half smile, and turned my attention back to the opening flap of the tent.

Park appeared a moment later. "I would appreciate it if, in the future, you would refrain from manipulating my MPs."

"Manipulating?" Zola asked. "Ah have *never* been accused of such deception."

Park crossed his arms and raised an eyebrow. Zola flashed a knowing smile.

"It won't happen again," she said. "Certainly not today."

"It's a little warm out," I said. "That rain really helped the humidity."

"That's all Missouri is sometimes," Park said. "Trees, hills, and humidity."

Zola dropped her pretense. "What are the tents and men doing down by the river?"

Park frowned. "Let's not talk about that here."

"Why don't you walk with us for a moment?" Zola asked.

Park hesitated, clearly weighing his options for a moment before nodding.

CHAPTER THIRTY-ONE

"**G**IVE ME A minute," Park said. He dipped back into the command tent. Zola and I had barely exchanged a glance when Park reappeared in the entryway.

"Let's go. I need to check on the troops. Walk with me."

We followed Park without further question. He walked to the southern edge of the tent, which gave us a straight path back to Main Street. Park moved fast, and I had to push my normal stride to keep up. Zola didn't have any such problems, and more than one soldier took notice of the lively octogenarian. We turned the corner, and Park marched in silence with us trailing him. His boots stomped on the old brick sidewalk, and it wasn't until the next intersection, that he looked behind him.

"Finally," he said with a sigh. "Every time I leave, every time I try to make a call, the major has someone on my ass. I can't get away."

"Why are they setting the tents up so close to the river?" Zola asked. "Ah believe yesterday's events prove what a bad idea that is."

"FUBAR," Park said.

"You've got tanks down there," I said. "It's a convenient box for drowning soldiers."

"The commanders want to control the point of attack by setting Casper's unit out as bait," Park said.

"Bait for what?"

"That's not clear. The captain who survived the skirmish at
our last camp took notice of how you charged in to protect us.
He's close with Stacy."

"Are you kidding?" I said, unable to keep the shock from
my voice. "Those people just went through hell."

Park remained silent as we passed the storefront of a print
shop. Brilliantly colored designs and papers hung in the
window, advertising sales that had expired over a week ago.
Beside it was Main Street Books, my go-to store for any
modern reading. It was a strange multitiered shop. Staircases
joined the various parts of it, leading up to landings and even a
second story, where display shelves mingled with a small
kitchen.

Times like this I, sometimes wished I could vanish into one
of those bookstores, and leave everything else behind. But the
threat to my friends and my city kept such thoughts in the
realm of fantasy.

Park led the way across the street, and we headed for the
visitor center that held the old museum. "Casper's setting up on
the second floor," Park said. "They tried to tell her she couldn't
go to higher ground, but we had it out. Not letting your snipers
go to high ground is idiocy."

The cobblestones on Main Street gave way to the rough
flagstone sidewalk in front of the visitor center. Long ago, it
had been the capitol building, when Saint Charles had been the
capital of Missouri.

Park pushed his way inside, and the humid air vanished in
a gloriously air-conditioned entryway. A gift shop waited inside
the front door, where stacks of books on the history of Saint

Charles lined the shelves to the right. A welcome desk sat on the far side of the room, directly across from the door. I hadn't visited in a long time, and I felt that I'd been neglecting my study of the city. I suppose I had a decent excuse, as chaotic as the last few years had been.

"Casper," Park shouted. "You here?"

Casper's voice came back, "Upstairs."

Park took a sharp right turn and led us up the old staircase. It leaned slightly, and I wasn't sure if it was a structural integrity issue, or if the footsteps of centuries had simply worn down one side of the staircase. Either way, it felt sturdy enough, though I was fairly certain buildings like this had to pass inspections to stay open to the public.

The top of the stairs left us in an open loft, where the banister surrounded all four sides of the room except for the entry to the stairs themselves. I glanced around the open area, taking in the plaques and diagrams and maps along the wall. Until my gaze fell on Casper. She'd built a nest of sorts, with a high table, and a series of gun mounts. It was an odd sight, seeing a modern soldier, with a .50 caliber rifle, set up among the old Civil War artifacts. We followed Park in and watched Casper as she sighted down the scope of the rifle and frowned.

"We don't have ammunition for that," Park said.

Casper nodded to the side, indicating the M16 in the corner. "Just keeping up pretenses."

Park crossed his arms. "Outstanding."

"I'm afraid they aimed two of the tanks at that pirate ship," Casper said.

"At Graybeard's ship?" I asked.

Casper blinked. "Was there more than one pirate ship out

there?"

Zola chuckled under her breath. "Oh, Ah like her."

"I've seen some of the skeletons running around. What are they?" Casper asked.

"Same as last night," I said. "Graybeard's crew can be a little unnerving at first, I know. But they're all right. Can't take them to the bar or anything, but they're all right."

Zola smacked me in the arm. "Just tune him out."

"It's funny you say that," Casper said. "Aideen said the same thing."

"What?" I said. "That's not very nice."

"People," Park said. "Let's focus on the issue at hand. The colonel has ordered troops to the riverfront. It's hard enough to keep order in the ranks. We *have* to show a unified front."

Casper looked out the window. "Maybe our pirate friends can give us a hand by the river."

"How so?" Park asked.

"Well," Casper said, "in my experience, if the men get spooked, they'll move. And even if they don't get spooked, it might give us quicker access to a warning."

"They're putting some of your squad down there," Park said.

"I know," Casper said. "They'll catch on fast." She gave Park a small smile.

Park stepped up to the window and looked down at the troops milling about on the riverfront. "Worth a shot. If anyone can make it down there without raising suspicion, it's you."

"Are you not coming?" Zola asked.

Park shook his head. "I'll leave it to Casper, and you." He

nodded to Zola.

Zola laughed without humor. "Ah'm not the best one to convince the pirate of anything. You'll need my student for that."

Park glanced at me. "If you're half as good as Frank says you are, then I believe Casper is in good hands." He hesitated at the door and looked back at Casper. "Take care of yourself."

And with that Park left.

CHAPTER THIRTY-TWO

C ASPER GATHERED UP a rucksack in the corner by her M16, and I led the way back out of the visitor center. We cut down the first street, where the cobblestones changed to bricks and eventually asphalt. Once we made it down to the crosswalk, I stopped at the edge of the street and looked behind us. The backs of Main Street's buildings weren't so uniform as the front. Decks and balconies protruded at irregular intervals, giving way to a mixture of wood and iron stairs.

At the highest point on more than one building, I could see soldiers making ready. Most of them milled along the balconies, but a few had braved the rooftops. I wasn't sure if they were taking up posts there. At least one was adjusting what appeared to be a telescope, and I suspected it was a camera, too.

"What are they placing on the roofs?" I asked.

"Cameras," Casper said.

We continued down the street, and about the time we made it to the entrance to the park where Graybeard was docked, I began to think we should have driven. Saint Charles's Main Street was not terribly long, but in the heat with the cobblestones, it could wear you out.

We passed the roundabout and had almost reached the docks when Casper paused. "That is somewhat more intimidating up close." Her gaze climbed the bone masts of Graybeard's warship, lingering on the ship's cabin, before sweeping back down toward the skull of the harbinger on the bow.

"Come on," I said. "You need to meet the parrot."

"I thought Foster was joking about that," Casper said.

"Oh no," I said. "He talks through a parrot. A dead parrot, but I guess it's an undead parrot. I'm probably not helping this, am I?"

Casper didn't answer. I looked back, and the look on her face said it all. Her lips were pulled tight, and her eyes narrowed.

"Just don't shoot him, and I'm sure you'll get along fine."

Zola blew out a breath and smacked her forehead, pulling the wrinkles out of her skin as I suspected she tried to control her temper.

"Right then," I said. "Let's go meet the captain."

Casper followed us onto the wooden docks, her boots much quieter than my own clunky footfalls. I wondered if it was the material of her footwear, or if her training was just that good. Casper jumped when a pale bony hand reached out of the water, and one of Graybeard's crew hurdled the railing, clattering to a stop a few feet in front of us. The skeleton rapped his forearms together, creating that familiar staccato that the crew used to communicate.

"Graybeard will be here soon?" I asked.

The skeleton nodded and dropped into the river once more.

"Was that Morse code?" Casper asked, taking a tentative step to the railing before peering down into the waters. The skeleton rose to the surface and raised a hand in greeting. Casper waved back hesitantly, and the shadowy skull vanished beneath the waters.

"You brought a guest," Graybeard said, his voice booming from the deck of the ship above us.

"Oh my god," Casper said.

"Lass," the parrot said before the skeleton tipped its hat.

"Let's not feed his ego," Zola said.

"How does his beard stay on?" Casper asked.

"Ye likely need to ask the two necromancers what stand beside you."

I grinned at the parrot. "Casper, Graybeard, Graybeard, Casper."

"I thought Park was leading you. Or did you cut out his heart and take his ship?"

"What? No." A confused look crossed Casper's face.

Graybeard sagged against the railing. "The military folk have no humor."

"Now now," I said. "Let's try not to scare off your new best friend."

The parrot danced on Graybeard shoulder. "A friend, eh?"

"She's the sniper some of your sailors saved. And she has rounds able to put down a water witch."

The skeleton straightened out and took a few steps to the plank, before descending that stretch of bone and sinew. "Perhaps I judged ye too quickly."

Graybeard's skeleton wasn't short, and with the hat on top, he cut a rather imposing figure. The parrot knew it, and I shook my head as he stepped ever closer to Casper, leaning over the young sniper.

"Does your crew communicate with Morse code?" Casper asked. If she felt any hesitation in the presence of the old pirate, she hid it completely.

"Why do you be asking?"

"Because I'm fairly certain the fine crewman that we met on the dock summoned you here by calling you a dingy piece of roadkill."

Graybeard's ship erupted in a clatter of bones and rhythmic staccato laughter. The teeth of two dozen skulls chattered together, before beating on the railings in an overwhelming tide of Morse code.

Casper grinned up at them. "It's a pleasure to meet you all."

"Aye," Graybeard muttered. "'Tis indeed how they communicate."

Casper smiled at the bird, and said, "I can tell they have great respect for you. I've served with enough units to know, to recognize that kind of respect."

"Well then, Miss Casper, what mad plan of Park's do you bring?"

"Not Park's plan," she said. "My plan."

The skeleton ran its bony fingers through its beard, while the parrot cocked its head. Casper ran down the idea, leaving out any extraneous detail, and only giving Graybeard what he needed to know to both understand and execute it, should he choose. I was impressed. She'd taken a rambling conversation with Park, and distilled it down to a few distinct orders. But she didn't deliver them like orders, and there would be no way for Graybeard to be insulted by it. Although I suspected Graybeard's crew would allow him to be insulted by it.

"I like your cut, lass. I like your cut."

Casper beat out a rapid staccato on the railing of the dock, and Graybeard released a haunting laugh.

"What was that?" I asked.

"She says I look good for a dead man."

"You *are* nicely feathered," I said.

The parrot's glowing eyes shifted to me, and he dead-panned, "It's more likely me beard."

"How will you signal us?" Zola asked. "If there's a sighting of the water witches?"

"If it is but one water witch," Graybeard said, "I doubt I'll be signaling you at all. But if we see more, there will be no mistaking the signal."

Some of the crew chattered up on the deck of the Bone Sails.

"A horn?" Casper asked, looking up at one of the crewmen.

"The boys are right," Graybeard said. "You'll hear the horn."

"A horn?" I asked. "You're riding on a ship made from a harbinger's skull, and your early warning system is a horn?"

"Aye."

I pursed my lips and nodded. "Fair enough."

"It's been a pleasure, sir," Casper said, bringing our introduction to Graybeard to an end. "I have to check on my squad. My superiors have placed them down by the river, and I'm afraid they're in danger there. Can you help us?"

"I'm afraid they're in danger everywhere, lass," Graybeard said. "Should've picked a different profession, if they did not wish to be in danger." Graybeard stared upriver, and the parrot danced on the skeleton's shoulder. "Reckon I could send another bag of bones your way. Might be helping you stay alert, and give me a better view of things."

Casper shot him a sideways smile. "Just don't steal any of my squad away for your crew. If you do that kind of thing."

"Not for a very long time. A very long time indeed."

"Thank you."

We were halfway up the dock when Graybeard shouted after us. "Boy! You might want to be considering cleaning out some dust bunnies."

I looked back at the parrot and nodded. Jasper had crossed my mind too, but if we were going to recruit the dragon, I had to be sure that Vicky was safe. And right now, I couldn't be sure. We didn't know where the water witches were coming from, or if they would strike Saint Charles. We still had Rivercene and Falias as likely targets, and our friends were in danger at both of them.

We made our way back up the dock and up to the little park before we began crossing a wooden bridge over the creek. The trees and branches intertwined overhead, creating a shadowy canopy that hid most of the light from above, but I could still make out a turtle and the ripples of the water.

"Look at the size of that turtle," I said.

"I've seen larger," Zola said as she leaned on the railing.

"Even here?" I asked.

She frowned for a moment, and then shook her head. "I suppose not."

Casper tugged on my sleeve. I turned to look at her, and she cocked her head to the side, gesturing for me to walk with her. I did, following her to the edge of the bridge.

"There's something in the water," she whispered.

"What do you mean?" I asked, shrugging my shoulders to readjust the excessively heavy backpack hanging off them.

"Look toward the center of the creek, directly in line with the turtle. There's an impression in the mud that shouldn't be there."

I figured Casper was being somewhat paranoid, which was pretty understandable after the events of the previous day. I sidled up beside Zola and glanced into the distance before letting my gaze slowly roll across the creek bottom. If we hadn't had the rains, and the level of the creek hadn't been so high, it might have been easier to spot.

Casper had been wrong, but she'd also been right. Water flowed everywhere except for one spot. Before I could turn to say anything to Zola, movement exploded in the water below us, and whatever had been there was gone.

"I suppose my eyes weren't playing tricks on me," Zola said.

"No," Casper said. "It's gone now."

"We need to tell Graybeard," I said.

"Give me a sec," Casper said. "I'm quite sure they'll be able to hear this." She rapped on the railing of the bridge, beating out an organized pattern with a baton she'd pulled from her belt. Graybeard's crew responded in moments. The hollow clack of bones banging together sounded a moment before the drums on Graybeard's ship came to life.

"What the hell is that?" Casper asked.

"Creepy ass drums," I said. "They're likely creepier when that thing's floating on a sea of fire, though."

Casper blinked at me.

"They got the message," I said. "Let's get down to your troops. We need to warn Aeros too. Foster and Aideen need to be ready."

I had my phone out and was texting Sam as we hurried back across the paths, passing a large statue of Lewis and Clark, and finally returning to the part of the Katy Trail that cut through the riverfront.

Something's here already.

It only took a moment for Sam to respond, but I'd be lying if each passing second didn't fray my nerves just a little bit. I breathed a sigh of relief at her response, and slid my phone back into my pocket.

"The vampires are coming."

"Let's pick up the pace," Casper said.

"Will Aeros hear us from here?" I asked Zola.

"Ah'm quite sure that Aeros heard the drums," Zola said. "If Graybeard's on alert, Aeros will be too."

Doubt bored into my mind. We were warning these men of the water witches, but what if the attack came from elsewhere? Or came from something else entirely? If the dark-touched descended on these people, it wouldn't matter what kind of munitions they had. They were all going to die. And there would be very little we could do about it. The dark-touched were brutally, efficiently murderous. It was all we could do to keep ourselves alive, and maybe divert them from the commoners, which would leave a whole lot of people to die.

"We haven't briefed him about the dark-touched," I said.

Casper frowned at me. "You mean the vampires you can only kill through the eye?"

"Who told you that?"

"Aideen gave us the rundown. Last night. And Foster told us about the harbingers, and I have to say, hearing about them from the fairy was a hell of a lot scarier than seeing them on film. And knowing that the hull of Graybeard's ship is carved from a *skull*, is frankly horrifying."

"Yeah," I agreed.

We passed the pavilion close to some old train cars, before Casper broke away from the paved trail, and led us down into the churning mass of national guardsmen. She greeted a few, and avoided some others, while Zola and I drew some strange looks from several of the soldiers. I suspected that meant that these weren't Casper's crew because her squad seemed quite familiar with us. And I would've thought that whatever company they came from would be familiar with us, too.

"Friendly greetings," I said.

"You and your friends have a reputation," Casper said. "Most of these people have probably been briefed about how dangerous you are. The rest have seen you in action. No training can prepare them for that."

I looked at Zola "We have a reputation."

"Pay attention to the task at hand, boy."

"What the hell," Casper said. "Ranger Rick is here, and he should still be at the hospital."

I followed her line of sight, and found the Army Ranger closer to the river. "Did you just call him Ranger Rick?"

Casper glanced back at me and said, "No." Her tone was deadly serious, and I couldn't detect the lie at all. For some reason, that amused me greatly.

CHAPTER THIRTY-THREE

I T TOOK AN effort of will, but I managed not to call the Army Ranger, Ranger Rick. "Hey, man."

He offered me a nod before turning to Casper. "I thought you were setting up the nest?"

"I did," Casper said, "but the civilians wanted a tour. And there is no greater duty than giving civilians a tour, Rick." The sarcasm—it almost dripped off her teeth, and that was a glorious thing.

"Is his name actually Rick?" I asked, nudging Zola with my elbow.

"Hush," she hissed back.

"Civilians," Rick said. "Are we using that as a story? I'm pretty sure everyone here knows who they are."

"I don't know how I put up with you," Casper said. "Your lack of appreciation for sarcasm is a real turnoff."

I looked around and recognized some of the wounded from the night before. I knew Foster and Aideen had returned to the hospital to help heal them, but some of them were clearly still in no condition to be on duty.

"What are they doing down here?" I asked.

Casper turned to look, her mouth tightening into a hard line. Her brow drew down, and the furious gaze flashed back to Rick. "What the hell are they doing here? Some of those soldiers were practically dead last night. They should still be in the hospital, or at least the infirmary."

Rick frowned. "I know. The colonel is trying to make a point."

"A point about what?" Casper snapped.

"A point about us," Zola said quietly. I almost missed it, spoken so softly, but Casper turned to look at her.

"Why you?" But her expression changed even as she asked the question. "Because we're working with the supernaturals."

"I suspect so," Zola said.

"You don't have to suspect it," Rick said. "They flat-out said it."

A string of curses exploded from Casper's mouth, and she stalked toward one of the tents. The closer we came to the river, the more uncomfortable I felt. I didn't think it was the presence of Graybeard's crew in the shallows nearby, though they could certainly be unsettling, but something felt off. Something felt wrong. Casper threw open the flap on the tent nearest the river and froze.

Inside was half the squad from the previous night. At least those who had survived.

"Hey, boss," one of the young female privates said. "Come to join the fun?"

"What the hell are you *all* doing here?"

"Orders. I don't think Park even knows. Sergeant Major said if the devils healed us, we should be hellish fighters."

"I'm going to cut that fucker's balls off so I can feed them to him before I rip them out through his chest, so I can feed them to him again." Casper's rant exploded, cutting through the relative quiet of the air, and bringing those around us into silence.

"Casper," Rick said. "Down a little."

Casper turned to Rick, approaching him with a fury that made him take a step backward. "If you have a problem with me being upset about my men being put in harm's way, you can go straight to hell."

"That's not what I meant," Rick said.

The earth shook.

Zola cursed. "We aren't ready yet."

I understood what was wrong then. I understood what had unsettled me. This was a place I'd visited often. A part of the river, flanked by a small copse of trees. Except the copse today was larger, broader, and taller. The earth rumbled when the Green Men moved.

✦   ✦   ✦

"FLAMETHROWERS!" RICK SHOUTED.

Someone shouted back, "Not delivered yet!"

A man at the edge of the tents sprinted toward us. "Signal the tanks—" Before he could finish his words, a vine three inches in diameter burst from his chest. He started to look down in horror at the bloody protrusion, but lost consciousness a moment later. It only took me a second to realize what the Green Man was doing as the vines wrapped around the dead man's arms and it appeared as if he was struggling against his wound.

"It's baiting us!" I shouted.

"Trap!" Casper echoed.

Some heeded the warning, falling back into the cluster of tents, the flimsy shelters that would offer no protection against the lumbering Green Men. Others charged. A series of vine-like branches erupted from the soil when they closed within a few feet of their fallen comrade.

The vines lanced up, cutting through torsos and skulls alike. Blood fell in waves, and the men never had a chance.

Zola raised her staff, taking aim at the men writhing in their final moments on the spikes of the Green Men. She unleashed a hellish vortex of fire, which ended the men's suffering in a heartbeat and lit up the nearest Green Man like a dried bale of hay. The creature screamed, trying to draw his vines and branches back into his body, but they sizzled and broke as the unnatural fire climbed his body, consuming the moisture inside it.

The Green Man stumbled and threw himself into the river, extinguishing the fires, but putting himself within easy reach of Graybeard's crew. They fell upon the tree like piranhas on the flesh of a freshly made corpse.

Casper, while frozen for a moment either in surprise or horror, moved into action with the practiced discipline of a career soldier.

"Get your soldiers out of here," I said. "Rick, help her."

"We can help," he said.

"No," I said as I dumped the shells out of my pepperbox, and slammed home a speed loader full of Mike's incendiary rounds. "Until you have those flamethrowers, you have nothing. Stay the hell away from those things. Their reach is a hell of a lot longer than you'd think."

The Ranger hesitated for a moment, but then he hurried after Casper. "Fall back!" The call for retreat echoed around the tents. It didn't come soon enough.

The horn on Graybeard's ship blared into life. I was surprised he'd sounded it for the appearance of the Green Men. As deadly as they were to the commoners, Zola and I could at least fend them off for a time. These were smaller, and appeared to be more flammable, than the ones we'd encountered the night before.

But the horn wasn't for the Green Men.

Down by the old railroad bridge, the river surged. At first, I thought it was an illusion, until some of the quarry equipment on the far side of the river vanished into the swelling mass. I could scarcely comprehend the sight as the waves roared higher, and I turned to fire two quick bursts of flame into the Green Men.

"Zola," I said, taking a step closer to her as her latest incantation died away. "Are you seeing that?"

"I see it," she said.

"Casper! Get out of here now! We can't stop this! Tell Graybeard to warn Alexandra and Nixie! The Queen's Army is here."

One of Graybeard's crew heard me, and the skeleton ran down the length of the now-still Green Man in the river. The bony figure banged its forearms together, and the rapid Morse code spread down the bank of the river until Graybeard's horn sounded again. This was not the roar of a single horn, but the stuttering growl of a march. The horn took on a stalking beat as the drums came to life, and the Bone Sails pulled away from the shore.

Casper sprinted out of the tent. "We can't get them all."

Her calm fractured, and she stared in plain horror at the monstrous wave bearing down on us. Even though it was moving slower than I had expected, it had split, and two dozen translucent forms burst from the water. They grew cloudy as their deadly forms took to the shoreline, and the thought of how many more resided in that wave made my skin crawl. I doubted we had more than half a minute before it crashed down on top of us.

My brain scrambled, trying to think of some way to buy more time for the soldiers.

Two large gray blurs streaked down from the sky, revealing themselves beside me a moment later to be full-size fairies. Foster barely had time to curse before Aideen said, "We don't have time to get them out of here. Casper!"

"What?"

"Fire into the wave when it closes!"

Casper dashed back into the tent. I came to the horrifying realization that the wave was far wider than the river, and we were going to be swept up in it.

"Circle shield," Foster shouted. "Now!"

Zola and I exchanged a glance before we each carved a narrow circle in the grass beneath our feet.

"Get out of here!" I shouted.

Foster drew the enchanted blade from his belt and raised it into the air as he and Aideen each grabbed a soldier and took flight. Casper and the others still hadn't made it back out of the tent. I glanced to the west and saw some of the soldiers running, trying to beat the wave.

"*Orbis Tego*," I said, keeping my toe on the line of the circle. Done right, it was an effective extension. Done wrong, and I would've cut my toe off. The glassy dome of energy snapped closed a split second after Zola's did the same.

The soldiers around us opened fire. I glimpsed Graybeard's warship slamming into the front of the waves. The ship didn't rise like it would have in normal water, unable to ride the wave as the witches didn't have the buoyancy to raise Graybeard and his crew. Instead, the bow cut into the wave, splitting the entire mass in two. The water crashed into us a moment later, and I lost sight of everything as a torrent of murky water tried to choke the life from my lungs. Forms drifted by. Some were clearly water witches, their translucent sneers as they smashed into the circle shield an unnerving sight before they dragged soldiers to the ground. My first instinct was to drop the shield when Casper's face was crushed up against that translucent dome. Sheer terror pulled her eyes wide as her focus flashed between me and the ground.

The strike wasn't smooth underwater. It was sluggish and slow, but the water witch didn't expect Casper's blade to be tainted with the metal of the stone dagger. The undine recoiled, leaving Casper to launch herself higher into the waters, where I hoped she could catch her breath.

Some of the others were not so lucky. I watched in horror and rage as those waters pulled soldier after soldier into the deep, the lithe translucent forms smothering their faces, watching their lives seep away, and capturing their last breaths. I met Zola's eyes, two beacons in that pit of water and death. She held up three fingers, keeping her middle tucked securely against her palm as she folded her arms across her chest.

It was a symbol I'd learned long ago. She meant to use a fire incantation. We hadn't needed to communicate with symbols in a very long time. Her gesture changed, and now she held up three fingers together; her index, her middle, and her ring. The first folded down, and a surge of adrenaline shot through my bones. This was it. She was going to drop a shield and attack from a most unexpected position. She wouldn't be alone.

Two fingers down.

I switched the pepperbox to my left hand and drew the focus from my belt.

Three fingers down.

Zola's shield vanished, and in that same instant, a hurricane of fire burst to life, turned on its side, and tore through the river of water witches. Steam and screams breached the muted sounds of the water around me. I could see the forms lifting, turning away from their prey to close on Zola as the weight of the river fell into the void on top of her.

I dropped my own shield and aimed the soulsword. It wasn't as precise as the demon staff I'd once had—a demon staff that had tried to kill me—but it would have to do. "*Magnus Ignatto!*" A maelstrom of fire, not so refined as Zola's, spiraled out into that abyss of murky water. In the back of my mind, I knew if there were any soldiers in front of me, they wouldn't survive it. But I also knew the chances of them still being alive were virtually nothing.

For a moment, I didn't understand what I was seeing as the water crashed in around me. I waited for the cold strike of a water witch's sword, but it didn't come. Instead, the waters burst to life. Massive streams of bubbles and flame fired downward at a sharp angle. Confusion overwhelmed me until the upturned skull of a long-dead harbinger cut through the waters not far away. Graybeard had brought the Bone Sails ashore.

The tide of water collapsed around me and surged back

toward the warship. I coughed and spluttered as the air suddenly returned to my lungs. A handful of clumsy steps brought me to the place Zola had been, but she was gone. I pushed forward, reaching the great gouges in the earth where tent stakes and larger things had been torn away.

What had been the edge of the bank before that wave struck was gone. The land that had been beneath both Casper's tents and her squad was no more. I didn't have time to mourn that loss or look for the dead. I turned toward the raging waters, and the soulsword in my hand grew into a blistering light.

The undines along the front line of those engaging Graybeard's warship were plain to see. I raised the pepperbox and fired into them. The hellish flame of Mike's rounds was enough to draw their attention. I holstered the gun and palmed a dagger. If they thought we'd been left defenseless, they'd been wrong. The weight of the backpack slowed me down, water-logged as it now was. But that didn't matter. It only added to the fury in my bones.

The nearest of the water witches vanished into a pool of water, only to resurface a few feet from me. I lashed out with a soulsword, and she laughed as her arm separated from her body, reforming a moment later. The inertia of her attack was too much for her to correct. All I had to do was raise the dagger in my left hand. The thrust hit her square in the chest, and I didn't wait to watch her turn to stone. I stepped to the side as she collapsed to the ground, and focused on the next witch.

A bellowing cry sounded from the warship, and I saw a vision of black and white Atlas moth wings diving toward the water, and lashing out with an enchanted sword. The next undine caught an arrow in the back of the head. She didn't have time to register what had happened before she was dead, the weight of her now-stone head collapsing through the rest of her body as her entire mass became a horrifically disfigured statue. I knew the fletching of Aideen's arrows when I saw them.

"Where's Zola?" I shouted.

I didn't need a response. I just needed her to know that we needed to find her. I didn't get an answer. Instead, I caught something sharp in the back of my left shoulder. It took everything I had to keep my grip on the dagger as I spun to find another water witch with a gleaming blade covered in my blood. She didn't gloat. She was silent and moved with a deadly grace.

I barely raised the soulsword in time to ward off another blow. The sword in her hand was imbued with enough magic to resist the power of my enchanted blade. A crackle of electric blue energy exploded between us, and she backpedaled. I scarcely registered the explosion of sound beside me, when the water witch's head jerked to the side, and a webwork of grey stone worked its way through her head.

I didn't hesitate. I slashed downwards with a soulsword, shattering the stone inside her, turning her into a lifeless mass of stone and water on the scarred earth.

With a glance, I found Casper staring at me. I raised my gun, aiming directly at her. I pulled the angle to the left, and she didn't so much as flinch. The explosion of fire tore through the through the undine behind her, sending the witch flailing back into the river.

I turned as quickly as I dared, while still giving myself enough time to study the pools and eddies around me. Anything suspicious was getting stabbed with a stone dagger.

Anything that moved was at least getting run through with a soulsword. It might not kill a water witch, but it would certainly slow them down.

"Where's Rick?" I shouted, glancing back to Casper.

She shook her head and nodded. A rifle came onto her shoulder, and she moved with the compact efficiency of a trained killer.

"Stay beside me," she said. "Some of the skeletons came into the tent as the water witches hit. We need to get back on that ship."

"Back on the ship?" I said pointing to a puddle that moved in a suspicious wave, against the current of the rest of the water. Casper unloaded a round into it, and I won't deny a bit of satisfaction as a webwork of stone formed underneath.

"The crew," Casper said. "They pulled some of us up on the deck. Some of the injured tried to run. Did you see them?"

"They didn't make it," I said as we moved closer to the ship.

Aideen took to the skies ahead as a curl of water lashed out beside her, swinging a sword in an impossibly fast arc. The noonday sun glinted through the translucent water witch. Aideen gave one mighty push of her wings and evaded the blow as she drew an arrow. She let loose and clipped the side of the water witch's head. Aideen shot forward, smashing into the undine's solidifying head with her elbow and snatching her arrow from the surface of the river.

The cannons along the starboard side of Graybeard's ship roared time and time again, lighting up the river and turning it into a boiling hellish mass. I didn't understand what he was doing at first, until the outlines of the undines became plain to see in that orange glow beneath the waters.

"This is insane," Casper said. "This is bloody insane."

I caught a glimpse of a gray cloak, tattered and burned, but it moved with a familiar gait. A flood of relief washed over me as Zola raised her arms at the bow of the ship, and sent another spiraling incantation of fire into the river.

"Shit," I muttered. Another Green Man surfaced near the Bone Sails, rearing one arm back and thrusting a series of spiked branches through one of the wooden panels on the side of Graybeard's ship. I drew the pepperbox and leveled it at the Green Man, taking careful aim before moving my finger to the second trigger, an unlikely Fae addition. I pulled the trigger and unleashed the remaining five barrels of hellfire.

A white-orange light filled the air and the scent of brimstone tore at my lungs. The Green Man roared when that beam of fire cut into his back, sending a tower of burning flesh up to its head. Graybeard shouted orders on the deck, as he swept his sword toward the burning Green Man. One of the smaller cannons near the bow swiveled around and took aim. The Green Man reared back again. Another boom thundered across the river, and the Green Man's head splintered. He fell backward like freshly cut timber, splashing into the diminishing waters.

The water swelled and crashed against the side of Graybeard's ship, the strange movement revealing the twisted drowned tanks now laying on their sides and upside down in the shallows of the river. Those men had never had a chance, no chance in hell.

Two more Green Men burst from the waters, and I stared in awful fascination as they closed on Graybeard's ship. They were bigger than the last, their arms looking more like oak trees than the whip-like saplings of the previous arms. The first lunged at the ship, only to be blocked by the sudden appearance of a stone wall. His fist shattered, only to regrow a moment later, with the fresh greens of a new sapling.

Aeros formed from that stone wall, flying out of it with a fury, even as the stones rearranged themselves into his body. The first blow fell on the Green Man's face before the creature could so much as raise its arms to defend itself. I imagined tons of stone crashing into a tree would have had much the same effect. The face splintered, and sap oozed from an exploded eye.

"Men of peace!" Aeros roared. "This day you have murdered the helpless. And for that, you die."

Aeros smashed the Green Man into the muddy banks with a two-fisted overhead blow. Graybeard's cannons fired on the other side of the ship.

And while I wasn't sure what they'd hit, the enormous wave began to recede. Graybeard wheeled the ship around, careful not to run aground in the shallows. The Bone Sails floated back to us, a bit scarred, a bit bloody, but victorious all the same.

I took in the sights around us, glancing back to see a line of soldiers along the side streets of Main. I couldn't see their expressions, but it didn't take much to imagine them. I suspected they didn't look much different than Casper's.

"Come on," I said. "It's over. For now."

Casper shook and watched the water recede upriver. What had been a titanic wave was now barely a swell in the retreating waters.

CHAPTER THIRTY-FOUR

GRAYBEARD DIDN'T BOTHER guiding his warship back toward the docks. Of course, from the angle we were at, I couldn't tell if the docks were still there. Instead, the pirate spun the bone wheel, and the ship glided toward the shore. The edge of the bank had been cut away in the raging waters, forming a natural dock. Graybeard dropped a massive anchor, and the Bone Sails slowed to a stop.

I walked with Casper, still eyeing with suspicion any puddle larger than a cup of water. A few I stabbed with a stone dagger just to be safe. The plank settled onto the bank of the river as we reached the worst of the erosion. Graybeard and Zola waited at the top of the bone ramp.

Casper hesitated, eyeing that plank with some trepidation. A rattling clack echoed out from the Bone Sails, and Casper's face split into a grin.

"What did they say?" I asked.

"That if I was scared of a little bone, I shouldn't stand so close to a dick."

I guffawed. "Are you serious? Did they just call me a dick in Morse code?"

"Pretty sure they did," Casper said as she took her first step onto the plank, and started up onto the deck. I followed her, feeling the strange give of the bone and sinew beneath my boots. The water had made some parts slick, but our issues with sliding and catching our balance ended when we set foot on the deck of bones.

"Thank you," I said.

The parrot ruffled its wings before settling down onto the skeleton's shoulder. "I thought we were here to deter water witches, not to engage an entire army of them."

"Surprises all around," I said.

"Lass," Graybeard said. He gestured toward the far side of the ship. "You'll find what crew we could rescue waiting for you."

"Thank you," Casper said as she hurried past Graybeard. One of the smaller skeletons, clad in leather shorts, gave Casper a slap on the back as she passed. She flashed the skeleton a grin, and I was fairly certain that was probably the skeleton who had called me a dick.

"Foster and Aideen?" I asked.

Graybeard's skeleton lifted its chin, and I followed the gesture up to the crow's nest. One of the skeleton crew gestured wildly to the two fairies standing on the edge of the nest.

"We were lucky," Zola said.

"Lucky?" I said. "Half the damn soldiers down there drowned."

"And imagine if we hadn't been there," Zola said. "In the time it would've taken to reach the riverfront from the shop, this engagement would've been over."

I hadn't thought of our timing as anything remotely like luck—more like our timing was just damn close to getting us killed, and watching our allies drown.

"They targeted you all, they did," Graybeard said. "You may

not have seen the shifting of the waters from down below. But from here, I could see every bend those witches took. They circled around you like a Titan come to swallow you all."

"Swallow us like a sheet iron cracker that got stuck in their throat," Zola snapped.

I remembered the waters closing around us, crashing against our shields; the soldiers dragged down to the grasses under the waves while the undines sucked away their last breaths.

"Yeah, maybe we are lucky to be here."

"The witches thought to neutralize us beneath the waters," Zola said, raising an eyebrow. "Ah would've thought our reputations required a larger attack."

A mournful, pained cry sounded from the huddle of soldiers across the ship. Casper had her arms wrapped around one of the younger privates, a man who couldn't have been more than eighteen or nineteen. I didn't need to hear the conversation to understand what had happened. That pained howl, the uncontrolled sob that told only of the loss of friends or family.

"They did enough damage," I said.

"Aye," Graybeard said. "But they could've done more."

I turned to Zola. "And where the hell was Alexandra? Nixie said she was coming back this way with support."

Zola frowned. "It is unlike Alexandra to be late. Ah wonder if the undines did not merely strike on one front."

Her words sent a frisson of anxiety tearing through my chest. I cursed and pulled the backpack off my shoulders. "We need to talk to Nixie. We need to talk to Falias."

"Foster!" Graybeard shouted.

The fairy perked up on the crow's nest, said something to

Aideen, and then swooped down toward us.

"What is it?" Foster asked as he glided onto Zola's shoulder.

"Have you spoken to Falias?" the parrot asked. "Any of Nixie's troops?"

He shook his head. "We just got done not dying. Why?"

"Because the water witches could've crushed you here," Graybeard said, "and yet they didn't."

Aideen followed Foster down. She landed on Graybeard's shoulder, opposite the parrot. "The queen is not known for subtleties. She is ruthless and murderous, and blunt though her tactics may be, they are deadly."

I already had the blue obsidian disc in my hand before Aideen finished speaking. I gave the fairy a nod, and started down the bone ramp, catching myself once when my boots threatened to lose traction. The cry of one of Casper's soldiers echoed out around me, and rage kindled in my gut.

I didn't bother to look for a smooth entry into the water; most of the sloping shore had been cut away by the raging river. I hopped down, keeping one arm on the bank, while I sank to my waist in the river. The old discs weren't the most secure communications we had. We had to be cautious about what went across them, but in an emergency, they were one of the best tools we had for reaching Falias.

The disc pulsed beneath my fingers, and I waited. The water rippled and shivered around me, and I began to question the sanity of hopping into the river when I had just seen a legion of water witches in those same waters. But the ripple did not become a deadly adversary. The ripple became a voice.

"Damian? What is it?"

"They struck Saint Charles."

"No," she said, a bald urgency in her voice. "That's impossible. They struck Rivercene. Ashley and Beth and Cornelius ..." She hesitated.

"Are they okay?" I was ready to fish the hand of Gaia out of the backpack and charge to Rivercene.

"They survived. But they only survived because Alexandra and our detachment showed up to help them."

"How many?" I asked.

She didn't answer.

I cursed and spat a string of profanity.

Nixie's voice came back, and whatever calm had been there shattered. "The queen is here!"

The transmission cut off, and the waters around me returned to their natural flow.

CHAPTER THIRTY-FIVE

I TRIED TO scramble out of the river, but the bank collapsed beneath my fingernails. It didn't stop me. I just dug my nails in deeper, and slowly pulled myself out of the mud and muck. I had the hand of Gaia out before I reached the ramp again. "Zola! The queen is in Falias! And the walls of the Obsidian Inn are unguarded!"

"Go with Gaia," Zola shouted. "We'll follow with who we can."

I shook my head. "No, we can't leave our home undefended."

"You're not going out there alone, boy," Zola said. "You don't know what's waiting for you."

Zola was right, and I knew she was right. Nixie had sent half her army to Rivercene. If she thought the attack was happening there, then what the hell did she think was happening here? What had she thought was coming for the Obsidian Inn?

"Get in touch with the innkeeper, Alexandra, anyone in Rivercene. Find out if they need you first!"

"Damian, no!" Zola shouted.

By the time her words reached my ears, I'd already wrapped my fingers into Gaia's and stepped into the Abyss. I walked blindly as Gaia formed beside me, the golden motes of light joining together, as the distant stars of the Abyss slowly swam into my vision.

"Falias. I need to get to Falias, and the Obsidian Inn."

"There is a great deal of power there," Gaia said, her voice echoing from nowhere and everywhere as her face grew more defined.

"The queen of the water witches has attacked them. I have to get there now."

"You should not."

I hesitated at Gaia's words. But she didn't understand, this was Nixie. This was Mike and the Old Man and Dell and the werewolves. I couldn't leave them. I couldn't abandon them to a wave like what had hit Saint Charles.

"I have to."

"You should not," Gaia said, a moment before she doubled over, releasing a thunderous shout as pain tore through her.

"Gaia!" I shouted. "What is it?"

"I have disobeyed," she said, her voice strained.

"No, you haven't. We're just having a conversation."

"It is not your word I disobeyed. It is the compulsion laid up on my hand. I will not send you to your death," Gaia snarled. "I do not care what this compulsion costs me."

"It's my choice," I said. "You can't keep me away. One way or another, I'm getting to Nixie. Put me somewhere close, but away from whatever threat you sense."

Gaia slowly straightened, the strain leaving her voice. "That would be a reasonable solution."

I eyed the Titan, horrified at the pain that had wracked her body simply for disagreeing with me, and terrified at what power she might have sensed.

"As close as you can get me, yet still believe me to be safe."

She narrowed her eyes and stared at the darkness around us. "I do not know if any place I put you will be safe. But I could do my best to keep you away from the largest of the powers."

"Do it," I said, "and no need for a soft landing. I need to be there yesterday."

I began to regret the phrasing of my request when the lights of the Abyss turned into stretched-out lines as Gaia whipped us through nothing. Gaia's hand started slipping away a moment before our connection severed entirely, and darkness became an explosion of daylight.

I slammed into the grass, rolling a few times before the inertia faded and I crashed to a stop. My backpack dug into my shoulder, and I grunted as I shifted it to redistribute the weight. I crawled up to my knees and tried to figure out where Gaia had dropped me. I pulled my phone from my pocket, before remembering that it had been underwater, more than once. There was no coming back from that.

A sound grew in the distance, an unmistakable crash. The battle cries of an army, charging another force. The earth shook beneath my feet. And the cries grew ever louder.

I turned slowly, orienting myself to the lay of the field Gaia had dropped me in. I tried to understand what I was looking at, and it didn't take long before dust in the distance told me which way the sound was coming from. The voice that sounded behind me nearly gave me a heart attack.

"You are a fool."

I rounded on the line of trees behind me. High in the branches of one of the evergreens was a face I hadn't expected to see here. The face of the fairy called Drake.

I wrapped my fingers around the focus on my belt and freed it. "You come to kill me?"

"What kind of idiot question is that?" Drake said. "My place has been in the shadows for far too long. I tire of my king's games. But you intrigue me."

I frowned at the fairy. Something didn't look right. The branch he was on bobbed up and down, not moving with the wind and the other limbs around him.

"Did you bring a Green Man?" I asked. "That your play? Have me get close enough to get impaled?"

Drake blew a laugh out through his nose. "You *are* a paranoid one." He slapped his perch, and I froze. It unwound from the tree, lowering itself into the field not thirty feet away. I'd only seen one before, one that had lived under my bed, a flash of silver teeth in the skull of a great beast.

"Shit."

"That was a good fight," Drake said. "You took down the Green Men far more efficiently than I've seen anyone do it before. I'd like to spar one day."

"Like today? While you're on your dragon? And I'm … screwed?"

Drake shook his head slowly, his eyes never leaving me, as if every moment he was anticipating an attack. For all his bluster, he was cautious. And he knew I posed a threat. That made me feel marginally better, considering the dragon seemed to be ignoring me completely. It nosed the earth beneath its front claws before releasing a mighty sigh and flopping to the field. Drake wobbled on the dragon's shoulder, but his gaze didn't waver.

"I guess one of us is bored," I said.

"As I said," Drake said. "Had I wished you dead, you would be so. I've come to give you a warning."

"From Nudd?" I asked.

"No," Drake said. "From me. I have no loyalty to either side of this conflict."

"Okay? And what does that have to do with me?"

"You've stepped into a trap. The battle over the hill is between the same factions. When you enter the fray, they will turn on you. Both sides."

I blinked at Drake.

"Nudd was right about you," he said. "You didn't receive a message from your mistress. That was masked by the Fae."

"But if my message wasn't real? Then anyone who uses those discs ..."

Drake nodded. "Those communiques are far less secure than you imagine."

I was about to charge over that hill, smashing into whatever conflict awaited me. But was Drake being honest? Was it just an ambush playing out? Now that I thought about it, Nixie hadn't shown her face. She almost always showed herself, even if it was just in the ripples of the water. I had no doubt the Fae could imitate her voice, but I didn't know the limitations of those actual projections. I cursed.

"Travel away from the battle," Drake said. "Your friends are less than a mile away. Do not use the hand of Gaia. The king will know, and a trap of a different sort will be sprung."

"That's how I came here," I said.

Drake gave a quick shake of his head. "The trap will only activate if you attempt to warp away. Your arrival was planned."

"Are you the same Drake that the fairies talk about? You served the Mad King?"

Drake placed a hand on his chest, covering the engraved symbols on his armor. "I still do."

I muttered to myself under my breath and pulled at a side pouch on my backpack. I slid out a bag of Frank's beef jerky and tore it open.

"What are you doing?" Drake asked.

"Making friends." I pulled out the largest piece of jerky I could find and tossed it underhand toward the dragon. The dragon's head snapped up so fast that he threw Drake off his shoulder, and the fairy yelped as he tumbled down the scaly back. The dragon, on the other hand, snapped the beef jerky out of the air with one quick strike. It made two exaggerated chews and then swallowed. Then it trundled forward, sniffing the air, until it was only about six inches away from me.

"Are you mad?" Drake shouted. "That is a *dragon*."

I held a handful of jerky out and let the dragon lick it away. It held its head upside down, and I poured the rest of the bag in. It chewed slowly, before finally returning to Drake, who wore an expression of absolute disbelief.

"If I don't find my friends," I said. "I'm going to train your dragon to chew your face off."

Drake climbed back up on his dragon's back and patted the beast's neck. "Interesting." The fairy gave me one nod, and then the dragon launched into the air.

I waited until they were out of sight before I blew out a shaky breath. To say the beef jerky had been a gamble would probably be the understatement of the year. That dragon could just as easily have bitten my head off, and if he was anywhere near as powerful as Jasper, I wouldn't have had very long to worry about it.

I couldn't be sure what Drake's intentions were, but the fact he didn't attack helped me entertain the idea that all was not as it seemed. The silhouette of the dragon vanished fully behind the tree line before I turned my back on the fairy and his mount.

I pulled the cold gray flesh of Gaia's hand out of my pocket and studied it. If Drake was right, I wouldn't be able to use the hand to escape the field. But did I truly believe that? Did I trust the word of a Fae who had so recently killed some of my allies? Killed Casper's men?

I took a deep breath and tucked Gaia's hand into my backpack. Running headlong into Nudd's trap might give me all the evidence I needed, but it also might get me killed a lot faster. The question was, did Drake set his own trap? I glanced behind me one more time before striking out through the long grass and heading into the trees.

CHAPTER THIRTY-SIX

THE DEEPER INTO the woods I traveled, the louder the whispers grew. The shadows of the canopy wrapped around me while the voices rose ever higher. It was disorienting, and I froze in place more than once to evaluate their source. With enough effort, and help from Zola's mantra, I could quiet all of them.

It didn't take long to realize those voices were all in my head. As soon as I stopped trying to tamp them down inside my mind, they rose to the surface over and over, and in more numbers than I could comprehend. If this was Drake's plan, to lure me closer into an ocean of lost souls, I might be in deep shit.

I didn't have a chance of traversing the forest floor quietly. Old groundcover, and newly fallen limbs, caused branches to snap under every footfall. Leaves crunched, and animals scurried away.

The forest grew more dense, and the vines of invasive plant species hung down around me like the willow whips of the Green Men.

I clenched my teeth and forged ahead. Ten minutes, twenty more. It was slow going in the denser woods, but I found it less and less likely that I would be seeing my friends on the other side of the shadows. When the forest grew dim enough, and my anxiety grew high enough, I contemplated summoning a ball of light. But if my clumsy path through the woods hadn't given me away, a floating ball of light sure as hell would.

The voices rose again. This time they shouted warnings, urging me to turn back, to run from that place as fast as I dared.

And as that became overwhelming, the forest finally gave way. I ducked beneath a log that had fallen at a forty-five-degree angle and lay propped on the bough of an ancient oak. When I stepped from the shadows and entered the field that waited beyond the woods, the darkness around me fractured. The voices gave way to silence, and I began to understand what was happening.

The flickers of power, and the sudden rise of the voices, hadn't been a natural occurrence. I'd crossed a line somewhere. A line of wards meant to misdirect or cause such a horrible sense of unease, they would send almost anyone fleeing from this place.

A hill rose in front of me, and I started up it. It wasn't steep, but it was enough that the trees beyond the hill were nothing but the peaks of evergreens on the distant slope of an old mountain. I turned away from that blue haze, and glanced back at the forest I'd come through. It looked normal, as welcoming as any I'd ever set foot in. But I shivered at the memory of those voices, and the dread that rose in my bones.

I drew the focus from my belt and held it at the ready. A dozen more steps took me to the crest of the hill, and I had my answer. I looked down into the valley of a river, at an encampment of chaos. But it was not the chaos of a pitched battle, this was an active camp. They were preparing, they were making ready for war. Something clanged in the distance, and it grew until it sounded as though a church bell had been rung inside my head. And by the time it quieted, it sounded again.

"Mike," I whispered. I'd only heard that sound coming from the Smith's Hammer. I'd never heard its equal. If this camp was a façade, someone had gone to insane lengths to create it.

I hadn't made it a quarter of the way down the steep slope before the soldiers below noticed me. Owl knights sounded the alarm. Two massive barn owls hooted at an unnatural volume, until it could have substituted for a tornado siren.

One of the owl knights shouted. "Take aim!"

A man grabbed the fairy's shoulder, spinning him around so the owl knight was face-to-face with the grizzled flesh and pale white beard of Leviticus Aureus.

"You try to cut that man down," the Old Man said, "and you'll be in a world of pain. And not for me, but for Nixie."

He looked up at me as the wide-eyed owl knight backed away from him. "What the hell are you doing here? You're supposed to be defending Saint Charles."

"Saint Charles was already attacked," I said. "If Graybeard hadn't been there, we would've been in trouble."

The Old Man cursed and spat. "Come on. You don't need to tell the story twice, I'll gather the others."

He led me through the camp of Fae. Towering Green Men wove their way between beautiful silken tents, while the knights marched and drilled, and voices shouted from inside those gilded tents. The Smith's Hammer rang out again, louder, and more deafening than ever.

Mike stood silhouetted by the forge as a burst of sparks

jumped off his anvil. The Old Man ducked inside one of the larger tents and said, "We have a visitor."

"Damian?" Nixie asked, surprise plain on her face. "What are you doing here?"

"I thought I was coming to your rescue."

Nixie stood up, revealing the gilded chair that should have been sitting in the corner. It was golden and studded with aquamarines, and I wondered why in the hell the Fae would've brought such a thing into the field.

"So you didn't get my message?"

"Message?" she asked, pulling a blue obsidian disc from a leather pouch at her waist. "No."

"Gaia brought me here. But not before I was intercepted by Drake."

Nixie lowered herself slowly back onto the throne. She was silent for a moment, and she looked to someone in the corner.

It was only then that I took stock of who was in the tent with us. Hess and Utukku stood close to Morrigan. A golden werewolf crouched beside them, a friendly smile on his face, but I knew what a deadly fighter Wahya was. He'd stood with us at Gettysburg, and mourned the loss of the Ghost Pack. More undines filled the tent, and in the far corner sat Euphemia. She nodded to me when I met her gaze, and I returned the gesture.

I told them the story of my encounter with Drake, and what he had said about still serving the Mad King. They seemed to take it all in stride, something which I hadn't been very good at doing. I told them about the false battle supposedly raging, staged by Nudd.

This drew expressions of surprise and shock from everyone

but Morrigan.

"It's a tactic he has used before," she said.

"That's what Drake said."

I told them of the woods, and the dread.

"That was Ward," the Old Man said. "Nixie had him lay down a barrier. The fact that Nudd knew we were here is disturbing."

"Why?" I asked.

Nixie drummed her fingers on the chair's armrest. "Because this is our forward operating base for the Obsidian Inn." She sagged back into the chair, propping her chin up on the edge of her hand. "We need to get eyes on that battle. I don't trust anything Drake says, but I don't trust Nudd, either."

"You can trust in who they are," Morrigan said. "Drake is loyal to the throne. Nudd will always move to return the Fae to power. I will go."

Morrigan said no more. She strode out of the tent with a purpose. One moment she was an old crone, and the next an enormous raven that launched into the skies.

"What about Rivercene?" I asked. "Are they okay?"

Nixie slid the obsidian disc into a bubbling pool of water beside the throne. "I've had no word." She closed her eyes and the disc pulsed. No one answered.

"It is not beyond Nudd's power to block those old discs," Wahya said. "That was established long ago."

"I know," Nixie said. "It's why the discs were abandoned to begin with."

The crashing of the bells stopped, and the silence was almost deafening as whatever work Mike had been doing in the forge faded. A moment later, the Smith entered our tent, glancing between me and Nixie.

"What are you doing here?" Mike asked.

"Long story."

He nodded to me before turning back to Nixie. "It is done. It will not kill, but any water witch it falls upon will be imprisoned."

A cloaked man slid through the entrance to the tent behind Mike. The sleeve of his cloak raised slightly, revealing the intricate tattoos of the man called Ward. He pulled back his hood, and his eyebrows flashed up when he saw me. "What—"

"Long story," Mike said.

Ward looked up at the demon and then turned to Nixie. "Mike's right." He held up a small gray disc. It could have been mistaken for a muddy disc. But it was etched with a hundred different wards. Two rings skirted the edge of the gray disc, encasing a series of runes not unlike those on the Key of the Dead.

"Have you tested it?" Nixie asked.

Ward shook his head. "I wouldn't do that to your people."

"Then do it to me," Nixie said, stepping forward.

"I don't think that's a good idea," Ward said. "This has the power to inflict intense pain."

"That's what you designed it for," Nixie said. "We need to be sure it works. Try it on me, and remove it quickly."

I stepped forward to protest, but Nixie stopped me with a glance. I didn't miss the tiny shake of her head, and I realized that there must be more here than I understood.

Ward held out the disc. Nixie turned her back and pulled her hair to the side.

"You sure about this?" Ward asked.

"Do it," Nixie said.

Ward touched the symbol etched in the center of the disc and then slapped it onto Nixie's armored back. An explosion of electric blue power shot out and wrapped around her in eight different angles, forming a sphere of power before the beam-like energy snapped closed around her. She stiffened, tried to take a step forward, and fell to the ground. The energy shifted to yellow and red and back to blue. She tried to stand, but all she could do was grunt, until a moment later she shouted against gritted teeth.

"Take it off," I hissed. "Now."

Ward reached down and lifted the disc away from Nixie as if it weighed nothing, as if those terrible beams of energy didn't affect him in the slightest. Nixie's body sagged with relief as the energy snapped back into the disc.

She took deep gasping breaths as she sat up. "I have not felt the power of a fire demon in a very long time. Well done. It is quite effective. It was a struggle to move at all, and any movement came with a heavy price."

"I'm glad to hear it," Ward said. "But I wish you wouldn't have tested it on yourself."

Nixie brushed a small tangle of grass off the vambrace on her left arm. "To not know what would happen until we were in the midst of the battle would seem unwise."

Ward nodded. "As you say."

Mike harrumphed. "I would still think there is a more sub-tle way to prove you trust your subjects." Mike's words put the entire exchange between Ward and Nixie in another light. She'd allowed herself to be incapacitated around armed Fae. Had she truly done it just to show her trust in them? Or had she done it to draw them out, and expose themselves while so many of our other allies stood beside her? Either way, I sided with Mike. It seemed like there were far less dangerous ways to accomplish that task.

"You planning on running me through with that?" Ward asked. He glanced down at my hand and then back up to my eyes.

I looked down and found a soulsword lit in my right hand. I frowned, and let my death grip on the hilt relax until the blade eventually receded and I could safely stash the focus in my belt once more. "Sorry. Habit."

Nixie frowned at me. "We generally don't encourage the killing of our allies." She turned to Ward before I could respond. "How many have you made?"

Ward handed it to her, careful not to activate the symbol at its center. "A dozen so far. I could likely have a dozen more by morning if I work through the night."

"If you can manage," Nixie said.

Ward waited, as if he would not move until she gave the word.

"You may return to the forge. Thank you both."

Mike gave her a nod before clapping me on the back and exiting the tent.

"Nice chair," I said.

Nixie glanced back at the ostentatious seat. "It's an old throne. And it has a great deal of meaning."

I bit my tongue, remembering where we were and who we were surrounded by. I wanted to ask her, and I hoped she'd say more.

"It's killing you, isn't it?" she asked. "Not opening your

mouth?"

"Maybe?" I said. "Maybe just a tiny bit."

She offered me a wicked grin, a break in her formal façade, as she turned back to the throne. "This one sat in the center of Atlantis. The head of a round table." She didn't turn back at me to see my raised finger, or my half-open mouth before she said, "Shut up." I lowered my arm and the Old Man chuckled.

"It was not a round table of equals. The chairs had meaning. The leaders of our separate clans, unified and still obedient to the throne. I would not demand that of my people, not that kind of obedience. Only that they do not drown the innocent of this world. And that they no longer war among themselves."

The water witches and Fae in the room slammed their closed right fists against their chests. It gave me goosebumps, and I wasn't sure if it was for appreciation of their loyalty, or the outright creepiness of how synchronized the gesture was.

"So it was raised from the wreckage," Nixie said. She met my eyes. "As my people will be, too."

The call of a great raven filled the silence that followed. Morrigan's winged form swept into the tent before a black vortex obscured her form and the old crone stood before us once more. "The necromancer is right."

It didn't really even bother me anymore that Morrigan just called me "the necromancer." It was a hell of a lot nicer than what some of the other Fae called me. Hell, it was nicer than what Foster called me sometimes.

"There was a battle," Morrigan said. "I don't think some of those armies understood that it was all for show. I saw more than one empty suit of armor on the ground. And what I am fairly sure was the helmet of a dark-touched."

"Would you recommend we strike?" Nixie asked. "We are not fully prepared, and Ward has many more discs to create."

"Nudd's deception is foiled," Morrigan said. "His people are on alert, and their focus is no longer on the battle he chided them into. His plot is foiled, as is the secrecy of this place."

The thundering alarm of the owl knights erupted a moment later. The drawn-out hoots of the owls echoed around the camp, raising a warning that I suspected I didn't need to ask about.

"He comes," Morrigan said.

CHAPTER THIRTY-SEVEN

N IXIE FOLLOWED MORRIGAN to the entrance of the tent, and I stepped behind the old crone. On the ridge that led to the woods stood a lone figure, shrouded by the dying sun, but unmistakable in his horned silhouette. Slowly, the negative space around him filled with the Fae and other creatures I could not identify against the darkness of the forest.

The Smith's Hammer rang like an enormous gong in the nearby forge. Mike had to have heard the alarm, but I wondered if he continued working with Ward simply to make his presence known. Ezekiel had once pulled trolls from the Burning Lands and Unseelie Fae to fight his battles. But he'd lost with help from the Fallen Smith. And Mike was leaving no doubt that he was with Nixie.

"Where is Lewena?" Nixie asked. "I seek only *her* head."

Nudd's antlered helmet tilted slightly to the side. "You are in no position to make demands. I come with an offer of peace. Surrender and I will—"

Surprise at Nixie's use of the queen's name gave way to the voices buried in my head. Millions of dead from the Gettysburg cataclysm rose in one calamitous screaming mass. They understood who Nudd was. Their cries overwhelmed me as they crawled their way up into my head, and I had to give them a release, or surrender my sanity.

The souls surged out into the world around me, calling to the mass of gravemakers that had been drawn to Ward's barrier. I hadn't felt them before, hidden as they had been by runic charms. But now that I understood, it was the easiest thing in the world to make the Hand of Anubis rise on either side of Nudd and slam down on him and his nearest allies, crushing them into so much mulch.

Nudd took a hesitant step backward from the nearest Hand of Anubis, righting himself and crossing his arms. If I hadn't been watching him, I might not have seen the trepidation. His voice showed no surprise or concern.

"We are here to establish an accord," Nudd said as the dead Fae beside him began screaming, their destroyed bodies siphoning away into the nearby ley lines. "I made no such threat."

"You tried," Nixie said. "And if you make another, you won't leave this place alive."

Nudd laughed.

"You do not understand what you have lost," Morrigan said, stepping up beside Nixie. "No songs will be sung of the great and fallen king."

"You go too far, Morrigan," Nudd said, his laugh dying.

"And yet you still live," Morrigan said, a sneer edging its way across the old crone's face.

I adjusted my feet as my boots slipped on the grass at the edge of the tent. I glanced down, surprised to see a pool of water coalescing beside me.

A voice whispered, so quiet it could have been a distant wind. "Say nothing."

All along the base of the hill, blades of grass moved the

wrong way with the coming of the wind.

Nudd raised his right hand, and his army drew their weapons. Or so they tried.

The voice that had been no more than a whisper grew into a cry, and became a voice I recognized. The pained shout of Ward. "It is done!"

I stumbled away from Ward as his cloak caught fire. A brilliant light lanced down into the earth, exploding outward into the shadows of the forest. The Fae on the hill screamed when the light reached them. It froze them in place, and I could hear the sizzle of power cutting into flesh from where I stood.

"This was never your trap," Nixie snarled. "Attack!"

The field around us turned inside out as water witches rose from a body of water that I couldn't see. In the blazing light of Ward's incantation, I could see the shock on Nudd's face. Whatever he'd expected, this wasn't it. I stared in stunned awe for a few seconds as Nixie's army dove into the enemy lines.

I understood the price the undines were paying, then. For as their swords and daggers pierced their enemy, they became a victim of Ward's trap just as much as the ones they had slain. It drew the attention of Nudd, who slowly lifted a leg from the earth. The power that held it in place cracked and fell away.

"You dare!" He raised his hand as the thick golden bond that had held him a moment before fell away. "You. Dare."

Nudd raised a mighty sword to strike out at his assailants. A volley of arrows erupted from the camp, sending a dozen Fae into a crumpled heap on the ground. Another volley, another dozen. The screams grew into a roar, and Nudd's army began to fail.

"I can't," Ward huffed. "I can't hold them."

I didn't need to hear more. Ward's warning jarred me out of my stunned silence, and I raced forward with the Old Man. A shield formed on his left arm, and I mimicked it. But the surge of power called out to the cacophony inside my head, and my shield became something else. The rusted flesh of a gravemaker surged out of the ground, covering my shield with damned darkness.

"Use it!" the Old Man shouted. The flesh along his right arm rippled and split, and the terrible power the Old Man kept bottled up inside rushed to cover his arm. As the nauseating, rolling tide subsided, he was left with a hand as black as onyx, and a sword formed of a gravemaker.

"Drake!" Nudd shouted. "I know this was your doing!"

Nudd snarled at me as I closed. It wasn't me he should've been focused on. The earth beside him spiraled up, and the Fae king doubled over as Nixie's sword flashed up, finding the seam in his armpit.

Nudd roared. It was not the sound of any Fae I'd ever heard. It was the sound of something primal, with the kind of power no being was ever meant to wield. Nudd reared back to strike at Nixie, and I had little doubt it would be a killing blow.

"Drop it, Ward," I snarled. My voice twisted as the flesh of the gravemaker crawled over my face. I fought back, keeping my line of sight open. I couldn't afford to slow down, one wrong move, one wrong move... The king had taken enough.

I reached forward my left arm, and the shield distended, expanding out like some comically large sword. Nudd's strike sank deep into the gravemaker flesh as Ward dropped the trap. Nixie fell to the ground as my soulsword arced up through the spot she had been standing a moment before. Nudd saw the attack at the last moment and lowered his helmet. The blade erupted as it struck his antlers, a blinding flash of power and souls and death.

"Now," Nudd began.

The corrupted sword in my left arm fell away to reveal the barrels of the pepperbox leveled at Nudd's face. His eyes didn't even widen as six rounds of hellfire detonated across his skull. He fell backward, but I raised the Hand of Anubis to catch him, wrap around him, and lock him into my mercy.

"This ends now!" Nixie snarled. Foot by foot the skirmish died away.

Morrigan stepped up beside Nixie and studied the king trapped inside the Hand of Anubis. "This is not Nudd."

"Who is it?" Nixie asked.

Morrigan frowned and reached out to remove the helmet. What waited inside horrified me. The dripping snout of a dark-touched vampire loomed inside the shadow.

We'd fought the dark-touched enough that I knew the Hand of Anubis shouldn't have been enough to trap it. "Why isn't it breaking free?" I asked.

"It is bound inside the armor," Morrigan said. "Destroy it. It is still a vessel of the king, and he can likely hear all we've said."

The dark-touched shook. Laughter echoed out of the damned thing's face, though its lips did not move. "Clever, clever Morrigan. I do not know how you realized what I intended, but I am impressed."

"If you are done," Morrigan said, "I will carry your creature off this field."

Ward hobbled forward, taking several deep breaths. He

studied the flickering lights around the dark-touched's head, which had been hidden behind the helmet. "He cannot merely communicate," Ward said. "He can feel."

Nixie struck like lightning. Her dagger slid into the dark-touched's eye, and Nudd's voice boomed in agony. She slammed the dagger home until the hilt was flush with the dark-touched's skull, and the vampire was still and silent.

"Are his people under compulsion?" Nixie asked.

"Not that I can see," Morrigan said.

"Me either," Ward said. He finally slid to the ground, and crossed his legs, hanging his head in exhaustion.

Nixie raised her head to the few survivors left on the hill. "Take your wounded, and those who did not brave the forest. Tell them of our mercy, and know that our doors are open. We welcome all who would stand against Nudd."

"You should not do this," Morrigan said. "It portrays weakness."

"Compassion is not weakness," Nixie said.

Nudd's Fae didn't move for a time. They exchanged glances, and flexed their wings, as if waiting for the ax to fall. They trailed off into the woods, leaving the armor of their fallen behind.

"I'll take the armor," Mike said. "You might want to change some of the imagery," he said as he held up and studied a picture of Nudd impaling the Mad King with his antlers. "But the craftsmanship's solid enough."

"The queen was not here," Nixie said.

"Neither was Nudd," Morrigan said. She turned her gaze to me. "Tell me again what happened with the attack in Saint Charles."

I told her once more of the wave, and how it swept out and curled around the soldiers.

"It is not like her," Morrigan said.

"I know," Nixie said. "She would've gone after more civilians, to throw the soldiers off their game."

I smiled when Nixie used modern slang, until the harsh reality of what she was saying sank in.

"She'd draw us out by killing bystanders?" I asked.

"Of course she would," Nixie said. "The fact that wave didn't hit deeper into the city means she wasn't there. And if she wasn't there, and she wasn't here."

"Rivercene."

"It will take us hours to get there," Nixie said.

"I can carry you," Morrigan said.

I held up a finger, silently asking the Morrigan to give me a moment. The potential consequences of that disrespect hit me a moment later, and I gave her a nervous smile. "Does anybody have a phone?" I asked, turning away from Morrigan and the last of the fairies vanishing into the woods.

"They are forbidden here," one of the owl knights said, brushing the back of his mount's head. "They proved too easy to detect."

"I do," Ward said. "It's not as if it matters now." He held out an old brick of a phone and slid a battery into the back. Until he'd done that, it might as well have been another piece of plastic he'd been carrying in his pocket without a signal for anyone, or anything, to detect.

I punched in Sam's number and waited. One of the fairies started arguing with Ward about why he'd had the phone. Listening to Ward try to explain that the battery wasn't in it, and that's why it didn't matter, made me want to laugh.

Sam answered. "Demon? What's going on?" The wind howled in the background, creating a constant buzz of static.

"Are you still in Saint Charles?"

"No, we're on Graybeard's ship. We're headed toward Falias."

"Have him turn around. This entire thing has been a misdirection. They're either targeting Rivercene or Saint Charles."

Sam cursed. Her voice became muffled as she shouted something and I heard the rapid staccato of a crewman replying. "I told them."

"I'm on my way," I said, turning to Nixie. "Come through the Abyss. Gaia will help."

"How many can she take?" Nixie asked.

"If you're wrong," Morrigan said. "They die."

"She's taken at least two before," I said. "Come with me. The others can find their way."

Nixie turned to Euphemia. "I charge you to protect the Obsidian Inn."

"It shall be done," Euphemia said. "My queen, it shall be done."

"Morrigan," Nixie said. "Please, aid Euphemia. Without Ward's circle, this place is vulnerable. We cannot lose the front to Nudd's men while we defend another from the queen."

Morrigan stood a little straighter. "You can be a fool, undine, but I will do this thing for you. May you ride upon the blood of the slain."

I pulled the hand of Gaia out of my backpack, not sure exactly what to make of Morrigan's words. I put one arm around Nixie and laced the other into Gaia's dead flesh. Both hands tightened around me, and we stepped into the Abyss.

CHAPTER THIRTY-EIGHT

"**W**ELCOME, BENEVOLENT QUEEN," Gaia said.

"Thank you for welcoming me into your realm," Nixie said, nodding at Gaia as if it were the most normal thing ever.

"What did I miss?" I asked.

"It is an old greeting," Gaia said. "One that should be reserved for true royalty."

"We need to get to Saint Charles," I said.

"And check on Alexandra." Nixie squeezed my hand.

"We don't have time," I said. "You sent her with a full company of water witches. Do you really think there's anything they can't handle?"

"A larger force of water witches," Nixie said.

I grimaced, and hoped she couldn't see the expression in the dim light of the Abyss.

"I can't leave her to her fate," Nixie said.

The thought of delaying a return to Saint Charles tightened the knot in my chest. But not only was Alexandra at Rivercene, so were Ashley and Beth. The words felt dry and wrong. "We need to make it fast."

"Fine," Nixie said. "I haven't heard from her, and I need to know what happened."

"Has the time of my awakening come?" Gaia asked.

"I rather hope not," I said. "Get us there fast."

"I warn you the jump will be unpleasant," Gaia said. "To walk through the Abyss twice in such a short time will not do you well."

"It can be a little disorienting," I said in agreement.

Nixie gasped. I turned my head to find one of the mountainous beaks of the leviathan known as Croatoan.

"It's maybe not as dead as the Old Man thinks," I said.

"No shit," Nixie said.

"I have a safe target for you," Gaia said. "But I warn you it is over the river."

"Hold on," Nixie said, squeezing me tighter.

Gaia gave no other warning. The distant stars of the Abyss streaked around us before spiraling into chaos. We stayed silent when the portal opened on the other side, and the river rushed up to greet us.

✦   ✦   ✦

I DIDN'T UNDERSTAND what had happened at first. I waited for the cold water, the loud splash, or for the landing Gaia had designated as safe to be significantly less than that. When I opened my eyes, I realized we were underwater. Nixie had somehow silenced our splash, and now we were racing through the shallow waters of the Missouri River.

"I can actually talk in this thing?" I said, staring around the bubble Nixie had stuck my head in.

"You don't have much air. You can tell me all about it later. I promise I'll act interested."

I grinned at her translucent face above me as we rose onto the edge of the river bank. "I don't understand how that could've been safe."

"Agreed. No river is safe when it's plagued by the queen's witches."

We hadn't yet exited the river when a voice boomed, "Be still your fleshy forms, or be crushed beneath the might of…"

I blinked up at Stump's imposing silhouette. The Green Man froze, glancing between me and Nixie. "You are not the threat we expected to see here. We have had many unwelcome guests," Stump said as he reached down into the river.

I cursed as the Green Man plucked me from the waters and set me gently on the bank. He extended an arm to Nixie, and she leveraged herself up beside me.

"Is Alexandra here?" Nixie asked.

"She has left this place to continue her journey elsewhere, and one was must wonder what sights she will encounter. What lies beyond the borders of these rivers and woods, and how I would enjoy the sight of your oceans."

"Is she okay?" Nixie said. "When she left, was she okay?"

Stump turned slightly, and the fading sunset revealed a pale wound on what constituted the Green Man's right cheek. "She was well, though most distraught over her inability to commune with her sisters. With you, in fact. Not all undines left this place."

"Cool scar," I said.

Stump blinked and slowly raised his right arm to run across the stretch of his cheek where the bark had been stripped away. "Why does your kind compliment our injuries? You are not the first today to do so, as the one called Cornelius said much the same. The sight of one's lifeblood spilled upon the battlefield does not seem like an event that should earn praise."

"Who is it?" A voice shouted from just over the rise in the embankment.

"The queen and her necromancer."

Nixie and I gave each other a bit of a double take before I cracked her a grin. "Come on, Your Majesty," I said. "Thank you, Stump. We need to talk to the innkeeper."

Nixie and I hurried over the hill, her muttering something about me being a pain in her ass, and the vista of Rivercene opened before us. My rapid strides stuttered as I took in the scarred landscape, and the sprawling form of one of the dark-touched harbingers.

"What happened here?" Nixie said, her voice raised as we stepped around deep furrows in the earth, and more than one shattered corpse of a water witch.

We jogged to a halt before the steps of Rivercene, the diminutive form of the innkeeper a strange contrast to her heavy presence.

"What are you doing here?" the innkeeper snapped, ignoring Nixie's question. "Alexandra has made for Saint Charles. And she's taken her soldiers with her."

"Did they leave you defenseless?" Nixie asked.

The innkeeper barked out a harsh laugh. "They were not the ones to bring down the harbinger."

"Ashley? Did she come here with Beth and Cornelius?"

The innkeeper nodded. "Most of your friends escaped. I didn't much like them torturing people on my front lawn, but they did leave a nice new garden of statues behind. Cornelius is resting upstairs. I will watch over him while you return to your home."

"Do you need a healer?" Nixie asked.

"We have our own ways," the innkeeper said. She paused a moment, and then said, "But I appreciate your offer."

"If you need us…" I said.

"Whatever Nudd has done to block the water witches' communications has not silenced my telephone."

I blinked at the innkeeper and suddenly felt rather stupid. A brief smile crossed her face before she snapped, "Now go. Your people need you."

I held my hand out to Nixie, and she wrapped her hand around my forearm before I laced my fingers between Gaia's.

"Tell the old Titan hello," the innkeeper said. "We will see you soon."

As Rivercene's broken sidewalk faded from my vision, I understood why the innkeeper said they were not unguarded. The massive willow tree-like creature, which I'd once seen walking down Main Street in Boonville, shifted near the old stump in the front yard. Blood and viscera dripped from the end of its vine-like limbs. And I saw the corpses of the dark-touched at its feet.

The light returned in the Abyss faster than I was accustomed to. Gaia coalesced beside us in an instant.

I fought down nausea, as it felt like my stomach was trying to escape through the top of my skull. "The innkeeper says hello," I muttered.

"It is always good to hear from an old friend," Gaia said, a serene smile passing over her face.

"What's happening?" Nixie said. She looked like she was about to double over.

"Are you okay?" I asked, worry rising in my gut.

"It feels as if the very earth beneath my feet is spinning."

"She will recover," Gaia said. "I do not believe the queen has experienced vertigo before."

Nixie looked up at me in horror. "Is this how you feel when you get dizzy?"

"Kind of," I said. "It's usually not quite this bad, though."

"By the gods," she said, grimacing. "Why do you continue to live?"

"Brace yourself," Gaia said. "This will not prove to be pleasant."

Nixie started to protest, and the Abyss spiraled into chaos around us. I would've laughed at the expression on her face if I hadn't known exactly how she felt.

CHAPTER THIRTY-NINE

I KEPT MY eyes open this time, not bracing for the impact of the river as I had before. Gaia released us from the Abyss not above the Missouri River, but inside it. Nixie once again made the entry into the water smoother than anything I'd experienced before. It was a strange sensation, diving beneath the waves without getting wet; shielded by Nixie's warmth around me, while the frigid waters rushed by.

We surfaced near the bank where the national guard units had incurred such great loss. Now it was an empty, muddy, and blood-soaked field. The carcass of the Green Man Aeros had slain waited like a fallen log. I blinked, and stared at it, in death unable to discern the difference between the sentient being and the driftwood around it.

Shouts echoed around us, but I couldn't pinpoint their source. Nixie stumbled beside me before hunching over, hands on her knees.

"This is awful," she said.

"Look on the bright side," I said. "We're still alive enough to know it's awful."

She laughed, made a pained noise, and slowly stood upright. "Come, no one is here. I pray we weren't wrong."

We struck out toward the scattered gravel and old railroad tracks that led back to the street. The shouting grew louder, and slowly I came to realize that we were hearing more than raised voices. Heavy equipment ground and squealed in the distance.

"Tanks?" I said, frowning as I looked either way on the street. I cursed when I saw the small clusters of tourists. The military might have been regrouping, but the gawkers and ghouls had come out to stare at the carnage.

The boom of a gunshot echoed around us, and Nixie and I exchanged a glance.

"This is bad," I said.

I ground my teeth as we hurried through the seething masses of soldiers, a level of chaos that spoke of their inexperience.

Aeros's voice boomed and cut through the noise of the street. "Stand down!"

Commoners screamed and ran away from the mass of rock and rage that formed the Old God. A still form lay at his feet, partway sheltered while Aeros faced down a tank rolling down the hill.

"Damian, we must hurry," Nixie said, dragging me forward. "We must clear the innocents out of harm's way."

"Shit, yes," I said, hurrying along beside her as fast as I could in the throng of soldiers.

"I don't know if you fully understand the consequences," Nixie said, her steps wobbling slightly under the vertigo of the Abyss. "This is a tactic Lewena used against Leviticus in the war for Atlantis. She drowned the innocent in front of the soldiers, drawing them out to die at her convenience."

I cursed and crashed through a line of soldiers. The commoners stood around us, stunned into silence. Two of them stepped behind me, and I thought I recognized them from the store when I heard the man say, "Stay behind Damian."

The machine gun mounted on the tank burst to life, cutting a line of chips across Aeros's chest while the bullets ricocheted in every imaginable direction.

The tourists and more stubborn locals weren't the only people in danger here. I raised my hand in a useless protest. Nixie held me back, preventing me from doing something stupid.

A flash of black and white wings caught my eye beyond the tank. "Angus!" The fairy looked up.

The tank's main turret fired.

Flames and death and smoke screamed from the barrel of that awful weapon. Aeros raised his fists, and a u-shaped wall of stone sprang up between him and the shell. The wall cracked in the following explosion, sending waves of shrapnel and debris skyward. Angus had barely escaped, shocking me with his speed as he grabbed two of the kids behind the wall and launched into the air with them.

One of the kids he'd had to leave behind screamed and went down, clutching his leg. Aeros glanced at the child, then turned back to face the tank. The Old God dropped into the earth, vanishing into a circle of green light. The tank adjusted its aim.

The next shot would take what was left of the wall of stone, and kill the half dozen people sheltering behind it. The commoners who had been protesting, the kids who had come to call Aeros a friend.

"No!" I shouted, sprinting forward. If I could get close enough, raise a shield, raise the Hand of Anubis, do something. I wasn't that fast. No one was that fast. "Run!" Angus dove back into the panicked crowd.

A loud thunk sounded from the tank. I wasn't going to make it to them in time. Where the fuck was Aeros?

He answered with a fury, rising beneath the tank. One stony fist grabbed the barrel and bent it toward the ground before the Old God flipped the tank over and slammed it against the earth. Stone flowed over the armored metal shell, and the tank squealed as Aeros tore it apart.

"They are *children!*" the Old God roared. "My stone will bear your names for all time, and the world shall call you murderers."

"Aeros, no!" I shouted.

He paused with his fist raised above the exposed soldiers, his eyes flashing between me and the terrified men below him.

"Don't kill them," I said.

"He's dead!" A voice screamed, cracking and rising into hysteria. I turned to see a child tugging at the arm of an older man. The endless, undefined wails of a survivor. There were the cries of grief, and then there were the primal chords of loss no person could put into words. The hiccupping, terrible sobs of lives broken, and a world that would never be the same.

"Murderers." Aeros turned away from the soldiers and looked down at me. "They should be held accountable. Would you not slay them if they were Fae or vampire?" He walked back toward the screaming boy.

I stepped up onto the flattened edge of the tank. "Okay, look, that's a big talking rock who wants to kill you now. Congratulations on pulling that off. You also just murdered someone's grandfather, so fuck you very much. The Fae who triggered Gettysburg are still out there, and they still want to kill you. Wise up before you find yourself alone in this fight."

The nearest soldier's hand reached for his sidearm. It caught on a mangled strip of metal.

The man next to him had a smarter approach. He placed his hand on his companion's arm, preventing any further attempts to draw his weapon. When the first man tried to protest again, the man I'd come to think of as the smart one stopped him more forcefully.

"Stop it. Do you want to see your family again? Or you want to die here?"

The man with the gun stopped fidgeting. I backed away, letting them climb out of the ruined tank. The wails of the child behind me cut through the silence of the men before me.

"Never forget that sound."

I turned away at that point, not wanting to see what the men would do. Or maybe I just didn't care anymore.

"Can you get them to the hospital, Aeros?"

"It will be done." He held out his hand, and the sobbing boy climbed onto it.

Nixie held her hand over the wound in the man's chest. "He's still alive." Her hand trembled, and a small orb of water congealed across the wound. "It will stop the bleeding for a short time, but you must be quick."

"I will be," Aeros said. The earth beneath the man shifted and surged forward, carrying all three of them past the overturned tank like a ship set upon the stones.

A familiar face caught my eye in the chaos. "Ranger Rick!" He didn't hear me, just kept walking.

Nixie raised her voice into a shrill, cutting octave. "Rick!"

CHAPTER FORTY

RICK FROZE, HIS gaze strafing the crowd around him until he found us. I raised my hand. He wove through the throng of people on the street and slipped past displaced cobblestones.

"Damian, is everyone back?"

"They're headed this way with Graybeard."

"How long?" Ranger asked. "Stacy has been preaching some ridiculous bull shit."

"Is that why your so-called soldiers opened fire and injured commoners?" Nixie asked. "It's disgraceful."

"You mean the protesters?" Ranger shook his head. "You have to understand, I think these morons hate the protesters as much as they hate their enemies."

"What are you saying?" I asked.

"I'm saying they're not referring to them as civilians anymore, but as the Devil's prophets or some such shit."

I clenched my fist and cursed. "And what good will it do bringing the others back here?"

"When they left to help you, the rumor is they were running away from the damage they caused with their own hands."

"What about Casper and the others? The unit we helped?"

"The soldiers they saved," Nixie said. She didn't pull punches, and she didn't dance around the point. "If Graybeard had not been there, far more would have died. Both the wounded and the defenseless."

"We can try to sort this out now that it's over," Rick said. "I'm due for a debriefing. I have to go."

"Ridiculous," one of the soldiers walking behind Rick muttered. "She's one of those witches that attacked us. Why is she walking around free?"

I didn't see the rock until it smacked into the side of Nixie's face. She grunted and held a hand up to the cut above her cheekbone. "Who?"

I found the cluster of men. And I started toward them, Nixie beside me, before Rick held out his hand.

The Ranger stalked over to the men.

"You like that shot, Ranger," the largest of them said. Rick said nothing, he simply struck the man with blinding speed. The soldier gasped and grabbed his neck before collapsing onto the ground.

"We do not fire on our own allies, be it with bullets or stones, so listen now. This is not over. Pull your shit together and make ready." Rick spat on this ground beside the man. "If you have a problem with it, you can have a big chicken dinner instead."

The two remaining hecklers stayed silent. They looked at the man on the ground, still working to breathe normally, as Rick walked away.

"God damn new recruits," Rick muttered. His eyes widened, and he took a hesitant step backward, and then another. "What in God's name is that?"

Nixie and I turned to find a shadow looming over the river; the titanic form of a dark-touched harbinger walking beside a towering translucent figure.

"That's a sentinel formation." Nixie frowned. "It's a calling card of the queen."

"That's why she cut the earlier attack short," I hissed. "Now Nixie is here without the force of her people." I turned to Rick. "Do you still have the daggers? The bullets?"

"I ... I don't know," Rick said.

"Casper had them before," I said. "And some of her soldiers. Find her, find Casper's unit, and get to high ground."

"Make for the shop," Nixie said. "Our best hope until Alexandra reaches us is the cu siths."

"Aye," Angus said, settling in on Nixie's shoulder. "I've seen a cu sith take down more than one water witch in my day."

"Run," Nixie said.

I didn't question it further. Angus and Nixie knew more about the history of the cu siths and the water witches than I likely ever would. I knew they'd been used in the Wandering War, and I knew they were heavy ground troops in that conflict. But as we dashed down the rough brick sidewalks, and the heads of the harbinger and the sentinel peaked above the rooftops, I worried what any of us could do against that force. I choked the doubt down and focused on my footing. Nixie could sprint for hours, while I didn't have that luxury.

The harbinger roared, the wailing cry of a dark-touched turned into a basso howl. The few commoners who were still standing on the streets turned and fled. Some dove into storefronts and restaurants. I hoped they were only gathering a few essential items before leaving. I feared what the coming battle could do to my city, and I promised myself I would do anything to keep these people safe.

✦ ✦ ✦

I HADN'T EVEN managed to get the front door open before
Bubbles shouldered it wide. The cu siths' fur bristled, and they
stared down at the river front. Our enemy was close enough
now I could see they stood in the center of the river. That they
had such height, beyond the depth of the water, was a terrible
sight.

"Why one?" Angus said. "Why one harbinger?"

"They're territorial creatures," Nixie said. "It's not uncom-
mon for them to attack one another. Though I would've
expected it to attack the sentinel."

I cursed. "Look at the sentinel's shoulders. Do you see
them?"

"Dark-touched," Nixie said, surprise plain in her voice.
"What is this? How is the queen controlling them?"

"There has to be a dozen of them. Bloody hell, how are five
of us going to slow that down?"

Nixie splayed her fingers across her breastplate, and said,
"Get your armor."

I dashed into the shop, throwing the closet open and pulling out the vest with "Cub" embroidered across it. Hugh's gift
had saved me more than once, but as I flattened the Velcro
straps, I remembered a weapon that might give us far more of
an edge than the cu siths.

I ran up the stairs, skipping one with each stride, and hurried to the wall at the end of the library. I slid the trunk out and
popped the latch, digging for the thick leather scabbard. I
grabbed a black leather sheath as well, and frowned at the Key

of the Dead and the splendorum mortem. The dagger I'd once used to kill a god.

I hesitated, and then slid the sheath for both the daggers onto my belt before securing it beside a thick iron buckle.

I hurried back to the front of the shop, and Angus stepped away from me as I exited. "What is that? The power, by the gods, I can feel it rushing off you."

Nixie frowned and laid her hand on my forearm. "You can't. You can't use that on the dark-touched. We don't know if killing one of those with one of Mike's weapons will break his oath, and end his life."

It was a terrible thought, that our most powerful weapon might only be used at the cost of one of our closest friends. I cursed. "If it becomes a matter of saving thousands, or taking that risk, I don't know that I can say no."

Nixie's hand fell away. "I understand. But you must not use that casually. If Nudd realizes you still have it, he will bring his army down on you all at once."

I looked away for a moment. "Let's just try not to die today."

"The power is not just coming from you," Angus said. "It's the cu siths. They're drawing power from the nexus."

"Will the queen sense it?" I asked.

"I don't know," Nixie said. "I don't have much experience with blood shields. The fact so few people know of the nexus tells me it is effective. But if Angus can sense it now, I don't know what will happen when the fireballs pull on it in earnest."

"Shit," I spat. "Let's move."

"Now this is a battle," Angus shouted, an edge of joy in his voice that made me somewhat concerned for the fairy's sanity.

"What are you talking about? We have no plan, no allies, no

backup, and we're probably going to die badly."

Angus launched himself off Nixie's shoulder, and exploded into his full-size form, sending a rainbow of fairy dust across the ground. "As your people say, ain't it grand?"

I exchanged a glance with Nixie. "He's lost his fucking mind."

"We're still running headlong into an army. I'm fairly certain we've all lost our minds."

Bubbles chuffed. And then she barked, only the sound didn't stop. The bark grew into a thunderclap, and the cu siths' fur began to glow. I hadn't seen them draw so much power since Stones River, when we'd been victorious over the Destroyer, but we'd paid with Carter and Maggie's lives.

Peanut's booming voice joined Bubbles's bark, and the cu siths grew into a glowing green comet. I couldn't hope to match their speed, and neither could the fairies. The thunderous howls became the snarling, gnashing teeth of creatures unhinged.

"Nixie," I huffed, unbuckling the belt at my waist.

She glanced over. "I hardly think this is the time."

I laughed and pulled the sheath for the splendorum mortem off my belt before re-securing the Key of the Dead.

"If something happens, like what happened to the Old Man? Just take care of it."

She took the dagger from my hand and frowned before nodding. She hooked the sheath into a heavy latch in the armor on her thigh.

"It won't come to that." She stared at me hard, the light from the cu siths becoming a blinding green sun. "I love you."

"I love you."

We crashed onto the riverfront about the time Bubbles and

Peanut crashed into the harbinger.

"For Cassie!" Angus howled. The fairy shot forward as though he'd been launched from a cannon, his wings tight as a sword lanced out at one of the dark-touched perched on the shoulder of the sentinel.

The sentinel turned to us, the shadow of one hundred eyes flashing throughout its body, as I came to understand what the sentinel was: one massive creature formed from a platoon of water witches. I slid the focus out after I flipped the pepperbox into my left hand.

Light bloomed from the side of the harbinger, and I could just make out the shadowy forms of the cu siths inside that light; tearing, biting, and doing enough damage to draw the thing's attention. The harbinger's progress stalled, and it turned to face the ever-growing cu siths attached to its side. It swung one mighty claw, but before it crushed the cu siths against its side, Bubbles and Peanut launched off and latched onto its arm, their claws cutting deep furrows into the harbinger's flesh as they rocketed toward its shoulder.

Angus circled back to engage another dark-touched, and he wrapped himself around the thing's neck, stabbing into its eyes over and over. The dark-touched nearest him got a claw in his thigh. The fairy yelped, and then all hell broke loose.

Two rounds from the surviving tanks cut into the sentinel. Fiery explosions lit the inside of the creature before the water witches scattered. We went from having two enemies facing us to hundreds. The water swelled, and I had little doubt of what was to follow. The undines would create the wave, and if what Nixie had said was true, the queen's attack would not be so precise. She would scour the city from the face of the earth, leaving only the dead in her wake.

CHAPTER FORTY-ONE

THE SENTINEL DISINTEGRATED like a glass sculpture, hammered and splintered. Angus slashed and hacked at the wrist of the dark-touched that had hold of him, eventually breaking free and taking to the air as the vampires all fell into the churning waters below.

Two of the dark-touched on the harbinger's shoulder eyed the hovering fairy. Angus was inspecting the wound on his thigh, and I didn't think he realized what was coming. I raised the pepperbox and fired two incendiary rounds, drawing the attention of the dark-touched, and, unfortunately, the harbinger. That massive Titan refocused on me and strode forward. My immediate goal was accomplished, as the dark-touched had now shifted their focus as well.

I cursed, watching the waters rise around the harbinger. Two massive green blurs sprinted from one of the harbinger's shoulders to the other, engaging the dark-touched and hurling them from their mountain-like perch.

The cu siths were fast, but I worried about their ability to engage the vampires. I didn't have long to worry, as the rising swell of the water closed on the shore. A small whitecap rose higher than it should have, and had I not been keeping half of my focus on the waters, I wouldn't have seen the sword flashing out of it.

"Impadda!"

The electric blue shield burst into life, redirecting the undine's strike, and leaving her open to an awkward slash from the soulsword. She howled as the water that formed her body boiled. It wouldn't do any real damage, but would buy me a few precious seconds.

The next thing I knew, something wet and heavy had slammed into my side. I crashed onto the muddy shore and scrambled to strike back at whatever had hit me. The undine vanished into the water as I realized I'd been hit by the corpse of a soldier we'd lost earlier in the day. Something howled in the water, and one of the water witches flickered, gray lancing through her body like an intricate webwork. Her sword vanished, and she collapsed into the river.

I rolled the soldier over and cursed. His bandages had been washed away, but I recognized him as one of the men Aideen and Foster had saved. One of Casper's, but if he was one of Casper's … I dug through his pockets, turning up knives and magazines of ammo that might have been useful against a mortal target, but it wasn't until I checked inside the Velcro pocket on his left breast that I found what I was looking for. My breath still came in ragged bursts, having been knocked away by the impact.

Another undine lurched out of the water and strode toward me, water dripping from a mass of intricately carved armor. I climbed back up to my hands and knees. I didn't have an M16 to even try the scavenged rounds with. All I had was a dead man, and a handful of death.

"Sorry, man," I said, reaching out to the dead soldier's aura. I touched him, not expecting a huge flash of knowing. But he'd been dead long enough that I got a stark glimpse into the life of the spy in Casper's ranks.

A good friend of Private Stacy, the man who'd tried to shoot me. I drew back in horror as the visions of what this monster had done came to life. Three sexual assault trials, no convictions, no court-martials, no consequences. Two suspicious deaths close to him, and I didn't need to see more. But there was no way to stop it. One of Casper's men had been lost on a training mission. This man … this man had lodged the shiv inside his neck. He was good, damn good, at fitting in, at hiding what he was. But now he was mine, and he had one last mission. A mission he would have recoiled from in life, and that drew a wicked smile from me.

I gathered his aura up into my hands, a technique I'd once used to cripple a demon that had come for my sister. Three undines shot out of the river, joining the one on shore.

"You'll make a nice statue," I snarled. I pushed my hands forward, the aura of the traitor stitched into the bullets in my hand. They launched forward, bouncing off the undine's armor.

"Fool," she said. "The full power of the queen's guard has—"

I snapped my hands into a fist, forcing the aura deep inside the metal that Mike had worked. It wasn't nearly dense enough to handle that kind of power, and instead of a handful of bullets, it became an explosion of shrapnel. The undines flickered and screamed and collapsed to the ground, all except for the leader. She caught enough of the blast for the stone dagger fragments to do their work.

I watched in satisfaction as her face shifted to gray. She would never speak again. A moment later, something with the force of a dump truck plowed into her, sending the rubble of a stony water witch across my field of vision. Bubbles turned and spun in place, looking for her next target. She found the undines on the ground and pounced. If there'd been even a chance the water witches would have survived the blast from the shrapnel, Bubbles made sure they didn't. Her claws tore into their bodies, separating the long gray stone fragments as she went, and carving up the muddy earth beneath. I wasn't sure if Bubbles had pulled all the pieces out, or if the witches would recover, but the cu sith pulled at their heads, and whatever she had damaged sent the water witches into oblivion.

The dark-touched followed, surging from the river as the wave from the sentinel reformed to the north. I glanced to the south at the ruined camp where the guard had lost so many. And I frowned at the spy at my boots. If more of them were left, if more of them still had the ammunition, I might be able to use it.

"Fall back!" I shouted. "Fall back!"

Bubbles pounced on one of the dark-touched as it closed on me. She worried at the vampire's helmet, her massive fangs clanging and screeching at the thing's head.

I couldn't find Nixie, and the thought sent a chill into my bones. Even if she fell, I doubted the queen's attack would relent. She'd want to make a statement, to utterly destroy Nixie's allies.

Almost at that thought, a fountain of water exploded from the center of the river, and I saw Nixie's form take shape. She reared back, screaming like a mad god as she plunged a stone dagger into the undine wrapped up in her arms. Her attacker turned gray and hard before Nixie smacked the statue of the undine away to shatter on the shore behind her. Nixie looked up at the harbinger, and then her eyes followed the shoreline.

"Fall back!" I shouted.

She shook her head and pointed upriver with the stone dagger in her hand. At first, I thought she was just indicating the harbinger, as if we couldn't leave that thing standing there. And while I agreed, I saw the true threat a moment later.

✦   ✦   ✦

THE TIDE SURGED through the river, taller and wider than what had come before. I had no doubt it was scouring buildings from the earth, no doubt that the land where we had fought Drake was being dragged beneath the waves, and the old junkyard, and maybe the bridge itself, had fallen to the queen's madness. I glanced back at the far bank. We'd never make it in time. The wave would reach us before we could find the stone weapons. And I knew of nothing else that could stop the undines.

I looked down at the spy at my feet. "Looks like you get to be useful more than once today."

Before Zola had taught me to use the power of auras and the basics of line arts, and coalescing a shield, she'd taught me about the truly dark places necromancy had come from. I pulled the Key of the Dead from my belt. The blade was dull, and that would make my work a hell of a lot harder.

I didn't have a lot of time, and I knew it was going to be sloppy, but I hoped it would be enough. I smacked the Key of the Dead into the side of the soldier's head, cutting one sharp line from his earlobe up to the corner of his eye, straight across his eyebrows, and down the other side. It wasn't perfect, but it didn't have to be. I needed something to magnify my pull on the dead. I might be able to use the mantle of Anubis to call enough of the gravemakers to me, but it could also get me and everyone else here killed.

"Did you know the eyes are the windows to the soul?" I asked the corpse as I dug my fingers into the lines on his forehead. "What they don't tell you is they remain the windows to the soul for hours after you're dead." I grunted and gave his face one harsh pull. The flesh had been in the water long enough that it tore away without too much effort, leaving his glassy eyes to stare up at me. I groaned and let the face flop down over his mouth.

"Gross, man." I lined the dull dagger up with the corpse's head chakra, and slammed it home. The knife might have been dull, but that was only in a physical sense. With the eyes of the dead revealed and the chakra points beneath its tip, it slid into the man's head like a sheath.

What had been the normal low buzz of Saint Charles' ghosts and dead became a beacon of power and terror and death. I let the gravemakers rise, closing over the corpse and my hands, circling the Key of the Dead. One thing Zola had always told me about ritual magic was that if I screwed up, it would be a lot more than me that died. I thought back over what I'd done, remembering the lines and patterns, and was fairly certain it was dead on. I hoped.

Communicating with the gravemakers was a strange feeling. I didn't think they truly understood words any longer, but they would respond to impressions and magic. In my head, I showed them what the stone dagger looked like, what the shards might look like, and the bullets Mike had forged. For the hell of it, I thought of the Damascus-style blades onto which Mike had melded the stone daggers. If they found one of those laying around, I could sure as hell use it.

Nixie streamed out of the river, smashing a dark-touched out of the air before it could sink its claws into Bubbles's neck. A water witch rose behind Nixie, a long gleaming sword ready to strike. But I couldn't break the spell. I couldn't risk what that would unleash.

Peanut roared as his fangs closed over the water witch. They didn't merely pass through. They cut a section of the witch away, and it did not reform.

"Good boy," Nixie said as she tossed the dark-touched to Peanut. The cu sith pounced on the vampire, creating a maelstrom of water and mud and fur. Nixie slammed her sword through the injured undine's head, and the water witch's body crunched as it solidified.

"Whatever you're doing," Nixie said, "you'd better do it fast."

I knew she was right. The harbinger was only a couple steps away from us, and the massive wave of undines would be on us in seconds. I wanted to tell Nixie to run, but if this didn't work, we were all dead anyway. I opened the floodgates inside my head and let the souls come screaming out, tearing through the Key of the Dead, and channeling their way down into the gravemakers. If anything good had come of those millions of voices inside my head. It was that they seemed to have agreed on one unifying purpose. The extermination of Nudd.

The visions and flashes of terror that entered my mind as those souls flowed to the gravemakers and wrapped their way around the corpses of the fallen soldiers, destroyed my ability to do anything but fight to stay conscious. My vision dimmed into a soundless gray tunnel. The roar of grief and the dying echoed through my mind. Until one voice cut through. The voice of the child who would have been the Destroyer. The voice of the child who would die if I died.

The scream that came from my mouth was not that of a mortal. It was something else, twisted and burned and tortured. But it was not alone. It came with friends.

Once a powerful-enough magic was summoned, it was as much instinct as it was skill to control it. And if you ever summoned something beyond your skill, good luck. The idea in my head was already formed. I'd done it before. But this was different. The undines were faster. I couldn't anchor them to one spot and expect them to stand still while I impaled them.

But the idea was the same. Someone grabbed my shoulders, and I realized it was Nixie. Saying goodbye?

"Not. Dead. Yet."

Pillars of the dead exploded from the river. They tore through the parking lot up on the shore, blasted a hole through Main Street, and one cracked the harbinger hard enough in the chin to send it stumbling backward and crashing down into the wave behind it.

"Now."

The wave reached the nearby pillars as that terrible web-work of brambles and spikes exploded from the towers. Only it wasn't the same thing that I'd used in the past. The gravemak-ers had picked up every bit of the stone dagger material they'd encountered. Now they wielded those fragments with deadly purpose.

With the souls inside, those towers took on a sentience of

their own. All I had to do was feed them energy to continue. The waves crashed into the brambles, and the brambles erupted into a cluster of thorns. I yanked the dagger out of the spy's skull before I wrapped my arms around Nixie and shouted, "Get us out of here!"

She started to run, and I looked back at the crashing wave and the flickering veins of stone and gravemaker inside of it. I was horrified to see it was still attacking the undines even after I had broken my connection with the Key of the Dead. But the undines crashed to the earth, some of them hit by enough of the stone dagger shards that their bodies shattered and were no more.

A series of booming barks sounded behind us, and I stretched my neck to see Bubbles and Peanut charging after us. The pony-sized cu siths looked more like grizzly bears, massive lumbering forms with the speed of a horse. Peanut flipped me and Nixie up into the air. Nixie yelped before we crashed onto Bubbles's back, one of us clinging to either side while Peanut charged along beside us.

"Stop, girl," I said, patting Bubbles on the head. "Stop." We stood on the edge of Main Street and watched the towers begin to collapse.

"It didn't stop them," Nixie said.

"I know," I said. "But it slowed them down."

CHAPTER FORTY-TWO

I CLENCHED THE Key of the Dead in my hand and called out to the souls. They were still there, still talking to me, still crying out for vengeance and blood. "You'll have it," I promised. "You'll have it."

Far above the carnage in the failing towers floated a lone fairy. Blood ran down his thigh, and one of his wings beat at a slightly odd angle, but Angus screamed at the waters. I couldn't understand what he was saying, but it sounded joyful. And it made me worry about the fairy's sanity again.

"Angus!" Nixie shouted. When he looked our way, she gestured for him to follow. The fairy gave one large flap of his wings and glided down toward us.

"What now, lass? That harbinger thing is getting back up. How do you intend to stop it?"

"Stall," I said. "Graybeard will be back soon."

"Come on," I said. "We have to move."

"The queen will regroup," Nixie said. "Though I saw a great many of her witches fall, I fear that will only strengthen her resolve."

"She's mad," Angus said, as we set off down Main Street. Some of the soldiers stared at us as we passed, but none of them dared approach. When one came close to us, Angus said, "Stay on high ground boys. And lass," he said as a female soldier passed by. "Not done yet."

Angus hurried ahead of us and glanced back. "I'll be scouting the perimeter. Scream if you need me." He launched himself into the air, gliding over the nearest roofs.

"I feel like we've been a bad influence on him," I said.

We reached the edge of the tent city before we started back down toward the shore.

"Damian!"

The voice sounded familiar, but it was higher than normal, as if there was some level of panic. "Park?"

"What the hell was that?" Park asked.

"Nixie's queen is here. Basically, you guys have a shitload of trouble. We need to stall them until Graybeard gets back."

"What can we do?" Park asked.

"Just make sure your soldiers have whatever weapons will work against the undines. It wouldn't hurt to be ready for Green Men." I started to turn away before I turned back to Park, "And maybe a dragon."

Park blinked and shook his head. "We'll do what we can. Can the tanks hurt that harbinger?"

Nixie and I exchanged a glance.

"It's only vulnerable in the back of its head," Nixie said. "Aim carefully, and stay out of its way."

I cursed when I saw the surging mound of gravemakers on the shore. I worried they were doing something more than I'd asked, but they slowly trailed away, seeping into the ground and into the waters, revealing a small hill of shattered gray fragments. I was both excited to see the man standing next to them, and terrified that he was standing so close to the waters.

"Edgar!" I shouted, raising my hand in greeting.

Edgar tipped his bowler hat and gave me a small smile. "If I didn't know better, I'd think you are glad to see me, Vesik."

"Yeah, well, don't tell anybody."

"I assume these are the fragments of the stone daggers?"

"Who told you?"

"Mike did. After I heard what he'd been doing, I thought you might need to expand your weaponry." Edgar handed me a fat aluminum gun case. I flipped the latch and pulled it open, frowning at the monstrosity within. "Is this a blunderbuss?"

"Technically, it's four blunderbusses," Edgar said, patting another gun case. "Should work fine for firing some rather small shards. Anything you stick in the end of that will become a deadly projectile."

"I don't think the military is going to know how to use these."

"I suspect not," Edgar said. "But I know someone who will."

A booming horn echoed over the waters, and I stared downriver as the Bone Sails appeared around the bend.

✦ ✦ ✦

THE SIGHT OF Graybeard's ship was a welcome one. The skeletal masts, their sails stretched in the crosswinds, was an intimidating presence.

"Watch the cases," Edgar said. Before I could protest, he had leaped from the ground and flown toward Graybeard's ship.

Foster and Aideen launched themselves from the deck and sped toward me. I could see Sam at the bow, and figured Frank wasn't far behind.

"Is that a harbinger in the river up there?" Foster asked.

"Yep."

"And it looks like the Queen's Army?"

"Yep."

"And a whole lot of dead stuff?"

"Yep."

Foster pursed his lips and nodded. "Glad you're not dead."

"Me too."

I reached down to close the case over the blunderbuss as Foster made to grab it. "Don't touch it. I don't know what it's made of. Edgar brought them."

Foster turned toward Graybeard's warship as Aideen crouched down to study the gun.

"Graybeard's crew is coming. A few of them at least," Foster said.

"A pirate's weapon for a pirate's crew," Aideen said. "Edgar put more thought into this than I would have expected."

"Really?" I asked. "It seems like all Edgar ever does is put thought into things."

"Yes, but he's preoccupied with the survival of the remaining Watchers. It's clear now that Nudd has placed a heavy price on them. I'm surprised Edgar stepped away to help us at all."

"What allies would the Watchers have left if they lost us?" The thought sent a shiver down my spine. I cursed and gestured to the pile of gray and black chaff close to the river bank. The first of Graybeard's crew surfaced and hopped onto the flood-torn grass with an unnatural agility. The skeleton clacked his jaws at me, but I didn't understand the code they used. I gestured to the boxes on the ground, and the crewman nodded.

His leather shorts stretched awkwardly over his bones as he

crouched down and spun the case toward him. The hinges squeaked slightly when he opened it to inspect one of the blunderbusses. He pulled out a few flasks of what I suspected were ammunition, and nodded to me before throwing the others to the skeletons who had just surfaced behind him.

I pointed to the pile of shattered stone daggers and then tapped the end of the blunderbuss. The skeleton cocked his head to the side. I pointed at the water and then drew my finger across my neck and the skeleton slowly tilted his head back and gave two sharp nods.

He clattered and clacked his bones and jaw together, and the crew hurried to the pile. It wasn't an overwhelmingly large quantity of metal, but I suspected there was enough to fill a few loads for the blunderbuss. One of the skeletons opened a gun case and shoveled as much as he could into it as fast as he could. They ran back to the edge of the river bank, and waited as Graybeard steered his ship closer. No plank extended, but once it was within fifteen feet, the skeletons leaped for it, easily clearing the railing Graybeard had swung open.

"Wow," Foster said. "They can jump."

The river surged, and Nixie's form exploded out of it, sailing past Foster to land between me and Aideen. "They've reformed the wave on the opposite bank," Nixie said. "But we're not alone."

"I noticed. Graybeard's ship isn't subtle."

Nixie bared her teeth in a vicious grin. "That's not what I meant." She turned to the river and bellowed an order. "Take them!"

The river churned into an ocean of whitecaps, crashing and rising onto either shore.

Graybeard's warship surged forward on a wave of undines. The pirate glanced at me, his beard lifting in the wind as the parrot stretched its desiccated wings. I raised my right arm and lit a soulsword. Graybeard raised his fist in response, and the battle began anew.

Nixie bounced on the balls of her feet, glancing between the roiling river and me. "We only need to kill the queen. Find her, execute her, and this all ends."

"As you wish."

I wasn't sure if Nixie would catch the reference, but she gave me a sly smile before diving headlong back into the raging waters.

"What the hell do we do now?" I asked Foster and Aideen as the river rose higher.

"This is a battle we should stay on the outskirts of," Aideen said.

Foster drew the enchanted saber that Mike had modified. He bellowed and then launched himself into the air, soaring for the heart of the battle.

"Idiot," Aideen said. She gave an exasperated sigh, glanced at me, and followed Foster into the chaos.

That left me on the shore with two very large cu siths. They danced back and forth on their paws, ready to tear something apart with their fangs. "Go on."

It was all the encouragement they needed. They plunged into the waters as their fur began to glow once more. I slowly straightened my back as the green glow grew brighter and more intense. They moved through the water nearly as fast as they had moved on land, something I hadn't expected.

The harbinger regained its feet after being knocked over by

the wave of its own allies. Edgar landed next to me as I watched the Titan surge toward us.

"I don't think we can handle that on our own," Edgar said. "Not unless you want to dive deep into insanity like the Old Man did. Do you?"

I blew out a laugh and shook my head. "No, but I have another idea."

"You better make it fast," Edgar said. "The dark-touched are closing on the military set up along Main Street."

I cursed and bolted for the cobblestone streets of my home.

CHAPTER FORTY-THREE

B EFORE I'D CLEARED the side streets, I saw the maelstrom of fire that Zola had conjured from the bow of the Bone Sails. She'd help keep Sam safe, but I understood the chaos around us, and I knew that everyone on that ship was in danger.

I hadn't made it fifteen feet onto the cobblestones before a green rocket appeared at my side. Bubbles slowed to a trot, continually glancing up at me as if asking me to hurry up. "We have to find Park," I said to the dripping-wet cu sith.

Bubbles chuffed at me.

"You've bitten Park before," I said. "Haven't you?"

Bubbles chuffed at me again.

"Find Park," I said. "We need him." Bubbles rocked into me with her thigh before launching ahead into the sea of soldiers. I watched in concern as a dozen soldiers went down like bowling pins. I sprinted after Bubbles as she led the way into the tent city. "Sorry, sorry. Ooo, you should get that looked that." I winced when I saw someone holding their bloody foot. I was pretty sure that was Bubbles's doing, though I doubted the cu sith had done anything like that on purpose.

Bubbles stopped outside one of the smaller tents and released a thunderous bark. Half the soldiers in the area turned to look at us. It wasn't awkward at all.

There wasn't anything to knock on outside the tent, so I figured I'd just take my chances and barge in. "Park?" I said as I entered the small tent.

Park sat in a low chair, beside a cot where two soldiers were perched beside him.

"Damian?" he said, jumping out of his chair. "What are you doing here? I thought you'd be down by the river with the others."

"Do you still have tanks in the area?" I asked, dancing around the question of whether or not he had command over them. I didn't know who the soldiers inside the tent were, and one of them wasn't in uniform. It was hard to tell what his rank might be.

"We do," Park said. "What do you need?"

"For one, Alexandra returned with some of Nixie's water witches. They'll be in the river battling the queen's forces. So, don't shoot any of them unless the soldiers are damn sure of which side they're attacking."

"How the hell are we supposed to tell that?" one of the soldiers on the cot asked.

"They'll be trying to kill you," Park said. "We've had enough friendly fire incidents, I think."

"The back of the harbinger's head is its weak point. Graybeard's better at fighting these things than anyone else, but he has his hands full with the water witches on the river. And I don't know if you can take them down alone."

"Casper's squad still has some of the ammo you provided. I'll put them on the rooftops. We'll help where we can."

"Good," I said. "You have dark-touched vampires moving in on the north side of Main. Your only chance is to hit them in the eye, or maybe repel them for a time with the flamethrowers. Either way, keep the harbinger off the street. Get the tanks down by my shop. They'll have a fairly clear target down to the river. Don't send anyone who isn't armed."

"Why are you listening to him?" the unmarked soldier asked. "He's one of them."

Park turned a glare on the man. "That's what you fail to understand. If they're killing the things trying to kill you, they aren't the enemies. And they are very good at killing things." Park turned back to me. "Tanks will be there. Now get out of here before your dog scares the ever-loving crap out of every soldier in this place."

I turned and found Bubbles glowing. She looked like a freshly cracked glow stick, and I could see where that might be a little concerning on a pony-sized dog.

"Come on, girl," I said. "Let's go eat some vampires."

Bubbles chuffed happily.

We jogged out of the tent city, the soldiers now giving us a wide berth. I hoped Park could hold up his end of the bargain. The harbinger laying siege to my home was one thing, but I didn't want to be the cause of that kind of devastation. I didn't want to summon the armor of the gravemaker and unleash that chaos on my own streets.

We hadn't made it all the way down to the shop when the first of the dark-touched reached us. One-on-one, the vampires were deadly. Two on one, I doubted I could hold my own for more than a minute or two. And that might have been optimistic.

Thankfully, the bristly green ball of death at my side had other ideas. Bubbles charged at the dark-touched, giving me time to raise a soulsword while she bowled through the slashing, hacking claws of the nearest vampire. I caught glimpses of the riverfront as we passed the side streets. A massive wave had swelled on the opposite shore and was threatening to crash down on top of the Bone Sails. Distant booms echoed out from Graybeard's cannons, tearing through the air, accompanied by the smaller explosions of what I imagined were the guns Edgar had brought.

The first strike I leveled at the dark-touched slashed through its eye. The creature roared and reared back, and I knew what was coming. I stepped into it with a shield, and the first two strikes glanced off either side. The terrifying power of the dark-touched sent fracture lines through the electric blue dome.

I let it fall as the vampire crashed into it a third time, only to raise a smaller one and bat its left arm away from its intended target, my neck. It brought me in close to the hissing, drooling face that hid behind that marred helmet. Time slowed as I aimed a soulsword at the dark-touched's eye.

It was one of those moments where I knew the blow would either land true, or Bubbles would be helping me pick up my entrails. It was a stupid move, but it was the only way to get inside the dark-touched's guard. The only way to put down one more of these demons before it reached the military, or the citizens who still lived there. I heard the hiss of flesh as the soulsword met its target. I felt the give as it pushed through the eye socket and rammed up through the dark-touched's brain, only to slam into the opposite side of the armor outside the back of the vampire's skull.

I remembered the sensation well from the battle in Greenville. With a quick twist of my arm, I was sure that the life force of the dark-touched had been extinguished. Its inertia, however, had not. The body crashed into me, flailing claws cutting into my vest—a vest that wasn't suited to stopping sharp objects, only the brutal impact of a firearm. We fell into a heap, but before the full weight of the dark-touched pinned me to the ground, Bubbles head-butted the vampire away. It took me a moment to understand what I was looking at, as the cu sith had the head of the other dark-touched snared in her mouth.

"Spit that out," I said. "That's gross."

Bubbles reared back and expelled the dark-touched's head with a surprisingly violent force. It cracked on the cobblestones and bounced up onto the sidewalk.

✦   ✦   ✦

I HESITATED AT the next block when I saw the dark-touched streaking across the rooftops. I wanted to climb up there, or use the Hand of Anubis to pull them down. But to stop now meant leaving the harbinger, and that could do far more damage than one or two rogue dark-touched.

Angus's voice boomed above us. "He's mine! Stay your course!"

Bubbles released a booming bark in reply. I held up my hand, exhaustion seeping into my bones so deep that I feared trying to keep up with the cu sith would result in me passing out. And certainly leave me without enough breath to respond to Angus.

The ranks of soldiers vanished almost entirely by the time we reached the shop again. The parking lot was almost even with the harbinger.

I cursed and watched as the massive form reached down and plucked a tank from the riverfront.

Three deep rasping breaths wheezed from my lungs, and then I followed Bubbles on to the side street beside the shop. I skidded to a halt as the massive tank in front of us grated its treads on the brick street, the metal squealing against the wheels. It pulverized the stone as it went, and part of me worried how much it would cost to repair the old road. Probably not a large concern at that point.

The hatch closest to me popped open, and I blinked when Rick's face appeared before me. "Park said to shoot the thing in the back of the head, right?"

"I thought you were a Ranger," I said.

"I am," he said with a grin. "But I wasn't always."

I nodded. "Back of the head. Hit it with the main gun, or you'll just piss it off. And it's smart about guarding itself. So wait until it's distracted."

"What the hell is going to distract it?" Rick asked.

"A boy and his dog," I said, offering a small smile before I sprinted away with Bubbles. Now I could see the battle clearly, as well as the crashing waves below. If I hadn't known better, I would've thought I was hallucinating.

Waves rose from the old quarry, surging forward and carrying towering equipment toward Graybeard's ship.

Still the harbinger closed on us, regardless of the undines attacking its shins and knees and climbing up to its eyes.

Still it came.

A massive conveyor belt lifted two dozen feet above Graybeard's ship, and I saw the skeleton crew raise their muskets.

The boom sent an unholy shot of gray through the wave, and I watched the waters collapse in on themselves, leaving the giant conveyor to crash into the side of Graybeard's ship and bounce off with minimal damage.

The pirate shouted as the waves rose again, and the cannons boomed over the side of the ship. What had been a towering tsunami collapsed in on itself completely, and I understood what had happened. The chaff of the stone daggers that was intended for the handheld weapons that Edgar had gifted us had been loaded into the cannons. It cut undines down like so much paper.

Still the harbinger stalked onto the shore. I could feel its footsteps as it crashed into the rocks and made its way toward Main Street. The road beside the river buckled and snapped beneath the weight of the thing. The Bone Sails lit up again, nearer the opposite shore, and its cannons erupted.

The harbinger's hand rose to shield the back of its neck, as if it had expected the attack. As if it had known exactly what to listen for. Two of the cannon shots rebounded off its hand. One caught a glancing blow on the back of the harbinger's skull, but the other sailed long, smashing into a storefront 100 yards in front of us.

Undines spilled from the river, hacking and slashing at the few still clinging to the harbinger that hadn't been swatted away by those massive hands. Some of them struck killing blows, and some managed to wound the others without killing them. I suspected they were using the poison blades instead of the stone daggers.

"Kill it," I said, pointing up at the massive harbinger.

Whether Bubbles understood or not, she charged at the

lumbering giant. She had a single-minded purpose and kept her eyes locked on the monstrosity before us. I drew the pepperbox and sent some of Mike's incendiary rounds screaming into any water witch who paid too much attention to the cu sith.

The one who made the mistake of getting in Bubbles's path ended up with her throat torn out, frantically clawing at the gaping wound. Bubbles streaked up the harbinger's leg, using claws and teeth to dig into the dark flesh. The harbinger slowed and looked down at the glowing green attack dog.

I tried to judge the angle of the tanks, but I still didn't think they had a shot. I raised the pepperbox and fired my last two incendiary rounds at the harbinger's face. Its attention swung from the cu sith back to me. It started to take another step before Bubbles leaped and hooked her fangs into the harbinger's eye. I cringed and flinched away at the sight of the cu sith clawing and scraping and digging into the harbinger's head.

The harbinger swung wildly, trying to dislodge Bubbles, but her head was entirely inside the thing's eye, sending a spray of vitreous fluid down its cheek. Still the harbinger swung and spun until the soft flesh on the back of its head came into view.

"Bubbles!" I shouted. When the first round of the tank fired, I screamed Bubbles's name even louder. The shell smashed into the back of the harbinger's head and sent a geyser of gore out the front of its face.

The second round blew clean through the harbinger's head as the whumph of the nearby tank deafened me to everything else. I couldn't hear myself scream the cu sith's name as the harbinger collapsed. There was no sign of her as the body tumbled forward and crashed down onto the edge of the river bank.

I charged the enormous corpse, instinct and rage and fear swirling in one mad thought. That surge of adrenaline was enough to chase the exhaustion from my bones, enough for me to reach out and grab the harbinger's aura. There was no flash of knowing, no horrible vision of whatever this thing had been. But inside I found no soul, no trace of what animated so much in our world.

What I found instead was power, raw, unfiltered. I used it to pull the head of the harbinger from the waters. The horrible gristly crack of that act froze the water witches in their tracks. The few who had been stalking toward me backpedaled.

They stared instead at the harbinger as its body rolled and roiled and what had been inside became the outside. Its massive skeleton fell away from the flesh as I lifted it. A soft green glow emanated from the left eye socket. I dragged the skull on sheer will alone, bringing it closer until I could reach the cu sith inside. She was panting, curled up in a ball, but I couldn't tell if she was injured through the splash of gore that permeated her coat. I let the skull come to rest on the parking lot beside me, and I waited for Bubbles to climb out of the blown orbital socket. She sniffed at me, and then shook herself off violently, the wet smack of meaty chunks slapping against me as all the tentativeness in her motions left. Gore coated me from head to foot, and I'd never been so happy to be so disgusting.

One of the tanks pulled up beside us, and I glanced over to see Rick. His face looked hesitant, but his voice was confident. "Where to next, boss?"

"Keep your guns trained on the riverfront. You might not

be able to kill them, but blowing them apart will slow them down. And if you see those vampire things with helmets on, just shut yourself up in the tank and wait."

"You got it." I heard Rick shout to his men, ordering them to keep line of sight on the riverfront and the north end of Main Street. I hoped they'd pulled back far enough to guard the hospital, when I remembered that the hospital likely had a guardian all its own. Aeros would be there. I had no doubt.

"Come on, Bubbles. Let's go eat some water witches."

Bubbles chuffed, shook out her rear leg and dropped a few more bits of gore on the ground. Her giant pink tongue worried at a large chunk of meat lodged between her fangs.

We made it down to the broken street, unopposed by the water witches, who appeared to have fled back into the waters.

A new line had formed upriver, and I could see Alexandra's black hair as she commanded the soldiers on the riverfront. Nixie's forces were driving the queen's water witches back into the Bone Sails. Fire and gunpowder stormed along the rails of the warship. Peanut's booming barks joined the gunfire as any undine that dared to board was cut down by the cu sith's fangs, or the flickering swords of Foster and Aideen. Graybeard commanded a nightmare army. Nothing could stand in their way.

The battle pitched and shifted, swaying upriver and back as Graybeard chased down an undine who'd tried to escape. Alexandra cornered her upstream. The sight had me transfixed, which was likely why I didn't see the pools shift at my feet, didn't see the translucent arms rising behind me, and didn't see the armored shape of the undine who pressed her blade into my throat.

"Call off your dog," the undine hissed in my ear.

"I'd rather have her just eat your face," I said.

The dagger bit into my neck, and it was done with such careful precision that I knew the witch would have no issues cutting my throat.

Bubbles finally noticed the water witch and barked like a thunderclap. Another water witch formed beside the cu sith, but this one I knew. Euphemia wrapped her arms around Bubbles and whispered to the cu sith, "No."

"I'm sure she can kill one undine," I said.

"It's not one," Euphemia said. "There are many."

"Summon your leader," the undine with the knife said. "Or her mortal dies."

Euphemia closed her eyes, and something in her breastplate pulsed blue.

"Don't," I said. "I'm not—"

"Silence, child," hissed the undine who had me.

Without seeing her position, I doubted I could summon a Fist of Anubis with enough accuracy to do any good. And by the time I called a suit of gravemakers, I'd be long dead.

Shit.

The fighting in the river drew down. Graybeard's ship wheeled around, and I wasn't sure if I felt better or worse with the cannons leveled at me. And blunderbusses weren't exactly known for their accuracy.

Nixie stood at the bow of the Bone Sails. "You kill him now, and you only seal your fate. I will take your throne *regardless*."

I stiffened at her words. I hadn't been caught by some random water witch—the queen herself had captured me.

"Millennia," the queen spat, "and you would throw it away

for flesh."

"Lewena," Nixie said, "your rule is not just. You never should have taken the throne."

"You handed it to me." The sneer in the water witch's voice was plain. A moment passed before I heard a pop come from behind us. Before I felt something sharp cut into my cheek. Before I felt the dagger drag across my shoulder to bounce harmlessly off my vest.

I spun to find Lewena standing behind me, a webwork of stone etching through her like lightning. I backpedaled, getting closer to the shore when another shot rang out. The witch who moved to grab the failing queen went down in a heap, half of her head disintegrated. A third shot. A third undine fell. Nixie held up her hand, and I suspected she was calling for an end to the shooting. I didn't know if the snipers would heed her call or not.

But I caught movement on the second floor of the welcome center. Casper raised her fist in unity, and perhaps respect. And no more shots came. Nixie leaped off the Bone Sails' bow, walking slowly forward until she was face-to-face with the failing queen.

I closed on them both, fumbling with a pouch on my hip. Most of the things inside Death's Door were for the greater good. Or to help, or defend, but some... some were meant to do terrible, terrible things.

Before any more was said, Nixie's stone dagger struck the heart of the queen.

A moment later, I thrust a fairy bottle into Lewena's mouth. As her life spasmed away, the witches around us reeled in horror when the vortex inside that bottle roared to life. It sucked away Lewena's aura, and eventually her immortal soul. I ripped the bottle out of her mouth before slamming the stopper home.

Nixie stared down at the ruin of her queen.

CHAPTER FORTY-FOUR

THERE IS A calm after every great battle, while the boiling passions and unstoppered violence slowly retreat into the darkest places of our hearts. Some of the military might have congratulated us, even celebrated with us briefly, as our mutual enemy fell.

But others looked at us as if we would betray them at any moment; an ally who with one hand offered peace and with the other sold their greatest enemy their most powerful weapons. Park and Casper's squad were formidable human allies, but I worried about the growing hatred and fear from Stacy and his ilk.

I winced away from Aideen when she pressed around the cut on my neck.

"Stay still. We have to heal this. I can't be sure that wasn't a poison dagger."

I gave Nixie a mournful look. "Can't you just tell if there's like bad juju in the wound?"

"Bad ... what?"

I let out an exasperated sigh and leaned on the wooden kitchen chair in the back room of Death's Door. "Fine. Do it."

The familiar sting of the healing began, like a line of wasps stitching my neck together, before the feeling changed. It burned, and the burning spread far past the wound. That odd sensation told me Aideen had been right.

The queen had sliced me with a poison dagger, which made me wonder where the blade had gone after she'd dropped it, after Casper had taken her with a shot to the head. And I wondered how that moment would be remembered by the water witches. Would they remember a human had brought down one of their strongest? Or would they remember Nixie plunging the dagger into the queen's heart? Or the horror of the fairy bottle?

The light of the healing, and the sting, slowly faded. "Okay, okay, you were right." I grunted and rubbed my neck.

"It will leave some trace of a scar," Aideen said.

"Really? I thought you were good."

Aideen huffed. "It was at your queen's request."

I smiled up at Nixie. "I knew you'd dig the scars."

"It is a trophy of our victory," Nixie said.

Frank's voice grew louder in the front of the room. "And then a freaking skeleton threw me a blunderbuss like an actual pirate. It blew that water witch to pieces!"

"Only because I didn't let the other one rip out your spine," Sam said.

"Tearing out spines is really hard," Foster said. "There is a serious art to it, and I doubt it could be accomplished on a moving ship in the middle of an undine storm."

I smiled and listened to them chatter about the battle as I stared up at Nixie.

She frowned slightly, and I didn't think I'd like what she had to say.

"I have to go back."

"For how long?" I asked.

"Until I prove Lewena is dead." Her hand cradled the fairy bottle, which hung on a thin chain around her neck. "And the coronation."

I nodded. "I'll miss you."

She put her hand on my cheek and smiled. "I'll miss you too. But the fight lies in Falias now. I'd ask you to come with me, but I know you can't leave your place in this war, either. One day it will end, and things will be different."

"You two are so sappy," Aideen said, a completely unmasked disgust in her voice.

I grinned at the fairy, and we slowly made our way to the front of Death's Door, and down to the damaged riverbank by the harbinger's body. Aeros stood close to its head, pointing out at the river and saying something to the soldier at his side.

The man shifted, and I could see it was Park, with Casper standing beside him. I raised my arm in greeting, and Casper waved back.

"We were just talking about how to clean up this mess," Park said. "Aeros seems to think he can rebuild the river banks without much of an issue. Although, I was more interested in his ability to rebuild that old road. I don't think the historical society will be thrilled with this."

I smiled. "Yeah, tanks and cobblestones do not mix."

Park rubbed the back of his neck. "I think it'll be good. If Aeros helps." He glanced up at the Old God. "After what happened with the tank, I think it'd help a lot in explaining things to my superiors."

"Your bullet saved the mortal prince of the water witches," Nixie said, turning to Casper. "I thank you, and am in your debt."

"The mortal what?" Casper and I echoed the same time.

"It's only a title," Nixie said. "I must go. Alexandra's waiting to escort me."

"I've given the order not to engage any water witches." Park paused, and then released a chortling laugh. "I've never seen a look on the general's face quite like when you said Damian is not to be fucked with."

"Yes," I said. "It was very subtle."

Nixie smiled. "Most of the water witches have disbanded. Though, should you have trouble with any of them, you need only ask."

"I thank you," Park said.

Nixie nodded before she kissed me, long and deep, until I grew a little uncomfortable with the eyes all around us. But that discomfort vanished as I realized I didn't know how long it might be before I'd see her again. I pulled her close and held her tight, until she finally broke away. She grew translucent, and stepped into the waters that had so recently been boiling with blood.

Note from Eric R. Asher

Thank you for spending time with the misfits! I'm blown away by the fantastic reader response to this series, and am so grateful to you all. The next book of Damian's misadventures will be arriving in spring, 2018.

If you'd like an email when each new book releases, sign up for my mailing list (www.ericrasher.com). Emails only go out about once per month and your information is closely guarded by hungry cu siths.

Also, follow me on BookBub (bookbub.com/authors/eric-r-asher), and you'll always get an email for special sales.

Thanks for reading!
Eric

Also by Eric R. Asher

Keep track of Eric's new releases by receiving an email on release day. It's fast and easy to sign up for Eric's mailing list, and you'll also get an ebook copy of the subscriber exclusive anthology, *Whispers of War*.
Go here to get started: www.ericrasher.com

The Steamborn Trilogy:

Steamborn
Steamforged
Steamsworn

The Vesik Series:
(Recommended for Ages 17+)

Days Gone Bad
Wolves and the River of Stone
Winter's Demon
This Broken World
Destroyer Rising
Rattle the Bones
Witch Queen's War
Vesik Book 8 – coming spring 2018*

*Want to receive an email on the day this book releases? Sign up for Eric's mailing list.
www.ericrasher.com

Mason Dixon – Monster Hunter:

Episode One
Episode Two
Episode Three – coming fall 2017*

*Want to receive an email on the day this book releases? Sign up for Eric's mailing list.

About the Author

Eric is a former bookseller, cellist, and comic seller currently living in Saint Louis, Missouri. A lifelong enthusiast of books, music, toys, and games, he discovered a love for the written word after being dragged to the library by his parents at a young age. When he is not writing, you can usually find him reading, gaming, or buried beneath a small avalanche of Transformers. For more about Eric, see: www.ericrasher.com

Enjoy this book? You can make a big difference.

Reviews are the most powerful tools I have when it comes to getting attention for my books. I don't have a huge marketing budget like some New York publishers, but I have something even better.

A committed and loyal bunch of readers.

Honest reviews help bring my books to the attention of other readers.

If you've enjoyed this book, I would be very grateful if you could take a minute to leave a review on the platform of your choice. It can be as short as you like. Thank you for spending time with Damian and the misfits.

Connect with Eric R. Asher Online:

Twitter: @ericrasher

Instagram: @ericrasher

Facebook: EricRAsher

www.ericrasher.com

eric@ericrasher.com

Made in the USA
Monee, IL
06 October 2022

15340533R00208